Time of Grace

Also by Clare Harkness

MONSIEUR de BRILLANCOURT

and published by Black Swan

Time of Grace

Clare Harkness

St. Martin's Press
New York

Library of Congress Cataloging-in-Publication Data

Harkness, Clare.
Time of grace / Clare Harkness.
p.   cm.
"A Thomas Dunne book."
ISBN 0-312-13611-0
I. Title.
PR6058.A6864T56   1995
823'.914—dc20   95-31435   CIP

First published in Great Britain by Macmillan

First U.S. Edition: October 1995
10 9 8 7 6 5 4 3 2 1

Acknowledgements

'One time of grace' from *Audible Silence* by
Laurence Whistler (Rupert Hart Davis 1961).
Reprinted by kind permission of Laurence Whistler.

Pages 20, 21 & 395: excerpts from 'Eloge de la
viçomtesse', 'Suite vive' from *Largeur des tempes*
(Editions Gallimard 1982). Reprinted by kind
permission of Patrick Reumaux and Editions
Gallimard.

Page 27: excerpt from 'Chapter 15' from *Another
Life* by Derek Walcott, copyright © 1972, 1973.
Reprinted by kind permission of Farrar, Straus and
Giroux, Inc.

Page 46: excerpt from 'What do you want to make
those eyes at me for' by Emile Ford and the
Checkmates; written by James Monaco, Howard
Johnson and Joseph McCarthy; Pye Records 1959;
© 1916/1944 Leo Feist Inc. Reprinted by kind
permission of Redwood Music Ltd., 14 New
Burlington Street, London W1X 2LR; CPP/Belwin
Inc.; and International Music Publications.

Page 85: 'In the firm blue of the unfolded sky' from
Image by Alberto de Lacerda (translated by Arthur
Waley and Alberto de Lacerda).

Pages 155 and 369: excerpts from 'Plus belle que les
larmes' by Louis Aragon. Reprinted by kind
permission of Editions Robert Laffont.

Pages 273 and 289: 'The Gorge' and 'Vanity' from
Collected Poems 1973 by Robert Graves. Reprinted by
kind permission of A.P. Watt Ltd. on behalf of the
Executors of the Estate of Robert Graves.

To my husband, my mother and my children, with all my love; and also, with love, to T.J.B. without whom my schooldays would have been infinitely less amusing and Jessica would never have existed

Contents

One time of grace,
And all the rest an angry muddle of effort:
Effort to find oneself in the right place;
Anger to find in life's vague hall of mirrors
No mirror framing the right face.

One shaft of glory,
And all before a darkness, and all after
A dimness, not so dark but that a hoary
Glimmer excites it from that urgent scene
Which holds the highlight of the story.

Life is to tease.
Life is a hint, a parable, a preview.
Life is a Rembrandt, where the Painter sees
Great procreative darkness big with light;
And there's no meaning unless darkness please.

Laurence Whistler

Prologue

The house was empty and frighteningly quiet. Jessica was sprawled on some cushions on the floor, still wearing a dress which my grandmother had worn as a young woman and which we had found in one of the trunks. I had forgotten its existence until we started clearing out the attic and came across it. Jessica had insisted on trying it on. 'If we're going to spend the afternoon reading all these old letters, we may as well wear old clothes,' she had said. A moment later, delving into another trunk, she had exclaimed, 'I remember you in this hat. Put it on. I want to see you in it again.' I had complied, of course. I always did.

All around us, on the floor, lay heaps of paper and a few old toys. I rescued a doll I had loved as a child and put it on a window-ledge, then picked up the first of the pile of letters in the box at my feet.

Darling Imogen,

You would have laughed if you could have seen me last night. I've won our bet, by the way, with the most amazingly eccentric man you can possibly imagine. His name is Gilles Estrangemaille de Brincourt and, I hate to admit it, but his Latin is better than ours. He writes endless tomes in Latin, all published, all frightfully important, all about mushrooms. He works in that laboratory in the rue Buffon – that place by the *Jardin des plantes*, do you remember? He adores all things English, has a wonderful sense of the ridiculous, and is terribly un-French in many ways. He likes people who are slightly mad; in fact, he only likes people who are a bit odd. He thinks Mervyn Peake is absolutely wonderful, and *The Third Policeman*, and Emily Dickinson. He can't stand Saint-Exupéry. He hates his family background, likes to dress like a tramp (well, not quite; but he likes shabby clothes), and tries hard to hide his birth. He never uses his full name, ridicules his class saying they are all buffoons, and shares my loathing of the *seizième*. However hard he tries, he gives himself away immediately because of his exquisite use of the language, his impeccable manners and the way he does the *baisemain*. He's a mycologist – quite a famous one – and he has only three obsessions: mushrooms, orchids and cats. I think he may just have added me to his list of obsessions, but only because, according to him, I look like a cat. He has the most beautiful hands you have ever seen.

We've met a few times at dinner parties and once at some scientific gathering which Dermot insisted I had to attend. I've always thought Gilles was quite mad and he has always thought I looked like a cat. We bumped into each other outside the CNRS just before lunch, yesterday, when I was dropping off some papers for Dermot; and instead of the normal kind of chit-chat people make on these occasions, Gilles said, with no preamble, 'I know a workman's café somewhere off the boulevard Malesherbes which nobody knows exists. They have an unlabelled red wine which, once tasted, you can never forget. It's out of this world. It really is nectar for the gods. The café owner says a friend of his supplies it direct from a vineyard in Burgundy, but he refuses to say any more about it than that. It seems so unlikely that this terrible little café should be there, right in the middle of the Grands Boulevards, let alone that it should have a *vin de table* for which one would willingly sell one's soul.

The food is of no interest, but I have to keep going back for the wine. I am always afraid the café will disappear, or that I shall be unable to find it and discover that it was all a figment of my imagination. Would you like to come and look for it with me and taste some of their magic wine?' Pretty difficult to resist, you must admit.

We found it, and the wine was indeed out of this world. We spent most of the afternoon there, talking. I learnt a lot about mushrooms and quite a bit about orchids. These are things which, in the end, will drive a person to insanity. In fact, Gilles told me that one of his colleagues, an ancient and respectable man, after a lifetime of crawling on his stomach through the marshes looking for a particularly rare orchid, recently blew his brains out with a shotgun in despair at never having found the plant in question. It is apparently far from certain that the orchid he was looking for exists. Gilles says there is only one recorded case of anyone ever having seen this particular orchid and he is convinced that the man who claims to have discovered it simply invented it to drive all other orchid men mad. It's the sort of thing mushroom men and orchid men do, apparently. They try to get rid of each other by driving one another mad.

By the time we left the restaurant, it was getting dark and beginning to snow. We walked round and round the place Saint-Augustin – not a good place for walking – trying to decide what to do next. I wanted to go home. Gilles wanted to go to bed with me. I half wanted to go to bed with him, too, but it's a pretty big decision to take if you married the first man you ever went to bed with and have never been unfaithful to him. The idea of going to bed with anyone else seemed rather frightening and, in some ways, rather repulsive. On the other hand, we had drunk a colossal amount of the magic wine and the idea of being able to lie down somewhere instead of

17

stomping about in the cold was pretty enticing. There was our bet, too, which is why I had allowed this whole thing to happen in the first place; and there was the thought of Dermot with that socially aspirant, point-scoring woman with the moustache and the hideous jewellery. I have to admit that the idea of him actually being attracted by someone so conventional and tedious rankled more than a little. I kept thinking about her prim, self-satisfied manner, her social pretensions, her extraordinary desire to dress like a well-heeled sixty-year-old and those frightful earrings (things like pink flowers with a pearl in the middle); and I felt positively insulted that Dermot could even consider being unfaithful to me for *that*! It has been going on for so *long*, too. There really didn't seem to be any justification for remaining faithful. Why be miserable when you could be having fun? 'What the hell?' I felt. 'It can't possibly make life any more frightful than it already is and it might make it a great deal more tolerable.'

I felt obliged to tell Gilles that the only reason that I was considering going to bed with him was because I was jealous. I told him all about it and he hooted with laughter. He knows the woman in question and thinks of her as being so insignificant that he couldn't understand how I could feel jealous of her. I don't think he has a very high regard for Dermot, either, though he's far too polite to say so. At any rate, he seemed to find the idea of them having an affair hilariously funny. His mirth was tremendously infectious and I soon found myself leaning against the *métro* railing clutching my sides in merriment.

'You haven't the faintest idea what jealousy really is,' Gilles said to me. 'I am sure, for instance, that everyone has always told you that there is nothing on earth as blue as the blue of your eyes. You've always gone around, serenely, knowing

18

they were the bluest blue on the face of the earth; but one day I will show you a wild gentian and you will pale with rage and envy. Then you will know what true jealousy is.'

I think it was the fact that Gilles made me laugh that finally persuaded me to say 'yes'.

Once that had been decided, we faced the problem of where to go. It was impossible to go back to either of our flats: mine because of the children and the 'au pair'; Gilles' because he has two co-authors working with him on a book on orchids and they have been using his flat as an office so they were likely to be there. There was little choice but to go to an hotel. I telephoned the 'au pair' to tell her not to expect me home until dinner, then we set off in the direction of the gare du Nord where we thought there were bound to be hundreds of hotels and one felt that they might not query the fact that we had no luggage and only wanted a room for a couple of hours.

We were not very successful. Most of the hotels looked awful beyond belief and the ones which were the least repellent had no vacancies. You remember what a horrible *quartier* it always was? Too grim for words and full of what your father would call 'suicide hotels'. Do you remember how he used to pick out hotels where one could commit suicide without embarrassing one's family? Well, he would have given these full marks. They would be ideal for it because no-one would know who you were and they certainly wouldn't bother to find out, so one could disappear without trace and without embarrassing one's relations. The whole enterprise began to seem terribly squalid and I started to have frightfully cold feet about it. In fact, by this point, I felt like bursting into tears and deeply resented Dermot for having pushed me to such extremes.

We did finally find a hotel and I felt paralysed. I

19

refused even to sit down because I had by then decided that all the hotels were filthy and that we would probably get fleas, or worse, if we touched anything. I ended up ringing Angelica and asking her to get us a room at the Ritz with no questions asked. She did and it was fabulous. I had forgotten how infinitely much nicer the Ritz is than the horrible George V or the Plaza-Athenée. No wonder Angelica lives there. And it's so romantic looking out on your favourite square.

When I got home, frightfully late, Dermot didn't even bother to ask me where I'd been; and when I got up this morning (before Dermot, fortunately) I found that an envelope had been pushed under our door. It contained a piece of paper on which was written:

> *Puisque vous êtes*
> *jalouse des fleurs*
> *en voici une brassée*
>
> *le bleu des gentianes*
> *vous fera pâlir de rage.*

When I came back from taking the children to school, I found another envelope. At first glance the paper inside looked blank; then I noticed, hiding in the bottom right-hand corner, the words:

> *Blanche de peau*
> *comme le sang bleu.*

When I returned once more, at tea-time, after collecting the children from school, I found yet another missive waiting for me. This one said:

> *J'aimerais simplement*
> *que le vent vous dévête*

pour pouvoir vous serrer
dans mes bras et vous tordre

comme si vous étiez le cou
et moi la corde.

Then the telephone rang and it was Gilles. He has kicked his co-authors out of his flat and we're meeting again tomorrow.

It's a long time since anyone wrote poems to me. I'm rather enjoying it.

Tell me about you.

All my love,
Jessica

Attached to this letter was my reply.

Darling Jessica,

Your letter arrived this morning. Wonderful. We have both won our bet, it seems, and both of us with a Frenchman. Isn't that odd? I made a point of avoiding both the English and the Italians like the plague. I feel I know all I want to know about both of them and I'm certainly not brave enough to attempt anything with either of them again. I should have listened to Granny on the subject of Italian husbands. She was absolutely right, only I didn't believe her any more after what happened with Anthony. She was so in favour of us marrying Englishmen, wasn't she? And although she did vaguely touch on the subject, I suppose, she didn't really warn me. Perhaps she thought André and Marguerite had told me. They did try but it must have been obvious I didn't have the faintest idea what they were talking about. Why didn't any of them tell me clearly?

Anyway, to revert to lovers, there didn't seem to be a huge amount of choice once one had discarded all the Italians and English. I hardly meet anyone other than Italians here, in any case, because for some reason everyone sticks to their own language groups – we all behave as if we were stranded in the middle of Africa, surrounded by natives and unable to speak their language – and the only Americans we meet are people from the State Department and I was certainly not going to start having an affair with any of them. There were a couple of Scandinavians who have been interested in me for ages but one was so dull and the other so gloomy that I knew I couldn't stand either of them for more than five minutes. So I picked a Frenchman. (I later discovered that he was the correspondent for *Le Monde*.) He was standing in the open doorway of the Embassy, shaking hands with someone, as we arrived for some dinner or other; and I saw him from across the street the moment I climbed out of the car. He was silhouetted against the light. I had never seen him in my life before and had no idea who he was, but the moment I saw him from across the street I knew he was going to be my lover. He knew too, he says. '*Cette chair est à moi,*' is what he thought, apparently. Was that, do you suppose, because I had decided he was going to be my lover or do you think he would have felt the same whether or not I had noticed him? I like to feel that I decided the whole thing.

He and Enrico had known each other for years; they'd known each other in Paris, in fact, so it was all very easy. Enrico mentioned that he was going to Rome the next day so Sébastien (his name is Sébastien) rang me the following morning and invited me to dinner. It was then that he told me that he knew we were going to be lovers the minute he saw me. The other thing that he said during dinner, which threw me slightly, was, '*J'ai remarqué tout de suite que vous aviez une bouche louche.*'

'*Louche?*' I asked, horrified.

22

'Louche,' he replied. 'Trop grande, très louche; et de trop belles dents. Une femme qui a une belle, grande bouche et de très belles dents, c'est trop.' Especially *louche*, he said, when the corners of my mouth went up. 'Une belle, grande bouche qui sourit et qui montre de très belles dents' – definitely *louche*, he assured me. And later, kissing me every few yards down the road, he said, 'Je me sens très bouche-à-bouche ce soir. Comment expliquez-vous que j'ai une telle envie de vous embrasser?'

'Parce que j'ai une bouche louche,' I replied.

He laughed and said, 'Quelle réponse parfaite. Oui, c'est ça. C'est une belle réponse.'

Once he kissed me for a very long time and then said, laughingly, 'Vous vous débrouillez pas mal pour une puritaine.' He looked at me for a moment and then added, 'Et puis vous avez des yeux d'une couleur qui n'existe pas. Ni bleus, ni noirs. Vous avez des yeux inimaginables.'

I told him that you always said I had navy-blue eyes. It reminded me of you saying to Anthony, 'It's because all her family have either incredibly black eyes or incredibly blue eyes. Imogen's eyes couldn't make up their mind which they wanted to be so they came out navy blue,' and Anthony laughed. Do you remember?

Sébastien seems obsessed with my mouth because, two days later, when we were making love, he suddenly whispered, 'sale bouche'. I was frightfully upset but when I mentioned it to him afterwards, he said, 'C'était le plus grand des compliments.'

I chose him solely for his looks. He has the most wonderful profile.

Love,
Imogen

It all came back so clearly. Jessica had been furious with Dermot. She had felt hurt and humiliated. 'I don't

23

know how you can stand it,' she had said on the telephone, referring to Enrico's incessant infidelities. 'How
can you bear him to touch you?'

'I can't,' I had replied. 'I used to feel physically sick
but now I just want him to leave me alone. I loathe his
presence in the house. I'm only happy when he's away. I
don't think I knew what it was to be miserable, really
and truly miserable, until I married. Do you remember
how unhappy we thought we were at school? And yet we
only cried about once every two years. Now I cry almost
every day. And I have a horrible feeling that I have
entirely lost my sense of humour. Why on earth did we
do it?'

'I don't know. I can't imagine. Do you remember your
grandmother telling us that her mother used to sit them
all down in the nursery and tell them that if any of them
ever married she would cry buckets? No wonder! I see
her point entirely. I shall teach my children the same.
"Centuries of carnal embracement." Isn't that what
E.M. Forster wrote? Well, that may be the male point of
view but as far as women are concerned it has been
centuries of intolerable bad temper, bullying and
astonishing selfishness; not to mention drunkenness,
infidelity and intimidation of children. What on earth
are we going to do about it? We can't go on like this for
ever. I can't see any end to it.'

We had agreed that we were stuck with it because of
the children. Then Jessica had suggested that we find
lovers. 'Perhaps we ought to take a lover to relieve the
utter ghastliness of life' was how she had put it. In the
end we had made that bet. We had bet each other that
we wouldn't find a lover within a week. And we had both
managed it.

Looking at Jessica lying there, I wondered what would
have happened if I had never met her. What would have
happened if neither of us had been sent to that school?

England

Still dreamt of, still missed,
especially on raw, rainy mornings, your face shifts
into anonymous schoolgirl faces, a punishment,
since sometimes you condescend to smile,
since at the corners of the smile there is forgiveness.

Derek Walcott

CHAPTER ONE

I first met Jessica when I was ten and disliked her on sight. She seemed, indeed was, precocious. She had extraordinary self-assurance for a child of that age. She was also very well aware of the fact that charm gets you further than good behaviour. She managed, by making people laugh, to be incredibly disobedient without ever seriously getting into trouble; and, by appearing totally vague, she always found someone to do for her anything she did not feel inclined to do for herself. In needlework lessons, for instance, the mistress inevitably ended up doing all Jessica's sewing for her so that at the end of every term she went home with a collection of beautifully embroidered table-cloths and napkins whereas the rest of us, a year later, were still struggling on with the same frightful old rag, knowing full well that we would never be able to use it even if we did manage to finish it.

Jessica was not a particularly pretty child. At times she was almost plain. On other occasions, she had the angelic fáce, upturned nose and sweet expression of a Renoir girl. She loved Renoir's paintings and I often wondered whether it resulted from a narcissistic love of her own image.

We were thrown together constantly from the outset. We were the same age, among the few non-Catholics in the school and the only 'new girls' in our class (most of the children having been incarcerated at the age of six). We had had similarly un-English upbringings, spoke three languages and had each just arrived from other countries, so we found ourselves ill at ease in the restricting atmosphere of an English boarding school.

Jessica's family, at that time, lived in Washington where her father was British Ambassador. His previous postings had been Madrid (where Jessica had attended a local nursery school) and then Paris (where she went to the *école primaire* in their area) so her Spanish and French were excellent. Although she had never lived in England, she had frequently spent holidays in her father's family house in Norfolk since it was the place to which her parents repaired whenever they were on home leave. For her, therefore, the 'culture shock' on arrival at the Convent of the Immaculate Conception – although considerable – was not quite as violent as it was for me.

I had been brought up in Milan. My mother, who was a pianist, was Italian and my father, a writer, was English. My immediate family consisted of my maternal grandmother, my parents and my twin brother, Simon. We lived in Milan in a large flat in the Via Alberto da Giussano, and spent every weekend and all of our holidays at Manta, my grandmother's lovely house overlooking Lake Maggiore. We grew up amid all the noise and music of Italy and all the love in the world so that when Simon and I were packed off to school in England (he to a preparatory school in Sussex, I to the convent in Berkshire), we were neither of us in any way prepared for life in an English boarding school.

With the exception of Latin and the sciences (which were astonishingly well taught) the level of teaching at the convent was poor. The nuns were far more interested in developing their own and each other's humility than in improving the academic standards of the school. They were particularly enthusiastic about a mysterious quality known as 'school spirit' and equally preoccupied with something they referred to as 'character-building'. Having renounced all possessions and all worldly desires, they could not allow themselves permanence of position or pride in their career. They had, therefore, worked out a system whereby no nun remained in the same job for any length of time lest she become attached to it or consider it her own. This resulted in some curious situations. The headmistress of one term would be responsible for scrubbing our backs in the bath the next; our geography mistress would, overnight, be put in charge of the linen-room; or our biology mistress would suddenly be asked to become novice mistress and so disappear into the Enclosure never to be seen again. For one wonderful term our chemistry mistress was put in charge of the kitchens and the food suddenly improved beyond all recognition, but the food bills increased accordingly and she was hastily removed and sent back to the classroom.

Very early on, Jessica and I made the mistake of correcting our French mistress in class. Not unnaturally, she was annoyed. Rather foolishly, she banned us from attending French lessons for a year and we were told we must spend the time in the library. The nuns hoped, I suppose, that we would instruct ourselves in something, though it is hard to imagine what they thought we could learn given that almost all the books were in Latin. We must have scoured the shelves hundreds of times in our search for something we could read but during that first year we never succeeded in finding anything other than endless lives of saints, a lot of whimsical fiction, a complete set of the Waverley novels (which, of necessity, we devoured in their entirety for lack of anything more interesting to read) and Dickens, who depresses me to this day.

We were, by comparison with the other children, well read for our age when we arrived at the school, so that until much later, when our Latin was good enough to attack the more interesting tomes in the library, we were constantly frustrated by the lack of reading matter available to us.

During the year of our banishment to the library, we rapidly came to the conclusion that it was more amusing to talk to each other than to read. The dislike I had originally felt for Jessica vanished during those endless conversations, during the course of which we temporarily forgot our French and discovered a friendship amounting to love. Had we only known, at that time, the value and the resilience of friendship compared with what is normally termed 'love', how different and how very much easier our lives might have been. It is probably true, however, that the pleasure we derived from each other's company was increased simply because we did not know what a precious thing we had found or how easily it could be threatened.

The horrors of school life, like the horrors of war, no doubt strengthen one's affection for fellow-sufferers; and community living seems to force one to search for a kindred spirit as solitary living never does. I loathed sleeping in open dormitories, bathing in groups, charging in hordes up and down the three-mile avenue before breakfast and around the playing fields after lunch. I could not understand why it was considered healthy and sociable to hit one another over the head with lacrosse sticks every afternoon whilst it remained 'unladylike' and totally forbidden to run down corridors, however late for class or prayers. Jessica was as bad at games as I was and as hopeless at gym. She asked too many questions. So did I. We were doomed from the start. Not only thrown together, we were obliged to defend our common, alien ideals against a world of monastic reproach. Life had suddenly become a mass of unwritten rules which we did not understand and constantly, unwittingly, broke. It took us some time to realize that the English way of life is entirely based on unwritten rules.

Meals were among the chief horrors of daily life at school. As in all English institutions, the food was uneatable. It was so awful as to be positively spectacular. The highlight of this remarkable cuisine was a notably unpalatable pudding known as 'Father Gallagher's Hat', which appeared with unfailing regularity on the refectory tables. It was a solid, slimy lump of suet the shape of which closely resembled that of our

32

school chaplain's hat. Almost as bad was another creation in suet which we called 'Reverend Mother's Leg'. This was a deathly white, cylindrical object which, when cut, oozed blood-red jam. Our favourite pudding, the only one we ate with any enjoyment, was disgustingly nicknamed 'Pus and Bunions' and consisted of a thin layer of rock-hard pastry covered with a sludge of uncooked margarine, sugar and chocolate powder. If to this list you add boiled silverside (memorable for its green-and-grey sheen); dehydrated potatoes, soaked and blown up again and full of black lumps; boiled tripe; winter greens floating in a pool of water; boiled liver (who on earth thought up the idea of boiling liver?); and a nameless, white fish in a nameless, pink sauce, you have convent cooking in a nutshell. Meals always seemed to have a sadly depressing effect on us.

Jessica and I had been brought up to fight for our ideas. The despairing nuns did not know what to do with us. We were made to go to Mass at six every morning for a term because we had been caught drinking gin out of a tooth-mug in a shrine to Our Lady of Sorrows. We were subjected to extra tuition in games on Sunday afternoons because we had had the bright idea of ruining a lacrosse match by finding a second ball and shooting it into our own goal. We broke silence incessantly; we smuggled food into the school and held 'midnight feasts'; we implored our parents to send us parcels of unsuitable books which were invariably confiscated; we declaimed Walt Whitman to an empty chapel at dead of night. We even broke into the nuns' Enclosure once, at three in the morning, by crawling along a beam above the chapel and through a hole in the convent attics. We had a wonderful time rummaging in their trunks and unearthing all the personal belongings they had had to abandon on entering religious life. There were photograph albums, diaries and newspaper cuttings, so we had a fascinating time discovering their real names and seeing what they had looked like before enveloping themselves in nuns' habits.

'Imogen! Do come and look! It's Sister Mary Agnes! Can you believe it?'

'Goodness, how incredible! She's absolute *heaven* in this photograph. And *do* look at Sister Monica James. What on earth is that thing she is wearing? How absolutely *weird* . . . What are those?'

'Newspaper cuttings about Sister Mary Agatha.'

'What *bliss*! Do let me see.'

From these we discovered that the nun in question had been the debutante of her year: very smart, fashionable and much talked about. She was, as we knew her, an elderly, very stout nun who wore spectacles and had an annoying habit of evading embarrassing questions in doctrine lessons. Her hobby was bee-keeping and we frequently collapsed in helpless laughter as, with bee-net over her veils and the skirts of her habit hitched up to her waist, she ran ponderously across the lawns in pursuit of a swarm.

While we were examining the nuns' treasures, the bell suddenly started ringing. I was frightened. Bells did not usually ring in the night. We decided we had better get back to the school and into our dormitory before the lightning struck. Having crawled back along the chapel beams (in itself a terrifying exploit since we were some fifty feet above the choir stalls), we emerged through a hole into the attics above the school to be met by a silently angry group of white-faced nuns. Had we been Catholics, we were told, we would have been excommunicated because we had climbed right above the Tabernacle without genuflecting. I tried to argue that we were crawling and therefore on our knees anyway and was given a look which would have struck terror to the depths of anyone's soul. I knew, from that icy stare, that I was irredeemably condemned to hell: that my parents were condemned; my brother and my cousins. The sins of the father . . . on the heads of your children and your children's children . . . I saw it all.

*   *   *

The community had worked out an efficient way of keeping the school clean. There were no maids or cleaning women because the pupils did all the housework. There were 'lay sisters' – as opposed to 'choir nuns' – to do the laundry and the cooking but we never saw them because they remained in the Enclosure and never came into the school. They were nuns who had come from working-class families and who were therefore supposed to be unable to understand Latin. This meant that they were not allowed in the school and could not attend the Offices with the choir nuns. We were barely aware of their existence.

At the beginning of term, we were each allotted a specific task in a particular room and this was our responsibility for the next three months. The tasks in each room were normally shared between two people. If it was a classroom, one girl was responsible for sweeping and polishing the floor while the other was supposed to dust and polish all the desks. If it was a dormitory, one girl would clean some fourteen handbasins and polish the taps while the other swept and dusted. On Saturdays, we all had to do an extra hour's housework in the form of polishing the silver and brass, brushing rugs with a carpet brush, and so forth. By the time we had been forced to our feet by a bell, stripped the sheets and blankets off our beds, turned our mattresses, washed from head to foot standing in front of our handbasins, dressed, brushed and plaited our hair, re-made our beds from scratch, been to Mass, had breakfast, run down the long avenue and back, done the housework and then had Morning Prayers, we were quite ready to go docilely to our lessons if only to sit down and draw breath.

The same principle was applied to the gardens. Everybody had a garden. That is to say, every girl shared with one other a small plot of earth which we were expected to cultivate and turn into herbaceous borders. This idea had the double advantage of keeping us healthily occupied out of doors during the little 'free time' we were allowed whilst keeping up the very beautiful school grounds without the aid of gardeners. In order to encourage us, a gardening competition was held half-way through each summer term. The girls who were judged to have the best garden were given a prize in the form of a picnic outside the school grounds.

When this was first explained to me, the prize did not seem worth the effort. My mother had put me off the whole idea of picnics when I was very young by telling me that they were one of the worst aspects of life in England.

'The English,' she said, 'have their charm but they also have some very tiresome habits. One of their worst characteristics is their insatiable desire to go on picnics. When you set off for a picnic in England, it is invariably raining and miserable. Nobody can ever agree as to where they want to have it. Tempers become frayed. You walk for hours looking for the right spot. No one would ever dream of giving up, of course, and you inevitably end up eating ghastly buns in a thistle-patch.'

Jessica and I were automatically allotted a garden together when we first arrived at the school.

'I don't know anything about gardening, do you?' I asked her.

'No. But it can't be very difficult. The basic idea seems to be that you stick something in the earth and it grows. Quite biblical. Anyway, the prize isn't very exciting, so what does it matter?'

The prize turned out, in fact, to be slightly more interesting than we realized at the time since, as we were later to discover, it was perfectly possible to spend eight years in that establishment without ever setting foot outside the school grounds.

Neither of us had any sense of competition. We thought gardening a bore; but we came to the conclusion that if we wanted to talk to each other without being overheard, gardening was the ideal cover.

We knew that our gardens were intended to be purely floral but, being permanently hungry, we hoped that we could get away with a few edible plants if we hid them carefully. I accordingly wrote to my grandmother asking her to send us packets of seeds and to include mustard and cress and radishes as well as flowers.

These arrived in due course. We planted them and watched with interest as the weeks went by. The radishes were beginning to show signs of life when, to our horror, a nun spotted them and uprooted the lot. Furious and disappointed, we determined not to let the same thing happen to our mustard and cress.

'It's ready to eat now, anyway,' I pointed out to Jessica, 'and the nuns will be so angry if they find it.'

Feeling very naughty, we sat down by our little garden and solemnly ate our way through two square feet of tasteless greenery. Neither of us liked to admit that it was not as interesting to eat as we had expected, although Jessica remarked that she had always thought mustard and cress was supposed to sting.

'I expect it is the wrong sort,' said I, convincingly. 'You know. Like tarragon.'

'What about tarragon?' asked Jessica, looking puzzled.

'There is a right and a wrong sort. I only know because my parents are forever growing tarragon that tastes of absolutely nothing. Year after year my father tears it out in a rage, shouting that those bloody imbeciles have sent him Russian tarragon again instead of whatever it is that tarragon is supposed to be. Perhaps this is Russian mustard and cress. Granny would say that the Russians are everywhere, scheming, you can never be too careful . . . God, their food must be dull!'

The day before the gardens were to be judged, we started to panic. We had stolen some flowers from the woods when we were out riding one afternoon and these had spread and looked healthy, but everything else seemed to be wilting or dead. Neither Jessica nor I was at all certain what to expect of the things we had planted but we agreed that the seedlings still seemed very small.

'Do you think we should have transplanted them?' enquired Jessica.

'I don't know,' I replied. 'They do look rather squashed.

On the other hand, they make a thick patch of green whereas they would look pretty pathetic if we separated them. They don't seem blissfully happy, do they? Perhaps we planted them at the wrong time of year.'

Jessica looked at me and laughed. 'Oh, God, we are hopeless!' she said, giggling. 'Anyway, it's too late to do anything about it now. They're obviously not going to be covered in blossom by tomorrow. What we've got to do is find a way of filling in the bare patches and adding a bit of colour.'

'Couldn't we dig up some of those delphiniums from behind the riding stables?' I suggested. 'There are hundreds of them. Nobody would ever notice.'

'Goodness, you are brilliant!' Jessica could turn on flattery as she could charm. 'Let's do it during Benediction, when they're all in chapel.'

We were unable to uproot the delphiniums when it came to putting my plan in action. They were growing in rough grass, our trowels were small and the earth hard. We decided to pick as many as possible, breaking the stems near the ground, and stick them into our garden in the vain hope that they would look as if they were growing there naturally.

The following day they were all lying dead on the ground but we did not have an opportunity to pull them out before we all had to assemble at the northern end of the gardens. The Mother Superior and the headmistress led us in stately procession from one plot of earth to the next, stopping at each to make whatever comments they thought necessary and to write down the marks in their notebooks. When they came to our garden, a look of annoyance mingled with despair crossed the face of the Mother Superior.

'Jessica Grantsby-Harte and Imogen Holt, please step forward,' she said in a dry voice. I can remember noticing for the first time that our names were always called together and that Jessica's was always called before mine.

'I would like you all to take a good look at this garden,'

the Mother Superior continued, raising her voice as she addressed the whole school. 'It is the perfect example of slovenliness, lack of effort and lack of school spirit. Are you not ashamed of yourselves?' Her fish-like eye settled on me for an instant. 'Weeds run rampant wherever you are in charge. Why, may I ask, did you not remove these red campions? As for the delphiniums! It is with deep distress that I discover you both to be dishonest as well as lazy. Yours is a double crime. You have attempted to deceive by cheating and you have stolen someone else's property in order to achieve your ends. I was watching you from the window of our cell as you stole those delphiniums.'

('Our cell' translated into normal English meant 'my bedroom'. The nuns, having renounced all personal property, could only use the collective possessive adjective or pronoun, a habit which caused considerable confusion on occasion.)

'Have you seen our pen, any of you?'

'Which our pen, Sister? *Your* our pen or Sister Winifred Martha's our pen?'

'Don't be silly, Jessica dear; the pen I was using.'

'But since all the pens are yours.'

'Ours.'

'Yes, I mean *your* our, or *yours* meaning *ours*. Why can't you use Sister Winifred Martha's our pen and let her worry about finding *your* our pen which is just as much *her* our pen if you are sharing everything?'

'You are really being exceedingly tiresome today, Jessica.'

'There is one last point I would like to make to you all,' said the Mother Superior, raising her voice again as her passionless, pale eyes swept the faces of a hundred little girls. 'I believe that I expressly forbade any growing of vegetables or edible matter in the gardens. These are supposed to be flower-beds. We are not bringing you up to run kitchen-gardens – you will presumably have someone to do that for you.'

'What did she mean about the red campions?' I hissed

39

into Jessica's ear. 'Are they our flowers from the woods?'

'I think so. I didn't know wild flowers were weeds, did you? Somebody might have told us!'

'Stop whispering when I am addressing you,' said the Mother Superior, glaring at us. 'I repeat that I believe I made it clear that you were not to grow vegetables. I said it again when you planted radishes. Not content with this, you have continued to disobey my orders by growing mustard and cress.'

'Those are calendulas, Reverend Mother, not mustard and cress,' I said with infinite assurance, pleased to be able to put her in her place in front of the entire school.

'Yes,' said Jessica firmly, taking courage from my bold move. 'They're calendulas.'

Reverend Mother looked at us coldly. 'I am sick and tired of you two trying to be funny,' she snapped. 'I am quite aware of the difference between mustard and cress and a calendula. Come to our office after Evening Prayers. I wish to speak to you both.'

The nuns moved on to the next garden with the children trailing behind. The procession wound on and on, pausing from time to time, until at last all the gardens had been visited and the winner announced. As the school trooped indoors, Jessica and I rushed back to our garden and pulled up a handful of our seedlings to taste. They were indeed mustard and cress.

'Oh, God!' sighed Jessica. 'Reverend Mother was right. We must have eaten the calendulas. Honestly, it is unfair! We tried so hard!'

Shortly after that, we set fire to our dormitory by mistake.

CHAPTER TWO

On Saturday afternoons we all had to wash our hair. For a short time, every handbasin in the school (and there was one for each child) had the figure of a girl bending over it, her hair, like Rapunzel's, hanging down into the water.

We also had to wash our brushes and combs, a job which bored us. Jessica and I often experimented with ways to speed up this part of the proceedings and on one occasion Jessica hit upon a scheme which we both thought a stroke of genius.

'Why don't we just burn off the dirt?' she suggested. 'That's how you sterilize needles and strip paint and all sorts of things. Our brushes will be unbelievably clean without us having to do anything. It'll only take a second and they'll be literally sterile; and then we won't have to go through all that tedious business of trying to get the soap out of the bristles, and of having to dry our brushes and combs afterwards. All we need are some matches.'

'There are some matches behind the statue of Our Lady in the Lady Chapel,' I said, 'but we'll have to put them back pretty quickly because the nuns use them for lighting that night-light.'

It was the one moment of the week when the nuns were not much in evidence. They spent most of the afternoon in chapel and supervision, left to the prefects, was minimal. It was not difficult, therefore, to put Jessica's plan into action. I went off in search of matches and then we waited until the dormitory was empty. As soon as each girl had finished washing her hair, she had to go up to the matron's office at the top of the building. There she would join the queue of people waiting to have their hair dried. There were only one or two hair dryers so one could wait a long time. As soon as everyone else had left our dormitory, therefore, it seemed likely that we would remain undisturbed for a reasonable length of time.

Once we had acquired the matches, the rest was easy. Jessica lit one and ran it along the comb which I was holding out and which, being made of some synthetic material, instantly burst into flames. I dropped it in astonishment and both of us watched, mesmerized, as the ancient floorboards started to catch fire. I remember staring at the spreading flames in disbelief and then suddenly realizing that we had a fire on our hands. I ran to the nearest handbasin, filled a tooth-mug with water and poured this on to the comb. It made a faint, sizzling noise, but there was insufficient water to extinguish the flames.

'Find a bucket, or a bowl, or something,' I whispered to Jessica, terrified that someone might come into the dormitory at any moment. 'A tooth-mug doesn't hold enough water.'

'Smother it,' Jessica insisted. 'Water's no good.' She ran to pull a blanket from her bed but by the time we had hurled it on top of the spreading blaze, a patch of floor was burning merrily. We jumped up and down in the middle of the blanket, hoping to stamp out the fire by stifling it. To our horror, flames started licking along one edge of the blanket as if encouraged by the additional fuel. The smell of burning plastic was overwhelming and the fire was spreading. Trembling with fear, I grabbed the eiderdown from my bed and used it to pick up the bundle of burning blanket and the remains of the comb. Shrieking at Jessica to open the door for me, I ran to the nearest bathroom and hurled the bedclothes into the bath. Jessica turned on both taps while I watched the flames subside. Soon there was nothing left of the fire but a lot of charred bedding floating in a bathful of water and a large, black patch on our dormitory floor.

By this time, the smoke from our dormitory had seeped across the landing and up the stairs; and the atrocious smell of burning wool and plastic had invaded the rest of the building. People soon started appearing from all directions and the first to arrive on the scene found me and Jessica on all fours, shaking with fright and trying to scrape the blackened floorboards with our nail scissors.

The result of this incident was that we were officially separated for what remained of the summer term. The headmistress then wrote to our parents explaining why we had been separated:

> not so much in order to punish them as for their own good and for the good of the other children. I am distressed to have to inform you that Jessica and Imogen have an extremely bad influence on one another and we can only hope that by being separated they will develop an interest in the school as a whole and that they will learn the importance of community of spirit as opposed to the whim of the individual. Until now they do not appear to have grasped the fact that rules are made for a purpose but I feel sure that in time they will adapt to community life and will develop the right school spirit.

Neither Jessica's parents nor mine appeared to take the incident particularly to heart. In the case of my parents, they seemed to feel that the nuns were making a great deal of fuss about nothing. They were on the point of writing to tell the headmistress that they disapproved of the idea of separating us when the bill for the damages arrived. Infuriated at having to pay a large sum of money for repairing our dormitory floor, my father changed his mind about writing and told me and Jessica that we richly deserved to be separated.

This decision, on the part of the nuns, to keep me and Jessica apart, was the beginning of half a lifetime of frustrated friendship, a friendship that for years was to be lived at long distance, against a background of endless partings. It was, I am convinced, during that first separation that we developed the indissoluble attachment that was to bind us for life. Certainly, it was a psychological error on the part of the nuns. Quite apart from the fact that one obviously wants most what is forbidden without reason, we felt that we had been singled out for a punishment that none of the other children had ever suffered and this reinforced our growing feeling that we were different from all the other girls. Total isolation and shared unhappiness welded us together until we developed a form of communication that might, by some, be termed telepathic. Our ability to understand one another without having to say anything formed the foundation of a friendship that would prove, at a later date, to be totally incomprehensible, and therefore vastly irritating, to our husbands and lovers. It was the kind of friendship which only an English boarding school can produce and which, for that reason, no Latin can ever understand. (This fact was brought home to me in later life when I read Jorge Luis Borges' brilliantly funny, passage in 'Tlön, Uqbar, Orbis Tertius':

> ... one of those close (the adjective is excessive) English friendships that begin by excluding confidences and very soon dispense with dialogue.

This sums up the Latin view of the English and their inability to communicate or to be friends.)

Jessica and I had, of course, long before we were separated, exchanged every possible confidence, so from that point of view our separation was of little significance. We became so intuitive that we could hold long conversations using only our eyes and, to everyone else's enormous irritation, we were frequently to be seen falling about laughing at our own, silent jokes. Only once did we resort to words during that period of separation at school. It was during an art class, when we

44

were both waiting to use the potter's wheel. I noticed Jessica writing something on her piece of clay, using the end of a paintbrush. When she had finished, she held it up so that I could see what she had written. 'Do you still love me?' was her question. I nodded and she pummelled her clay into a ball again.

Once we had emerged from our silence and were finally allowed to speak to each other again, we felt constantly obliged to test one another's affections. It was a phase which lasted for more than a year. Every sentence was preceded by the words, 'If you love me ...' ('If you love me, you'll help me clean my shoes', 'If you love me, you'll wait while I brush my hair', 'If you love me, you'll help me look for my vocabulary book', 'If you love me, you'll eat some of my spinach for me.') There seemed to be no limit to our love for one another, and no limit to the number of times we had to prove it.

It was not until long after we had left school that we understood the reason for so many of the rules that had previously seemed incomprehensible. We did not, at the time, realize how frightened the nuns were of close friendship or love. As far as I know, there was not one single case of lesbianism while we were at school or, indeed, before or after we were there, but the nuns must have been constantly watching out for signs.

During all those years, the nearest that Jessica and I ever came to having any kind of physical experience together was a farcical incident which occurred when we were about fifteen. By the time we were that age, we were allowed to spend a certain amount of time on Saturday afternoons unsupervised (Sundays were almost entirely taken up with letter-writing in class, plain-song practice and lengthy sessions in chapel). On this particular occasion, ten of us, Jessica and I included, were in the Common Room playing records and lounging around when someone had the bright idea that we should close the curtains, turn out the lights, form couples and dance to the music, pretending that we were with boys. It seemed a perfectly good idea at the time so we all proceeded to fall into each other's arms and shuffle about the floor to the strains of the Everly Brothers, Buddy Holly, Paul Anka and the like.

Because of our exceedingly protected backgrounds and the rarefied atmosphere of the school, we had only first come into contact with 'pop' songs at about that time. We considered all that brand of music to be in bad taste, but we thought it extraordinarily sexy. We were ashamed of ourselves for listening to it, but found the temptation hard to resist. The fact that the singers all had working-class accents made them seem doubly attractive to us. (It appears to be human nature to imagine that every other race, creed, nationality, colour or class of person is more sexually exciting than one's own kind. Why this is, who knows? Nevertheless, the myth persists; and we were convinced, in those days, that our brothers and cousins and all the boys of our acquaintance were totally inhibited – which they were – but that working-class boys were the unashamed possessors of unbridled passions and animal lust.)

By the time we had listened to Edith Piaf singing 'Milord' (a record that Jessica was responsible for bringing back to school) we were all well into the swing of things and happily imagining ourselves as French tarts (to be a French tart seemed an extraordinarily romantic notion in those days, too, of course). Then someone put on a record which we all thought the epitome of sexuality. We could hardly bear to listen to it, it seemed so blatantly sexual. The words went, roughly, as follows:

Oh, what do you want to make those eyes at me for
If they don't mean what they say?
But, baby, all right, I'll get you alone some night;
And, baby, you'll find you're playing with dynamite . . .

46

While dancing to this record Jessica suddenly said to me, 'Don't you think we ought to practise kissing, too? I mean, this is all very well, but we know how to dance. What we don't know is how to kiss and it's going to be frightfully embarrassing if we suddenly get kissed at a dance or something when we've never kissed anyone in our lives.'

'OK,' I replied, 'but you do it first.'

'I can't,' answered Jessica. 'Anyway, we've got to do it together. We must close our eyes and pretend the other person is a man. I'll count to three and then we kiss, all right?'

'All right,' I said.

We closed our eyes, counted to three and bumped noses rather hard.

Jessica giggled and said, 'Try again.'

Soon, we were glued to one another, swaying to the music. It reminded me suddenly of an incident I had forgotten until then which was that when my twin brother, Simon, and I were about four we had, at his suggestion, touched tongues as an experiment and then spent the next ten minutes washing out our mouths and squeaking about how disgusting it was.

After a while, Jessica unglued herself and said, 'I can't keep this up any more. How long do kisses go on for?'

'Absolute *ages*,' I said, 'but I think we've got the hang of it, don't you?'

'Yes, except for the breathing. It's jolly difficult to breathe. There must be a technique, like breathing when you're swimming, but I suppose that comes with practice.'

'It's pretty disgusting, isn't it?' I asked. 'Imagine doing that with somebody you don't know. I don't think I could, could you?'

CHAPTER THREE

The life of a convent, not unnaturally, centres around religion. A fair proportion of our day was therefore taken up in prayer and in religious instruction. Probably more time was devoted to the study of Latin than might have been the case in other schools and since Church Latin differs in pronunciation from classical Latin we were made to practise both; but the texts we studied in each were equally powerful. Soon our heads were ringing with magnificent lines and we found ourselves reciting long passages in our sleep. Everything we learnt was dramatic. Our childhood dreams were filled with Menelaus bristling with spears and Camilla baring a breast for battle.

Through our childish determination to discover what was contained in the more interesting works in the library, Jessica and I devoted an inordinate amount of time to the perfecting of our Latin. At first the nuns were pleased. They thought our Latin excellent and held us up as an example of the results of diligence to the rest of the school. Soon they began to suspect that our reading was leading us into areas they would have preferred us to leave alone. They were not sure whether to be delighted or worried when we told them we had discovered that Theodolfus (the first great name in the schools of Orléans that later produced numerous poets and scholars) had been languishing in prison, suspected of treason, when he wrote 'Gloria, laus et honor tibi', the hymn we always sang on Palm Sunday. They were re-assured when we announced that it had become obvious to us that Shakespeare owed a lot to Horace and even to Virgil. They were far from amused when Jessica, asked in class to give an example of an emphatic *tu*, and expected to quote something quite different, stood up and recited in Latin, 'would you take all that rich Achaemenes owned, or the Mygdonian wealth of teeming Phrygia, or the well-stored houses of the Arabs, for one hair of Licymnia, when she bends her head to your burning kisses, or with mock cruelty refuses what more than the asker she would love to be snatched, and sometimes snatches first herself?'

The matter of what we were or were not allowed to read came to a head during class one January afternoon when we were about fourteen. The lesson started badly.

'Imogen,' our Latin mistress snapped the moment she came through the door, 'I understand from Sister Martha Eugenia that you made some airy reference, in your English prep, to the fact that Shakespeare "stole all his ideas from Horace and frequently copied him almost word for word". You did not, apparently, substantiate this in any way. Perhaps you would like to illustrate this remark for the benefit of the rest of the class by giving us a couple of examples.'

'Of course,' I said, rising to my feet and feeling thoroughly smug at being able to show off what I had purposely learnt by heart. 'I feel certain that everyone will agree with me when I say that the lines:

> Three winters cold
> Have from the forests shook three summers' pride,

from the Shakespeare sonnet that we had to learn yesterday are remarkably similar to:

> *Hic tertius December ex quo destiti*
> *Inachia furere silvis honorem decutit.'*

'I think you will find, Imogen, that Shakespeare's lines were about the passing of human beauty whereas it is

49

highly unlikely that Horace intended a symbolic meaning. What other example can you give us?'

'Jaques' famous speech must have been taken from Horace's passage about the ages of man,' I said.

'Let us hear Horace's passage, then,' Sister Simon Thomas said, 'and let us have it in English so that everyone can understand.'

I recited it, ending,

'And so to every age belongs its part;
Youth must not play the dotard; nor the boy
Ape manhood. Nature's law must rule the stage.'

'Not the most poetic of renderings,' commented Sister Simon Thomas. 'Accurate, Imogen, but a very literal translation.'

'It was intended to be literal, Sister,' I pointed out, 'and, anyway, it isn't my translation. It's by someone called Alfred Noyes. I found it in the library. I can do Shakespeare copying Virgil too if you want.'

'No, thank you, Imogen. I think we have all had quite enough of the sound of your voice for one afternoon. You may sit down now.' She turned to Jessica. 'Now, Jessica, let us hear the piece of Virgil I set you. I want it in English please.'

' "Allecto then, in Gorgon poisons steeped",' Jessica launched forth. By the time she reached, "On her a serpent from her blue-black locks the Goddess threw", I had recognised the translation and sensed that we were heading for trouble but Jessica ploughed on, oblivious, ending,

"Ere yet the flame o'er all her bosom spread,
Mildly she spake and mother-like, and long
Wept o'er her child and Phrygian bridal day . . ."

When she finally came to a halt there was an iciness in the silence that followed.

'It's rather sad, don't you think?' asked Jessica blithely.

50

'It is certainly not your own translation, Jessica,' said Sister Simon Thomas in an ominously calm voice. 'I think I asked you all to translate that passage yourselves.'

'I did and you would have hated it. You would have said exactly what you just said to Imogen: "Not the most poetic of renderings. Accurate but very literal." You're always complaining about us all being too literal so I found this version which, you must admit, is far more poetic than anything I could produce and it's a great improvement on our boring old textbook, too. I think it's very moving.'

'And where precisely did you find this translation?' enquired Sister Simon Thomas, looking stonily at Jessica.

'In some old book in the library. I can't remember the name of the man who translated it. It was done some time last century, I think.'

'I know the book, thank you, Jessica. I was asking where you found it.'

I could see from Jessica's expression that she had realized, too late, the pit she had dug for herself. 'In the W section of the library,' she replied, in a subdued voice.

The W section had for a long time intrigued us both. It was a locked, mahogany-fronted, rather than glass-fronted, bookcase which took up the whole of one alcove in the library. Only girls in the Upper Sixth were allowed to have access to the books therein contained and the only reason for staying that long in the school seemed to be to find out what exotic and unsuitable reading might be hidden within this solid piece of carpentry.

Curiosity overwhelmed us until we could bear it no longer. We took to shadowing members of the Upper Sixth (there were only five girls in the class so it was not a particularly onerous task) until we found out where the key was kept. As we had suspected, it was hidden in the headmistress' study where it hung on a hook beside her timetable board. This board was right next to the window which was almost always open and was not, in any case, difficult to force open from outside. The path leading from our gardens to the tennis courts led right past it, so it was easy enough to saunter by at regular intervals and, when the coast was clear, to lean in and help ourselves to the key. We tried to choose times when we knew the headmistress was in chapel saying the Offices because we knew that she locked the door of her study when she was elsewhere for any length of time. The chances of anyone else walking in were, therefore, slight. We had been doing it for months.

'And how did you obtain a book from the W section?' asked Sister Simon Thomas.

'I sort of borrowed the key,' replied Jessica.

'What do you mean "sort of borrowed"? There is no such thing as "sort of borrowing". Either you borrowed it or you didn't and, if you did, who lent it to you?'

'Well, I took it really.'

'So did I,' I interrupted. 'It was my idea in the first place and I took it just as often as Jessica did.'

'You mean you have taken it more than once?' the nun enquired, turning to me.

'Yes,' I replied.

'And how did you get hold of the key?'

'Through Mother Winifred's window,' I said, adding, 'but we've been asking her for ages and ages if we could read those books because we've read everything else in the library so many times and we can't go on reading the same books for the next four years, can we? I mean, how do you expect us to learn anything if we just go on reading the same old books over and over again? We know them all by heart already. And what on earth will our parents say? They are paying to send us here so that we can learn something. My father would have a fit if he saw the library.'

'The books in the W section are not the sort of books you should be reading at your age and I imagine your father would be more likely to "have a fit", as you call it, if he could see what you have been reading without permission. I imagine he'll be thoroughly displeased when he hears.'

'You don't know my father,' I retorted. 'I told him last holidays that the Abbot of Cluny gave Peter Abelard absolution for all his sins and had his body removed in secret and sent to Héloïse, and my father, who was previously unaware of this, was delighted. I bet *you* didn't know that, did you?'

Sister Simon Thomas looked appalled and said, 'It is not a subject we discuss in this school, still less in class. I shall have to report all this to Mother Winifred and she will probably have to tell Reverend Mother.'

'Well, I can't think why you should be so shocked. Abelard was a fearful old prig anyway. Have you read his letters? In one of them he told Héloïse that the reason he had wanted her to become a nun was because he didn't want her to go on enjoying "sins of the flesh", or meet other people, or have any kind of life. And then he was hypocritical enough to go on lecturing her in all his letters about how sinful she was and how wonderful it was that he'd had all his revolting appendages removed.'

'Imogen!'

'*I* didn't say they were revolting; *he* did!'

'Imogen, I *forbid* you to continue this subject! Please go and stand outside the classroom until the lesson is over.'

When the lesson was over, Jessica and I were told to wait in class while Sister Simon Thomas went to talk to the headmistress. I did not feel particularly worried because I mistakenly thought that, since all the books my father had given me to bring back to school had been confiscated the instant I unpacked but had never been mentioned again, the headmistress did not really mind what we read but felt obliged to make the gesture of removing them.

Jessica was far more accurate in her appraisal of the situation. 'I bet Whinny will be furious,' she said, 'and I bet she brings up the subject of those other books of yours.'

'I'm sure she won't,' I contradicted. 'She'd have said

something before this if she were going to say anything. It's ages since they were confiscated.'

'She's probably been reading them all herself,' said Jessica. 'I expect all the nuns have been reading them.'

'Even if they have, I can't see that they can object,' I said. 'They're all books one is expected to have read: *Tender is the Night, For Whom the Bell Tolls, The Constant Nymph*, a collection of Aragon poems and some short stories by Elizabeth Bowen – I can't remember what else, can you?'

'There were some Prévert poems, too, and Strachey's *Elizabeth and Essex* and Edith Sitwell's *Fanfare for Elizabeth*. Your father seems rather keen on you reading about Elizabeth. He's forever giving you books about her.'

'It's his favourite period in history. I think he imagines he would have liked to have been Drake – a dashing pirate on the high seas coming home from time to time to flirt with a highly intelligent and powerful woman. He likes the high seas, he likes intelligent and strong-minded women and he's a bit of a pirate at heart so I can see why the idea attracts him.'

'I've just remembered one book they might object to,' said Jessica, returning to the problem of our forthcoming interview. 'That book of correspondence between Lawrence Durrell and Henry Miller.'

'Well, they've obviously forgotten about them or thrown them away, although it's jolly mean of them and Daddy will be furious when he hears. If we didn't have to leave our letters open for the nuns to read, I'd write and tell him immediately.'

At this moment the classroom door opened and Sister Simon Thomas reappeared saying, 'Mother Winifred would like to see you both in her study right away.' We tried to guess from her expression what the headmistress' reaction was going to be but our Latin mistress was not intending to give anything away.

When we entered Mother Winifred's study, she did not look up from the papers she was correcting.

'Close the door behind you, please,' she said and continued to write for a full minute before she finally looked up.

When she did at last raise her head, she surveyed us both with an expression that one could only classify as one of revulsion.

She was a dignified and stately woman who rarely betrayed any emotion, so it was a shock to realize, after all those years, that not only was she not fond of us, she apparently regarded us with positive loathing. My heart sank. The look in her eye was not encouraging.

'Well, Jessica and Imogen, I hear that you have taken to stealing as a way of life. It is extraordinary that it is always the same two girls who end up in our study. You seem incapable of keeping any rules, you appear to make a point of being disobedient, you cause havoc in your classes and dominate them to such an extent that the other girls barely have a chance to express themselves, and you are an extraordinarily bad influence on one another and on everyone else. I am seriously thinking of writing to your parents to suggest that you might do better elsewhere. However, I feel that that would be admitting defeat and that we ought to make one last attempt at turning you into something of worth. You both have very good brains which you are wasting so I have decided to allow you to learn Greek and to form a play-reading society as you requested last term. I expect to be present at the play readings, so you will have to hold these at times that suit my timetable as well as yours. I suggest Saturdays after tea and Wednesdays after supper.

'Since you have already helped yourselves to the key to the W section, I am going to make an exception in your case and allow you to continue to read books from that part of the library on one condition and that is that you do not share the books with anyone else for whatever reason and that you do not refer to any of those books in class. I am going to check which books you take out each time and I am going to give you weekly written work to do on each of the books you read. I may also set passages for you to learn by heart which you can recite to me just before your play-reading sessions.

'You must include everyone in your class in the play-reading society, if they wish to join; and I expect you all to perform a play, properly acted and directed, on the penultimate day of each term. You may ask Sister Matthew Dominic to help you with the costumes and to let you use the stage for rehearsals. She must be present at all rehearsals but you two are to be responsible for everything else including the casting and direction. The play must have my approval before you start rehearsing and may I suggest that you don't try anything too modern. I am unlikely to approve anything that has been written recently. We want something with some content, something that has stood the test of time, not a collection of inert people exploring the limits of the pregnant pause.

'Lastly,' said the headmistress, her hands still neatly folded on her lap, 'we come to the matter of your own personal books. I think it has always been made quite clear that you are not to bring books back to school and certainly not the utter rubbish that you brought back, Imogen: very shoddy literature, obviously bought on a station bookstall. I am disappointed in you.'

I longed to tell her what I thought of her literary judgement but was far too frightened to do so. There seemed to be easier ways of making the same point. 'They weren't bought on a station bookstall, actually, Mother. My father gave them to me to read and my mother suggested that I bring them back to school because she said she thought the library sounded totally inadequate.'

'In that case, I can only say that you have thoroughly irresponsible parents,' was the headmistress' astonishing reply.

The play-reading society was, from our point of view, a success. Hardly any of our class wanted to join it and, of those who did, many dropped out again after a couple of weeks so that we ended up with a small group of genuine enthusiasts. Because of the many demands made on her time, the headmistress was frequently unable to stay for more than ten or fifteen minutes so that as soon as she was out of the way we abandoned Molière or whatever we were officially supposed to be studying and changed to *Murder in the Cathedral* or some other play that we really wanted to read.

The first play we performed was equally successful. We chose, with the headmistress' approval, *The Importance of Being Earnest* and as Jessica and I were responsible for the casting, we gave ourselves the best parts. I played Lady Bracknell and she played Algernon and we both hugely enjoyed ourselves.

At the end of the performance the headmistress congratulated us but added, 'I think that next term you must give the main rôles to the others. I look forward to seeing what you can do with a minor part, Imogen.' Worse than this, she insisted on choosing our next play. It was a dull, one-act affair about Joseph of Arimathea arriving in England and planting a piece of the true cross. It was written in what was supposed to be ancient English and I was lumbered with the worst line in the whole play.

Dressed as an old man and hobbling across the stage with the aid of a stick, I had to cup my hand to my ear and announce in a quavering voice, 'Hark! I hear a voice upon the loo.' 'Loo', we were told, was an old, English word for 'hill'; but inevitably when, during our end-of-term production, I uttered this line, the entire school shrieked with hysterical laughter and from then on continued to giggle whenever I reappeared on stage.

From that day onward, I developed permanent, incurable, stage fright so that our essays in acting, which had started so light-heartedly, ceased, for me, to be anything but agony.

CHAPTER FOUR

Neither Jessica nor I understood why we had been sent to the Convent of the Immaculate Conception. Both our mothers were what is known as 'lapsed' Catholics and, since both our fathers were agnostic and violently anti-Catholic, we had neither of us been baptized or brought up as Catholics.

We came to the conclusion that our mothers must feel guilty about this and that they somehow imagined that they could save the situation by sending us to a convent boarding school. What seemed incomprehensible was that both our fathers should have agreed to the idea. There was no question of my brother being sent to a Catholic school and all of Jessica's three sisters were in the French lycée system. Why, we wondered, had we alone been singled out for different treatment?

'They obviously don't like us,' commented Jessica. 'That must be the reason. And I suppose our mothers think they are going to save our souls by sending us here.'

'Well, even if that is true, it doesn't explain why our fathers allowed it. Mine has never had a good word to say about Catholicism. He is contemptuous of all religion but he really loathes the Catholics.'

'That's what I mean,' said Jessica. 'He obviously doesn't like you. Both our fathers must hate us.'

It took Jessica years to admit that she was being unfair to our parents. The Grantsby-Hartes knew that they were shortly to return to England and felt that of their four daughters (who had all until then frequented

French lycées wherever Sir Reginald was posted because the syllabus remained the same from country to country) the two youngest were still too young to be sent to boarding school and the oldest too old to change systems.

As to my father, I overheard him telling a friend that he had purposely sent me to a convent boarding school rather than to any of the more obvious girls' public schools because he was damned if he was going to have me turned into a hockey-playing female with a voice that shattered glass. 'England,' he said, 'is riddled with hearty, back-slapping women hurling manure about with pitchforks and I do not intend to add my daughter to their number.'

'Well, he's quite right,' commented Jessica when I repeated this conversation to her. 'How lucky you are to have such a sensible father.'

'He isn't sensible. He's not in the least bit sensible,' I said. 'He believes exactly what he wants to believe in life and it has nothing to do with reality most of the time. Do you know what he asked me last holidays? He asked me how I was getting on with my pillow-lace.'

'What did he mean?'

'He thinks we are taught to make pillow-lace. He is determined to believe that the nuns are teaching us to sew a fine seam and to cook like angels, and that we spend our days drifting about peaceful cloisters to the dull hum of the bee and the distant sound of chiming bells.'

'Golly! Did you tell him it wasn't like that?'

'No, I didn't dare. He gave me such a lecture about the advantages of combining faultless Latin with an ability to cook that I didn't have the courage to tell him that no-one has made pillow-lace for generations and that the kitchens are in the nuns' Enclosure so we are never allowed within miles of them. He'd be appalled if he realized how much time we spent charging about in the mud chasing a ball, our bare legs blotchy with cold; but I don't suppose he'd believe me if I did tell him and he certainly wouldn't believe me if I told him that the only reason no-one plays hockey in this school is because the nuns think it is common. He'd be just as furious to think that we had to spend our afternoons playing lacrosse.'

'Well, at least he's *tried* to send you somewhere nice. It makes it all forgivable at least. I know my father sent me here to get rid of me.'

'Have you ever asked him?'

'Yes, of course. He gave me some feeble story about how he was not going to be in Washington much longer and how we'd be coming back to England. He said that I wouldn't be able to continue in the Lycée because the Lycée is in London and we'd be living in Norfolk, so the only solution was to send me to boarding school. But I know that was just an excuse to get rid of me.'

'Why is he coming back to England? He can't be retiring yet, surely?'

'He seems to think he's going to be head of the Foreign Office.'

'But then you'll have to live in London, won't you?'

'No. He doesn't want us to. I told you, I'm sure he doesn't like us. He wants Mummy to live in our house in Norfolk and to be able to come there at weekends. He's intending to have his own flat in London but we won't be allowed to live there. I'm not even sure he's going to let my sister, Lavinia, live there. She may have to board with one of the other girls from the Lycée.'

'How much longer has she got before she finishes school?'

'Two years.'

'Wouldn't it be more sensible for your mother to stay in London with her until then?'

'Of course it would be, and there would probably be much better day schools for Fenella and Jane, but it's the tradition in England to banish wives into forced exile on some frightful piece of land miles from anywhere. You'll soon find out. Everyone does it. It's a sort of undeclared divorce that Englishmen impose upon their wives. They all hate women and only marry them in order to breed heirs. All they ever want to do with their wives is dump them in the country, as far away from London as possible, and then run to the City or hide in their dreadful clubs. I'm sure those clubs only exist because they want somewhere where no-one can get hold of them and where they can drink and play snooker and pretend to be back at school again. I wouldn't be the least surprised to discover that they all dress up in grey flannel shorts and give each other canings.'

'I suppose that's why my mother hates Englishmen so much. She says they're the most ghastly men on earth and that that is why Englishwomen always have that desiccated look. She keeps telling me that we're going to find English balls deadly and that if we do, by some miracle, manage to entice an Englishman out on to a moonlit balcony or anything romantic of that sort, they will be bound to start talking about shooting, or marine insurance, or stockbroking, or something equally frightful.'

'But your father is English, isn't he? Does she think he's ghastly?'

'No, she's potty about him but, in many ways, he isn't typically English. He simply takes the bits he likes from every country and ignores the rest. He has lived so long in Italy that the England to which he thinks he belongs vanished ages ago without his noticing. He's like someone out of another century. My mother always says he's "Byronic", whatever she means by that. A friend of theirs told me once that he couldn't understand how my father could bear to live in Milan, and when I tried to explain about Mummy's music and the importance of Italy, la Scala, my grandmother and everything that matters to her, this man said, "But that can't possibly satisfy your father. He's so ineffably English." I thought "ineffably" was rather a good word: I think I might add it to my vocabulary. Anyway, whether or not Daddy is ineffably English, he certainly never talks about shooting, or insurance, or stockbroking and I should think he's charm itself on a moonlit balcony. He does seem to miss

61

his club, though. He always rushes to it the moment he arrives in England.'

'Why, do you suppose?' asked Jessica. 'Has he ever told you why?'

'He says he likes male company and that what he misses in Milan is conversation, and that Milanese women are a lot more interesting than the men; but I'm not quite sure that it is as simple as that,' I added as I began to give the matter scme thought.

My father's attitude to men's clubs had always struck me as ambivalent. He frequently extolled the merits of this excellent, English institution which permitted men to escape from their wives and enjoy the stimulating company of other men in a totally female-free environment; yet, he was probably his club's most active member in trying to change the rules so that women might be allowed to pass through its hallowed portals of an evening. He was irate and profoundly shocked when the majority of the members voted against such a radical change.

'Ironically,' he had said, 'it is the young members who are most against it. You'd think they'd have more sense.'

When my mother asked him why he minded so much he replied, 'Well, you know what clubs are like – full of the upholstered dead. The place is unspeakably gloomy at night. One wouldn't want women around in the daytime, of course, and one would have to restrict them to the bar and the dining-room. Couldn't have them twittering in the library or messing up a game of snooker. Still, the place is depressing in the evenings and a few women in the bar would liven up the club a bit.'

To me, on another occasion, he gave a different explanation. Smiling slightly maliciously, he patted my hand and said, 'Since members apparently only commit adultery with the wives and daughters of other members, it seems only reasonable that they should each have a fair chance to inspect the field.'

62

When I repeated this to Jessica she simply said, 'Goodness, your father must be civilized.'

I reminded her of this as we sorted through another trunk-load of letters and photographs. 'Well, he *is* civilized,' she replied with a laugh as she crossed the attic with a bundle of photographs and installed herself once more on her comfortable cushions.

'Did you ever tell your parents how much you hated it at school?' she asked suddenly.

'No', I replied 'Did you?'

'I tried once but they didn't believe me. Daddy said it was a complete volte-face on my part and that if I'd really been that miserable I would have said something earlier; and I overheard Mummy once telling a friend of hers that children always cried when they said goodbye at the end of the holidays but that they stopped crying the moment your back was turned. If you crept back and peered at them through the carriage window when they didn't know you were there, she said, you'd find them babbling away to their friends nineteen to the dozen, as happy as grigs (whatever grigs may be) having completely forgotten they were in floods of tears a few minutes before. Children always try to make you feel hideously guilty and worried, she said, and the next thing you know they have forgotten your existence. Why didn't you tell your parents?'

'I was afraid to tell them. Daddy would have been furious. You know perfectly well how angry he would have been; and I was terrified of him. And then I knew they had tried their best to find a good school for me and that they were paying through the nose for it, so it seemed rather churlish and ungrateful to tell them I hated it. Now I come to think of it I did try once to say something to Mummy and she asked me whether I really thought I'd be any happier in any other school. "You're not cut out for institutions," she said. "You're too much of an individualist and you don't like rules and regulations. You loathe being told what to do so you'd find any

63

school impossible. You'd be just as unhappy anywhere else. I hated my school, too. It's all rubbish about school being the best years of your life. School is frightful, there's no doubt about it; but people have to go to school. It makes everything seem much nicer afterwards, if that's any consolation. There's virtually no situation, however unpleasant, in which one cannot cheer oneself up instantly by thinking 'At least I'm not at school any more.' "

' "But why couldn't I have gone to school here?" I asked her. "Why did I have to go to school in England? Why couldn't I have gone to a day school in Milan?"

' "There were several reasons," she replied. "First of all, you were paralytically shy. Something had to be done about it. You may have forgotten but you used to cling to Granny's skirts and hide if anyone other than a member of the family appeared. The only solution seemed to be to throw you in at the deep end and force you to fend for yourself. Then there was the problem of your English. You really didn't speak it terribly well. You were obviously thinking in Italian; and your written work was dreadful. You know Daddy wouldn't put up with any of his children being less than perfect in English and the only way to learn a language is to go and live in the country concerned. You never learn it properly, however hard you try, unless you live in the place. And it's much easier the younger you are." She didn't mention Granny's reasons for wanting me to go to school in England, but I'm sure she was aware of them.'

'Well, she was right about your father, anyway,' remarked Jessica. 'Do you remember how furious he became every time we said the word "Mass"?'

We both laughed remembering my father turning puce with rage. Nothing irritated him more than our Catholic pronunciation of certain words. Upper-class Catholics having developed an idiosyncratic pronunciation of the language, we were taught at school to say the word 'Mass' as if it rhymed with 'pass', and 'confessor'

64

with the stress on the first rather than the second syllable, 'refectory' similarly with the stress on the first rather than the second syllable, and so on.

'Since when has M-A-S-S been pronounced with a long "a" in the English language?' my father would roar at us and then turn purple when Jessica and I replied that only Irish peasants pronounced 'Mass' as if it rhymed with 'gas'.

'Actually, to be fair,' we would add, smugly, 'it is generally understood that non-Catholics and converts mispronounce it and that this is no indication of their class. It's simply that they weren't brought up as Catholics and don't know any better; but for a born Catholic it is the exact equivalent of saying "perfume" instead of "scent", or "toilet" instead of "lavatory", or "dessert" instead of "pudding".'

'I've never heard such utter rubbish!' my father would explode. 'I can't think why I'm paying to send you to school in England if they can't even teach you to pronounce the language correctly.'

'And do you remember how angry he was when we neither of us knew the opposite of "zenith"?' continued Jessica. 'I thought he was going to have an apoplectic fit. I've never been so scared in my life and we can't have been more than about eleven at the time.'

My father had developed a habit of testing our knowledge to find out if we were learning anything at school and, on this occasion, he had asked us what the opposite of the word 'zenith' was. When neither of us could produce an answer, he said, exceedingly quietly, 'Has neither of you ever heard of the word "nadir"?' Then, as we shook our heads, he rose to his feet, hurled his newspaper across the room and shouted 'Christ Almighty! You two are completely ignorant! What in God's name are we paying to send you to that school for? They aren't teaching you anything. I've never met such a pair of illiterate, ignorant, hopeless creatures. I despair of you. They don't even seem to teach you your Bible. Ever heard of Moab? No. I didn't think so. Washpots? Shoes?

Any of it ring any bells? Good God, what on earth do you learn in that place?'

'Funnily enough,' I said to Jessica as I remembered the scene, 'I reminded my father of that incident recently and he seemed astonished. "I must have been having money problems at the time," was his explanation.'

Upton Hall

CHAPTER FIVE

The return to school in September, for the start of our
second year, was an occasion of unrelieved gloom.
Simon seemed frozen when we kissed our parents goodbye; my mother cried on seeing us off, and I felt leaden
with despair. The train journey was long and uncomfortable, and made worse by the fact that my mother, who
had always accompanied us during our first year, was
forbidden by my father to come with us this time. He
thought we were quite old enough to travel by ourselves
and, since we could speak French, saw no reason for us
to be nervous about changing trains in Paris and crossing that city by ourselves. He felt the same about us
making our way across London to our school trains. He
had no patience with worried travellers and no time for
children who could not look after themselves.

'For Christ's sake,' he snapped at my mother, 'they're
eleven years old. I was sent to prep school by myself
when I was eight. They speak three languages fluently.
They're perfectly capable of making a telephone call in
an emergency and they've got each other for company. I
can't think what on earth all the fuss is about. You
Italians can't let your children grow up. That's why you
end up with all these ridiculous men who are still living
with their mothers at the age of forty. No child of mine is
going to be tied to your apron-strings, let me tell you. The
discussion is closed and I'm not having any more nonsense from any of you.'

We took the night train from Milan and arrived in
Paris in the very early morning. Simon was under the

impression that, because we had been made to pay for the pillows in our *couchettes*, we had bought them and we therefore refused to hand them back when we arrived at the gare de Lyon. We had to find a porter to help us with our trunks and an unpleasant struggle ensued as we tried to walk past the ticket barrier with our pillows under our arms.

We had two hours to wait at the gare du Nord so we left our luggage and went in search of breakfast. While we were munching our *croissants* Simon suddenly announced, 'I'm going to run away. I'm trying to work out whether it would be better to do it here or in London.'

'Oh, Simon, you *can't*. You mustn't. *Please* don't,' I begged. 'Where would you go? How would you survive? I'd die worrying about you. So would Mummy, you know she would. Anyway, you said your new school wasn't as bad as the other one.' (Simon had been removed from his first preparatory school at the end of the previous Easter term because of my father's conviction that the headmaster was mad.)

'Well, it's only slightly better. I still hate it. You can't imagine how much I hate it.'

'I hate my school, too, but it would be stupid to run away. I've often thought about it but we'd never survive a minute. It's too dangerous. We haven't any money; we haven't anywhere to hide. We'd be caught immediately and we might even be arrested, or kidnapped. I don't think I'd even be able to get out of the school grounds without being caught.'

'Well, it doesn't matter so much for you. It's different for you because you have Jessica.'

'Yes, that's true, but if you ran away I'd still have to run with you. I couldn't let you go by yourself. Don't you have *any* friends at school?'

'Not really. There's one boy who's all right but we don't talk to each other much. We only know each other because we hide under the same tree. It's a weeping willow so it has long branches and it is really the only place where one can hide from everybody, so we share it.'

'How often do you hide there?'

'Every day.'

'What, both of you?'

'Yes.'

'You must know each other quite well by now, then, if you sit there talking every day.'

'We don't talk. We cry.'

'You sit there crying?'

'Yes.'

'Not every day, surely?'

'Yes, every day.'

'Both of you?'

'Yes.'

'How awful! You can't stay there. Why on earth don't you tell Mummy? She'd be so miserable if she knew.'

'There's no point in telling Mummy. She can't do anything about it and there's no point in making her miserable for nothing. It was Daddy's decision, not hers. She didn't want me to go to school in England in the first place but Daddy wouldn't listen. Granny didn't manage to make him change his mind so Mummy doesn't stand a chance.'

'Are you sure Granny tried?'

'Yes, I know she did. She was dead against it but Daddy was adamant. He said it would toughen me up and that it was a mistake for boys to grow up surrounded by women; but it's really because he wants to have Mummy to himself. He can't stand having me around. I know he can't. He has always wanted to get rid of me.'

'That's not what he really feels, it's just what it looks like to you. It's only because Mummy is away so much that when she is there, he wants her to himself. He's just the same to me.'

'No, he's different with you.'

'He *isn't*, Simon, I promise you. He's forever blasting off at me. You know he is.'

'He doesn't do it the same way, partly because you're

71

a girl and partly because he's proud of you. When he yells at you, it's only because he expects so much from you and because he wants you to be perfect, but when he shouts at me it's because I get on his nerves. He doesn't expect *anything* from me – or he only expects disasters. He can't stand me. I know he can't.'

'Well, you're wrong; but, anyway, you're not to run away because if you do I'll have to run away, too, and I don't want to: I'm too scared.'

'Well, I'll try a bit longer, but I can't promise. If I do run away, do you promise you'll come with me?'

'Yes, of course I will, but I still don't want to and, in any case, how would I know if you decided to run away?'

'You'd know. You'd feel it. I'd concentrate very hard and then you'd know. And you wouldn't have to worry. I'd look after you somehow. I don't know exactly how but I'd do it, I promise.'

'Could I bring Jessica?'

'If you want to, yes.'

'Where would we meet you?'

'In London. You could get as far as London, couldn't you?'

'Yes, but where in London?'

'Under Big Ben. I'd wait there until you arrived.'

'OK. If you ever run away that's where we'll meet, but you've got to promise that you won't leave before I get there.'

'I promise.'

'Swear?'

'I swear.'

The remainder of the journey, with Simon silent and forlorn, was given the final ghastly touches by the English weather. It was pouring with rain from the moment we alighted on English soil and, as I looked out of the train window at the London suburbs glistening in the wet, I failed to understand how anyone could choose to live in such a country. It was as if one had gone from summer to winter in a day.

Simon and I parted in London to head off in our separate directions and by that time I felt so dejected that even the knowledge that I would find Jessica on the school train did nothing to improve my spirits. When we reached our final destination, a coach drove us the five miles from the railway station to the school. As it turned through the gates and into the drive my stomach was in my mouth and I felt as if I would die. In our misery, Jessica and I could see no difference between our lives and those of the infant factory workers or orphans in Dickens. David Copperfield, we felt, could not possibly have been more unhappy.

It was as we were grinding our way through that first term of our second year that Jessica's parents returned to England. They had barely installed themselves in their house in Norfolk before they kindly invited me to spend half-term with them, and they soon came to a happy arrangement with my parents that, half-terms and Easter holidays being short, and air travel expensive, I was to spend half-terms, Easter and a couple of weeks in the summer with them. In return, Jessica would spend the rest of the summer with us in Italy. It was to Upton Hall, therefore, that I set off with Jessica when half-term arrived.

I loved the Grantsby-Hartes immediately, and was made to feel one of the family from the moment I first met them. I particularly loved Jessica's mother who in physical appearance was what Englishwomen are always supposed to be and yet so seldom are. She was one of those fine-featured blondes with bone-china complexions whose entire beauty lies in their skin and hair. In twenty years' time one would be unable to guess that she had ever been beautiful, but in those days she had the fragile perfection of a lily just before it fades. Her hair, which had never been cut, was piled upon her head where it was held in place by countless hairpins which she scattered liberally wherever she went.

(Lady Grantsby-Harte was so immensely feminine

73

that for years her daughters felt very masculine by comparison. As Jessica entered her teens, she became horribly anxious about herself.

'Goodness, Imogen,' she kept saying to me, 'do you think I am turning into a man? I'm getting hairs on my legs. Thank heavens I'm fair and you can hardly see them. Come and have a look. I think I really *am* turning into a man. Will you still love me if I do?'

'Of course,' I would reply, and we would both giggle.)

Upton Hall was an enormous Elizabethan manor-house which had none of the cottage atmosphere usually associated with architecture of that period. It was lugubrious, very dark and far too large to be reassuring. The halls were immense and the lead-paned windows seemed to keep out all but a faint glimmer of light. The drawing-room was filled with frightful furniture and oppressive paintings; the sitting-rooms so cold that one huddled in vast armchairs around fires where whole trees were burned with astonishing speed. We all had scarlet faces as we sat, scorching, our knees practically in the flames and our backs frozen. We were permanently aware of the acres of icy room stretching away behind us. Everyone took to drinking gin and tonic to keep themselves warm.

Jessica's mother used to send us on frequent expeditions to obtain further supplies of gin from Grandpa. Grandpa had a wing of the house to himself, with a servant to look after him. He was exceedingly deaf and more than a little dotty but he had one irresistible attraction – limitless supplies of gin. A large quantity of this vital liquid was hidden about the place: behind books in the library, under his bed, in the coal-shed, even in the cloakrooms, used as boot-blocks in the riding-boots. The places changed constantly and Grandpa could sometimes be quite ingenious in his attempts to outwit us. Open war was never declared. We never admitted to stealing his bottles and he never mentioned the fact that they were disappearing. Jessica and her mother were convinced that he never noticed. I was certain that he was perfectly aware of what was taking place.

With the words, 'Darlings, go and fetch some gin from Grandpa, will you?' we were packed off on a terrifying expedition into enemy territory.

Grandpa never knew who I was even after years of meeting me every day at luncheon and he always bellowed loudly, 'Who is that girl? How long is she going to stay?'

He intensely disliked people appearing in his quarters, especially children. Jessica's job was to distract him while I had the task of finding his latest hiding-place. She would try to keep him busy talking about Trollope – he was very fond of Trollope – while I rummaged under his bed and helped myself to whatever I could find. I would then creep downstairs on tiptoe, past the library, along the passage and start running as I reached the main hall. Across this I fled, up the front stairs and along more corridors until I finally reached the drawing-room where I triumphantly presented my hostess with the results of my foray. Jessica would wander in a few minutes later, looking vague and saying, 'God, Grandpa is boring! I *hate* Trollope.'

Poor Grandpa was grossly mistreated. He joined us every day at luncheon where the conversation passed entirely over his head and nobody made the slightest attempt to look after him or make allowances for his deafness. He used to bellow in my ear about the poor drainage on the farms whilst one of Jessica's sisters would be pinching my arm and hissing, 'Grab the gravy before Grandpa gets it!' The most fascinating discussions were constantly interrupted by one or other of the members of the family exclaiming, 'No, Grandpa darling, the treacle tart is for the girls. You know you don't like it. There's a nice custard for you,' or 'Quick, Imogen, pass the potatoes before Grandpa sees,' and 'No, Grandpus, you *know* you're not allowed roast pheasant; your teeth aren't up to it . . . you can't have any port: it's bad for your gout.' As Grandpa looked longingly at the vast quantities of food we were demolishing, he had to be content with disgusting-looking concoctions resembling multi-coloured baby food.

About one thing Grandpa was absolutely adamant. At Christmas, the poor had to be given a side of beef and a sack of coal. It was the custom for the local landowner to look after his tenants to that extent and nothing was going to prevent him from doing his duty. Useless it was to point out to him that he had lost the entire family fortune years ago, investing in some non-existent coal-mine in Wales, whereas all his 'tenants' lived in comfortable council-houses and had cars and televisions. Every Christmas, without fail, each family in the village received a side of beef and a sack of coal. Few of them, if any, still had coal fires but Grandpa was unaware of the existence of electric fires and he presumably imagined the villagers gratefully roasting half an ox on spits in their meagre dwellings. He walked through his own grounds wearing a splendid cape and brandishing a silver-topped cane. Not one of us ever had the courage to ask him for a bottle of gin; no one dared refuse his Christmas bounty.

Upton Hall was a house where one was very aware of the seasons. Like all respectable English houses, it was icy in winter. Bathing was a nightmare, going to bed was agony. I used to dread changing for dinner because it meant leaving the drawing-room fire to traverse miles of dark and freezing staircases and halls, only to be faced with a haunted room and glacial bathroom. In true English fashion, the bath water was always boiling in spite of the sub-zero temperature of the surroundings. My bathroom smelt of rising damp which depressed me almost more than the cold. I used to lie in the water until I was lobster-coloured in the vain hope that I would store up enough heat to survive the ghastly process of drying myself and dressing for dinner. Once ready, I fled from my terrifying room back to the fire and the gin – hearing, as I went, the nuns' voices in my ears saying, 'Ladies never run, Imogen,' and muttering to myself, 'To hell with being a lady.' Jessica's mother used to sing dirges in the bath. It was the only time she ever sang, so one assumed she was enjoying herself.

Meals were delicious and the wines divine. Conversation was eccentric and highly entertaining. No-one ever went to bed before two in the morning. No-one ever rose before noon. As we had our last drinks, vast kettles were being heated in the kitchen; and, when we finally retired, we each went to our rooms armed with a cup of hot chocolate and a scalding hot-water bottle. Neither of these could in any way alleviate the cold of the bedrooms or the icy touch of the sheets. Unable to sleep, I used to move the hot-water bottle from one bit of my bed to another, trying to decide whether it was worse to have a cold back or frozen feet. It was in that ghostly and unwelcoming room that I first read Henry James' *The Turn of the Screw* and my terror was complete. The beams creaked at night and ivy tapped against the leaded panes in the wind. I turned out my light, hoping to be swallowed by death before the ghost appeared and the monster pounced.

Spring was always charming, with the gardens coming to life again and the grounds a mass of bluebells and daffodils. There were peacocks and geese wandering all over the lawns. We were always told by the gardeners that peacocks loved cedar trees and needed lots of wives if they were not to die, forlorn, of a broken heart. Whether or not this is true, I do not know to this day, but they had an abundance of both cedars and wives at Upton. Over the years, the strange, rather disturbing noise emitted by these birds became inextricably associated in my mind with the smell of the English countryside and the sight of fields and paddocks stretching away beyond the ha-ha.

While the peacocks were drifting about looking elegantly half-witted, the geese tended to settle comfortably in the rose-beds where they appeared to have a permanent supply of large eggs upon which to sit. I do not remember ever seeing an egg hatched, nor do I remember anyone ever eating any of them. I rather suspect that the Upton geese only laid one clutch of eggs in their lives and that they were always the same ones we saw in the flower-beds year after year.

There was only one gander, Egremont, and he scared the daylights out of me. He was better than any guard-dog. As soon as he heard a car coming up the avenue, he would start moving towards the front of the house where he would stand, poised ominously, with his neck stretched forward. The moment the car drew up, Egremont would start hissing and the person unwise enough to descend from the safety of his vehicle before one of the family appeared, found himself confronted by an irate bird who was quite capable of viciously attacking any intruder.

All the local tradesmen knew Egremont's habits and sat tight until one of the family came and called him to order. Jessica and her mother both adored him and, vast though he was, carried him about in their arms, where he looked perfectly ridiculous. I can still see the frail, beautifully dressed figure of Jessica's mother teetering about the lawns in absurdly high heels, carrying an enormous, white gander in her arms and apparently whispering sweet nothings in his ear.

Summer was heavenly. Long days outdoors: tennis on the north lawn, croquet on the south lawn; picnics, bathing, decorating the local church with an abundance of flowers; tea and cucumber sandwiches under the cedars; then Pimm's on the lawn before we sauntered in to change for dinner. Every day was a long succession of familiar events. Life became immensely agreeable and the house became less frightening as the temperature rose.

There were outings in plenty. The most complicated was going to the sea to bathe. The sea was only a few miles away, but the hours of preparation this expedition required made one feel as if one were about to set off for the uttermost ends of the earth. Jessica's family had a terrible car which was falling to pieces. Amongst its other charms, it had a large hole in the floor between the front and back seats. 'Jump, Imogen, darling,' Jessica's mother used to say and I obediently hurled myself from the gravel drive to the back seat without so much as a toe touching the car floor. Into this dilapidated vehicle we were expected to pack a large number of things: huge hampers of food, enough books for the whole family, extra towels, wine, chocolate and – most important of all – hats. Whilst in the sun (whether in the garden, or on the beach, or while swimming) all the women were expected to wear hats to protect their complexions – not just any hat, but large straw hats with ribbons. It must have seemed extraordinary to the other swimmers, in the early sixties, to see a bevy of graceful, behatted women wading out to sea and drifting about like swans, their heads held high above the water.

('The English are quite mad,' I could hear my mother saying. 'Charming people. Delightful very often. But quite, quite mad.')

White skin was not something you acquired. It was simply something you were born with, like blue blood. Nobody would ever have dreamed of saying it was common to be brown, but it was understood. Once, when we were about eighteen, Jessica came home after staying with my parents in Italy. Although one could hardly have called her suntanned, she was very slightly golden. I was enchanted. She looked ravishing. Her mother looked at her with stunned horror.

'Jessica, my darling!' she said, almost in tears. 'Whatever are we going to do with you? You had better find yourself some good books and sit reading in the cellar for a couple of weeks.'

Another incident I remember vividly occurred at a point-to-point. As with swimming expeditions, a great deal of preparation was required before setting off to a point-to-point. Once again, we packed hampers of food and wine in the boot of the car; but we also packed in blankets, shooting-sticks, binoculars, local newspapers, a tarpaulin and multitudes of hats and coats. We all had to have a warm coat in case it was cold, a macintosh in case it rained, a smart coat in case the weather was clement enough to dress correctly (in England, it seemed that dress was of greater importance in the country than it was in town); and we had to have a suitable hat to accompany each of these outfits, not to mention gloves, bags and all the other accoutrements. There were so many hats that we could barely see out of the rear window of the car.

Grandpa came to point-to-points with us largely, I believe, because it provided us with a second car. I could never make out which was the more frightening: to be driven by Grandpa, who had a Toad-of-Toad-Hall complex on the roads, or to be driven by Jessica's mother who could not see a thing and drove firmly on the wrong side of the road, peering blindly at the approaching traffic.

On this particular occasion, we arrived after a hair-raising drive and pulled up amongst the other cars in an area which seemed to be knee-deep in mud. It was an exceedingly cold day. There was a biting east wind and the ground was sodden. A rawness entered our bones; the damp rose up and embraced our thighs. Our legs soon became blotchy and our hands blue. With one gloved hand we clutched our hats in the wind while with the other we desperately tried to hang on to our fluttering race-cards.

By about five in the afternoon the situation became intolerable. Teeth clenched, we studied our cards. The last race was at five thirty and I was longing to abandon everything and go home. The thought of crumpets and tea was irresistible but there was apparently no question in anyone else's mind of giving up. Jessica's mother was beginning to wail and become fractious. It was at this point that Jessica decided to produce one of her most characteristic brain-waves. She announced to the assembled company in the most authoritative manner that it was a known, scientific fact that the nearer one was to the ground, the warmer it was, and that the earth was giving up large quantities of heat which were being wasted in the cold air. She was very insistent about it and added that we could increase the warming procedure by blowing on one another.

She finally convinced us; and so it was that we finished the afternoon face down in the mud, in a circle, our heads practically touching and our feet splayed out along the ground, furiously blowing at each other.

We lost a lot of money on that last race and Jessica's father was in a bad temper for the rest of the evening.

Italy

In the firm blue of the unfolded sky
I shall decant the limpid magic
Of the purest sensations, melody
Of childhood, where I was only I.

No firme azul do desdobrado céu
decantarei a límpida magia
das sensações mais puras, melodia
da minha, infância, onde era apenas eu.

Alberto de Lacerda

CHAPTER SIX

Our holidays in Italy could hardly have been more different from our holidays in England. Jessica fell in love with my family and with my grandmother's house as totally as I fell in love with Upton Hall and its inhabitants.

Manta had huge and very beautiful grounds. There were walks and fountains, walled gardens and ponds, greenhouses and kitchen-gardens, orchards and vines. There were sun-drenched terraces and shady alcoves, swings and hammocks slung here and there. Those who liked the heat put deck-chairs in the blazing sun, those who found the sun too harsh sought out cool, stone benches half-hidden under trellises of overhanging grapes. The lawns ran down to the water's edge and by the lake, almost hidden by weeping willows, there was a summer-house. It was a paradise for children.

My grandmother was the central person in our lives. My mother was away so often, playing concerts, that it fell to my grandmother to provide the permanent presence and rock-like security that mothers are normally supposed to provide. In the daytime she would sit reading in the shade, or walk in the gardens with us telling us anything she thought would be useful to us in life. In the evenings, she would sit on the terrace looking out across the lake. Both Simon and I adored her and it was to her that we turned for information and advice, on her lap that we laid our heads in moments of despair.

She said to me once that the real reason that she had been in favour of my being sent to boarding school in

England was that she wanted me, when the time came, to meet men who were not Italian. 'It was only by sending you into that society at an early age that you were ever going to be able to stand Englishmen or have a chance to escape,' she said, 'and of course you have to grow up there and know people from childhood in order to be invited to the right houses and dances when you are older. You wouldn't meet a soul if you went there for the first time at eighteen. Englishmen don't like women much but they do leave them alone to get on with their lives. Italians keep their wives imprisoned. *Never* marry an Italian, darling child. They make wonderful lovers but *terrible* husbands.

'You should have a look at the French and the Americans, too, of course,' she continued, 'but I think you'd be bored by the Americans – they're such babies – and the French are all so frightfully irritable and bad-tempered. They're quite exasperating and they won't believe there is anything worth seeing or knowing about outside France, which can become very tiresome.

'Of course, you don't have to get married,' she added with a sigh. 'In many ways you'd be better off not marrying; but I don't think many women are satisfied on their own and to be childless is not a happy state for any woman. Even the ones who think they don't want children usually regret it in the end. No,' she sighed again, 'I don't think you'll find a better compromise than an Englishman. It has a great deal to recommend it, as long as you don't want anyone to pay you too much attention. That's why I encouraged your mother to marry one. It has been a very successful arrangement on the whole. Of course, he's never been faithful to her, but then nor would an Italian have been. No man is. At least he allows her to be herself and have her own career, her own friends; to be a person in her own right, not just a possession. No Italian would ever have allowed her the same freedom and independence.'

She paused for a moment. 'A lot of Englishmen are homosexual, of course. Simon's headmaster, for

88

instance. He's supposed to be an excellent teacher and the boys all adore him, but he's obviously homosexual. He's hopeless with parents and so ill at ease with the mothers. I'm not sure I think it was a good idea to send Simon to school in England, but I do think it was a good idea to send you.' She relapsed into silence but behind the resigned exterior I glimpsed, for a second, a look of deep sadness as she turned her gaze once more towards the lake.

The Italian lakes are not happy places. Their beauty is profoundly melancholy and I always sensed in my grandmother an identification of spirit with the wistfulness of Maggiore. It was almost as if she and the lake shared a tragic secret and exchanged their melancholia back and forth, commiserating with one another. It seemed as if my grandmother sought the lake not so much for consolation as for confirmation of her understanding of the world, confirmation that life really was as sad as she had discovered it to be.

One of the many myths about the Italians is that they are light-hearted. It may be true of the south of Italy but it is certainly not true of the north. The northern Italians have a deeply depressive streak as one realizes instantly if one reads even a few of their suicidally gloomy novels.

I often wondered whether it was something to do with the climate – the atrocious fog and damp, the night-like darkness of winter, the simultaneously ghostly and hellish quality of the place. England, reputedly the country of fogs, has never produced anything to compare with a Milanese *nebbia*. The Italian word for it is far more evocative of the true spirit of their fogs than is the English translation: *nebbia* sounds like the nothingness and desolation that it is.

My grandmother was an exaggerated example of the northern Italian spirit. She had long since ceased to believe in anything. She had tired of travelling, tired of the theatre, tired of all but the slow movements in symphonies and the minor key in music. She no longer wanted new experiences. She had found out all she wished to know about life. She, once such a devout and faithful churchgoer, had ceased even to believe in God. 'I wish so much that it were true and that I would see you all again,' she would say to us, 'but I'm afraid, darlings, that when we die we simply snuff out like candles.'

She had been greatly admired as a young woman. She and her two sisters had been generally recognized as the three most beautiful girls in the Milan society of her youth, and she was supposed to have been the most beautiful of the three. I had seen pictures of her dressed in complicated dresses, the loops and plaits of her black hair piled in heavy masses upon her head, and a cameo on a ribbon around her lovely neck. There was a great serenity about her in those pictures. Her wide mouth looked gentle and as yet unharmed by life, and her dark eyes had not yet acquired the wistfulness that in later years they were never to lose.

In her early twenties, she had fallen desperately in love with a charming and good-looking Florentine from a very old family. Her parents totally disapproved of him for they saw instantly what kind of man he was; and his family utterly disapproved of my grandmother, the Florentines in those days being snobs about the rest of Italy and not wanting their sons to marry girls from Milan. Against everybody's wishes, my grandparents married and my grandmother felt humiliated and betrayed when her husband turned out to be an incorrigible philanderer who was happy to live off her fortune but seldom bothered to come home.

'We could have been extremely happy,' she once said to me. 'It was so silly of him. I thought I had married a man and discovered that I had married a baby.'

My grandfather always maintained that he loved my grandmother – until the day he died, he never ceased to reiterate that she was the only woman he had ever loved – but my grandmother, who was hurt beyond all bearing, gave up believing him after a time. She

gradually withdrew from life and, disabused, watched
the world go by from some distant pinnacle, surveying
the scene with amusement and irony but always with a
complete lack of involvement. She never loved anyone
else except her daughter and grandchildren; and she
feared greatly for me, her only granddaughter, as she
had done for my mother, for she knew that I, too, in my
turn would be hurt.

With the untroubled confidence of youth, it never
occurred to us to give the matter a thought but, had we
done so, it would have seemed inconceivable that a time
might come when my grandmother would no longer be
there. She seemed part of the foundation of life itself,
that wise old lady with the wry sense of humour and the
faraway look in her dark eyes.

Jessica always thought that my grandmother preferred me to her grandson, and perhaps she was right
since my grandmother did not trust men whatever their
age; but I think it more likely that she saw me as an
extension of herself and that she hoped, through me, to
redress the balance and to teach me how to escape the
tragedy that is woman's lot. Whatever her reasons, and
in spite of very convincing efforts not to show favour-
itism, she seemed more concerned about me than about
Simon.

My mother, on the other hand, without any shadow of
doubt preferred her son to her daughter – not that she
did not love me passionately, but she adored Simon in
the highly possessive and emotional way in which Latin
women tend to love their male offspring. She was
immensely proud of him and took what Jessica called the
King Priam view ('better that Troy should burn than
that my wonderful son should die') as far as he was
concerned.

My mother ought to have been irritating but was,
in fact, the opposite. She was the most endearing
person – dramatic, noisy, affectionate, untidy, over-
excitable, anxious and tremendously appealing. She
had her mother's beauty but her father's blue eyes

which looked astonishing under her very dark hair. A great many men passed through our house, most of them musicians – composers, conductors, violinists and singers – and, as I grew older, I had the impression that the majority were in love with my mother, but she never appeared to notice. I imagine that my grandmother had brought her up to expect the worst of men and that, rather than waste her life wondering about their motives, my mother chose to ignore them completely except in a professional capacity. All her tempestuous love was, therefore, concentrated on her children.

Had it not been for her music, my mother would have stifled us with her love but, fortunately, the piano absorbed huge amounts of her passion and energy. Without realizing it at the time, we lived on music. The house was filled with it. My mother practised for hours every day and when she was away playing concerts, my father listened to symphony after symphony on record. In any other country, people would have complained about the noise, but in Italy noise is taken for granted. At all times of day, echoing round the courtyard and up and down the stairs one heard people playing records full volume, or practising some instrument, or singing scales; or, as in any house in Italy, simply bellowing bits of opera as they bathed or shaved. It was not until, as an adult, I was transplanted to Washington, that I realized how much music I had absorbed as a child and woke up to the fact that it had become an addiction.

My father had nothing in common with my mother except an equally great love of music. He was a very private man, and as unemotional as my mother was emotional. He was one of those deceptively quiet people with exceedingly short tempers but although irascible in the extreme, he was a man of great generosity and persuasive charm. He was considered eccentric by most people, partly because he held such strong views – some of them rather unusual – and partly because he had absolutely no time for social conventions. He simply loathed the socially aspirant and it was a loathing which he passed on to his wife and children.

The Italians liked my father. He was their idea of the perfect English gentleman: at ease in any society, impeccably dressed, immensely well read, charming to one and all and yet, by their standards, totally eccentric. They were always amazed by the intensity of his irritation with people or things he did not like and his impatience with anything which bored him. 'I simply will not tolerate being bored,' he used to say as, throughout our youth, he dragged us out of theatres or concerts in the middle of performances because he thought them indifferent. 'I cannot understand how people can spend good money to sit through such utter rubbish,' he would complain at the top of his voice as we scrambled over the feet of the other spectators. We were always near the front which made us doubly conspicuous; and anyone who has ever attempted to leave la Scala in the middle of a first performance will realize that my father frequently achieved the virtually impossible. We became adept at jumping ropes and scrambling down fire-escapes.

My father made a point of being direct so it was easy to tell whether or not he liked someone. If he disliked them he made no attempt to hide the fact. He always concentrated on the person he was addressing as if they were the only person in the world, and he had a penetrating stare which people often found disconcerting. If their eyes wavered for a second, my father immediately suspected them of being shifty. He thought eyes highly indicative of character and formed some rash judgements as a result. He took a violent dislike to the headmaster of Simon's preparatory school, for instance, and insisted on removing him and sending him elsewhere; but he never gave any of us a reasonable explanation for this. All he would say was, 'The man's totally insane. He has yellow eyes, exactly like a mad gundog.' He was greatly in favour of wall-eyes, for some reason, and of anyone with eyes that did not match. He seemed to think it went with originality and brains. He talked fondly of someone he had once known who had had a glass eye.

The most important person in our household, after my grandmother, was Clémence, our governess. She was a Frenchwoman, from Tours, who had been in my grandmother's employment for twenty years or more at the time that I was first sent to boarding school in England. Originally, she had been my mother's governess but had gradually changed rôles as my mother grew up. After my mother married, Clémence stayed on at Manta as my grandmother's housekeeper-companion; and, then, when we were born, my grandmother sent her to us, in Milan, where she became our nanny and then governess.

Clémence was extremely upset when Simon and I were sent to school in England – 'ce pays barbare', as she called it. I suspect that she took it as a personal insult and in some way a slight on her teaching abilities. Worse than this, however, was her conviction that we were bound to fall ill in a country where, it was well known, medicine was so backward that no-one had yet discovered suppositories and where they all ruined their intestines with pills and chemicals. To Simon's and my hideous embarrassment, she bombarded us both at school, for years, with terrible parcels of suppositories – suppositories for sore throats, suppositories against influenza, suppositories for constipation, suppositories to make you sleep, every type of suppository known to man. We begged her to stop sending them and tried to explain how mercilessly we were teased as a result, but her reply was always the same. 'It is only because of their unnatural practices that the English are so prudish about sensible medicine. Normal, well-balanced people are not afraid of the anus.'

At the end of Jessica's first holiday at Manta, she said to me, 'I'm not surprised you and I made friends so quickly. I honestly never believed that I would meet another family as mad as mine; but yours is just as mad, if not madder.'
'Do you think our families are any odder than anyone

else's?' I asked. 'Don't you think all families are probably as odd, if one knew?'

'No, I don't,' said Jessica, firmly. 'I don't see how they could be. I think our families are very peculiar.'

'Do you suppose we'll end up completely insane?' I asked her, suddenly worried. 'We must have inherited enormous doses of battiness.'

'Pleasantly eccentric is what I intend to be,' said Jessica. 'Actually, what I'm longing for is to be *really* old because I've got all these plans. For a start we're never going to have to stand at art exhibitions any more. Think of it. We'll be able to go round every art exhibition as slowly as we like, in perfect comfort, in a wheelchair. I shall bop people with my umbrella to make them get out of the way and you can wear an ear trumpet and squawk at them. I want you to push me along the promenade des Anglais, in Nice, in a wheelchair, too. It's my absolute dream. I'm going to be in the wheelchair and you're going to be pushing me, wearing a large hat and white gloves. If you get really exhausted, I might relent occasionally and let you have a ride in the chair while I put on the hat and gloves. Then we can go to the casino – I assume there is a casino in Nice, isn't there? If not, we'll have to borrow a motor-bike and go to Monte Carlo. One of the good things about being old is that you can afford to lose lots of money. It doesn't matter losing it because you're going to be dead soon, so we can have a wonderful time losing our money and behaving disgracefully. I do think the idea of a motor-bike is a good one, don't you? I like the thought of surprising everybody; and two old ladies in hats on a motor-bike would be much more interesting than two old ladies in a car.'

Simon came into the room as Jessica was saying this and his arrival on the scene brought our conversation to an abrupt halt. He did not like Jessica; or, rather, he disliked the fact that she had caught my attention.

I had always been afraid of my twin. He was an unhappy and secretive child who, when no-one was looking, wrought vengeance on me. While I was still small enough to be impressed by such things, he told me stories of ghosts and monsters hiding at the foot of my bed, ready to devour me. He locked me in dark cupboards to tease me. He hit me and punched me as if I were a boy; he took all my toys from me and broke them.

Occasionally, my grandmother or my parents would discover signs of bullying – inexplicable scratches all down my back, or bruises all over me – and then he would be punished. Nothing made my father angrier. It put him into an instant rage and his fury against my brother was frightening for all of us. Inevitably, I ended up feeling guilty at having been the cause of it.

I loved my brother in spite of all this, for twins are close companions, however difficult their relationship; and I understood, behind his behaviour, the war that he was waging against my father and their joint frustration at having to share my mother.

I was also aware that he was having a much worse time at school than I was. Whatever my criticisms of the Convent of the Immaculate Conception, and however mistaken the nuns' judgement on occasions, they were gentle and kindly women entirely motivated by good intentions and it was plain, even to a child, that there was not the smallest trace of the sadistic or malicious in them. It was their true saintliness, so removed from the outside world, that often made them blind to the workings of simpler human beings. At Simon's school none of this applied. Not only were some of the masters true sadists, the whole system was built to attack the weakest, the foreigners, the ones who were different; and little boys are far crueller than little girls. Things improved slightly for Simon when he progressed from preparatory school to public school, but only because by then he had been beaten into something resembling the other English boys. His tales of the canings, the tortures, of being hung by the feet upside-down in lavatories appalled me; and his letters to me were a constant cry for help.

Like many twins, we could sense when the other half

of our couple was in distress and I frequently felt physical jabs of pain for no reason and knew that something terrible was happening to Simon. There was nothing I could do about it but it added to my misery and my hatred of England.

When I first produced Jessica, Simon became desperate. He felt, I think, that the only person who really cared for him or knew him had dropped him for something more amusing. At first he clung to me, following us everywhere, trying to form a trio, but apparently he felt excluded. He accused me of having been seduced by England, of having shifted emotionally from Manta to Upton. It was perhaps for this reason that he took to ridiculing me and, during our teens, making me uncomfortably aware of my sex. Only in our late teens, when we started going to dances together, did we rediscover the closeness and uncanny telepathy we had experienced as small children. Until then, for many years, I felt his presence as an overwhelming burden and his interest in me extremely threatening.

As far as I was concerned, the advent of Jessica in my life had been a godsend. She replaced my need for Simon as a companion and she was strong enough to represent a barrier between him and me. She did not dislike Simon. Rather, she was intrigued by him. 'Your brother is extraordinary,' she would say to me. 'Why is he so angry all the time? Are all boys so violent?'

As she grew older, however, her interest altered. 'Has Simon stopped thinking that girls are silly?' she asked me when she was about fifteen. 'He's so good-looking. It seems such a waste.' And, after the first dance we all three attended together, she whispered to me, 'I think I've got a bit of a crush on your brother. Do you know if he still hates me? I had the feeling while we were dancing that he really quite liked me.'

I watched them with interest the following morning as the three of us had a late breakfast in a café together. Jessica was shocked at the way in which Italians simply knock back an *espresso* standing at a bar, and that there is virtually never anywhere to sit down. 'I must say,' she remarked critically, 'I think Italy is heavenly in almost every way, but I do think your breakfast habits are hopelessly uncivilized. I know you all like to hit the ground running when you get up in the mornings, but this is ridiculous. Why is no one ever allowed to sit down? And why are all your *croissants* made of *panettone*? I rather like *panettone* at tea-time, but sweet *croissants* at breakfast are really too disgusting. You have the best coffee in the world and then you don't allow anyone to enjoy it. No wonder everyone suffers from stomach ulcers. It would put me in the most fearful bad temper and give me an ulcer immediately if I had to start the day like this every morning.'

'You're not being at all fair,' laughed Simon. 'People don't normally have breakfast in a café. It's our fault that we got up so late and couldn't be bothered to make our own breakfast. Cafés are only for people in a hurry. We never eat these disgusting *croissants* at home, do we? And I can't think of anywhere where breakfast is more civilized than at Manta.'

'Everything at Manta is utterly civilized, but we all know that Manta is completely untypical and that your family does everything differently from everyone else,' retorted Jessica.

'I suspect that the same could be said of your family,' I interrupted, and we all laughed.

Jessica was particularly ebullient and full of wit that morning, I remember, but Simon seemed to me to be his usual self. I would have loved him to regard her as an object of desire: for reasons I did not care to analyse, it would have been a relief to me; but I could see no signs of reciprocal interest on his part.

Upton Hall

CHAPTER SEVEN

'Did you really have a crush on Simon in those days?' I asked Jessica as we battled to force open the lock on what appeared to be a metal hat-box.

'Yes, I did for a while. I thought I was madly in love with him; but I didn't get much encouragement so it petered out,' she said then added, with a laugh, 'Just as well as it turned out.'

The rusty lock finally gave way at this point and we opened the lid of the box to find it crammed full of old photographs.

'Here's a picture of Egremont,' exclaimed Jessica with delight, holding it out for me to see. It was very faded and one of the corners had been torn off, but it was unmistakably Egremont.

'I was always terrified of him,' I said.

'Were you?' enquired Jessica, sounding surprised. 'I thought you adored him.'

'No. It was you who adored him. You and your mother.'

'I hated him quite a lot of the time. He was always foul to me when Mummy was away.'

'He was, wasn't he? Especially that first time when Mrs B. was away and we got drunk, and your mother was so cross with us. I used to think about it quite often when I was living in Washington. I used to force myself to think about it in order to cheer myself up. It was one of the few things that made me laugh when I was feeling really depressed.'

'I wish I could have seen you. You must have looked

very eccentric laughing all by yourself in Georgetown, or in the gardens of Dumbarton Oaks, or wherever you happened to be at the time.'

'I don't think I laughed out loud in public, or made an exhibition of myself,' I protested.

'Of course you did. You're doing it now. Just look at yourself. If I didn't know you, I would think you were very peculiar sitting there in that hat, laughing to yourself.'

I suddenly realized that I probably had laughed aloud in the streets of Georgetown. I found it almost impossible not to laugh aloud, even now, when I thought about it.

It had happened one summer, when I was paying a brief visit to my father's sister in Essex. Jessica's parents had had to go to Cambridge for a few days and her sisters were staying with cousins in Scotland. Grandpa was away on one of his periodic and disastrous jaunts to London (these trips were always in some way connected with unfortunate flutters on the stock exchange) and so Jessica found herself alone at Upton Hall for the first time in her life. She felt abandoned and telephoned me daily. She excelled at sounding pathetic when she wanted something. Unlike most people, she became positively seductive when feeling sorry for herself.

'Do come, Imogen, please. It's so frightening here at night and Egremont is being horrid to me. He's missing Mummy and being absolutely beastly to me, as if it were my fault she'd gone away. Imogen, I know I saw the ghost last night. It was petrifying. If you love me, please come. Otherwise I shall die. I know I shall die and it will all be your fault.'

'Why don't you come here?' I asked. 'Aunt Miranda won't mind.'

'But, Imogen, I can't!' wailed Jessica. 'I promised Mummy I'd exercise the horses and look after the ducks. It would be too awful if she came back and found them all dead!'

'All right, I'll come. But only if you meet me at the station. You'll have to tell me how to get there. I've always been driven, don't forget, so I've no idea how to get to you by train. Where do I change for Little Upton?'

'It's frightfully easy. You change in Norwich and ask anyone for the train for Little Upton. Ask them for the Upton Flyer: that's what everyone calls it. You normally just have to cross to the other side of the platform and it should be waiting there.'

The Upton train only had two carriages and one could not buy a ticket for it beforehand.

'You'll have to pay the station master at Little Upton,' I was told.

The Upton line was permanently threatened with extinction. The government wanted to close it because it only served four villages and was not, to use their term, 'economically viable'. Every six months or so, a census was carried out on the number of people using the line and with equal regularity the entire population of the county turned out to defend it. The train, which, as Jessica had said, was known as the Upton Flyer, was dear to their hearts and for the two or three days of the census it was crammed to bursting. There were farmers with their wives; bankers and stockbrokers who normally travelled by car and who looked conspicuously out of place with their bowler hats, pin-striped suits and umbrellas; there were women with children and strange parcels; the odd tradesman; the occasional pig or crate of chickens; a collection of youths wearing winkle-pickers and imitation leather jackets; and the local Member of Parliament. These faithful travellers went back and forth between Great Chipping and Norwich as many times a day as the Flyer for as many days as the census took to complete. The ticket collectors, local inspectors and station-masters all confirmed that the train was in constant use by hordes of locals. The government was baffled by the fact that the number of people using the train regularly did not coincide with the amount of revenue the line was producing, and eventually became suspicious. After years of discussion, a major meeting was called in order that the government investigate the arguments for and against closing the line.

It turned into a formidable debate. The highlight was reached towards the end when a local vicar rose to his feet and in a barely intelligible accent launched into an impassioned defence of the Upton Flyer. His argument, expressed in almost incomprehensible English, was that before the line existed the villagers had been unable to move very far afield. Bicycles, he pointed out, were not the same thing. You thought twice about bicycling twenty miles. Ten miles there was one thing, but ten miles back again was another. The local population had, therefore, been inclined to commit incest. Marriage between cousins, or even sisters and brothers, was common. It was difficult for the local prelate to draw the line since everyone was intermarried and those who seemed to be descendants of quite separate families were frequently half-sisters and half-brothers. Many children were the result of regrettable incidents between grandparents and grandchildren ... The vicar waxed poetic as he described the copulating habits of the peasantry. It was, he pointed out, clearly disastrous. Every village in the area was full of monsters – grotesque children with huge heads, adult men being wheeled about in perambulators by their half-witted daughters. The railway had at last brought salvation to the countryside. Men from Blixton could court girls from Great Chipping. There were even those who went as far as Norwich. Take away the Flyer, he exclaimed, and you will once again find young men raping their own grandmothers, aunts sleeping with their nephews, fathers with their daughters. To abolish the line would bring back immorality and incest to the area.

The government inspector in charge of the enquiry had been listening with the bemused air of one who is not quite sure he is hearing correctly. He was finding the accent heavy going and the drift of the argument unexpected. He strained forward in an effort not to miss any vital point and seemed at a loss for words when the vicar finally sat down. Wiping his brow with a spotlessly clean handkerchief, he cleared his throat, pulled from his breast-pocket a pair of half-spectacles which he placed precariously on the end of his nose, and surveyed the hall of upturned faces with an air of total despondency.

'Am I to understand, Reverend Peabody, that if one were to abolish this uneconomical branch-line, the government would be directly responsible for encouraging incest, that it would be putting the official seal of approval on marriage between blood relations? Is my interpretation of your argument correct?'

'Arr,' said the vicar, rising abruptly to his feet and equally abruptly sitting down again.

'These are very curious arguments, Reverend Peabody, which shed a new and perplexing light on the whole problem. You have just exposed an aspect of the matter which the government had not, I feel sure, fully appreciated previously. I sense difficulties ahead which I had not foreseen. We shall have to ascertain the facts. There will have to be studies carried out,' the government inspector continued wearily. 'Precise statistics will have to be drawn up on the population, the relationships between one family and another, the rate of incest before and after the construction of the railway line. It will be some time before we have sufficient information to come to any accurate conclusions.' He drew a deep breath, polished his spectacles and continued. 'You have brought a most surprising and unexpected element into the argument, Reverend Peabody, and I fear the decision on the closing of the line will have to be postponed until we have had time to look fully into the matter.'

Loud cheers greeted this last remark and the meeting broke up in an atmosphere of joyous festivity. The vicar of Hadfield-St-Mary, not normally very popular with his flock, suddenly found himself the recipient of warm congratulations and enthusiastic applause. He was led off, in triumph, to the Ox and Crown where his parishioners

105

stood him endless rounds of bitter. Never before had the Reverend Peabody been the centre of such festivity, never before a popular hero. Light-headed with the sudden attainment of glory and euphorically tipsy on ale, the vicar mistook his way to the gentlemen's lavatories and contentedly urinated into the fruit-machine to the loud cheers of his drinking companions. Only the publican disapproved, calling 'You'd better get the Reverend home now before he does any more damage. Disgraceful I call it. Unsuitable, 'im being the vicar and all.'

The congregation in Hadfield-St-Mary's little church was double its normal size that Sunday and its vicar enjoyed his unaccustomed popularity for some time afterwards.

I changed trains in Norwich and had no trouble finding the Upton Flyer, tiny though it was. I was profoundly happy as I watched the English countryside rolling by, knowing that Jessica would be waiting for me upon my arrival. I was to make this journey by train many times during the years that followed, and always had the same reception – but, that first time, I was taken by surprise. Jessica had bicycled over, wheeling another bicycle beside her for me. Apparently, she had not thought of the problem of my suitcase. She had, however, told the station-master I was coming and, devoted as he was to his station and to Jessica's family, he decided to receive me correctly. As the train came to a halt at Little Upton, I remember thinking that the station looked like a toy station – tiny and beautifully decorated, with carved and painted wood – and the train was like a toy train. As it stopped I saw Jessica, wearing a large, floppy hat, hanging on to two bicycles. Then, to my astonishment, I noticed the station-master rushing to open the door of the carriage for me.

'Don't move, Miss,' he said, the moment he had opened the door. Then, he gave a great blast on his whistle and waved a red flag at the engine-driver who gave me the impression that he was quite used to this sort of thing and was, in any case, apparently in no hurry to proceed.

Repeating, 'Don't move, Miss, till I get back,' the station-master whisked away and produced from some hidden shed three solid, wooden steps on wheels which he rolled up to the train door so I could step down gently, he giving me his arm as if I were the frailest creature on God's earth. I was not allowed to touch my case ('Leave it to me, Miss'), so I went over to where Jessica was standing, smiling, and kissed her under her floppy hat.

'What a sweet station,' I said, 'and what an adorable little man. I've never been to a station where they produce steps on wheels before.'

'I told the station-master that you were my best friend and he was duly impressed. You looked terribly funny stepping down out of the train. You looked so surprised. I wish you could have seen yourself,' Jessica giggled. 'I've brought you a bike by the way.'

'Yes, I can see,' I replied, 'but what am I supposed to do about my case?'

'Oh, God!' sighed Jessica. 'I forgot about that. I suppose we'll have to leave the bikes here and walk. What a bore. And I thought I was being so organized.' She thought for a moment. 'We'll have to walk all the way back here again and then bicycle home. Or we could bicycle home first, walk back here and then walk home with the case; and, by then, someone might have decided to bring it for us,' said Jessica, always optimistic.

The station-master having first climbed into his little signal-box to change the signal and then waved his green flag just to make sure everyone understood, the train was finally allowed to continue its journey. Looking quite flushed by all the exertion, he then came towards us carrying my case.

Jessica smiled sweetly at him and said, 'I'm terribly sorry to bother you, Mr Turner, but do you think you could look after Imogen's luggage for half an hour? It's all my fault, you see, because I brought two bikes and I completely forgot about the problem of luggage, so now we're going to have to bike home, and then walk back here, and then walk back home with the case which, as you can imagine, is going to take a little while and is going to be quite exhausting for Imogen after her journey. It was so silly of me . . .' Her voice trailed off, leaving all sorts of suggestions hanging in the air.

'You don't need to do that, Miss Grantsby-Harte,' said the station-master reassuringly. 'I'll ask my son to drive it up later when he goes over to the farm.'

'Oh, do you think he really could?' enquired Jessica, looking helpless and relieved. 'It would be incredibly kind of him. I can't tell you how awful I feel: it was so terribly disorganized of me and poor Imogen is not much good at carrying things so I couldn't possibly let her manage it by herself.' She smiled blandly at me and I had the awful feeling that she was about to invent some fatal illness for me which made me incapable even of walking.

Fortunately the station-master prevented her by saying, 'That's all right, Miss. It's a pleasure and it's no trouble at all for my boy. He drives right past your gates. Only, if you wouldn't mind keeping an eye out for him because he don't much like your gander. 'Fact he's right scared of him which I tells him is silly, him being a grown man and all and that being only a bird.'

'Of course, Mr Turner. Please tell your son it will be quite safe. I'll lock Egremont in the paddock for the afternoon. He's been awful lately, anyway, so it serves him right. You are absolutely angelic. I'll never forget how kind. It's really so sweet of you. Imogen's immensely relieved, aren't you, Imogen?'

'Yes, it's exceedingly kind of you,' said I, feeling embarrassed.

We wheeled our bicycles into the lane, still waving 'goodbye' to the station-master, and at last found ourselves pedalling towards Upton Hall.

'You see. I told you,' said Jessica, with immense self-satisfaction. 'It's always better to put off anything disagreeable as long as possible. I find if one procrastinates long enough, there always conveniently appears someone who is just longing to do whatever it is for you. You end up making someone else feel useful, too, so you are really performing a good and charitable act for which, no doubt, you are duly rewarded in heaven. All in all, I find it a most satisfactory system.'

My heart sang as we turned into the gates of Upton Hall. The drive went steeply downwards at first, before rising again, and we let our bicycles sail down at full speed, enjoying the sensation of racing between the trees without having to pedal.

As we started up the opposite slope, we were carried some of the way by the momentum already gathered and instinctively we knew that we were racing against each other. We leant forward as if on horses, except that our legs were moving furiously. By rights, Jessica's hat ought to have blown off but her hats always seemed to stay glued to her head as if they had grown there and had always been part of her.

As we reached the top of the hill and the drive levelled out to wind between the lawns and cedars, I was well ahead of Jessica. She managed, as she always did, to turn the situation to her advantage.

'Why on earth are you going so fast?' she shouted. 'Honestly, it's utterly exhausting trying to keep up with you. Anybody would think you were training for the Olympics or something. How do you except me to make polite conversation if you keep charging off into the middle distance?' She sounded positively pained. I slowed down to allow her to catch up with me and was rewarded with her most beatific smile.

'Oh, Imogen, I *am* glad you came. You can't imagine how awful it has been without you.'

Egremont was waiting for us. He liked me, a sentiment which I was unable to reciprocate, and waddled fast in my direction, making snapping noises with his beak. As he snapped and nudged my hands, Jessica pushed him away, saying, 'Stop it, Egremont! She's my friend, not yours.'

We left the bicycles propped up outside the front

door – something we would never have done had Jessica's parents been there. Jessica then preceded me into the hall and let out a shriek of horror.

'Honestly, I don't believe it! Egremont's been in here and he's shat all over the hall. Oh, God, I hate him! He always does this when Mummy's away, just to show he's annoyed – as if I hadn't noticed!' She ran outside again, shouting, 'Egremont! You're a beastly bird and I absolutely hate you! How can you be so horrid to me? Well, you're going into the paddock and that's that!' She picked him up in her arms and, staggering under his weight, ran with him to the paddock. He docilely allowed himself to be thus transported, happy no doubt to have made his point and to be the centre of attention again. The horses, however, were none too pleased, and moved smartly to the other end of the field.

Jessica came back, still looking furious. 'I told you he was being utterly horrid to me. It's been ghastly. You can't imagine—'

At this point, we were interrupted by the cook calling us. She seemed flustered when she finally appeared.

Jessica suddenly said, 'Oh, I forgot to warn you. Mrs B. is going away for the night. She says her sister is ill. It seems odd that her sister is only ever ill when Mummy isn't here, but I'm quite pleased really. It means we'll be all on our own, for once, with no servants spying on us.'

'If you'd care to come into the pantry a moment, Miss,' said the cook to Jessica, 'I'll show you where everything is.'

'Come on, Imogen. You come too,' said Jessica, pulling me by the arm.

I followed her through the kitchen into the pantry where stupendous quantities of food seemed to have been prepared.

'Darling Mrs B., you are wonderful!' exclaimed Jessica as the cook explained patiently, item by item, that this simply needed warming for fifteen minutes in the bottom of the Aga, that those could be eaten cold, that those just needed boiling up and that the sauce was all ready in the blue bowl in the refrigerator.

'Are you sure you are just going away for one night?' enquired Jessica with the apparent innocence which I knew covered considerable sarcasm. 'It looks as if you expect us to fend for ourselves for several weeks – or did you think we might be holding a house-party?'

'It's just as well to be prepared, Miss Jessica,' replied the cook, totally unaware of the sarcasm. 'I don't know what your Ma would say if I didn't leave you enough to eat.'

'I wonder what Mummy will say when she hears,' remarked Jessica afterwards. 'I shouldn't think she'll be at all pleased.'

We were both excited at the prospect of being totally on our own together for the first time in our lives. Every detail of the following thirty-six hours seemed a miraculous adventure. The greatest adventure of all was being allowed to mess about in the kitchen. For children brought up in boarding schools and fed for years on the repulsive food provided by those institutions, ovens and sinks became symbols of pleasure rather than tools of slavery so that the idea of cooking for ourselves became for us a hedonistic dream, and the entire kitchen-scullery-pantry area an enchanted world of unlimited self-indulgence.

Those children of our acquaintance who did not share this enthusiasm for cooking and eating remained entirely indifferent to food as adults and, as far as one could see, equally indifferent to all sensual pleasures. I later came to the conclusion that it is probably impossible to be sensual in one area without being sensual in all areas and that those who are not interested in any one form of sensual enjoyment are probably not sensual at all. How can someone who dislikes the feel of water possibly love the feel of silk; and how can anyone who does not love the feel of silk enjoy the touch of someone else's skin against their own?

During the afternoon we played tennis (Jessica insisted on calling it 'ping-pong' which was doubtless all our tennis deserved), then we played a game of croquet at which we both cheated by common consent. We made a habit of cheating at games. Jessica maintained that rules were made for, and kept by, idiots and that games only became amusing and a test of one's intelligence if one had to do battle with cheats – the whole point, she claimed, was to out-cheat a cheat.

While we were still cheating at croquet, the station-master's son arrived. We heard his van coming up the drive and ran round to the front of the house as he drew up, honking furiously on his horn. He was an anxious and blotchy-faced youth.

'It's all right,' shouted Jessica. 'We've heard.'

'It's the goose, Miss, what I was honking at, not wanting to get out and be bit, if you follow me.'

'That's a goose, as you so rightly surmised,' replied Jessica. 'She won't hurt you. The one you are afraid of is a gander and he's in disgrace so he's shut in the paddock. You're absolutely safe.' Again, that innocent voice and gently mocking smile. I suddenly realized that I would be unable to bear it if she ever mocked or despised me. (When I said this to her, years later, she seemed surprised.

'How could I possibly ever mock or despise you? You're so frightening.'

'Frightening?' I asked.

'Yes, frightening. You've always absolutely terrified me.'

It was difficult to tell whether she was laughing or serious.)

'I think we could let Egremont out now, don't you?' enquired Jessica as we watched the van disappear between the trees. 'He's probably bored stiff, poor love, and the horses will never be the same again if we leave him with them much longer. Thinking of which, I promised Mummy I'd exercise them and I haven't done it today. Could you bear to ride Tarquin for me if I ride Gawain? I can't be bothered to take them out now: it's too late; but we could ride them over the jumps.'

I agreed and we spent the next hour cantering round the paddock and hopping feebly over some small fences.

It was only as evening approached that the house began to feel frightening again. The departure of the cook made us feel very alone all of a sudden. Although we were perfectly used to travelling by ourselves and changing planes and trains in foreign countries, we had neither of us been in a house without adults before; and Upton was a long way from any other human habitation.

Jessica suggested gin, the eternal remedy in that house. This seemed a good idea. We had several quite large ones whilst listening to some ancient jazz records that we had found in a cupboard. We danced for a while until we felt dizzy, at which point we sat down and helped ourselves to another gin and tonic. Jessica started giggling. Her laugh was infectious and we soon found ourselves doubled up in mirth.

Amongst the jazz records, curiously, we found a record of two of Hitler's speeches. We put this on and listened to it several times. Neither of us spoke a word of German but for some reason we found it hilariously funny. Our stomachs were aching; we clutched our sides, and the house was echoing with the peals of childish laughter when suddenly the telephone started ringing loudly. The sound made us jump. It was totally unexpected and seemed louder than usual. Jessica had just collapsed on a sofa.

'You answer it, Imogen,' she said. 'I don't think I can stand up.'

I was still giggling as I picked up the receiver and my 'Hello' must have sounded somewhat garbled.

'Hello?' enquired a shrill, educated voice in my ear.

'Hello,' I repeated and then 'Hello' again since there seemed to be no response the other end.

'Do stop saying "hello",' called Jessica from the sofa. 'You sound perfectly absurd.'

'Well, some woman said "hello" to me but now she seems to have gone away again,' I answered just as the voice returned saying, in anxious and irritable tones, 'Hello? Who is that?'

'Who are you?' I asked, adding – for Jessica's

benefit – 'I don't like this at all. It's very suspicious. She's trying to find out who I am without saying who she is or to whom she wishes to speak.'

'Why don't you put the receiver down?' asked Jessica and at exactly the same moment the shrill voice in my ear said, 'Imogen, is that you?'

I suddenly recognized the voice as that of Jessica's mother and felt so embarrassed that I tried to sit down on a nearby chair. In doing so, I succeeded in pulling the telephone off its tiny table.

'What are you doing?' giggled Jessica, as I tried to pick it up.

This question started me giggling again, and when I finally managed to collect the telephone off the floor, I could hear Jessica's mother calling my name anxiously and repeatedly.

'Oh, golly, I'm so sorry,' I said, still laughing.

'Are you all right, Imogen? You sound very odd.'

'No, no. I'm quite all right. I just knocked the phone off the table . . . No, it isn't a wrong number.' I was trying to answer Jessica at the same time. 'It's your mother.'

'My mother has been dead for some years,' retorted Jessica's mother, rather coldly I thought. 'Imogen, darling, are you sure you're all right? You don't sound quite normal to me. Is Jessica there?'

'Yes, but she can't get up.'

'What do you mean, she can't get up? Is she in bed?'

'No, she's on the sofa, but she's exhausted.'

'Well, she can't be so exhausted that she can't cross the drawing-room.'

'She's dizzy. I think she'll fall over. Jessica!' I suddenly shouted, much louder than I had intended. 'Your mother's dizzy. I mean worried. I mean she wants to talk to you. I told her you were in bed but she says she's too exhausted to cross the drawing-room.'

Jessica moaned, but rose to her feet as I suddenly announced at the top of my voice, 'I feel terribly sick. I think I'm going to faint.' I left her to pick up the telephone and collapsed in a heap on the floor. My head was spinning and I did not pay much attention to my surroundings, though vague half-sentences of Jessica's drifted through the alcoholic haze.

'No, Mummy . . . it's just that we're feeling a bit sick. I think we ate too much apple charlotte . . . oh, yes, and we tried one of Grandpa's cigars when we were listening to Hitler's speeches. They were so funny. Goodness, you were lucky to be alive then! He must have been a scream . . . What? . . . Oh, yes. Yes, of course I know he was awful and mad and the most sinister phenomenon ever to come out of the Western world – What? . . . Yes, of course I realize. I just meant he sounded so hysterical and it must have been so terribly funny . . . I wasn't being flippant! I say, Imogen,' she suddenly said to me, prodding me with her foot to make sure I was listening, 'Mummy's sounding terribly cross for some reason . . . What?' she addressed the telephone again. 'No, I can't call her . . . I'm not being thoroughly exasperating: I really mean I can't call her – literally. She's away . . . Yes, that's what I'm trying to tell you. Mrs B. is away for the night – or it might even be for several nights judging by the amount of food she left us . . . Yes, all right . . . We were going to bed anyway . . . Yes, I promise we're going to bed right now . . . Mummy, I promise . . . All right, Mummy darling, but please don't ring too early because Imogen and I want to sleep late . . . She's OK. She's asleep now. It was just the cigar. No wonder Grandpa's dotty if he smokes those things all the time . . . OK. Goodnight. Talk to you tomorrow,' and she finally put down the receiver and sank to the floor beside me, groaning.

'God, what an effort. I feel quite drunk. I hope Mummy didn't notice. She sounded cross about Mrs B. and she was furious about the record. She also seems convinced you must have fallen off one of the horses and given yourself a nasty bang on the head. She says she's coming home tomorrow night and that she'll ring first thing in the morning to see how we are.'

*　　*　　*

We had had a long discussion during the afternoon about where I was to sleep. A bed had been made up for me in the haunted room but I had absolutely no wish to sleep there and Jessica did not want to sleep alone either.

'I told you on the telephone that I'm sure I saw the ghost. It's really too frightening. It would be so much friendlier if we slept in the same room.' (Jessica tended to class all people and things into one of three groups – 'friendly', 'tedious' or 'jungly'. The last term was reserved for people or behaviour considered to be beyond the social pale or for occupations she disliked such as playing lacrosse) 'Why don't we sleep in the Oak Room? It's so much friendlier than the others.'

It was to the Oak Room, therefore, that we staggered off to bed, feeling unbelievably ill. Jessica's last words, as I fell asleep, were, 'I don't think that cigar was a good idea, do you? Perhaps cigars go better with brandy than with gin but I don't think I could bear to try.'

I had been sound asleep for what seemed like a long time but woke up with a start. I sat up in bed, wondering for a second where I was. Jessica was sitting bolt upright in her bed, clutching her knees and calling my name in a loud whisper.

'What's the matter?' I whispered back and then, startled into wakefulness, 'Have you seen the ghost?'

'Listen!' whispered Jessica.

We both held our breath and listened to the distinct sound of heavy footsteps coming up the drive.

'Someone's coming up the drive,' I whispered, unnecessarily.

'Do you think it's a burglar?' whispered Jessica.

'It could be an escaped convict,' I suggested, helpfully, 'or somebody coming to murder us.' Our imaginations were beginning to run riot.

'What do we do?' asked Jessica.

'I don't know,' I replied, feebly. 'Perhaps we had better hide. We could go down the secret staircase' (Upton boasted a priest's hole and a hidden staircase) 'but we might bump into the ghost.'

'Maybe it *is* the ghost,' suggested Jessica in a tight little voice.

We listened again. The footsteps were coming nearer the house.

'I don't think it can be,' I said. 'You can't hear ghosts' footsteps.'

'Why not?' asked Jessica. 'You can hear their chains and their groans. Perhaps our ghost makes a noise on gravel.'

By now we could hear the footsteps immediately beneath our bedroom window. We sat absolutely still, hardly daring to breathe, as the person below abruptly stopped moving. There was total silence for a full minute during which every imaginable picture of horror floated through my mind. I imagined that it was really the ghost and that he had simply floated through the wall downstairs and was about to appear in our room; I imagined a murderer standing, pistol drawn, waiting for the first move from us to shoot us down; I imagined the corpse of some intruder who had managed to reach the house only to be strangled by the ghost; I imagined monsters and rotting bodies, ghouls and maniacs. The silence was more terrifying than any noise as we waited for something frightful to happen.

The stillness was abruptly broken by the noise of a plant being crushed under a heavy boot in the flower-bed below. This was immediately followed by the sound of someone trying to open the window downstairs. Jessica's hand suddenly shot across from her bed and clutched mine.

'Do you think we should be brave and go and look out of the window?' she whispered.

I nodded and squeezed her hand for reassurance.

We crept out of bed, still holding hands, and tiptoed cautiously across the room. We had almost reached the window when all hell broke loose below. First there was a wild fluttering and hissing, then a deep yelp, then more fluttering and scrabbling followed by a male voice saying,

117

' 'Ere. Get off!' and a loud thump succeeded by another yelp.

'It's Egremont!' whispered Jessica excitedly. 'Good old Egremont.' We stuck our heads out of the window and looked straight down on the most surprising sight. A large, helmeted policeman, torch in hand, was sitting in the flower-bed wildly kicking his huge, booted foot at Egremont who was attacking with gusto. After one brief second of surprise, we both laughed out loud with relief.

Jessica immediately called to Egremont to stop. 'You're a good bird, Egremont,' she called down to him. 'You're an absolute angel, but you can stop now.'

'Angel, indeed!' stormed the policeman. 'That bird's a public menace. I have a good mind to take him up to the station. I'm going to put him in my report you can be sure. He's a public danger and you ought to keep him locked up.'

At the words 'locked up', Egremont took another sharp nip out of the policeman, this time getting him full in the thigh. The bobby let out a bellow of pain and rage and Jessica, rather flustered, shouted, 'Egremont! Stop it immediately! I'm coming right down. I'll only be a second,' and then, as she heard the policeman hurling dire threats at the gander, she added, 'Don't you touch him! He's saved our lives. You might have been a murderer or a criminal for all we knew. Which reminds me, who are you and what do you think you are doing trying to break into our house in the middle of the night?'

'I'm the sergeant from the village, Miss.'

'No, you're not,' retorted Jessica who was still hanging out of the window but who had finally let go of my hand. 'I know the village policeman perfectly well. In fact, I've known him all my life. His name is Perkins and he's afraid of mice.'

'Perkins is in hospital, Miss. Fell off his bike, he did. Yesterday. Had a very nasty fall so I was sent from Great Chipping.'

'That still doesn't explain what you're doing here at this time of night – and caught in the most suspicious

118

act,' said Jessica, adding in a hoarse whisper in my ear, 'He might be an impostor. I don't think he's a policeman at all.' She put her head out of the window again, calling, 'Egremont, you stay right there. We're coming down and we might need you again.'

The policeman winced as he heard this but Egremont just stood hissing as if waiting for the next move before attacking again.

We skipped down the back stairs as fast as we could, pulling on dressing-gowns as we went, and rushed out of the scullery door and round to the flower-bed under our bedroom window. I half expected the figure in the rhododendron bush to have disappeared but he was still there, although he had at last succeeded in struggling to his feet. As we approached, he pulled himself up, stuck out his chin, took a deep breath, then turned to Jessica saying, in monotonous tones, as if he were reciting a prayer for the dead, 'I will 'ave to file a report on this and I shall be putting in a complaint about the bird. I shall need to explain your presence 'ere so you will 'ave to come down to the station but I'll take your names and addresses first.'

'What on earth are you talking about?' asked Jessica. 'I happen to live here. My name is Jessica Grantsby-Harte and this is my guest, Imogen Holt. It is outrageous that you should come snooping about here at dead of night. In fact, I want proof that you really are a policeman and an explanation of your extraordinary behaviour. Egremont!' she suddenly shouted. 'Stand guard! Imogen, go and ring the police station and tell them to send someone up here as fast as possible.' Jessica's voice had suddenly acquired a tone of command I had never heard before and I realized for the first time that her vague and helpless airs covered an iron will.

'I think there has been a misunderstanding, if I may say so,' said the policeman looking thoroughly uncomfortable. 'Are you saying that you are Lady Grantsby-Harte's daughter?'

'Of course I am. Who on earth do you think I am?'

'Well, you see, Miss, it was your Ma what asked me to check. Said the house was empty, she did, and asked me to keep an eye. Funny she never thought to tell me you was 'ere. When I saw a light I said to myself, "That's suspicious," I said and I proceeded to inspect. I left my bike up the top there and came on foot so as not to disturb any suspicious party.' ('As if anyone could have failed to hear the heavy thud of his approaching boots,' Jessica later remarked) 'I proceeded cautiously around the house,' continued the policeman, 'until I came to the kitchen window when, looking through it, I saw to my surprise plates what hadn't been washed up and other signs of activity around the Aga. The Aga top weren't shut which weren't normal, were it? So I went to the scullery window and there I saw more plates and a frying pan too – all dirty! "Arr," I says to myself, "Mrs Burton wouldn't never go away and leave things dirty." Not the type, Mrs Burton, to do a thing like that. I know Mrs Burton what works 'ere you see; she's married to my wife's cousin. Very suspicious I thought it, what with your Ma being away and all. And the funny thing is that it was Perkins she had spoken to, not me, but Perkins told me about it, and then your Ma rang the police station late this evening to remind Perkins. Worried, she seemed, so I thought I ought to take a look. We've 'ad a lot of complaints about the gypsies lately and it seemed fair to me they might 'ave seen an empty house and decided to use it for their own purposes, if you follow my meaning. I was going to climb through the window and take a quick look about when that bird of yours flew at me. A right brute 'e is and no mistake. Bruised me all up me legs 'e did! You want to watch 'im or you'll be in trouble. I'll 'ave to put 'im in my report like I said, and I shall 'ave to ask both you girls for a statement just for the record.'

'Why?' asked Jessica as the bobby pulled out a large notebook from his jacket pocket.

'Need it for the record,' he repeated. 'Could be as you

120

weren't meant to be 'ere for all I know. Your Ma didn't mention there was any children here.'

After a great deal of argument we agreed that he should telephone Jessica's mother, as a result of which he was reassured about our identities.

'How stupid of Mummy,' Jessica stormed as the policeman left at last. 'What on earth did she mean by calling the police? She might at least have warned us. We might both have died of fright, and Egremont might have been clubbed to death with a truncheon. I think it's outrageous. I shall tell her so, too.'

As we clambered back into bed, we could hear the policeman's thunderous footfall gradually growing fainter as he made his way back down the drive. Egremont had stationed himself in the flower-bed under our window and obviously intended to remain there for the night. As if to remind the world that he was still on guard, he let out one last hiss before we all succumbed to sleep.

When Jessica's mother returned the following evening, we told her what had happened and Jessica complained bitterly about the whole thing.

'I' was worried, darling,' her mother said. 'You sounded so odd; and Imogen sounded most peculiar, too. I thought you might be suffering from shock of some sort, or that you had fallen off one of the horses, or that you were terribly ill and feverish. Then, when you couldn't produce Mrs B. I had this terrible idea that you were being held up at gunpoint and couldn't say what was happening and that Mrs B. was probably lying bound and gagged somewhere.'

'Goodness, Mummy, I never knew you had such a fevered imagination! And you complain about me inventing things!'

'You get it from me, I'm afraid, darling.'

'If you thought that, why on earth didn't you tell the police? And why didn't you tell them we were here?'

'To tell you the truth, darling, I thought there was

121

another possible explanation and I didn't want to get you into trouble. I just wanted to be sure you were safe.'

'What other explanation? What are you talking about?' asked Jessica, looking completely mystified.

'I had just the tiniest suspicion you might have been taking drugs,' said Lady Grantsby-Harte to our astonishment. Jessica and I gasped. We had barely heard of the existence of drugs and had certainly never come into contact with them.

'Honestly, Mummy!' Jessica exclaimed, sounding genuinely shocked.

'We've never taken drugs,' I said, horrified at the idea. 'We wouldn't ever, would we, Jessica?'

'Darlings, I'm sure. It's just that you did sound so very odd and I hear such terrible stories about teenagers smoking "pot", or is it "hash"? After all, you are very young and you might be silly enough to try. I thought that if you had taken something you would probably be asleep by the time the policeman arrived whereas if there were anyone else in the house he would soon see and force his way in. If it had been Perkins, I wouldn't have minded telling him and asking him to talk to you both, but since it was some unknown creature from Great Chipping, I didn't want him finding out that you had been smoking pot or whatever and getting you into trouble. I just wanted him to check that there hadn't been a burglary, or a murder, or anything of that sort. In any case, darlings, the important thing is that you should both be all right which you seem to be, so we don't need to worry about it any more.'

'Of course we're all right,' I said, still appalled that anyone should suspect us of drug-taking. 'It was only the gin that made us feel peculiar.'

'The gin?' queried Lady Grantsby-Harte, her pretty face suddenly anxious. 'Was there anything wrong with it? I don't think gin goes off. I can't ever remember hearing that it did. Where did you find it?'

'It was Grandpa's gin. We found it in his bathroom. We didn't think you'd mind. There wasn't anything wrong with it, it was just that we drank rather a lot of it.'

'But, darling child, you're used to gin,' said Lady Grantsby-Harte. 'It can't possibly have turned you into the gibbering idiot you seemed to have become last night.'

'I don't think we've ever drunk that much before,' I said, trying to defend myself against accusations of battiness. 'And then there was that awful cigar of Grandpa's which we found in the library. Perhaps cigars don't mix with gin. Jessica thought we should have tried it with brandy instead.'

'Of course,' sighed Lady Grantsby-Harte, looking relieved, 'I'd forgotten about the cigar. That explains everything. *Never* smoke cigars. They always make one feel *so* ill; and Grandpa has particularly large ones. Stick to gin, darlings, will you? It's so much safer. Now I simply must have a bath. The train journey from Cambridge was really too frightful and, when we changed on to the Upton Flyer, I found myself cornered by the new MP for Sutton Chiswell. He's *such* a dreary young man. You can't imagine . . .' Lady Grantsby-Harte's voice faded into the distance as she drifted from the room scattering hairpins in her wake.

CHAPTER EIGHT

'You never believed in marriage when you were a child,'
I said to Jessica as we put back the last of the photographs. 'Why do you think you changed?'

'Because we were brought up to think it was the only
thing to do. We were made to believe in it. Generations
of indoctrination taking their toll, I suppose, plus the
fact that your father kept telling us how ignorant we
were so that we didn't really believe we were capable of
anything else. It might have been better if I'd hung on to
the views I held as a child; but, then, I wanted children,
and so did you. Perhaps it was your fault. You had such
romantic views about it all. I expect you influenced me,'
she laughed. 'Everything has always been your fault, but
I forgive you. I'm jolly glad we both had children. It
would have been awful not having children.'

'Did it never occur to you that you could have children
without marrying?'

'No, not at the time. I was highly unimaginative.'

'It occurred to me but I wasn't brave enough.'

'You didn't need to think about it. You were always in
favour of marrying. You thought all men rode on white
chargers. You were the one who had imagination. I'm
sure you must have influenced me.'

Jessica, I noticed, had not lost her knack of extricating
herself from all responsibility but it was true that when I
first knew her she had been entirely against the idea of
marriage. 'I can't imagine why anybody marries,' she
used to say to me. 'Just when you're free at last with no
school rules, no teachers pestering you, no parents

deciding your life for you, why should you choose to get married and have some horrible husband telling you how to live and expecting you to wait on him hand and foot and do all the work while he goes out and has a nice time with his friends?'

'Well, he wouldn't be horrible if you chose him, would he?' I contradicted. 'He'd be romantic and exciting.'

'That doesn't last,' said Jessica gloomily. 'Look at our mothers. They must have thought our fathers were romantic and exciting originally and look what they're stuck with. Actually your father *is* rather romantic, I have to admit, but mine certainly isn't and yours still expects your mother to do all the work while he has a nice time. The only reason for marrying, as far as I can see, is in order to have children. I want lots of children, don't you? I want at least six; but I think I've found the solution to the problem: I'm going to marry a sailor when I grow up so that I can have children but my husband will never be around. With a bit of luck, he might be shipwrecked by the time I'm in my thirties.'

'I'd *hate* to marry a sailor,' I exclaimed with feeling. 'Apart from anything else, I can't stand beards. I want to marry someone chivalrous and strong who will carry me off . . . Someone like Ivanhoe, or Launcelot, or Richard Coeur de Lion,' I mused.

'Richard wasn't chivalrous! He wasn't the least little bit chivalrous!' exclaimed Jessica. 'He barely noticed Berengaria's existence. He hardly ever bothered to visit her. In fact, your grandmother told us he didn't like women at all. Don't you remember?'

'Well, you know what I mean,' I replied. 'Someone like Napoleon or William the Conqueror.'

'Honestly, Imogen! Napoleon would have been far too small; and he was horribly unfaithful! And William the Conqueror beat Mathilde, didn't he?'

'That was before she was his wife and it was only because she refused to marry him and he loved her so much he couldn't bear to live without her.'

'I thought it was something to do with her referring to

125

the fact that he was illegitimate. But anyway, even if you're right, it's a jolly strange way of showing someone you love them. I wouldn't marry anyone who beat me, I can tell you. I think a sailor is a much better idea.'

By the time we were fifteen, however, boys had become of paramount interest and we thought of little else. At about the same time we began to speculate a good deal about our parents and their lives.

'Do you suppose they've ever had affairs?' Jessica asked me about my parents.

'I shouldn't think so,' I replied. 'Although Granny always says that Daddy has never been faithful and a lot of men seem quite keen on my mother. I don't think Mummy notices, though. She's so much more interested in her music than in people. What about your parents? Do they have affairs?'

'No. They're far too boring and respectable. Your parents are far more interesting.'

'I thought you said your mother had had a Red Indian lover?'

'I'm not sure he was a lover exactly,' replied Jessica. 'More of an admirer, really. I only saw him once. He turned up at the Embassy, quite drunk, and rushed up to my mother shouting, "Annabel! The only woman I've ever loved!" and fell flat on his face. Mummy was furious and said, "Get him out of here," to my father – but Daddy didn't seem to mind at all: if anything, he seemed rather amused.'

I always found it extremely difficult to predict whether Jessica's father was going to be amused or infuriated by any particular incident and I was nervous of him, as a result, in spite of the fact that I liked him. He had an explosive temper and was easily irritated; but like so many irascible characters, he was far more patient with people who were unafraid of him than with those who were frightened of him. I had the opportunity to discover this aspect of his character fairly early on in my childhood because I was witness to the curious case of Vince and Sir Reginald's change of attitude towards him.

Vincent was the postman and one of the most familiar figures about the village. He was what is euphemistically termed 'simple in the head' and inclined, as a result, to rub everybody up the wrong way. When he was not delivering the mail, he gardened for Mrs Twistleton-Brock, an elderly lady of uncertain temper. Whenever we bicycled past, we would hear her clarion tones echoing over the wall, baying, 'Vincent! You are an imbecile, a complete dunderhead! How can you be so stupid?' or 'Don't you talk to me like that, my good man. If I fire you, nobody else will ever employ you.' Once we heard her simply saying, 'Vincent! How *dare* you?' and for ages after we wondered what it was he had dared to do.

Everyone found Vince hard to bear but none found him so utterly exasperating as did Jessica's father. The latter's annoyance was, I suspected, caused by Vince's terror both of Egremont and of the dogs. (Sir Reginald's Collie had once bitten him in the leg and pulled him off his bicycle, at which point Egremont had joined in the fray with more than usual enthusiasm. It was an incident which Vince had trouble forgetting.) Sir Reginald – not a patient man at the best of times – had absolutely no time for stupidity or fear. It infuriated him, therefore, to see Vince sidling up the drive, quivering in every limb.

'For God's sake, man, come here and stop shivering!' he would bellow as Vince dropped all the mail. 'Don't be so totally useless,' he would roar as Vince, espying the approaching dogs, flattened himself, moaning, against a tree. 'Those animals haven't as much brain as a peahen. They certainly haven't the wits to bite you' (this in reference to the Labradors).

It was all the more surprising, therefore, when one Sunday morning at seven we were all roused from slumber by Vince thundering on the kitchen door. Not provoking any response, he went on to the door of the gunroom where he thumped again for a time. When this produced no result other than to bring a hissing

127

Egremont, full speed, from the shrubbery, Vince hastily opened the wrought-iron gate in the wall surrounding the rose-garden. Closing the gate behind himself just in the nick of time, he set off past an ornamental pond and fountain and raced round to the front of the house where he made such a noise on the front door that no-one could ignore it any longer. Sir Reginald stuck his head out of an upstairs window, bellowing, 'For Christ's sake! What the hell is going on?' Seeing Vince, he went purple with rage. 'What the devil do you mean by making such an infernal racket?' he demanded. 'Do you realize what time it is? Perhaps you are unaware that today is Sunday?'

Fearless at last, Vince looked up at Sir Reginald with all the confidence of someone who knows that he is bearing tidings of the utmost importance. His moment of glory had arrived and he could barely contain his excitement, so bursting was he to impart his news.

' 'Ave you 'eard about our George?' he enquired of Sir Reginald, knowing full well that the answer could only be in the negative. George was Vincent's brother and not much brighter than his sibling.

'No,' exploded Sir Reginald, 'I have not! Nor do I have the faintest wish to hear.'

'Arr,' said Vince, preparing his bombshell undaunted. 'That's been took to train to be a Druid.'

Sir Reginald was slightly taken aback by this information. 'How very enterprising,' was all he managed to reply.

We later discovered that George had taken a job as a cleaner in a Benedictine monastery. The difference between Catholics and Druids was apparently non-existent in the Norfolk mind. From that day forward Vincent walked with a new gait, his sense of importance manifest, his terror gone; and Sir Reginald never shouted at him again. From then on he appeared to regard Vincent with amused benevolence.

Jessica's mother was delighted with this change of affairs. She was extremely protective of Vince as she was of all those she considered to be downtrodden. She had a strong social conscience, in total contradiction with her political opinions and voting habits, and this frequently caused her to behave in a way that was considered odd by her friends and relations. She seemed to feel it incumbent upon herself, for instance, to broaden the minds of her servants and was forever dragging her cook or her housemaid up to London to the opera or the Chinese exhibition, or whatever of interest was on at the time. When her husband periodically queried her about the utility of this operation, she would say, 'Mrs B. has a very good mind. Had she been given any education, she might have been quite something.'

'Well, I don't think you can claim that Diggers has much of a mind,' Sir Reginald would complain.

'Poor Diggers has done nothing but cleaning since she was fourteen and her mind needs broadening, that's all that's the matter with her,' Lady Grantsby-Harte would reply firmly.

After a time Sir Reginald gave up questioning his wife on the subject and Jessica's mother continued her mission unimpeded.

'Do you think your parents had any more in common with one another than you did with Dermot or than I did with Enrico?' I asked Jessica as we were reminiscing on all this.

'Not really,' replied Jessica, 'but I think they were more tolerant of each other. They didn't try to change each other, or give up the things they loved, or do everything together, did they? Mummy never pretended to understand anything about politics, yet Daddy never criticized her for it. He didn't try to educate her or interest her in world affairs, but at the same time he never made her look ignorant or uninformed. He went out of his way to cover up for her, in fact, whereas our husbands never missed an opportunity to make us look small. And Mummy never seemed to mind that Daddy couldn't understand her putting so much effort into the gardens; it didn't seem to upset her that he never appreciated what an incredible job she had done on the place. I can't even remember ever hearing her complain about having to give all those boring dinners for his shooting friends, either, can you? She hated them but she never moaned about it; and Daddy never tried to make her go with us on shoots even though all the other wives trailed along. I will say that for our husbands: at least they never went shooting. Imagine if we'd married someone like Daddy. We might have spent every weekend of the winter up to our ears in dead birds. Do you remember how awful it was?'

I remembered all too clearly. During the shooting season at Little Upton we were expected to accompany the guns and the first time that Jessica and I were forced to take part was not an occasion that I was likely to forget. It was one of those days that started badly and that one sensed from the beginning could only become worse. Sir Reginald was thundering about at the crack of dawn bellowing at everyone to get a move on and making endless forays into the gunroom. Lady Grantsby-Harte – miraculously up betimes and dressed in a heather tweed suit which made her look even more delicate than usual – was floating about the dining-room supervising an endless supply of coffee, tea, porridge, eggs and bacon, kidneys, kedgeree, crumpets, toast and butter, marmalade and a multitude of home-made jams. Sir Reginald had invited six people for the weekend and a great many more for the day (all of whom had decided to take advantage of Lady Grantsby-Harte's invitation to breakfast) so that when Jessica and I appeared in the dining-room in search of a little sustenance we were confronted by a sea of unfamiliar faces. It was a daunting beginning to a terrifying day.

Lady Grantsby-Harte insisted on everyone eating a hearty breakfast, pointing out quite rightly that it was exceedingly cold outside, that the weather forecast predicted snow later, and that we were going to be out until sunset. Gargantuan amounts of food had to be wolfed at high speed because Sir Reginald, who must have breakfasted very early, was eager to get going and kept shouting, 'Will someone kindly come and put collars on the dogs?' or 'Annabel! Where the hell have you put my shooting gloves?' He eventually put his head around the dining-room door and roared, 'Good God! You're not all still eating, are you? If any of you wants to come shooting, you'd better get weaving. We're leaving in three minutes.'

There then followed the battle of the gunroom. This was probably the most important room in the house. All the family's favourite occupations were herein represented. One entire wall was devoted to riding-boots, hats and crops with, at its far end, a couple of pairs of waders, some fishing tackle, a pair of flying boots, and a collection of croquet mallets. On the opposite wall were rows of pegs upon which hung a motley collection of macintoshes, riding jackets, shooting jackets, a tweed cape, a navy-blue overcoat and various deerstalkers, caps, sou'westers and other assorted headgear. On a shelf above these were a number of tennis racquets and several boxes of tennis balls. Beside the passage door the third wall was taken up with shelves on which were all the guns, cartridges, gun-cleaning equipment, saddle-soap, linseed oil, boot polish and an impressive array of thick, woollen socks. Lastly, at the far end of the room, by the door leading out into the courtyard, was another great rack containing a good twenty pairs of wellington boots, neatly organized according to size, and, below these, a gigantic collection of apparently identical women's shoes. On closer inspection one could see that there were, in fact, two different types of shoe: some were heavy lace-ups of the kind always known as 'clodhoppers', and the others were square-heeled pumps generally nicknamed 'flatties'. All of them were brown. I never understood why we needed so many of them.

In the middle of the gunroom was a table which was intended to be used by people polishing boots, cleaning guns, emptying cartridges out of cartridge belts and the like. It was never used for any of these purposes for the simple reason that Lady Grantsby-Harte always had it completely hidden under pots of growing bulbs. As soon as the hyacinths were far enough advanced to distribute around the house, the tulips would be under way and a new collection of bowls would appear on the table. Even in the summer, when the bulb season was long since over, Jessica's mother would use the table for flower cutting and arranging. It was always littered with sprigs of this and that, basket-loads of cuttings, secateurs, gardening gloves, and half-filled vases.

It was unfortunate that the shooting season coincided with the bulb-growing season. Lady Grantsby-Harte never did things in a half-hearted fashion. Not only was the table in the gunroom covered with sprouting bulbs, every available inch of floor was covered with pots and bowls. One had to pick one's way carefully towards the boots and hats. Sir Reginald, who considered the situation intolerable, tended to kick priceless pieces of porcelain out of his way, muttering furiously to himself. Occasionally he would break something valuable and yell at his wife, 'Why the hell do we have to have all these blasted plants in here? For Christ's sake get them out of here before I break the lot. What in God's name are the greenhouses for?'

'Sorry, darling,' Jessica's mother would reply, totally unperturbed. 'Did you hurt yourself? The bulbs have to stay here, I'm afraid. Greenhouses are *hot*, darling, whereas this room is lovely and cold.' The fact that the last of the Meissen had just been broken seemed to be a matter of complete indifference to them both.

By the time Jessica and I went to find our boots, on that particular morning, the gunroom was a milling throng of people messing about with cartridge belts and accusing each other of having taken the wrong gloves, scarves or shooting sticks. Jessica's mother was distributing boots to anyone who did not have any (some of the women seemed to have come ill-prepared) and was shrieking hysterically at anyone who looked like treading on any of her bulbs. I was about to put on my boots when Lady Grantsby-Harte whipped them away from me and gave them to a tiny, vacant-looking girl whose feet happened to be the same size as mine. I was told I would have to borrow one of the other pairs, all of which were far too big for me. 'They'll be perfectly all right if you wear a few more pairs of socks,' said Lady Grantsby-Harte gaily, 'but for heaven's sake move away from those hyacinths.'

At that moment Sir Reginald reappeared and handed me a shooting stick, two very heavy leather bags full of cartridges, and a silver hip-flask. 'Take these for me, will you? There's a good girl,' he said. 'I may need you to hand me more cartridges later this morning, so you and Jessica had better stay with me once we get there. Oh, and you might take these, too, while you're at it,' he said, handing me a tin of toffees and an unpleasant-looking device for hanging huge numbers of birds over one's shoulder. I looked at him aghast, unable to tell him that the mere thought of a dead bird made me feel sick.

As I walked out into the courtyard, feeling thoroughly the worse for wear before the day had started, I was struck by the absurdity of the scene. Standing around the Land-Rovers, in groups, were twelve of the most inelegant men I had ever seen. They looked like a bunch of second-rate comedians. In Italy, no-one thought of the English as particularly good-looking; in fact, they were known to be rather plain. We were all brought up, however, to believe that Englishmen were beautifully dressed. It was the women, we were always told, who were so dowdy, with their hideous bags and head-scarves and their total lack of style. It was not until I had spent a couple of holidays in England that I began to understand that Englishmen made a cult of decrepitude and that baggy corduroys, shapeless grey flannels, shabby jackets, patched elbows, dilapidated breeches and filthy shooting jackets (nowadays it would be Barbours) were *de rigueur* among the upper classes. It seemed unexpected from a race of men so obsessed with clean shirts and polished shoes. I was soon to discover that a total revolution would take place before dinner when the disreputable figures one had seen ambling about in the daytime would disappear to plunge into boiling baths and to re-emerge, in time for drinks, totally transformed.

Englishwomen, of course, were another matter and no Latin would ever understand how they could dress the way they did. The Italians held the theory that it was all the result of Englishmen being so indifferent to women that they had lost heart centuries ago and could no longer be bothered to make the effort. Even allowing for this probability, one felt it required enormous determination and a certain talent on the part of the women to find such spectacularly awful clothes and mind-boggling colour combinations. Jessica's mother was one of the very rare exceptions and one wondered where she had acquired her irreproachable good taste.

Emerging from the gunroom into the crisp morning air and not yet aware that to be shabby was to be smart, the shock was considerable as I surveyed the assembled company. They were an unattractive group. Most of the men were middle-aged and going bald. They were almost all gingery or nondescript in colouring, with blotchy faces covered in broken veins and an unappealingly puffy look beneath the eyes. The majority of them had gigantic stomachs and those who still retained some semblance of shape had already acquired that unhealthy, flabby look that soon turns to double chins and waistlessness. All but the very young had, from a steady excess of drink, developed complexions ranging from ruddy to puce. The younger men looked thin and undernourished. One could see how the word 'weedy' had crept into the language. Their gangly legs looked scrawny, their boots apparently too big for them and their heads disconcertingly small for their height. Several of them had pimples; one of them had protruding eyes. They were extraordinarily reminiscent of guinea fowl.

All the men, whether young or old, thin or fat, were wearing identical clothes: terrible old plus-fours, scruffy jackets, bedraggled scarves that had once cost the earth, thick olive-green socks showing over the top of serviceable boots or stout brown shoes, and truly lamentable hats. The slimmer ones had cartridge belts slung around their hips; the portly ones had leather cartridge bags hung over their shoulders. It was difficult to imagine how the former would, in time, develop into the latter but this was apparently the normal growth pattern of the species. The only man who could claim to be fairly respectably dressed turned out to be the keeper.

To the far right, noticeable because his was not the standard uniform but a remarkable variation of it, stood a rotund figure wearing mustard-coloured knickerbockers, a suspiciously new-looking jacket in ochre twill and a hat which looked as if it might once have been a cross-channel swimmer's black bathing cap. His face was purple from a lifetime of serious drinking and his nose looked as if it would soon leave no room for the rest of his face. Jessica's father later described him as having 'a colour never previously achieved by anyone except my sister Harriet. The only difference is that Harriet doesn't have a bottle nose,' he said. Neither Jessica nor I ever found out the man's name and we steered clear of him all day. He looked as if he might have a diabolical temper.

Behind the men stood a collection of tough-looking women wearing pork-pie hats or trilbies with feathers; and, behind them, stood a trio of very young women with hefty thighs and vacuous expressions. Jessica, her older sister and I appeared to be the only children present. Jessica's two younger sisters were thought too young to join the expedition.

Amongst the female contingent was Sir Reginald's sister, Lady Berkhamsted, nicknamed 'Uncle Harriet' by Jessica who had often spoken of her. Jessica introduced us. It was apparent that she adored her aunt and that her sentiments were reciprocated. Lady Berkhamsted had a brisk manner and a powerful personality. 'My niece always calls me "Uncle Harriet",' she boomed at me, 'so you might as well do the same. Those boots look ridiculously large for you and you need a sensible hat. What can Annabel have been thinking of, letting you come out with that? Better go back and get one. A good felt hat is what you need. Something to keep the top of your head warm.'

Lady Berkhamsted was a fine example of the flower of English womanhood. Her face was square and not unlike a bulldog's. She had a snub nose and not much in the way of cheekbones. Her hair was the colour of dried grass and was the sort that becomes more and more colourless with the passage of time but never turns grey. It was cropped in haphazard fashion, too short to be classed as dishevelled but with no recognizable shape so that one would never be able to tell whether or not it had seen a comb lately. She had an amused and kindly eye of the palest forget-me-not blue. The other eye was also pale blue, but it was expressionless for it was made of glass. Jessica's father later told me that Lady Berkhamsted's husband had shot out his wife's eye, not in anger but by mistake during a shoot. Lady Berkhamsted had apparently divorced him on the strength of this, not because she had lost an eye but, or so she claimed, because she could not bear to be married to a bad shot. Her whole demeanour was merry and determined. She looked as if she might prefer dogs to people but did not hold it against people that they were so lacking. Her face was a remarkable colour that made her eye look even bluer. It was obvious that she had spent her entire life out of doors.

One was tempted to think that Lady Berkhamsted had no breasts but I rapidly realized that this was an optical illusion created by the fact that her bosom had long ago merged with her stomach which protruded in balloon-like fashion above her muscular, stocky legs. Seen from a distance, she might have been blown up with a bicycle-pump and then draped in heavy tweeds. Her delightful

136

smile was unspoiled by the fact that she appeared to have double the normal number of teeth. She had a voice like a fog-horn and her hat was a jaunty affair with a curious assortment of feathers stuck at random into the brim. I adored her the moment I clapped eyes on her.

'You two had better come with me,' she bellowed when I reappeared with another frightful hat. 'Reginald and the others have all gone and the beaters will go home again if we don't get there soon. I've already got a bevy of women in there, so you'll just have to squeeze into the back as best you can. That looks a more sensible hat,' she said, thumping me on the shoulder as I clambered in.

The other women had chosen to go in Lady Berkhamsted's car because they did not want to be squashed amongst guns, shooting sticks, dogs and the like. They had never been driven by Sir Reginald's sister before and had no idea what was about to hit them. Lady Grantsby-Harte wisely stayed at home. 'I can't bear dead birds,' she said firmly, 'and, anyway, someone will have to drive up with the lunch at the end of the morning.'

Lady Berkhamsted climbed behind the driving wheel with the look of a woman about to go to war. She had trouble starting the engine and looked self-congratulatory when it suddenly exploded into action. 'I've never understood the gears of these things,' she said cheerfully as she brought down a sturdy left foot, clad in a heavy leather shoe, on the unsuspecting clutch. She proceeded to attack the gears as if she were trying to uproot brambles from her garden. The Land-Rover suddenly shot forward, hiccoughed, then started a series of kangaroo-like bounds out of the courtyard and round to the front of the house. 'I don't think it's in first gear,' said Lady Berkhamsted accusingly. 'I don't think it's got one, so we'll just have to go fast.' An unmerciful right foot bore down on the accelerator as if intending to reduce it to dust, and we hurtled towards the front drive, then down the hill between the cedars. As we

137

started to race up the far slope towards the gates, Lady Berkhamsted said, 'Keep your fingers crossed that nothing is coming. We can't stop or we'll stall and never be able to get out into the road. Better to take it fast, anyway.' For the next few minutes, all one could hear was the unbroken sound of Lady Berkhamsted's horn and faint, whimpering noises from some of the women.

There was nothing coming past the gates as we shot out into the road and, to everyone's relief, Lady Berkhamsted drove quite sensibly for the next few minutes. She apparently had no problem changing gear from third to fourth and back down to third again. There was not another car to be seen and the countryside was pristine white from the heavy frost that lay on the ground. It was a perfect, although very cold, day. The hedges and fields sparkled in the brilliant morning sun.

'Right,' said Lady Berkhamsted as she suddenly turned left on to a deeply rutted, very muddy track which headed steeply downwards between two fields. 'This is where we leave the road. It's terribly rutty so hang on everyone.'

The next ten minutes were excruciating. Becoming more and more bruised by the minute, we bumped and swerved our way over and around huge rocks, deep tractor ruts, patches of thick ice and dangerous-looking tree roots. 'This bit's rather bad, I'm afraid,' remarked Lady Berkhamsted casually. 'Lucky it's so icy. Much worse when it's muddy.' As she spoke the Land-Rover skidded, slid up a bank, nearly overturned, righted itself and shot towards the opposite bank, heading for a large tree. 'Damn!' exclaimed Lady Berkhamsted. 'I've forgotten how you stop these machines. Oh, yes, I think you pull out the choke (or is it the clutch?) and stall it.' She decided to do both and her long-suffering vehicle made a noise like an erupting volcano and came to a grinding halt about three inches from the tree.

We all climbed out. As Lady Berkhamsted explained, there was no point in starting the motor again since she was not too sure how to put the gears into reverse and the likelihood was that she would drive straight into the tree. 'You must all push it backwards down the bank and get it on to the track again,' she said. 'I'd better stay at the wheel and steer so that we end up heading in the right direction. Good for you all to have a bit of air and exercise before the last bit.'

We managed to push it down the bank without too much trouble, although it was clear from the expressions on all the women's faces that this was not the kind of outing they had expected when they set off that morning, blithely, in the direction of Upton Hall. Once on the track again, and facing roughly in the right direction, the Land-Rover refused to start. 'You'll all have to push again,' shouted Lady Berkhamsted from her seat behind the wheel. We pushed to no avail. We were not strong enough to move it an inch. 'I'll have to give you a hand,' said Lady Berkhamsted after a while. 'One of you come and push at the side so that you can hold the wheel. I'll come round to the back. I'm stronger than the lot of you and one can put more force against the back.' A solid woman in a green felt cape offered to push at the side and hold the wheel. Inevitably, one push from Lady Berkhamsted and the Land-Rover set off fast down the hill. The woman in the green felt cape could not begin to keep up with it. 'Run!' shouted Lady Berkhamsted then, seeing that the woman was not a good sprinter, she started to hare after the Land-Rover herself. She reached the woman, pushed her out of the way, and galloped at astonishing speed down the track in pursuit of her departing vehicle. It was a comic sight. One would not have thought that Lady Berkhamsted was the right shape for a rapid sprint but she was obviously far fitter than anyone had realised. She took off like a rocket from a launching pad and hurtled into the middle distance, hitting a patch of ice here and there which made her skim at high speed for a couple of feet every now and then as she raced along the track. She seemed to have the balancing capacity of a trapeze artist as she sped along treacherous ruts full of boulders and roots, her elephantine form leaping, gazelle-like, up and down the banks when the track became too slippery. She finally disappeared from sight as she plunged round a sharp bend.

When we eventually caught up with her, she was sitting in the Land-Rover which had come to a halt as a result of the curve in the track. It was firmly embedded in the bank. Lady Berkhamsted looked thoroughly cheerful. 'We're practically there now,' she said with satisfaction. 'We can walk the rest of the way. The men can dig the motor out in due course.' Then, turning a concerned eye towards the woman in the green felt cape, she enquired, 'Suffering from arthritis, are you? No? You seemed to have trouble moving. I'd see a good doctor if I were you and have a thorough check. You don't want to wait too long. Better to get it sorted before it gets worse. Harrison's a good man, if you want to have a sensible opinion. Remind me to give you his number when we get back.'

The recipient of this advice was speechless with irritation. Jessica heard her, later in the day, complaining to her husband about the episode and I, later still, heard her husband saying to someone else, 'I gather Lady Berkhamsted's a bit tricky. Mad as a March hare and an absolute menace on the roads. Poor old Reggie. Damned awkward for him.'

The shoot was well organized. We all stood about talking for a while at the start of the drive. One might have imagined that nothing much was happening, but on the far side of each slope and behind every copse the place was a hive of activity. As soon as we started to hear the tapping of the beaters' sticks, we all moved smartly to our posts. Everyone was silent, waiting. Jessica and I stood just to the left of Sir Reginald. Suddenly, a bird flew out and flew straight back over the heads of the beaters. All at once the birds started flying out towards us. Jessica's father fired two shots in swift succession. There was a second's pause, then a loud thud right behind us followed instantly by another dull thud. All around us shots were being fired and birds came tumbling out of the sky to hit the ground with a sickening thump. In a matter of minutes, ten, fifteen, twenty birds fell from the sky. Men with dogs were rushing around behind us picking them up. I had not expected the birds to make a noise as they hit the ground. I had not realized it was going to be a complete massacre. Feathers started drifting towards us on the breeze. As one landed on my shoulder, I turned to Jessica and said, 'I think I'm going to be sick,' and saw that she was staring behind me with tears pouring down her cheeks. I followed the direction of her eyes and saw a man pick up a half-dead bird and beat it several times over the head. He seemed to go on and on hitting it, fairly feebly, and I wondered why he could not give it one great clout and put it out of its misery. Two more wounded birds were twitching on the ground. One of them tried to run and was chased by a dog who looked as if he was mauling it before he took it to his master. I could not stop myself imagining what it would feel like to be shot and in great pain, only to be scooped up by a huge mouthful of teeth and carted off to my enemy who would then club me to death, slowly and half-heartedly. As the world started to turn and yellow stars flashed before my eyes, I saw another bird right at our feet. It was lying on its back, jerking violently, as if in a state of perpetual spasm. Jessica was bending over it and calling to her father, 'Daddy, please shoot it. Why can't you shoot it?' Sir Reginald turned round in surprise and I added, 'That bird is not dead.'

Sir Reginald picked it up, shook it and said, 'Dead as a doornail. It's just nerves,' and turned back towards the coppice.

I fell on top of Jessica as I fainted.

Lady Berkhamsted picked us both up. She must have seen us from her position at the bottom of the slope and done one of her sprinting acts for she was at our side almost instantly. 'Reginald, I'm taking the girls with me,' she said. 'Come along, you two,' and she marched us back to where she had been standing. Once there, she said, 'Didn't Reginald give you his hip-flask to carry?'

'Yes,' I replied, 'it's still in my pocket. It's lucky it's silver. It would have broken if it hadn't been made of metal.'

'Right, well let's have it,' she said, plunging her hand into my coat pocket. She unscrewed the top, handed it to me and said, 'Take a good slug of that. It'll make you feel much better. Then Jessica had better have some. Ghastly business, this shooting lark, but you have to let men do it or they'd all be killing each other. Go on, my dear, have some more of it. A good big gulp is what you need.'

I did as I was told and nearly choked. It was the first time I had tasted whisky and I did not like it.

'All right, now you can give it to Jessica,' said Lady Berkhamsted, walloping me on the back in an effort to stop me coughing. 'You'll probably have to put up with a lot of this in your lives, so I'm going to give you a lesson in how to cope with it. Cork up that whisky, Jessica m'dear, will you? We may need it again. Reginald will just have to survive without.

'Now, the important thing about shooting is to concentrate on the art of aiming. Don't think about the birds and don't look at them when they're down. If you're watching someone shoot, try to watch the bullet. There's a grey smudge you can follow and which they don't have time to see. You can tell them if they are shooting too high, or behind the birds, or whatever. The moment you have noticed where the bullet went, look for the next bird. It's easier if you are actually shooting; that's why I took it up. It's like not feeling car-sick if you drive yourself. No use doing it unless you're going to do it properly, though. There's no excuse for wounded birds. Your father is a good shot, Jessica. Virtually always kills them stone dead. I'm a better shot. Couldn't live with myself otherwise. And don't let anyone give you that argument about how all the birds would be extinct if there weren't people breeding them to shoot.

They'd only be extinct because we had shot them all.

'As I said, you have to let men do it or they'd all be killing each other. They're complete brutes, really, but perfectly manageable as long as you're better at everything than they are. You'll find they can be quite good fun as you get older. Now, the birds are coming in this direction again. Keep to my left, please, both of you.'

We had been told that she was a good shot but I had somehow never believed that any woman would go near a gun. She looked conspicuous on this occasion, being the only woman shooting, but she must have been conspicuous so frequently in the past that she was unaware of the fact.

'Right. Feeling better? I'm going to put the lesson into practice now or the men will be furious. I've let four go over untouched while I've been talking to you. Concentrate on my aim. Imagine you are doing it.' I felt tearful and Jessica had a face as pale and frozen as the ground.

Very soon a hen pheasant flew in our direction. We were at the bottom of the slope, in the dip, and the bird was flying low. 'It would be easy to shoot that, do you see?' demanded Lady Berkhamsted. 'But I can't because it's so low. I'd be aiming straight at the beaters.' She waited until the hen was high in the air and slightly behind us to the left, then fired one shot and it plummeted to the ground too far away for us to hear the sound of its fall. It landed in the thicket. Another bird came over, again flying low. This time she waited until it was even higher and further behind us. Again, she fired one shot and it fell instantly into the woods. 'While I reload, I'd like you both to have another swig of whisky,' said Jessica's aunt. 'Then I want you to get cartridges out of the bag and have them ready to hand me when I need them. How are you feeling? Tell me if it's too much and I'll hand over to someone else and take you back.'

The thought of facing another drive with Lady Berkhamsted made the shooting seem less awful. We survived the rest of the morning without too much difficulty. Jessica's aunt killed everything outright and never missed a thing. Later, during our picnic lunch, all the men congratulated her. One of them said, 'Why don't you take them when they're in front of you? It would have been much easier to hit them while they were still close.'

'The beaters happened to be standing in my direct line of fire,' said Jessica's aunt coldly. 'The birds were just about at the level of their heads.'

'The beaters were too far back to be hurt,' insisted the man.

'They certainly wouldn't have been seriously wounded, I agree,' retorted Lady Berkhamsted. 'But they might have found it discouraging to be constantly peppered with shot.'

'I told you Uncle Harriet was wonderful,' whispered Jessica.

The picnic arrived, delivered by Jessica's mother, who had come up in a jeep. She was waiting for us when the last drive of the morning was over, and had spread the contents of four large hampers upon a wooden table that stood at the edge of the wood. We were all frozen so the sight of a colossal thermos full of hot soup was exceedingly welcome. Jessica's mother made sure that each boiling mugful was heavily laced with sherry, so that Jessica and I, who had already had a fair amount of whisky, began to feel pleasantly tipsy. 'I think you'd better eat a lot, you two,' boomed Lady Berkhamsted, 'otherwise you'll start to feel sick again.'

As we waded our way through sausage rolls, baps, hard boiled eggs and thick slabs of fruit cake, I was reminded again of my mother's warnings about the English and picnics. No other race on earth would stand about in the freezing cold, their breath hanging in clouds in the frosty air, cashmere scarves around their necks in an attempt to keep out the biting wind, clutching a bun which they held alternately in their left and right hands in order to give the other hand a chance to warm up in a pocket for a few minutes.

I was also reminded, as I tried the fruit cake, of one of

144

my grandmother's remarks: 'The English have never been able to make cake; just the dullest, driest slab. It's rather like their hats. I can't imagine why they should have such frightful hats. I think they must make them themselves.'

The picnic was eaten rapidly so that we could return to the serious business of killing. It was a perfect January afternoon and Jessica and I were delighted to note that, being the end of the season, a large number of birds had learnt the trick of flying straight back behind the beaters. Unlike the men who were keeping count of the number of birds they had shot, we took to totting up the number of birds that escaped. It was encouraging and by the end of the afternoon we were feeling reasonably happy again.

The last drive was timed to end just before dusk and it was only then that the full horror of the occasion hit us again. Men and dogs started appearing from every direction carrying birds which they heaped in piles upon the ground. Some of the men had contraptions such as the one Jessica's father had given me to carry: they seemed to hold about twelve birds, all hung by the neck. When all the birds had been collected up and piled in heaps, a couple of men went through, counting. The total came to one hundred and fifty, bringing the total for the season up to two thousand, six hundred. Jessica was in tears again.

Nobody wanted to drive home with Lady Berkhamsted. Only Jessica and I thought it would be preferable to travelling with the men who had embarked on a discussion, which was to last for hours, about how many pheasants they had killed, who had missed what and why, and the difficulties of hitting low-flying birds. We overheard some snide remarks thinly disguised as compliments.

'Beautiful shot, that, George,' I heard one of them saying. 'That hen was flying very high. Pity you had to let the next three go. Tricky, those low shots.'

Somebody else was blaming the man in mustard

knickerbockers for having shot a white pheasant. They had all been told not to shoot any of the white ones. (Their behaviour was not unlike that of bridge players after a rubber; but bridge, fortunately for us, was something we would never have to play since both our families considered it frightfully common. The only time I ever heard bridge mentioned at Upton Hall, Jessica's mother said, 'It's the sort of game that's played by businessmen in this country and, in France, by bored women living in Versailles whose husbands work in petrol – you know, Total or Elf or one of those things.'

My mother, who very rarely gave advice, said, 'There is one piece of advice I feel I must give you. Whatever you do, never learn to play bridge. If you ever make the mistake of learning it, you'll find yourself constantly besieged by the most dreadful people wanting you to make up a four. People change, too, when they take up bridge. Even those who, however dull, are normally perfectly worthy souls become very unpleasant when they play bridge. It's a simply frightful game. Avoid it at all costs.' Neither of our fathers ever thought it worth mentioning.)

The next task was to dig Lady Berkhamsted's Land-Rover out of the bank. A group of men undertook to do this but none of them wanted to be driven back by Jessica's aunt.

Once back at Upton Hall, we found a magnificent tea awaiting us. It was by then five o'clock and we were ravenous. The crumpets, always delicious, seemed even more delectable than usual and better still were the great piles of buttered toast covered in Gentlemen's Relish. Long after all the food had been demolished, people were still sitting about drinking cups of tea and reading the papers. From time to time someone would rise to their feet and say, 'What I want is a hot bath.'

Little by little people drifted off until one could hear, all over the house, the distant sound of running water. I ran my bath rather late only to discover that, even with the addition of gallons of cold water, it was absolutely scalding. I could not even put my hand in to pull out the plug so that I could let out some of the hot water and add some more cold. I had to lie on my bed and read for half an hour before it had cooled enough to be manageable. After everyone had reappeared, dressed for dinner, the water was still boiling. It was one of the mysteries of Upton Hall.

Jessica's mother loathed shoots. She hated everything about them but whereas she could refuse to accompany the guns, she could not avoid the dinner afterwards. She particularly disliked her husband's shooting companions. To be fair to Sir Reginald, he disliked them too but, since he loved shooting, he had to take what offered in the way of other guns. The people he invited to shoot with him were not the people he would normally have chosen as his dinner guests, but he was prepared to put up with them every Saturday evening during the shooting season. At dinner, although politeness itself, he appeared vague and distracted. He had perfected the technique of appearing to be somewhere else entirely. Jessica always claimed this was a result of his diplomatic life. ('It's because of the Official Secrets Act and all those things they're made to swear,' she would say. 'He's so afraid of giving anything away or being asked any questions about his work that he looks as if he hasn't heard what you said and starts talking about opera.')

I had a different theory. Sir Reginald was not an easygoing man. Volatile and thoroughly irritable, he did not tolerate fools easily. His manners, on the other hand, were irreproachable. His way of dealing with the unintelligent when he was host, I suspected, was to think hard about something completely different and to refuse to listen to the remarks being made around him. This was a technique which Jessica's mother would have done well to acquire. She, too, found the conversation exasperating. She longed to be back in Paris or Washington and to be discussing Marguerite Yourcenar or the Phillips' Collection. She had, on this occasion, managed to persuade her sister to come for the night so

147

that she had someone to whom she could talk at dinner. It was a vain hope since there was bound to be very little opportunity for them to talk to each other.

Lady Grantsby-Harte had placed, on her right, the person she thought the least awful – an amiable character who tried to interest her in the pleasures of salmon fishing – and, to her left, out of a sense of duty as hostess, the person she thought most unbearable – a huge man with an apparently limitless supply of poor jokes. Her sister, who was as lovely to look at as she was, spent the whole dinner being ogled by the man of the mustard knickerbockers (his evening dress was unremarkable except for the size of his bow tie which would have been perfect as the bow on a girl's party frock). He leaned heavily towards Lady Grantsby-Harte's sister whose expression clearly stated that she was finding his attentions unwelcome.

When the ladies finally rose to leave the gentlemen to their port, Jessica's mother turned to me and her two oldest daughters (the two younger ones had been packed off before dinner) saying, 'It's time you three were in bed. Will you say good-bye to everyone and then go to bed as quickly and quietly as you can. Don't wake Fenella and Jane whatever you do. Nanny says they're both exhausted.'

On my way upstairs, I overheard Lady Grantsby-Harte saying to her sister, 'I don't think I can stand much more of this. Do you want to come up to my room and have a stiff drink while they're all powdering their noses? The coffee won't be served for a while and Harriet is such a brick I'm sure she won't mind coping with those frightful women until the men appear. I'll go and ask her. I'm sure she'll do it. I wish I could get the gin out of the drawing-room without anyone seeing, but I know Reggie's got some Scotch upstairs. We can always pretend you had something in your eye, or a nose-bleed – we'll think up some excuse to explain our absence.'

Jessica's mother had a small sitting-room off her

bedroom to which she retired when she wanted to be alone, or when she was writing letters. It was situated immediately above my bedroom and it was to this room that she and her sister repaired that evening, after dinner. Both of them were inclined to become tipsy when they were bored and that evening they were noisier than usual. As I lay in bed ruminating on the violence and cruelty of the masculine sex, my thoughts were frequently disturbed by muffled giggles and the sound of tripping overhead.

The discovery that men enjoyed killing was something that I had trouble digesting but as I considered this new and dangerous aspect of the male, my mental meanderings were constantly interrupted by sounds of skipping and hilarious laughter coming from immediately above my room. It was hard to concentrate and I needed to concentrate for I was battling with an idea I had held, buried, for years but had never consciously formed until then. I thought of men throughout history, I thought of the way my grandfather had treated my grandmother, I thought of my father and his temper, I thought of Simon's bullying, I thought of Sir Reginald's explosiveness, I thought of all the men I had watched that day. It was the first time I had seen grown men tense and excited, and I knew it was not just the thrill of the chase: the smell of blood was in their nostrils; they had become hounds baying for blood.

While the sisters' merriment became steadily louder my train of thought drifted until I found myself thinking about the convent. Was there, I wondered, a more fundamental, earthly, reason for becoming a nun than the explanation we had always been given of an inexplicable, miraculous, religious vocation? Was escape from men their real motive? And what were the fathers' motives in shutting their daughters away for life?

Many of the Catholic ceremonies struck me as preChristian but none more so than the nuns' Clothings and Professions which were terrifyingly pagan in outward aspect. Unlike their sisters in larger convents, who

149

usually favoured collective Professions, our nuns made their vows individually on entirely separate occasions. The nun in question, although she was entering a community, always seemed to me to be an appallingly lonely figure. The bride in white being given away by her father was reminiscent of other, ancient, sacrificial offerings: Abraham 'tempted' by God to take his son into the land of Moriah and there offer him upon a mountain top for a burnt offering; or Agamemnon slaughtering his daughter as a bribe to the gods for the winds of war.

What kind of a mother was Clytaemnestra? Did she feel she had made the ultimate sacrifice? Would she have given anything to die in her daughter's stead? Was she born a murderess or did she become so as a result of Agamemnon's behaviour? God knows, she had reason enough to loathe her second husband before ever he sanctioned the sacrifice of their child (and it was not the first time he had killed a child of hers) but did she, in fact, loathe him and despise herself, or did she simply accept it as the will of the gods, Man's usual behaviour and Woman's fate?

Where were the mothers in this no less barbaric ceremony that required a modern Iphigeneia, a sacrificial lamb? Once again, it was the father who led her to the altar where she was removed from the world amidst a ritual of frightening primitiveness and breathtaking beauty. The symbolic cutting of her hair, the wedding ring, the replacement of the bridal gown and wreath with the black habit and veil; the solitary figure singing solo to her God in an otherwise silent chapel; the slim, black figure lying prostrate, face downwards in the aisle between the ranks of her sisters, her arms outstretched in the shape of a cross – these were the symbols of an age-old cry, a call from the deep unconscious where Man listens to the palpitations of the universe and Woman abandons herself entirely. Small matter that the wind would have risen without Iphigeneia's disappearance: the beauty and the horror of it would have been lost. The ships would have sailed to Troy in a

150

different mood. Man's lust is to kill and Woman has chosen to find ecstasy in sacrifice because it is something she cannot escape.

I did not want to be part of that sacrifice. Like a bird struggling to escape from its cage, I wanted to find my wings and fly; or, like the phoenix, use womankind's experience to rise from the ashes and soar into the sky. I could see full well who my gaolers were likely to be and, while Lady Grantsby-Harte and her sister made merry above me, I was forced to the conclusion that I was afraid of men.

Over my head, the noise continued and I could distinctly hear piano music in the background. They must, I assumed, have turned on a wireless. The whole thing was absurdly like something out of Beachcomber for the last things I heard as I fell into a troubled sleep were the distant sound of girlish laughter and the fall of a dancing slipper.

Paris

Je ne sais plus vraiment où commencent les charmes
Il est des noms de chair comme les Andelys
L'image se renverse et nous montre ses larmes
Taisez-vous taisez-vous Ah Paris mon Paris

Lui qui sait des chansons et qui fait des colères
Qui n'a plus qu'aux lavoirs des drapeaux délavés
Métropole pareille à l'étoile polaire
Paris qui n'est Paris qu'arrachant ses pavés

Paris de nos malheurs Paris du Cours-la-Reine
Paris des Blancs-Manteaux Paris de Février
Du Faubourg Saint-Antoine aux côteaux de Suresnes
Paris plus déchirant qu'un cri de vitrier . . .

Louis Aragon

CHAPTER NINE

The years wore on; our prefects left and we in our turn
became prefects. The last two years seemed interminable and by the time we sat our 'A' and 'S' levels we
had almost ceased to believe that school would ever
come to an end. The day inevitably dawned, however,
when we drove for the last time down the tree-lined
avenue towards the gates and freedom. As we turned out
of the drive, the whole world seemed to open before us.
Anything and everything seemed possible. No one was
ever more optimistic than we were that day. We firmly
believed that, from now on, we would be able to do anything we wanted, be anyone we wanted, achieve anything we wanted. As we bowled along in our railway
carriage, bound for London, it never occurred to either
of us that anything awful could ever happen to us again.

Added to the general excitement of leaving school
was the prospect of facing our first English ball.
Jessica's mother had written early in the term to tell us
that some neighbours of theirs were intending to hold a
summer ball and that we and Jessica's older sister had
all been invited. She added that we had been asked to
come with partners, if possible, since they were apparently short of men, and suggested that I might like to
invite Simon and that Jessica could ask one of her
cousins to join the party.

We spent more time and energy preparing for that
ball than for any of our exams. We felt sure that this
would be the occasion when we would meet the man of
our lives and that, like the heroines of some fairy tale,

after years of being imprisoned in some ghoulish tower or dungeon, we had finally reached the part where we were going to live happily ever after.

Little did we realise the agonies that lay in store for us. When the idea was first proposed, we confidently assumed that we would somehow acquire a certain grace and poise before the day arrived; but as the evening approached our excitement turned to terror. We knew nothing about boys. Simon, perhaps because he was my twin, perhaps because close proximity wears down the differences, never seemed like a real boy to me. Or perhaps it was simply that having known him as a child, he remained to me a child, and I had not taken in his new rôle of young man. I was, however, uncomfortably aware that he was much better taught than we were and that Jessica and I must seem exceedingly ignorant to him and his friends. We were convinced, in any case, that boys were much cleverer than girls so we started the evening with the belief that we were at a severe disadvantage.

Then there were those mysterious warnings that the nuns and Father Gallagher had given us. The nuns never mentioned kissing but Father Gallagher had once told us that it was a mortal sin to open one's mouth when kissing; and the nuns made it clear that 'arousing men's passions' was a very grave sin, adding that since men's passions were uncontrollable it would be entirely our fault if anything untoward occurred. To make matters worse, one of our fellow prefects had told us that there was a sign language that you had to learn before you could understand what men expected of you and that if you did not know the language you might inadvertently give an encouraging response to some outrageously daring and embarrassing question.

All in all, it was pretty nerve-racking. Would we know what was happening? Would we seem so absurdly ignorant that our dancing partners would be forced to abandon us and go in search of more interesting prey? What did we do if they became uncontrollable? No one had ever thought fit to give us any guidance as to how to behave if this apparently all-too-common situation arose. The only thing that I had ever been told which seemed to have some slight bearing on the subject was that only very common girls slapped men's faces. Jessica insisted that someone had told her that the important thing was never to faint. If you fainted they might take advantage of you, apparently. (What might this really entail, we asked one another? We had visions of having most of our clothes ripped off as we lay in the middle of the ballroom floor, and lots of boys standing around staring at us.)

Jessica's mother was determined to make sure that we were the best-turned-out girls ever sent to a dance so the preparations as we bathed, dressed and put up our hair, took most of the afternoon. In the course of trying on most of Lady Grantsby-Harte's jewellery, I tried to extract from her some rather more precise information about what lay ahead but her answers, as always, were vague.

'Not a very good age for boys, I'm afraid,' she said with a sigh. 'I'd try to keep away from the spotty ones if I were you. They're always much more difficult to get rid of afterwards, for some reason. You might want to take a spare pair of shoes, too. Young men are always strangely disconnected from their feet so your shoes are bound to be ruined in no time. Try to make friends with some nice, sensible boys that you can invite here for tennis parties.'

Simon had arrived by this point and was listening to the conversation with astonishment. 'I can't imagine why you think it's going to be so bad for you. It's much worse for us. We have to make all the moves and invite girls to dance and try not to tread on their toes and all that sort of stuff; and we haven't the faintest idea what to talk to them about.'

'Are you going to try to kiss them?'

'Certainly not! What a frightful idea. Nobody's going to try to kiss you, don't worry. Boys can't stand girls, anyway; and even if they did, they wouldn't admit it in front of other boys. Everybody would think they were cissies. Why would anybody want to kiss you, anyway? There's nothing that special about you.'

'Can we have one of our pacts?' I asked. 'If it's all too frightening, will you rescue me?'

'As far as I'm concerned, I'll be happy to dance with you all evening. I haven't the least wish to meet anyone else.'

'What about me?' enquired Jessica. 'You can't leave me on my own all evening. You've jolly well got to take turns with me and Imogen, Simon. It's not fair, otherwise.'

'Oh, all right,' said Simon.

'I think you're all being very silly,' interrupted Jessica's mother. 'There will be lots of nice boys and girls and the whole idea is to meet new people. You'll all be fine when you get there.'

She was wrong. We were overcome with panic. Every time anyone asked me to dance I broke out into a cold sweat and, as we swept around the floor, desperately tried to interpret every shift of hand or arm, convinced that my partner was giving me one of those secret signs and that I might be giving the wrong response.

Most of the boys present, Simon included, were about to go up to Oxford or Cambridge and were, I felt sure, brilliantly clever. One of them, a young man who exuded ease and social grace, talked to me at length about *Bonjour Tristesse* and his admiration for Françoise Sagan. He employed the words 'mistress' and 'lover' frequently during this discourse and all the while, as we danced, his thumb massaged the palm of my hand with an odd, circular movement. What on earth did this mean, I wondered frantically? Was he asking me a question? Was he about to kiss me?

If such a thought occurred to him, he rejected it. To my secret disappointment, we finished our dance with nothing unusual occurring. I decided that he had been waiting for me to make some sign-language reply which I had obviously failed to give. I had the unpleasant feeling that I had made myself appear ridiculous. The thought of having to repeat this routine again and again all evening was more than I could bear. I decided to go off in search of Simon.

Simon was finding the whole thing equally difficult, apparently. He had been cornered by a huge girl who plainly terrified him. I managed to steal him from under her nose and we then agreed that we would only dance with each other for the rest of the evening.

We danced well together because we had had ample practice. We had attended ballroom-dancing classes together in Milan in the holidays and had converted our old nursery at Manta into a room for practising the steps. Often, in winter, when the weather was bad, we took ourselves off to the nursery and danced.

As a result, we were immediately conspicuous. People stopped to admire us sailing about the floor, unaware that we were hissing, 'Slow, slow, quick, quick, slow,' in each other's ear as we danced. The dance floor began to empty and couples stood round the walls watching us. Overcome with embarrassment, Simon whispered, 'Can't you pretend to have a stomach ache or something? We've got to stop dancing. This is frightful.'

I thought a stomach ache might be embarrassing so I pretended to sprain my ankle. Simon looked concerned and held me gently by the arm as I hobbled from the floor. It was a technique we were to polish to a fine art over the next couple of years. Every time we were invited to a dance, I very early on developed some mysterious ailment which necessitated a speedy departure; and Simon, always a gentleman, inevitably felt obliged to take me home. I discovered, years later, that we had been famous for it in Italy and that we were generally known amongst our Milanese contemporaries as 'the twins with the sore foot.'

That night, in Norfolk, people probably believed us but whereas I was then able to languish on a sofa looking pale and interesting, Simon was almost instantly called into action again. We had barely sat down before we noticed Jessica frantically signalling to us. She was dancing with a thin, gangly creature who appeared to have her locked in a tight embrace, his cheek glued to hers, his right hand squeezing her hard against his chest. One could almost feel his hot breath and perspiring brow.

'Oh, God,' complained Simon, 'I suppose I'll have to go and rescue her.'

'Say I'm in agony and that we've got to leave,' I suggested.

'Good idea,' said Simon. 'I can't stand any more of this in any case.'

The gangly youth did not give up easily and, when he did, followed us to the front door demanding Jessica's telephone number. I could see that Jessica's mother had been right. He was evidently one of the spotty ones of whom Jessica would have difficulty ridding herself.

'Honestly and truly,' said Jessica in the car on the way back to Upton, 'what a frightful evening. Thank God we're getting out of England and going to the Sorbonne. Your mother was quite right. Englishmen are ghastly. If all the boys are like the ones we've met tonight, there really is no hope for us in this country.'

'The girls weren't any better, I assure you,' said Simon.

'Well, at least they didn't leap on you and squash your bosom to a pulp,' said Jessica.

'They kept trying to get me to go out into the garden with them, which was just as bad,' replied Simon.

'Well, I feel jolly sorry for you going to Cambridge,' remarked Jessica. 'You'll have a horrible time. I think you're mad. There must be somewhere else where you can read biochemistry, somewhere not in England.'

'Not as good and not anywhere that I could get into with only English qualifications,' answered Simon.

'Well, poor you,' said Jessica. 'Did you realize that most of those boys this evening were going either to Oxford or to Cambridge? They'd practically all been accepted; can you imagine? You're going to be stuck with those sort of people for years – and it doesn't say much for this country if they represent the flower of England's youth and the pick of the nation's brains, does it? I can't think how they manage to be so conceited when they're all so spotty and uncouth.'

'Who is to say that the boys at the Sorbonne won't be just as bad?' said Simon. 'And, God knows, the French are conceited, too. I can't see why you think it's going to be so much better in France. It'll be just as bad.'

'No, it won't,' Jessica insisted, 'and, anyway, there is so much else to do in Paris, so many things to see, and the food will be good. It will all be much more fun.'

'What do you suppose would have happened to us if we hadn't gone to the Sorbonne?' I asked Jessica as she reminded me of this conversation. 'If we'd gone to university in England, would we have avoided marriage, do you think?'

'No, of course not,' replied Jessica. 'We wanted to marry. We were in the mood to fall in love with almost anybody. But I think we would have picked very different types. It's most unlikely we would have fallen for such aggressively left-wing people. In fact, I have a horrible feeling we would still be the appalling little snobs we were at school. We wouldn't have had any reason to change if we had stayed in England. Going to France was the best decision we ever made from the point of view of learning anything useful.'

Viewed with hindsight, it seemed hard to believe that we should have been so innocent and so totally unprepared for life, but nothing in our upbringing had had any bearing on the modern world. We were a generation behind our time and unaware of the existence of nine-tenths of the human race.

'I bet you,' said Jessica, 'that nobody would believe us if we told them that there weren't any newspapers at school, and that they didn't have any wirelesses or televisions. We never heard the news, did we? The nuns

163

never told us anything about what was going on in the world.'

'Well, they probably didn't know what was going on. After all, they didn't hear the news or read newspapers either. It wasn't really their fault. In a way, it was our parents who were at fault.'

'That's perfectly true. It's very odd, when you think of it, that your parents never stopped discussing music, and art, and literature, but they hardly ever mentioned current affairs. Your father read his *Times* and his *Corriere della Sera* pretty thoroughly every day but I don't remember him ever making any comments on world affairs, do you? Perhaps he thought it would bore your mother.'

'I don't think either of them was the least interested in politics. Mummy certainly wasn't. What is much odder is that your father always avoided political discussions like the plague which, given his interest in the subject, seems strange to say the least. He always went out of his way to avoid expressing any opinion, as far as I can remember.'

'Yes, but that was because he was always so worried about giving anything away which should have been kept secret.'

'Well, whatever the reasons, the results were disastrous. We held the most obnoxious views and we were completely unaware that all around us lay a world of appalling poverty, political torture, racism, anti-semitism, starving children, civil wars, decimated families, mothers and babies machine-gunned down in cold blood. We hadn't even taken in that there were millions of ordinary, working-class families who struggled all their lives just to earn an honest living and to feed their growing children. What kind of an education was that?'

'It was unforgivable,' sighed Jessica, 'but then supposing we had been aware of all that, think how miserable we would have been. We couldn't possibly have enjoyed Manta and Upton: we'd have been feeling

164

much too guilty. It's an awful thing to say but by growing up in such a protected environment and in such total ignorance we were given a magical childhood, and it's difficult not to be glad of that.'

'It was odd of our parents, all the same, don't you think?' I asked.

'Not really. They obviously knew that sooner or later we would have to come face to face with the harsh truth that this world is not a pleasant place and I think they wanted to give us a happy childhood first: to allow us to be real children – children who believed in fairy tales, and ghosts, and Father Christmas – rather than children who were forced to be adult before they had learned to read.'

'Yes, perhaps,' I agreed. 'Was that, do you suppose, why they encouraged us to go to the Sorbonne when one might have expected them to want us to follow in their footsteps and go to Oxford?'

'Yes, I'm sure it was. They must have realised that if we stayed in England we'd never change and that the only hope of ever making us wake up was to send us somewhere else before it was too late. What I don't understand is why your parents allowed Simon to go to Cambridge when he had had the same conventional, unintelligent English upbringing and was in just as much need as we were of being forced to reassess all his ideas.'

'I imagine they thought he was intelligent enough to get there by himself; and where could he have gone? He didn't want to go back to Italy, if you remember. He was determined to keep a safe distance between himself and Daddy. And he couldn't have gone to France. He'd never have got into any of the Grandes Ecoles with just his 'A' and 'S' levels. He was going to have to earn his living at the end of the day, too, whereas we were just girls mucking about and filling in time. Do you remember how frightened we were when we arrived in Paris? And do you remember that ghastly hotel?'

Jessica laughed. 'The hotel was rather an unfortunate beginning, I must admit,' she replied.

'If we hadn't stayed there, we might never have contacted André,' I pointed out, 'and we certainly would never have met Edward Blight.'

'That would have been a relief,' said Jessica ruefully; 'and if we hadn't been involved with André and Edward we would never have met Anthony or Enrico, or even Dermot, if it comes to that. Golly, I'd never really thought about it before but the hotel can be blamed for everything.'

It was odd to think that an insignificant, squalid hotel could have been the cause of so much trouble, but we did not have much choice when we arrived in Paris. We had very little money and we had to stay somewhere while we looked for a flat. The hotel in question was cheap and within manageable distance of the Sorbonne, and it was a degree less awful than the *chambres de bonne* we had visited. It was, however, far from clean and having just emerged from eight years of frenetic housework in a building so immaculate that a baby could safely have eaten off the floor, Jessica and I both hated dirt. Not only did we hate it, we were terrified of it. We imagined ourselves going down with cholera and bubonic plague. Jessica, I remembered, had thought she might be developing botulism from using the tap water when she cleaned her teeth.

'You can't get botulism from water,' I had pointed out. 'At least, I don't think so. You get it from sausages, don't you? I believe it's a particularly German disease, perhaps because they eat so many sausages.'

'Well, in that case, I'm getting diphtheria,' said Jessica firmly. 'There's something wrong with my throat and I know it's the water. We'll have to clean our teeth with Evian and we'll have to do something about this room.'

We cleaned our room as it had never been cleaned before. We bought gallons of *eau de javel* and spent fortunes on disinfectant sprays, flea powders, rat poison ('just in case', as Jessica said) and a variety of strong

166

soaps. After days of scrubbing, the room still looked dirty although the repulsive odour of stale Gitanes had been replaced by an overwhelming smell of bleach. We bought our own sheets and towels which we took to the laundry ourselves, but still we felt unhappy.

'It's the mattresses,' I said to Jessica. 'I think they need to be fumigated.'

'There's the bathroom, too,' replied Jessica, 'and that frightful loo. Whatever either of us does to clean them, the other people make them dirty again. It's really too jungly. I don't think I can stand it any longer.'

'I'll go and talk to the manager about getting the mattresses fumigated, if you like,' I suggested to make her feel better.

It never occurred to me that the manager might object.

'Pas question! Vous êtes complètement maniaques, vous deux!' he exploded. 'Vous dérangez tout le monde avec vos histoires. J'en ai marre! Allez voir un psychiatre! Ne m'en parlez plus ou je vous sortirai d'ici tout de suite, je vous jure. Vous êtes sérieusement malades! Complètement folles!' he shrieked after me as I beat a hasty retreat.

In despair, Jessica and I went to the nearest post office and made two telephone calls: one to my grandmother, the other to Jessica's parents. Both calls produced immediate results. Jessica's father contacted the British Embassy and my grandmother telephoned an old family friend called André Brillac d'Hocquincourt. The latter was an elderly baron with peculiar habits but my grandmother knew that we would be perfectly safe with him. He adored children, particularly girls, and his greatest regret in life was not having any of his own. He also loved my family more, probably, than he loved anyone else; and, in any case, my grandmother was perfectly aware that he reserved his private fetishes for Arab café boys.

I had known André since I was a child and although, as a small girl, I had greatly disliked him, I had grown fond of him during my teens. Jessica, too, having spent so much time with my family, knew André and was devoted to him. Over the years we had learnt to accept his one, vastly irritating foible. He loved titles and was an expert on family trees. It was fatal, with André, to mention anyone by name, whatever their nationality, for he would immediately launch forth into a complete history of both sides of the person's family: cadet branches, false claimants to the use of the name, total impostors, extinct branches, the whole works. He was particularly fond of princesses and collected them as he might have collected Fabergé eggs. Fortunately, his love and knowledge of literature were stronger than any of this and my parents had taught me early in life how to divert his attention: the mention of Racine was more powerful than any family tree.

André was horrified when he saw our hotel. 'Your parents would be scandalised if they knew,' he said to me. Within no time he had moved us to a thoroughly respectable little *pension* near the Odéon, saying 'This is not the height of luxury. It is very simple but it is more convenient for the Sorbonne and at least it is clean. It won't cost you any more than where you were and you will be in safe hands. I have had a word with the manager and asked him to keep an eye on you both. You are going to have to share a very small room until the end of the week, I am afraid, because all the other rooms are taken; but you'll be moved into a much bigger room on Friday. There shouldn't be any problems but let me know if there are. Now, let's go and have a hot chocolate at Ladurée. I think our wonderful summer may finally be coming to an end. It feels positively autumnal today. There's quite a sharp nip in the air.'

Just before André appeared and rescued us from our first hotel, the manager of that establishment suddenly summoned us to the front desk. I thought he was going to make another blistering attack on our efforts at cleaning but instead he handed me the telephone saying, rather grumpily, '*Quelqu'un de l'ambassade de Grande-Bretagne pour vous.*'

'It must be for you,' I said to Jessica, handing it to her.

While she took the receiver from me, Jessica handed me the *écouteur* so that I could listen to the conversation.

'Hello,' she said.

'Is that Jessica Grantsby-Harte?' asked a male voice.

'Yes,' replied Jessica.

'My name is Blight,' said the voice. 'Edward Blight. Your father has been in touch with the consul and asked if we can give you a hand finding somewhere to live. Accommodation in Paris is quite problematic and I understand you want to live near the Sorbonne which is the worst area, particularly at this time of year when it's milling with students all looking for accommodation. Still, I'll see what I can do. It might be easier to find you somewhere in the Marais, if you don't mind crossing over to the Right Bank. There are perfectly good buses that run from the rue de Rivoli to the *cinquième* – much easier than the *métro* where you would have to change. Otherwise, I expect we could find you somewhere in the *Quinzième*, although it's not so convenient, of course; or perhaps around Denfert-Rochereau. As I say, I'll see what I can do. You had better come along to my office. How about Friday morning? That should give my secretary time to rustle up some information. Do you know how to get here?'

'The Embassy's in the Faubourg-Saint-Honoré, isn't it?' asked Jessica.

'That's right, although my office is not in that building. It's only a few yards away on the other side of the street. Ask the man at the main entrance to the Embassy. They all know who I am and they'll point you in the right direction. You have to go through an archway between the shops. You can't miss it once you are in the court-yard. I'm on the second floor. Come about twelve fifteen. I should be free by then.'

'Thank you very much,' said Jessica.

'Do give my regards to your father, by the way,' added Edward Blight as an afterthought. 'I used to know him quite well, years ago, when we were both just starting at the Foreign Office, but I haven't seen him for years – not since he was first posted abroad, in fact. I was very fond of him. I'd love to see him again. We all travel too much in this business. Right, I'll expect you on Friday. Goodbye.'

'Goodbye,' echoed Jessica.

By the Friday morning in question, André had moved us and we were safely ensconced in our new *pension*. We were told that we were being given a much larger room at noon that day, when the previous occupants checked out, so we agreed that I should move our belongings while Jessica was seeing Edward Blight.

André offered to take us both out to lunch but Jessica declined, saying, 'I think it would be too much of a rush for me. I'm supposed to be in the Faubourg-Saint-Honoré at twelve fifteen. What if this Blight character doesn't see me straight away? It'll be far too late to meet you anywhere.'

'What I suggest,' said André, 'is that we leave a message at the hotel to say where we've gone and then you can join us if you are back in time.'

'All right, but don't count on me. Let's say that if I haven't appeared by the time you leave the restaurant, I'll meet you, Imogen, at the hotel at four thirty.'

On that happy note, we parted. I moved our belongings to our new and very pleasant hotel room; then André took me to Lipp for lunch.

Jessica did not manage to join us. Instead, she returned to the hotel at five o'clock, looking furious, and burst into the room saying, 'God, what a ghastly man! You can't imagine what an awful time I've been having. And I didn't even have a chance to see anything of Paris after all that, except out of taxi windows. Goodness!' her tone suddenly changed. 'This is an improvement. What a nice room. Good old André. You were jolly lucky to have lunch with him, I can tell you, and not with the ghastly Blight. I don't believe a word of what he said about being an old friend of Daddy's. I can't imagine what they could ever have had in common and Daddy has certainly never mentioned him. His name suits him entirely.'

I asked Jessica what had happened and she gave me a blow-by-blow description. She had been asked to wait for nearly forty-five minutes, but when Edward Blight had eventually ushered her into his office, he had welcomed her very pleasantly, repeating his tale of having known her father in London years ago. He had seemed to Jessica organized and efficient and had produced a list of possible addresses for us to visit, all apparently checked by the Embassy and all very reasonable.

'When you ring the landlords, mention that you were sent by the Embassy,' he said. 'There are always hundreds of people running after every room and flat in this city and it will probably help to mention us. You can use my name if you like. If there are any problems, or they require a reference, ask them to ring me; and do let me know if there is anything else I can do. Your father wanted us to check that your allowance was coming through all right. Yes? Good. If there is ever any problem on that score, let me know and I'll have a word with the bank. Now, I expect you'd like some lunch.'

Jessica was surprised that he wanted to waste any more time with her but, realizing that she was too late to join us, she accepted. ('In any case, at that point I thought he was rather kind and sweet, if a little pompous, she explained to me.)

'Have you any preference as to where we eat?' the Blight had asked.

'Not really,' replied Jessica. 'I hardly know Paris. I've only been here two and a half weeks.'

'Well, I cannot abide eating in the same place twice,' said the Blight, pulling out a restaurant guide and flicking through its pages. 'Here's one I haven't tried,' he exclaimed enthusiastically after a slight pause. 'Right, let's go.'

He helped her on with her coat, chatted to her as they went out of the building, hailed a passing taxi and asked its driver to take them to an address in the quinzième. As Jessica pointed out to me when describing her afternoon, it seemed an unnecessarily long way to go just for lunch, but apparently the Blight had no urgent engagements that afternoon.

As the taxi pulled up outside the restaurant, the Blight leaped out, saying, 'Wait there a moment. I have a sneaking suspicion that I *have* been here before. I'll just check.' He vanished inside briefly and then reappeared saying, 'I thought it looked a bit familiar. I have definitely been here before. We'll have to find somewhere else.' He had brought his restaurant guide with him and clambered back into the taxi to study it. Finally he said, 'That looks OK. We'll give it a try,' and asked the taxi driver to take them to the place des Ternes. The taxi turned back on its tracks, crossed the Seine once more and headed for the *dix-septième*. This time Jessica was allowed to descend.

The minute they walked into the restaurant, the Blight reared back. 'There's a man smoking,' he said accusingly. Jessica agreed that there was indeed a man smoking, even two men smoking. 'Well, I can't possibly eat with people smoking,' he said and signalled to the head waiter. The *maître d'hôtel* looked astonished when the Blight demanded that he tell the two people in question to put out their cigarettes. He explained to the Blight that he really could not force his clients to give up smoking or he would not have any clients left.

'*Je suis désolé, Monsieur*,' he said politely.

The Blight looked outraged. 'This is intolerable,' he complained. 'Well, we can't stay here.' Jessica followed him out into the street again and the Blight hailed another taxi.

They made two more abortive attempts before finding a restaurant where Edward Blight had never before set foot and where no-one was smoking. ('Miraculous in Paris, you must admit,' Jessica said to me when telling me about it. 'There can't be more than about a hundred non-smokers in the whole of this town and we seem to have found them all in one place.'

'Perhaps it's the place where they all congregate,' I suggested.

'Perhaps,' replied Jessica. 'At any rate, I was terrified the whole way through lunch that someone would suddenly decide to light a cigarette and I'd never get my pudding.')

After they had had a moment to study the menu, the Blight looked up and enquired whether Jessica was ready to order. 'Any feelings about whether you want red or white wine?' he asked, affably.

'I was thinking of having the *lotte*,' replied Jessica, 'so I'd rather have white – unless, of course, you want red, in which case I'll happily choose something else. It all looks utterly delicious.'

'Do you enjoy drinking wine?' the Blight enquired. Jessica replied that she did.

'Know anything about it?' he asked.

'Not nearly as much as you must do, but my father did go out of his way to try and din in the basics. I'm quite good at decanting, and pulling out champagne corks, and that sort of thing but I don't think Daddy is terribly proud of my palate. Still, I suppose he has managed to give me some idea of which wines are worth drinking.'

The Blight looked sceptical. 'All right,' he said genially, handing her the wine list. 'You choose.'

Jessica, inevitably, picked a wine she knew. She chose a Corton-Charlemagne 1952 saying, 'I expect you'll think it's too old for a white wine, but I know it's all right because I have tasted it recently and it was absolutely delicious. Perfect, in fact. The only other white wine I can think of that lasts as well is Le Montrachet, but they don't seem to have it on this list.'

The Blight looked startled. 'I think we'll have red wine, don't you? I never drink white wine if I can help it. Gives me a headache,' he said as if he had not heard her.

'In that case, I'll have the duck instead of the *lotte*, if you don't mind,' replied Jessica. 'In actual fact, I'd rather have duck because I have just noticed that they

173

have my absolutely favourite red wine. It's exactly what I most want to drink.'

'Which one is that?' asked the Blight.

'Pommard '45,' replied Jessica.

The Blight reeled. Jessica, who had not been taught to look at prices, mistook the Blight's expression and added helpfully, 'I know it was undrinkable even a few years ago. In fact, lots of Daddy's friends sold off their 1945s in despair in 1961 and 1962. I expect it tasted as hard as nails the last time you tried it but I promise you it's absolutely *perfect* now. It's the most wonderful wine you have ever tasted. Don't you think it's extraordinary that it can take a wine twenty years to be drinkable and that it can then become so delicious? It's a sort of miracle, don't you think?'

'I can see your father has done a good job on you,' commented the Blight, drily. 'Excellent choice, excellent, I must say.' He paused and then said, 'Will you excuse me a moment?' and added, as he rose to his feet, 'Nature calls, as they say. If the waiter comes for our order, you can give it to him. I'll have the *blanquette* and I'll try their *pâté maison* to start with.' He headed towards a door marked *Messieurs* at the back of the room but stopped on the way to talk to the wine waiter. They seemed to have an interminable discussion, poring over the wine list and pointing to various items on it but when the Blight finally continued on his way he looked quite satisfied.

'No joy with the Pommard, I'm afraid,' said the Blight on his return to their table. 'They only have it in far larger quantities than we could possibly drink so I've ordered a Lafite instead. It should be pretty good I think.'

The food arrived in due course, and so did the wine. The waiter's face was impassive as he held the bottle for the Blight's inspection and approval before opening it. It was indeed a Lafite but it was the smallest bottle that Jessica had ever seen – the same size, she assured me, as the bottles one is offered in an aeroplane. The Blight tasted it, nodded, and the waiter poured half the contents into each of their glasses. The empty bottle was removed. It had filled roughly a third of each glass.

'I always think it is infinitely preferable to drink a small amount of a very good wine rather than a large amount of a poor one,' remarked the Blight, looking thoroughly content. 'Well, to your very good health and welcome to Paris. Your father is a fortunate man to have such a pretty daughter' ('and he positively ogled,' said Jessica, describing the scene). 'You hardly know Paris, you say. Well, we must do something about that. We must have dinner some time and I'll show you the sights.'

By the time they had finished their coffee, it was after four thirty and Jessica was desperate to escape.

'Too late to go back to the office now,' commented the Blight. 'How about a stroll? We could go up to Montmartre if you like. It's very pretty and the view of Paris is wonderful. Then, we could find somewhere pleasant and sit outside and have a drink later if you like.'

Jessica explained that she had promised to meet me at four thirty and was already late. She thanked him for his help with information about flats and fled.

'Sure you can make your own way back to your hotel?' asked the Blight. 'Right. Well, I hope to see you again very soon. I'll give you a ring in a day or two to see how you are getting on.'

'Who exactly is the Blight?' I asked Jessica when she had finished her tale. 'What does he do at the Embassy? He doesn't seem to have to work very hard.'

'No, he doesn't, does he? I didn't like to ask him what he did. I felt it would be rather rude of me, but I had the impression that he wasn't very important. It was something to do with the way the staff reacted when I asked for him, and the way they left me sitting there for such hours without asking me whether I wanted a coffee or anything. In Washington when anyone asked for Daddy they were treated as if they were important just because they were seeing him. Well, with the Blight it wasn't at all like that. I think that building is only the Consulate anyway and I'm sure that if he'd been important he would have been busier and he wouldn't have had time to take me out to lunch; probably wouldn't have wanted to, either.'

CHAPTER TEN

Shortly after this, Jessica and I found a tiny flat that we could afford in the rue des Carmes. We loved the place on sight and the fact that it was one of the addresses supplied by the Blight was a drawback in terms of indebtedness amply outweighed by the excitement of having our own flat for the first time in our lives. We were also very aware of our luck in finding anything so conveniently situated. It was just yards down the hill from the bibliothèque Sainte-Geneviève, where we were to spend so many hours; if we took the short-cut down the tiny and picturesque rue de Lanneau, we found ourselves on the steps of the Collège de France; we were only minutes away from the rue Saint-Jacques, the boulevard Saint-Michel and the whole of the quartier Latin; and it was a short and very pleasant walk along the rue des Ecoles to the Sorbonne.

The Sorbonne was not as we had imagined it to be. The first few days were utterly bewildering both because it was extremely difficult to find out where one was meant to be at any given time, and because it was impossible to find one's way about. The building was a labyrinth of passages, tiny classrooms, staircases and amphitheatres. All the wooden doors looked identical, all the marble corridors looked alike. It took a long time to learn one's way to the right amphitheatre, or to recognize it when one had reached it; and we had had no idea, beforehand, of the number of people we would find packed into one building. The first day was memorable for the throngs of lost undergraduates milling around helplessly.

More intimidating than all the rest, or so we thought at the beginning, were the other undergraduates. The girls seemed extraordinarily self-confident; the boys seemed cynical and unpleasant. They all roamed about in gangs of their own sex. The girls, looking very attractive, seemed able to ignore the boys entirely; the boys were extremely conscious of all the girls and lounged around smoking and making sarcastic remarks about anyone who passed. Occasionally, one of the girls would swing round and shout some extremely cutting retort at which all the boys would start talking to her and she would then become very aggressive. It soon became apparent to us that this ritual was a form of flirtation. A crossfire of unpleasant remarks would fly back and forth, and one could see that it was the height of excitement for all concerned. Eventually, the girl would toss her head, make some last remark and waltz off to join her waiting friends. As the group of girls moved away, they would keep looking back over their shoulders at the boys, giggling as they did so.

Since Jessica and I were not reading the same subjects and were frequently not in the building at the same time, we each had to face the frightening mob on our own. Neither of us felt the least able to cope with the wolf-whistles and personal remarks, so we spent the first few months in a state of perpetual embarrassment.

Every undergraduate's life is one of discovery but ours, that first year in Paris, was largely one of political discovery. Until then we had never encountered anyone who claimed to be 'left-wing', but in Paris the entire world seemed to be socialist or even, in many cases, Communist. Here, anyone with the minimum of brains was left-wing. Anyone right-wing was assumed, generally correctly, to be stupid. The small number of right-wing undergraduates came almost exclusively from the much despised Jesuit schools (anti-state, anti-intellectual, snobbish, homosexual) and from aristocratic families. There was one exception: a tiny group of clever, right-wing students who did not fit into this category and who claimed to be *anarchistes de droite*. There were only a handful of them, fortunately, for they were exceedingly disagreeable. Their political views were fascist and their sexual attitudes misogynous. When they were not making vile remarks about *youpins* (yids) they were boasting about their repulsive behaviour with prostitutes. Jessica and I saw them walk purposely into a black student one afternoon and, saying '*Pousse-toi, Blanche-Neige*' ('Move over, Snow White'), knock him right across the passage so hard that he hit his head on the far wall. When I tried to remonstrate with them they rounded on me, spitting '*Ferme ta gueule, petite conne!*' The experience was salutary: our left-wing friends had no trouble persuading us to join them. We were instant converts.

One of the first to befriend us was a boy called Olivier who came from Toulouse. As far as we could tell, Olivier was an exception in that there appeared to be very few students from the provinces, and it was perhaps the fact that he was not Parisian which made him seem so much friendlier than the others. He was enormously entertaining but always desperately worried about his finances. He kept vanishing from the Sorbonne for weeks on end because he needed to earn money, but would drift back again as soon as he had enough to survive the next month. He had some useful attributes: he could type, work a telex machine and write good English, so he usually managed to find work quite easily; but since he always made it clear that he did not intend to stay longer than was absolutely necessary, people seldom offered him jobs of great interest. He was in his second year when we arrived and we had only been at the Sorbonne for a term when he announced that he was abandoning the university permanently because he had been offered a temptingly well-paid job in Tahiti. 'You're mad,' we told him. 'You've only got one more year after this before getting your degree and surely you don't want to live in Tahiti for the rest of your days? What will you do afterwards if you don't have any qualifications?'

'Well,' he replied, looking thoroughly dejected, 'I haven't really got much choice. I've been chucked out of my lodgings once again, I can't pay for the books, I can't go on bumming food off you two and I certainly can't afford to buy food myself. This job is amazingly well paid, so I should be able to save up fortunes in a couple of years and then come back and do what I like. They're paying my fare out there, obviously, and at least it will be a change. The women are supposed to be lovely, too; sloe-eyed, with swaying hips. I'll write to you both and send you my address so that when you're rich and famous you can come and visit me there.'

'The climate's supposed to be horrible,' said Jessica, trying to discourage him from leaving. 'It's frightfully muggy and it's always overcast.'

'The beaches are fantastic,' replied Olivier, more to encourage himself than to convince us.

'I thought they were supposed to be littered with stonefish or whatever those things are that first turn you mad and then kill you,' I interrupted.

'They have wonderful food – fish and fruit that are absolutely out of this world,' continued Olivier, ignoring us both. Nothing would dissuade him, so off he set.

A couple of weeks later, Jessica received the following postcard:

This is a nightmare. The flowers are amazing but everything else is dreadful. The insect life is driving me demented and I'm covered in lumps and bites and bleeding scratch marks. The weather is humid and grey. The clouds haven't shifted since I arrived so I have yet to see a chink of blue sky. The man I am working for is dreadful and his wife is worse. As for the women, they all turn out to wear size 47 sandals and it isn't just their gigantic hips which sway. What nobody bothered to warn me was that they all have moustaches and mouths full of gold teeth. Love to Imogen, O.

Shortly after this, Olivier reappeared again saying that he was going to sue the company in Tahiti because he had not been paid the whole time he had been there and he had been thrown out of the country by the police because his employer had not filled in the necessary documents. 'The only good thing,' he said, 'is that they had to pay my ticket home because I couldn't pay it and they couldn't keep me. I think they were about to go bankrupt anyway, so I'm well out of it.'

For a while, after his return, Olivier seemed to go into a decline. He was as broke as ever, he seemed unable to find any work, the girl he wanted to marry decided to make a brave gesture and marry a Rumanian in order to help him acquire French nationality and the Rumanian apparently had every intention of staying with her permanently. Olivier became positively suicidal. He vanished completely for about a month but reappeared one Saturday morning in the bibliothèque Sainte-Geneviève.

'Hello, Olivier,' I whispered. 'How nice to see you. We were really worried about you. Where have you been?'

'I've got a job,' Olivier replied, looking ecstatically happy.

'Wonderful!' I exclaimed. 'I'm so glad! What is it?'

'I'm working in an hotel.'

'A nice hotel?' I enquired.

'Rather an odd sort of hotel,' he replied.

'Where?' I asked.

'In the dix-huitième.'

'Are you enjoying it?'

'Tremendously. It's great fun.'

'What do you do there, exactly?'

'Well, I listen to everyone's life history and I make endless bowls of soup. I'm a sort of night porter. It's very interesting. Some amazing people stay there and they all tell me their life story.'

People were beginning to hiss at us to be quiet and one of the supervisors rose from her desk and started heading towards us. We left the library so that we could talk in peace and it soon transpired that Olivier was working in an 'hôtel de passe'.

'I have another job too,' he said enthusiastically.

'Another job?'

'Yes. I work in the daytime for their Serene Highnesses.'

'Which Serene Highnesses?'

'Some people who call themselves the Prince and Princess Rudolf zu Hohentrecht. They're Belgian. I look after their little girl. They don't know about my night job at the hotel and they mustn't find out, so don't tell anyone but Jessica about it please.'

'May we come and visit you at the hotel?'

'Yes, of course. You can help make soup and join in the party. Come any night after eleven. You'll love it. So will Jessica. You can have some of the soup too if you're hungry. I must go now. I just came to look something up in the library. I've decided to try for my degree after all but I can't come to the cours magistraux as long as I continue to work for their Serene Highnesses all day, so I'm having to swot among the tarts and the soup bowls at dead of night. I really need to borrow notes from someone who is reading history and is in their second year. You might ask Jessica if she could befriend one of the second-year students and wheedle them into letting me borrow their notes. The hotel has a photocopying machine, so I could copy them and return them very quickly. I hear that some of the lectures are being given by an Englishman from Cambridge. He's supposed to be brilliant. I'm furious to be missing them. I wonder whether anyone is taping them. Do you think it's allowed? Anyway, I must run because their Highnesses are not at all Serene when I'm late. Here's the address of my hotel,' he added, handing me a piece of paper on which he had scribbled the details. 'Do come. It's hilariously funny. Love to Jessica,' and off he dashed.

At lunch-time, when I returned to the rue des Carmes, I gave Jessica Olivier's news. 'I've heard about the Englishman,' said Jessica. 'He doesn't lecture to our year, unfortunately; and although I vaguely know some of the second-year students by sight, I don't know any of them well enough to ask them if I can borrow their notes. I'll see if I can find anyone else who does; and I'll try to find out about taping lectures, too, although God knows who one has to ask. By the way, I want to go to the PUF or Gibert this afternoon. Will you come with me? There's a book I want by Leroi-Gourhan who seems to be the big name in archaeology here. Apparently he lectures at the Collège de France so I thought we might go and listen to him some time, but I'd like to read something he has written first.'

'That's good because I want to buy another of Janké's books. He seems to have written an awful lot and it's going to take me for ever, but I've decided I'm going to read every word he has ever written. I'm practically at the end of *L'Ironie ou la Bonne Conscience*. I shall have finished it by tomorrow. Let's go to Gibert,' I suggested, 'because it's less expensive than the PUF; and also I need some new exercise books. Why do you suppose all French *cahiers* have squared paper? I can't make out which is worse, the paper with little squares or the paper with big squares. It's driving me potty. I'm sure we're going to develop squints from it.'

Jessica could not find the book she wanted at Gibert so that, as soon as I had bought my exercise books, we crossed the road to the Presses Universitaires de France. There, Jessica went downstairs to the art and *beaux-livres* whilst I went up to the first floor to browse in the sections devoted to politics and philosophy.

Some time later, as I was flipping through the pages of a book by Raymond Aron and wondering whether I should also read every word he had ever written, Jessica suddenly reappeared at my side with several enormous art books. 'You're going to have to help me carry some of these,' she said. 'I've found lots of really wonderful books downstairs, but they're all frightfully heavy. I still haven't found the one I came here for, so do you think

183

you could hang on to these for me while I go and ask the manager or somebody to help me? I won't be long,' she added encouragingly as she handed me her books and disappeared again.

While she had been speaking to me I had noticed a tall, grey-eyed man turn away from a shelf of history books to stare at us. It was as if the sound of English voices had disturbed him. As Jessica vanished down the stairs and I moved to the shelf which contained Jankélévitch's books, I felt his eyes following me and when, after a moment or two, I turned around to look, he was still watching me. Our eyes met for an instant before I blushed and turned back to the philosophy titles. It was the first time in my life that I had been aware of overt sexual interest in a man's expression. Feeling hideously uncomfortable, I grabbed the first book I could see and raced downstairs to the desk where the manager was writing something down for Jessica.

'It's going to take for ever before they have this book in stock again,' she said gloomily. 'Every archaeology student in Paris wants a copy, apparently, and it's reprinting at the moment. Just my luck. Considering that archaeology is only practised by amateurs here, it seems to be an astonishingly popular subject. Anyway, I'd better go and pay for those other books. Thanks for keeping them for me. I'll take them back now.'

While we stood in a queue waiting to pay for our books, Jessica took mine out of my hands and asked, 'Is this all you're buying? What is it anyway? May I have a look?' After glancing through it, she said, 'It looks jolly turgid to me but I'm sure it's the sort of thing we ought to be reading. Can I borrow it after you've finished with it?'

'May I, not can I.'

'Oh, Imogen, don't be so boring. You know I always get it wrong and I really can't see that it matters. It's only because you're a foreigner that you mind so much.'

'I know,' I said, laughing. 'But I do mind. Anyway, of course you are welcome to borrow it; although it may be awful. I can't tell you the first thing about it. I only chose

184

it because of the title, *La Musique et l'Ineffable*. It's a wonderful title, don't you think? Why isn't the queue moving, by the way?'

At this point, we realized that something had gone wrong with the till and that we were going to have to wait while someone was found who could fix it. I opened my book at random and read a bit. Somewhere in the middle my eye alighted on the following passage:

> *Le nativisme n'a pas tort: il y a un espace concret que tous les sens concourent à édifier. Mais l'idée d'une voluminosité et, on l'a vu, d'une profondeur musicale, n'a elle-même de sens que par rapport au temps: c'est le temps qui rend le charme évasif et diffus, qui fait de l'ipséité musicale une présence absente infiniment fugace et décevante . . .*

'I see what you mean,' I said to Jessica. 'I think I may have bitten off more than I can chew. Still, I suppose I'd better read it. I'm sure I'll learn something from it and he does have the most wonderful use of words. I like *"infiniment fugace"* as an expression, don't you? I must remember to use that some time. It's going to be jolly hard work, though. I shall feel frightfully saintly when I've finished it.'

'Forgive me for interrupting,' said an English voice behind us, 'but some of his other books are much more entertaining. There is one in particular which I think you might like and which has an equally good title. I wouldn't bother with that one if I were you; unless, of course, you're particularly interested in music, in which case it's well worth reading.'

I turned round to find, standing in the queue behind us, the grey-eyed man who had been watching me earlier.

'I *am* particularly interested in music. It's one of the things I'm *most* interested in,' I replied, I hoped frostily, feeling foolish and annoyed that someone should have listened to our conversation.

185

'In that case, you must certainly read it,' he said, politely; but for a fraction of a second I thought I caught a gleam of amusement in his eye.

'If there is another one which you think is better I'd like to buy it as well,' I said, thinking that perhaps I had been ungracious, 'but I have already read *La Mauvaise Conscience*, *L'Aventure, l'Ennui, le Sérieux* and *L'Ironie ou la Bonne Conscience*.'

The queue suddenly started moving again at this moment.

'I'll see if they've got the one I'm thinking of,' said the man. 'You stay here. I'll be back in a minute.'

He soon reappeared with a copy of another book by Jankélévitch. This one was called *Le Je-ne-sais-quoi et le Presque-rien*. 'Try this,' he said. 'It's excellent.'

I thanked him and was again extremely conscious of admiration in his regard. I looked down in embarrassment.

'Come on, Imogen,' said Jessica suddenly. 'They're waiting for you to pay for your books.' The girl behind the till, no doubt discouraged by the machine's earlier technical hitch, snapped at me that if I wanted to daydream there were other places in Paris where I could go to do it, that she did not have all afternoon to waste, that she had other customers to serve, and a string of equally helpful remarks. I felt flustered and promptly dropped my money on the floor. I bent to pick it up but the Englishman was there before me. He handed it back to me, looking as if he wanted to laugh. I felt idiotic.

When we emerged into the street at last, my only desire was to escape as fast as possible. I walked so quickly that Jessica had to run to keep up with me.

'Whatever is the matter?' she asked as I shot along the rue Cujas. 'You seem very peculiar all of a sudden.'

'It was that man,' I said. 'He kept staring at me. He started staring at me upstairs.'

'Yes, he did, didn't he? I noticed that too. It was probably just because we were talking English. There aren't many English people about. In fact, I haven't noticed any other English students around, have you? I suppose they're all at the Alliance française. I expect he was simply wondering what you were doing in Paris, buying books in French by stodgy French philosophers. I wonder how he came to know so much about Jankélévitch, if it comes to that. Anyway, we're miles away now. Do you think we could slow down? I'm going to drop all my books if I have to run any further.'

CHAPTER ELEVEN

We had intended to go to the cinema that evening but when we returned to our flat with the books, we discovered a letter that had been pushed under our door during the course of the day. It had obviously been delivered by hand and we recognised the writing immediately. I was a letter from the Blight.

Since Jessica's lunch with him shortly after our arrival in Paris, the Blight had refused to leave her alone. She loathed him and made little attempt to hide the fact, but he seemed impervious to the heaviest hints. We were extremely vulnerable because, not having a telephone, he felt free to turn up without warning whenever he pleased. Jessica always produced the wildest excuses for not being able to accept his incessant invitations, but he was never the least discouraged. He suggested theatres, dinners, concerts, sight-seeing trips, expeditions to Reims and Rouen and even an intimate weekend in 'a pleasant little hostelry I came across in Sologne last year'. Jessica declined every invitation but still he would not give up.

Jessica's recent excuses had all been along the lines that she had promised my parents never to let me out of her sight, that I did not know a soul in Paris, that I was hopelessly unable to manage by myself and that she did not like to leave me on my own. It was hardly surprising, therefore, that the Blight had hit upon the idea of inviting me along as well. His letter read:

My dear Jessica,
 I feel it is time that you and your friend saw

something of the real Paris – a Paris which is a great deal more glamorous than your present existence permits you to realize. You and Imogen must, I am sure, be tired of the squalid area around boulevard Saint-Michel, and the revolutionary conversations of the Left Bank. I have therefore planned what I hope will be an agreeable evening for you both. We shall be going to the Opéra and then out to dinner and I shall pick you up at seven because we have to collect someone else on the way. You might tell Imogen that we shall be hearing a performance of *Rigoletto* conducted by one of her own countrymen. I have invited an acquaintance of mine from the Italian Embassy to join us. I thought it would be pleasant for Imogen to be able to speak her own language since you tell me she is so lonely. He is a charming young man, in any case, and I am sure you will both like him. A *tout à l'heure*.

Edward

'Oh, God!' said Jessica. 'What a pestilential man. What ever did I do to deserve him? I'm going to get Daddy to do something about it if he doesn't give up soon. What are we going to do? He's going to be here in three-quarters of an hour. I suppose we could go out again and pretend we never came home and so never found his letter. What do you think?'

'It would serve him right if we did,' I said. 'After all, we could easily have gone straight to the cinema and not found the letter until later tonight.'

'On the other hand,' Jessica ruminated aloud, 'he'll only come up with some other frightful idea and sooner or later I'm going to have to say "yes" to one of his invitations. Given that fact, I'd far rather say "yes" to one where you're invited too; and I like *Rigoletto*. At least, I like the music. The story is completely daft with that ridiculous woman bellowing in a sack when she ought to be dead from stabbing and Rigoletto with the blindfold thinking he has lost his sight, or it's too dark to see. How could he not have felt the blindfold? The whole thing is absurd. But, anyway, the music is OK and much less hard work than that thing in Latin that you dragged me to last term – you know that Stravinsky opera about Oedipus that you liked so much. I couldn't sit through *that* with the Blight; but Verdi, with you there as well, I can just about manage. I think perhaps we'd better accept this invitation. It's much the least awful of his suggestions to date and compared with un *petit séjour intime en Sologne* it's absolute bliss. There will be the other man, too, which should make things easier. Do you think your Foreign Office coughs up such utter pills as the Blight? Let's hope the Italian Embassy can produce something more dashing.'

'He couldn't possibly be worse,' I said, 'and we'd better hurry up and get changed if we're really going.'

Our doorbell rang at seven on the dot. Jessica opened the door and Edward Blight breezed in looking pink and clean. He had one of those shiny, English faces that always look as if they have just been scrubbed by an energetic nanny and have seen many a bar of Pears' soap in their time. You could tell, the moment you clapped eyes on him, that he washed behind his ears twice a day, slept with his window wide open even in the coldest weather, went for a brisk walk every morning and sang in the bath. His wavy, grey hair was neatly brushed and his mouth looked slightly wet. Jessica winced as he kissed her. He appeared to be aiming at her cheek but managed to hit the right half of her mouth, possibly by accident. I held out my hand to make it clear that I was not intending to be kissed.

'We're meeting Enrico at the Café de la Paix for a quick drink before the opera starts,' said the Blight. 'His name, by the way, is Enrico Emanuele de Mitis. He's the Press Attaché at the Italian Embassy although his speciality is economic affairs and one hears that they are going to ask him to be Economics Attaché. He is reputed to be exceedingly clever and is expected to make a brilliant career for himself. He claims to be a socialist although he comes from a very rich family. He's very good-looking. I think you'll like him.'

When we arrived at the Café de la Paix, the Italian Press Attaché was already installed at a table with a bottle of Krug in a bucket beside him. ('I'm getting a bit muddled about socialism,' Jessica said to me afterwards. 'I didn't think socialists were supposed to loll about the Café de la Paix drinking Krug.') He rose to his feet as we approached and, after we had all been introduced, pulled out a chair for me, saying, 'I hope you all like champagne.' Then, seeing the Blight's expression, he added reassuringly, 'I'm afraid I ordered it and paid for it the moment I arrived. I thought it would save time and it seemed the only thing to drink before facing an evening of gigantic *soprani* falling in love with stout tenors.'

'Don't you like opera?' I enquired a little later, whispering so that the Blight, who was talking to Jessica, would not overhear.

'Loathe it,' he replied with a wry smile.

'How extraordinary,' I said. 'Why did you come here tonight, if you loathe it?'

He looked at the Blight who was still heavily engrossed in his conversation with Jessica, then leant towards me and whispered, 'Because dear old Edward is *forever* asking me to the opera. He seems to have an *idée fixe* about Italians needing music in order to survive and he is *determined* to be friends with me – I can't think why: he must be very lonely. Anyway, I've refused so many invitations that it was becoming positively embarrassing; and when he said he was bringing along two charming and very pretty girls, I decided that this was the moment to accept. I'm glad I did. You're not just very pretty: *Lei è veramente bella.*'

Italians always feel obliged to tell every woman they meet – whether young or old, fat or thin, pretty or plain – that they are beautiful. It is simply a question of good manners. I therefore paid no attention to this

191

remark. Enrico noticed this and seemed irritated by it. 'I mean it,' he insisted. '*Lei è veramente bellissima.* There is something very unusual and touching about your looks. You have the rather haunted look of a wild animal that has been trapped. Is it the blue eyes under that dark hair or is it the expression in your eyes? I don't know.'

For the second time that day I saw undisguised admiration in a man's eyes. This time they were hazel rather than grey, but the look was the same. It was unmistakable. I wanted to escape. I felt embarrassed, and uncomfortable, and frightened. (When I discussed it with Jessica later, she said, 'I think it must be something to do with the weather. I believe spring affects men very oddly – all that stuff the nuns used to tell us about men's uncontrollable passions, wasn't that something to do with spring? You must know that from your music. Stravinsky obviously suffered from it badly and, although it's still quite cold, we are in March so I suppose it is the beginning of spring. Maybe they'll all calm down when summer arrives.')

I looked at Jessica, hoping she would notice and come to my rescue but she was trying to disentangle her hand from the Blight's at that moment.

Enrico, following my gaze, said, 'Your friend looks like the girl in *La Baigneuse*. She has a perfectly sweet face.'

'The girl in *La Baigneuse* was Renoir's wife, did you know?'

'No, I didn't. No wonder he painted her so much.' He took the champagne bottle out of its bucket as he said this and started to refill our glasses. A waiter appeared instantly and took the bottle out of his hand, saying, '*Permettez, monsieur.*' Enrico said, in English, 'Waiters always hate one to help oneself for some reason. How long have we got, Edward? When does the performance start?'

'We should be going in a few minutes,' replied the Blight, 'but we've got time to finish our champagne first.'

I watched Enrico during this exchange and decided

that he had an unusual face for an Italian in that his features were neither regular nor aquiline. He had a lopsided mouth and a boyish expression. The Blight had told us that he was about twenty-eight, but he might just as well have been sixteen. It was only when he was talking about politics, later, over dinner, that his expression changed, making his face look suddenly middle-aged.

Music, in Paris, is always unpredictable. The opera, that evening, was a very poor production but it had its entertaining moments. The conductor seemed to be having a great deal of trouble with the members of the orchestra who, in true French fashion, had obviously decided that it was more important to demonstrate their individuality than to act as a group. The violins seemed to have chosen a different tempo from the rest of the players and were totally ignoring the agitation of the conductor; the flautists and oboists talked loudly amongst themselves whenever they laid down their instruments; and the entire brass section walked out the minute they had played the last note that was going to be required of them until after the interval, not bothering to wait until the curtain came down. One assumed they were heading for the nearest bar because they seemed to be in a hurry as they clambered over one another's feet, knocking music stands as they went. A more powerful conductor would have broken a few *bâtons* and stormed out in a rage but this little man (who turned out to be American, not Italian – the Blight had got it entirely wrong) simply waved his arms frenetically in all directions and looked as if he wanted to burst into tears.

The singers were no better. Gilda must have been a good fifteen years older than her father and was apparently suffering from a sore throat. It was difficult to tell, from where we were sitting, whether she had simply been badly made up or whether she was one of nature's freaks and ought really to have been born a man. The Countess, on the other hand, was definitely female, but on the scale of a Fellini woman. She could barely stagger about the stage and the Duke practically vanished under her armpit when he had to escort her off as she left for Ceprano. When he burst into his gay, lilting air,

> Questa o quella per me pari sono
> a quant'altre d'intorno mi vedo,
> del mio core l'impero non cedo
> meglio ad una che ad altra beltà . . .

one felt that he had a point. Not so much a man of easygoing morals, one felt, as a man faced with an impossible choice, surrounded by women who richly deserved to be dumped in sacks and left to die.

I saw Enrico rolling his eyes to heaven the moment the curtain rose. Within a couple of minutes, Jessica and I developed uncontrollable giggles. The Blight alone seemed blissfully unaware of the absurdity of the evening. He leaned back with a peaceful expression on his face and moved his hands in time to the music. Only occasionally, when Jessica and I were completely unable to stifle our merriment, did he wake from his reverie and glare at us.

I was surprised to discover that the French, normally so demanding and so intolerant, are far more restrained in these situations than are the Italians. At la Scala, the performance would have been booed from start to finish. At the Paris Opéra, everyone remained silent and clapped politely when it was over. Enrico kept his eyes shut most of the time but groaned aloud when, in the third act, the Duke started singing, 'La donna è mobile . . .'

'I think this is the piece of music I hate most in the world,' he whispered to me. I entirely agreed with him and felt that here, at last, was someone who had the courage to say what he really thought.

'I hope you don't mind, Edward,' said Enrico as we emerged into the night air once more, 'but I felt that since you had been kind enough to organize tickets for this splendid performance' (the Blight took this remark at its face value) 'it was incumbent upon me to take you all to dinner afterwards. I have, therefore, booked us a table at a favourite haunt of mine in the rue Saint-Martin. They discourage people from smoking and the food is excellent.'

As we climbed into a taxi, Jessica whispered to me, 'Enrico must have had dinner with the Blight before!'

The Blight was delighted to discover a new restaurant and the food was indeed excellent. There was a particularly delicious fresh *foie gras d'oie* which had been marinated in cognac for days and was served hot with red berries – and the surroundings were delightfully old-fashioned, with plush seats, brass rails and art deco looking-glasses. The Blight seemed genuinely satisfied. There was nobody smoking and he had never heard of the place before. His only complaint was that the tables were too close to each other but he agreed that, given the size of the room, this was inevitable.

'Better than anything you've experienced in Paris, so far, isn't it?' he enquired of me and Jessica. 'It's extremely important to eat well, you know. I always think that the most important attribute a woman can have is the ability to cook well. I wouldn't tolerate a wife who couldn't cook, would you?' he asked Enrico, continuing, before the latter could reply, 'I'm on the look-out for a nice girl who can cook and who is ready to settle down and have children. It's a lonely life, this, without a wife and children.'

Jessica caught my eye and made a face. 'Was that a heavy hint?' she asked me afterwards.

It was fortunate that the restaurant itself was so pleasant because the conversation soon became tricky. Enrico and the Blight began to discuss politics and it was clear from the start that they disagreed profoundly on every aspect of the subject. Enrico became quite disagreeable about it and seemed to be incapable of allowing the Blight to hold his own views. The Blight became ratty to begin with and later rather offended. Jessica tried to change the subject a couple of times and on each occasion the Blight turned to her, leering disgustingly, but returned immediately to the discussion with Enrico. At one point, I noticed the Blight's hand slide towards Jessica under the table where, as far as I could tell, Jessica must have pinched it because he pulled his hand back quite violently. Jessica later told me she had scratched him as hard as she could. ('He kept messing about with my knee,' she said, 'so I had to scratch him.') This did not stop him trying again between courses and again while we were drinking our coffee. Jessica's eye met mine over and over again and it was quite clear that she was asking me to help. I toyed with the idea of kicking the Blight's hand off her knee, but could think of no credible explanation for such an action; I wondered about spilling my hot coffee over him but could not bring myself to do that either. Jessica was shifting uncomfortably opposite me and looking more and more desperate. I eventually decided that the only solution was to be blunt.

'Do you like Jessica's knee?' I enquired. 'It's a jolly nice knee, isn't it? She has very pretty legs, don't you think?' The Blight removed his hand smartly and Enrico laughed aloud.

'Serves you right, Edward,' he said. 'You can't go around squeezing pretty girls' knees in public or you'll give your Embassy a bad name. I think it's time we were all leaving now, in any case.' He asked for the bill and then, turning to the Blight, said, 'I'll take these two home, if you like. It's more or less my direction, in any case, and quite the wrong direction for you.'

The Blight agreed and, after effusive thanks and 'goodbyes' all round, during which he clasped Jessica for an unnecessarily long time, he set off in search of a second taxi. Enrico had already found one for us and Jessica and I piled in, feeling heartily relieved that it was not the Blight who was seeing us home. We giggled in the taxi as we discussed him and Enrico joined in our mirth.

I felt rather mean suddenly and, as the taxi approached the rue des Carmes, said, 'He's just an awful bore and he certainly doesn't understand the first thing about music, but he's trying to be kind. I'm sure he really means well.'

'What makes you think that?' asked Enrico, laughing. 'I doubt very much whether he means well. I suspect him of the worst possible intentions. It is quite obvious what he has in mind – and who can blame him? The real danger, my dear girl,' he said suddenly, looking at Jessica very seriously, 'is, as he made perfectly clear, that he is looking for a wife – a good, well-behaved wife who "wants to settle down" and who will cook for him and give him children. He would not be nearly so persistent, and therefore not a fraction as tiresome, if all he wanted was a light-hearted affair or a quick romp in bed. If I were you, I would say that you loathe children and that you have no intention of ever learning to boil an egg. That should do the trick. Now, is this where you live? Right, I'll just tell the taxi-driver to wait a second, then I can see you safely to your door.'

After Enrico had departed and as we climbed the stairs to our flat, Jessica said, 'Enrico seems terribly friendly, don't you think?'

'You mean "friendly" in your sense, I take it?'

'Yes. I mean not tedious and not jungly,' replied Jessica as she opened the door to our flat, 'He liked you, too, I could tell. He liked you a lot but he was civilized enough not to slobber all over you like the disgusting Blight. You're so lucky. I really can't think what I've done to deserve Edward. You'd think it was punishment for some really frightful sin, wouldn't you? And yet I don't think I've done anything terrible for ages. The last thing I can think of was on Prize Day when we stuck straws into all the trifles and sucked up the sherry from the bottom – but it *was* our last day at school and trifle is such a disgusting pudding that I'm sure none of the parents would have wanted to eat them in any case. What is that wonderful name you have for it in Italy?'

'*Zuppa Inglese.*'

'Yes, well there you are. That's exactly what it is. English soup. Revolting! Anyway, I can't believe that stealing sherry really merits the Blight. How am I going to get rid of him? I think I'm going to ask Daddy to do something about it. Perhaps he'll know of some dreadful secret in the man's past that we can hold over him. Do you think it's pathetic of me to ring Daddy? I don't think I can stand it much longer and I have tried for five or six months to get rid of him by myself.'

'I'd have done it ages ago. Your father won't mind. I expect he'd be jolly annoyed if he knew that someone at the Embassy had been making your life a misery.'

'Will you come with me to the post office at lunch-time on Monday?'

'Yes, of course. I've got some sort of oral exam that morning but it should be over by lunch-time. By the way, I forgot to tell you. André wants us to have dinner with him at his flat on Monday evening. He has a new Arab cook about whom he becomes positively lyrical – I couldn't quite make out whether it was his culinary talents or his person that André was speaking about with such enthusiasm, but anyway, he seems to want us to have dinner there and says he has invited some other people to amuse us. I said I'd come definitely and I thought you probably would, but that I would let him know tomorrow morning if you couldn't.

'Well, I can and I will. Apart from anything else, I want an excuse to wear that necklace he gave me. And you must wear yours, too. He'll be so pleased and flattered.'

On Monday, exam over, I met Jessica at the top of the steps leading down from the main entrance of the Sorbonne to the place de la Sorbonne.

'How did it go?' she asked.
'Fine.'
'Did you pass?'
'Yes.'
'Easily?'
'Quite.'
'Over eighty per cent?'
'Yes.'

'I told you. I knew you'd be OK. You always are. Good. I'm glad. It would be awful if you suddenly became stupid overnight.'

'Would you still love me?'

'I expect so but it would be jolly boring all the same. Now, you've got to come to the post office with me. Then I want to tell you my plan for Saturday.'

There were always long queues at the post office whenever we wanted to make a telephone call. For local calls, we used bars and cafés, but long-distance calls had to be made from the post office.

Jessica had no trouble getting through to the Foreign Office but it seemed Sir Reginald was not at his desk. He was working at home, she was told. 'What a bore. I'll have to call the operator again,' she said to me. As she put down the receiver, I was aware of the queue jostling and pushing outside. The mob expected us to emerge and made their displeasure quite clear when we did not do so.

The next attempt at calling England proved more difficult. Little Upton might not be far from Paris as seen upon a map, but Jessica might as well have asked the operator for a village on the Tibetan frontier for all the success she had. The operator maintained that there was no such place as Little Upton and no such place as Chipping Draycott (the local exchange). After endless expostulations and disagreeable remarks, she was finally persuaded to telephone the operator in Norwich to ask for help. When Jessica was at last put through to Upton Hall she looked triumphant. She handed me the écouteur and we both turned our backs firmly on the furious queue outside.

The first person to hear the telephone ringing at Upton Hall was the cook. She it was who answered it. ' 'Allo, Miss Jessica,' she said, sounding incredulous, when she realised who it was. 'Calling all the way from France, are you? My goodness! Your Ma's in the garden and your Pa's in the library working. I think he's got someone with him. We'll be having lunch soon so your

199

Ma would be coming in now anyway. I'll go and call her.'

'It's Daddy I want to talk to, Mrs B.,' said Jessica, but too late, for Mrs B. had already gone off in search of Lady Grantsby-Harte. The queue outside had started to agitate. An angry man with a moustache kept tapping on the glass door with a coin and behind him were several other people who grimaced and gesticulated wildly whenever I dared turn round and look in their direction. By the time Lady Grantsby-Harte had come to the telephone, Jessica was feeling harassed.

'Mummy, darling, I can't speak to you for more than a second. There are all these horrible people outside looking like the mob must have done just before they stormed the Bastille. I *have* to talk to Daddy. There's this ghastly man at the Embassy who seems to think he owns me just because he helped us find our flat. He pretends he used to know Daddy and he seems to think this gives him the right to paw me, and invite me to hotels for the weekend, and plaster me with wet kisses and generally behave disgustingly. He's revolting and he *won't* leave me alone. Imogen and I have tried everything, but he won't give up. A couple of nights ago he took us to the opera and started making heavy hints about how he was looking for a wife and he's *ancient*! Please go and get Daddy and make him do something about it.'

'Poor darling. How perfectly frightful. What is the man's name? Edward Blight? I've never heard of him. I'm sure Daddy doesn't know him but you can be certain he'll put a stop to it. I'll get him to come and talk to you. Hang on a second.' We heard her calling her husband, 'Reggie! Reggie, come quickly! It's Jessica calling from Paris. Her life is being made intolerable by some disreputable character from the Paris Embassy who claims to know you. You must do something about it immediately. It's outrageous!'

When Sir Reginald picked up the telephone, he sounded thoroughly amused.

'What's all this about, darling?' he asked Jessica. 'You can't expect people not to take an interest in you, you know. You're very pretty.'

'But he's *awful*, Daddy. He's really disgusting. And he's terribly old, too. He must be at least fifty. It's positively *malsain*.'

'Fifty isn't terribly old, I'm afraid, darling, however antiquated it may seem to you.'

'Well, it's jolly old to be looking for a wife and wanting to have children. I think it's disgusting. He keeps saying he knows you, too. Do you know him? Was he really a friend of yours?'

'What's his name?'

'Edward Blight.'

'Blight. Blight. Yes, that name does seem to ring a bell of some sort. Let me think. Something to do with UNESCO, was he? And now at the Consulate? Yes, yes. It's coming back. I do have a faint recollection of him but it dates back to about thirty years ago. I think he caught mumps at the wrong moment and was relegated to the B stream. Poor old Blight! That's what it was, I'm pretty sure. And now he's infatuated with you . . . Well, I think that's terribly funny. Poor old Blight,' he repeated and laughed uproariously.

'It's not poor old Blight at all!' wailed Jessica. 'It's poor old me! You've absolutely got to do something about it. *Please*, Daddy.'

'All right, darling, although I can't think how. Pretty awkward. Still, I'll see what I can do. What on earth is all that noise?'

'It's the French rabble about to lynch us. I must go or we'll never get out of here alive. I'll talk to you soon and I'm counting on you! Lots of love; and from Imogen. 'Bye!' and Jessica finally put down the receiver. 'Right,' she said to me, 'we'd better put on our French act and hurl a few insults at these people before they start insulting us,' and she marched out muttering loudly about the incompetence of French operators, the hopelessness of the French telephone system, the impossibility of hearing anything when you did get through because of unhelpful and inconsiderate people making a din all around you and the overall ghastliness of this rude and barbaric country.

It worked. There were a few unpleasant remarks from

201

the queue but nothing like the disagreeableness that one might have expected. We had learnt very quickly that to survive in Paris one must become as aggressive as the Parisians themselves. The Parisian way of life is based on the rule that one should never be kind, never be polite and never apologize. The most important thing of all, we learnt, was to attack people before they had done anything because if you did not they might mistake you for a fool and attack you instead. We had become adept at all this but still found it unnerving.

'God, I feel exhausted,' said Jessica when we had paid for the call and emerged at last.

'What do you think I feel?' I asked. 'I had an incredibly long oral exam this morning before coming to do battle with the furious crowds. Why are they always so angry, the French? Why do you think they are all so bad-tempered?'

'It must be because they don't get enough sleep,' replied Jessica. 'Everybody becomes ratty when they're tired and the French spend the whole of their lives dead from exhaustion. Look at the way they live. They all leap up at the crack of dawn because they have to be at work so early and the schools start at eight fifteen, and lots of shops are open before that. Then they leave their offices so late that they can't be home before eight at the earliest.'

'That's only because they spend such hours over lunch,' I interrupted. 'If they didn't stay late, they would have hardly got back to the office before it was time to go home.'

'Possibly,' said Jessica, 'but it doesn't alter the fact that by the time they've got home, bathed, changed and got themselves to wherever they're going, or cooked a wonderful dinner, and finally sat down to eat, then argued about absolutely everything, cleared up the mess and at last persuaded their impossible children to go to bed, it's almost time to get up again.'

'They have school on Saturdays, too,' I added, 'so they

still have to get up early and it means they can't ever go away for the weekend, or not very far at any rate.'

'Their livers seem to be a permanent source of worry to them, as well, poor things. Do you think liverishness makes one bad-tempered?' Jessica enquired.

'I should think so,' I replied.

'What I haven't worked out yet,' said Jessica, 'is why the Italians aren't the same. Their life-style, at least in the north, is virtually identical and they seem to worry about their stomachs and intestines in the same way the French worry about their livers. Why aren't they bad-tempered?'

'I expect they get it out of their system by making a lot of noise,' I suggested. 'That may be why they sing.'

'Do you think singing gets rid of bad temper?' Jessica asked. 'I shall have to think about this. "So by my singing am I comforted, even as the swan by singing makes death sweet." Do you remember? I shall have to study the Italians when I've finished examining the French.'

I laughed. 'I'm so glad you're here,' I said, 'and that I'm not in Paris without you. I wouldn't be enjoying it half as much on my own.'

'Listen, I want to tell you my idea,' said Jessica, abruptly changing the subject. 'I think we should visit Olivier in his hôtel de passe on Saturday night. We can't do it on a weekday because it's too far to get home and anyway we'd be too tired to attend our lectures in the morning. But on Saturday it doesn't matter if we stay all night – in fact, it's probably better if we do because I don't know what time the métro stops and, anyway, I don't much like the idea of getting on the métro at place Clichy or Blanche at dead of night, do you? It's quite frightening enough getting on at the gare Saint-Lazare in broad daylight. I think we should find some man to go with us, too, just in case. Supposing Olivier weren't there, for some reason? And we don't really know what a maison de passe is like, do we? The real problem is who do we ask to go with us? We can't very well ask André, can we?'

'What about Pierre?' I asked. 'Wouldn't he come with us?'

'I don't know,' replied Jessica, 'but I suppose it's worth a try.'

Pierre was a young Communist who had been doing the same course as Jessica but had left the Sorbonne to go to Sciences-Po' (Institut d'Etudes Politiques de Paris). We had become close friends with him while he was still at the Sorbonne and continued to see a lot of him in the evenings and at weekends. He was often to be found lounging around our flat, giving us impassioned lectures on French politics and we were immensely impressed by his commitment to Communism and his belief that he and his party were going to turn the world into a better place. He was thin and pale and always looked ill but his eyes blazed as he explained what was wrong with the world and what he was going to do to change it.

'I have a feeling he may disapprove of Olivier's job,' Jessica remarked as we munched a sandwich before returning to the Sorbonne, 'but perhaps we could convince him that Olivier needs help and encouragement if he is not to abandon his studies entirely.'

'The real problem,' I said, 'is to find someone to lend Olivier their notes. Isn't there anyone you could ask?'

'I thought I would try to organize an introduction to the English lecturer but I don't quite know how to set about it,' said Jessica. 'I suppose Pierre must still know some of the second-year students. Perhaps we should ask him first. Golly, we're going to be late. I must run. See you this evening. What time are we supposed to be at André's?'

'Eight thirty,' I answered, 'and he minds frightfully about punctuality.'

'OK. I'll meet you back at the flat at six. See you later,' and she raced up the front steps and disappeared from sight.

CHAPTER TWELVE

André lived on the île Saint-Louis, at the corner of the quai d'Orléans and the rue Jean-du-Bellay. His flat took up the entire top floor of the building and from his drawing-room windows one looked out at Notre-Dame, its spire rising like the mast of a galleon above the slate-grey roofs. In spring and summer, when the leaves were out, its flying buttresses were partly hidden behind the trees, giving the impression that they were huge, fat fingers plunging down into the horse chestnuts.

Opposite André's flat, on the far side of the pont Saint-Louis, the wall of the île de la Cité was covered with overhanging plants. Above these stood a weeping willow, its branches hanging down until they trailed into the water. To the right of the bridge was the quai aux Fleurs where Jankélévitch, the most notable and brilliant of the philosophers at the Sorbonne, held court and, beyond this, across the water, on the Right Bank, stood the Hôtel de Ville. To the left, the grey-green waters of the Seine divided around the tip of the île de la Cité and, on the far bank, the lovely houses of the Rive gauche stood, higgledy-piggledy, behind the double row of poplars and horse chestnuts which provided the *bouquinistes* with their only shade in summer, their only shelter in the rain. Amongst these houses of the Left Bank, two were particularly noticeable because of their ancient, brown, tiled roofs and dormer windows. Beyond these again, the dome of the Panthéon rose, huge and solid, into the sky where it remained silhouetted against the passing clouds. Somewhere, in the distance, a clock struck on the hour, every hour.

The interior of André's flat was surprising. The over-all effect was of acres of blue and gold with, here and there, a touch of light relief in the form of a wrought-iron bench, painted white. One had the impression that André, when visiting one of his cousins' châteaux, had raided the grounds and removed the ancient garden furniture to resuscitate it, repaint it, and bring it to life amid the Louis XVI.

There were looking-glasses everywhere: some with delicate, gilt frames; some with more ornate frames of that deeper colour known as 'old gold'. Standing about on exquisite pieces of furniture were ormolu clocks and rare candelabra. The latter were all of solid brass and the candles they held uniformly dark blue. To the right of the largest window, beside heavy satin curtains, was a perfect Louis XV table on which stood two jewelled chalices that looked as if they must have been stolen from a church. Here and there, in apparently haphazard fashion, André had placed a *banquette* or a *chaise-longue* to fill the empty spaces.

In the left-hand corner of his vast drawing-room there lay upon the floor a large piece of looking-glass, kidney-shaped and surrounded by pebbles. Bordering it and embedded in the pebbles were rush-like plants, and palms, and grasses, creating the effect of a pond among the reeds. Here, from time to time, a passing guest would pause to contemplate his own reflection; or, like Narcissus, stand pining and lost in admiration at the sight of his own face floating among the bulrushes.

A sly-looking boy met us at the door and took our coats. He had a neat little backside and narrow hips. When André came to greet us, the boy giggled and disappeared.

The drawing-room was full of people but two stood out immediately. The first was a very frail old lady, beautifully dressed, with limbs so thin that one felt they would snap if touched, and an ancient head of striking beauty. She sat, bird-like, perched on the edge of her chair, her

206

bright eyes darting hither and yon, looking at every-thing, noticing everything. When Jessica and I were introduced to her, she held out an arm no thicker than my wrist, but her grip was firm and her hand steady and warm.

The second person who was immediately noticeable was the grey-eyed Englishman who had made me feel so uncomfortable in the bookshop two days earlier. He was standing at the far end of the room as we entered it, apparently admiring the chalices, but turned to look in our direction as I followed Jessica through the door. For a second a puzzled expression crossed his face, instantly followed by a look of recognition and surprise. Then, half-smiling, he bent to replace the chalice he had been examining. As André introduced us to the old lady, I could feel him watching me just as I had felt it on that previous occasion. I knew that his eyes were on me as André led us through the room, presenting us to one person after another, so that by the time we finally reached the end of the room and I found myself face to face with him for the second time, I was as flustered and unhappy as I had been in the bookshop.

'Anthony, I would like you to meet Imogen Holt,' said André, 'Imogen, je te présente un cher ami anglais, Anthony Metcalfe.'

As we shook hands, I looked up to see on Anthony Metcalfe's face the same amused expression I had seen two days earlier.

'So,' he said, 'we meet again. What an unexpected pleasure.'

'You have already met each other?' enquired André.

'No,' replied Anthony Metcalfe. 'That is to say, we have never been introduced, but we have seen each other before. We bumped into one another at the Presses Universitaires de France only two days ago and exchanged a few words. I would happily have continued the conversation but Miss Holt was apparently inordi-nately pressed for time.' As he said this, his eyes were brimming with laughter and I felt myself blushing.

'What strange coincidences life produces,' commented André. 'Well, now you have met properly I hope you will be friends. Anthony is almost as dear to me as you are,' André continued, turning to me, 'although I have not known him for as long as I have known you.' Then, turning back to Anthony, he explained, 'I have known Imogen since she was born. Her parents are my oldest and most cherished friends. And this is Jessica Grantsby-Harte, Sir Reginald Grantsby-Harte's daughter. *Elle est aussi délicieuse que ma petite Imogen*, but you must also have seen her when you met Imogen, yes? I thought so. They are quite inseparable. They have made my life so delightful, these two girls. I have been enjoying myself enormously since they came to Paris. How did I manage before I had *mes deux filles* to brighten up my days, I ask myself? *Elles sont très drôles*, you will see, *et tout à fait charmantes*. Now, I must ask you all to excuse me a moment while I look after my other guests. I particularly want to make sure that my dear Marguerite is happy. She is so frail and it is such a struggle for her to go anywhere these days; but she so loves seeing other people that she would be desolate if one didn't invite her. I am putting you next to her at dinner, Anthony, because I know she will be charmed by you. I think you will find her company most agreeable, too. She is very clever and witty. Her mother was a Rochefort and one assumes that Marguerite inherited her brains from that side of the family. Her father, as you know, was a highly respected man and the title is, of course, one of the oldest and most famous in France – one of the very few families to have survived the Revolution – but I don't believe any single one of them was ever noted for his intellect.'

As André moved away, Anthony Metcalfe turned to Jessica and asked, 'How long have you two been living in Paris?'

'Since last September,' replied Jessica.

'And what brought you here?' he enquired.

'The Sorbonne,' said Jessica. 'We're both at the Sorbonne.'

'So that is it,' said Anthony Metcalfe. 'I wondered what two English girls were doing buying incomprehensible French philosophy books. Are you reading philosophy?'

'No,' replied Jessica. 'I'm not; but Imogen is. She's not English, by the way. At least, she's only half English.'

'What's the other half?' enquired Anthony, addressing me.

'Italian,' I answered. 'My mother's Italian and my father is English, but we live in Italy.'

'That would explain it,' said Anthony. 'I was astonished to hear you speaking English the other day. You don't look at all English. When I first saw you, I was sure you were Italian, then I thought you must be French, but I was completely baffled when I heard you both chatting in such very English English. I am delighted to have had the chance to meet you again and to unravel the mystery. I must admit that I was curious and intrigued. Are you both enjoying it here?'

'Yes, tremendously,' we chorused.

'What about you?' asked Jessica. 'Do you live here, too?'

'No. At least, not permanently, although I'm living here at the moment and seem likely to remain here for some time. I'm on a sabbatical from Cambridge and I'm doing a bit of lecturing at the Sorbonne. I only came here because I'm trying to write a book which requires a lot of research, most of which has to be done here.'

'What kind of a book?' enquired Jessica.

'It's a biography. For various reasons with which I won't bore you, I have committed myself to writing the life of a very obscure Napoleonic general. He spent the first half of his life in France, mainly in Paris, then there is a gap of ten years during which he seems to have disappeared without trace; then he reappeared in northern Italy – first in Piemonte, having joined the Waldensians, and later in Milan. He also popped up in the States at one point and I'm having a job to find out why he went there or what happened to him during those missing ten years. Most of my sources of information are here but I may eventually have to do some research in Italy as well. The curious aspect of all this is that I have, as a result of my research, amassed an enormous amount of information about the Waldensians and I have become extremely interested in their history. I am seriously toying with the idea of writing a history of the Waldensian movement when I have finished the General's biography. So, what with one thing and another, I suspect I shall be in Paris for quite some time.'

'You must be the English history lecturer we keep hearing about,' said Jessica. 'How do you know André? Did you meet him here, or did you know him before?'

'Oddly enough, we're vaguely related by marriage. A great-aunt of mine married one of his cousins; but although I always knew of him, I had never met him until a few years ago when I ran into him at some family get-together. He has been extremely kind and helpful in putting me in touch with the few remaining descendants of my Waldensian and he has provided me with a lot of other useful contacts as well. He himself has supplied me with some surprisingly useful information. He's an erudite old man and his obsession with family trees has, in this instance, been extraordinarily useful.'

At this moment, the last guests arrived. 'Good heavens!' exclaimed Jessica. 'Look who has just walked in!'

I turned to see Angelica, a Peruvian girl who had been in our class at the Convent of the Immaculate Conception, walking through the door on the arm of a middle-aged man. She was wearing false eyelashes, a strapless, red dress and massive amounts of matching jewellery. This last was so overwhelmingly flashy that we wrongly assumed it was not real. Rubies, like rocks, hung around her neck and wrist. More rubies, pear-shaped and surrounded by pearls, hung from her pierced ear-lobes. On her left hand she wore a ring consisting of one large, single ruby set in platinum and on her right hand another ring made up of a cluster of smaller stones –

rubies and diamonds – in the shape of a heart. She was heavily made-up and looked supremely satisfied as she clung to the arm of her male companion who was clearly South American or Spanish. He was square in build and on the fleshy side, with very black hair to which scented oil had been liberally applied. His dinner jacket was made of a particularly shiny, black material and was narrow at the waist, with wide lapels and built-up shoulders. His stout thighs bulged under a narrow trouser leg and on his feet he wore black boots with heels. He, too, was wearing jewellery: a diamond pin amid the ruffles of his shirt-front and a heavy signet ring which looked uncomfortably tight on his plump finger.

Angelica noticed us immediately and crossed the room to greet us.

'What are you doing in Paris?' I asked. 'I thought you had gone back to Lima.'

'I did and then I met Antonio and we got married. We came here on honeymoon a couple of months ago and I fell in love with the place. Antonio has to come here often on business, so I shall be coming over all the time.'

We were unable to pursue the conversation because at this point dinner was announced and everyone started drifting towards the dining-room. I watched André, himself old and frail, bow to his ancient princess then take her hand and help her to her feet. Once she was standing, he appeared to make her some compliment then, offering her his arm, he led her towards the dining-room. On the way there, the old lady paused and patted André's hand as if approving something he had said. They looked at each other and smiled with the tender complicity of very old friends. Something in my expression made Anthony Metcalfe say, 'Yes. Very touching.'

At dinner, I found myself sitting between a pompous lawyer in his mid-fifties and a prickly young man who claimed to be a television journalist. Jessica was seated diagonally across the table from me, with Anthony Metcalfe on her right and a sour-looking man on her left. On Anthony's other side, between him and André, sat the old lady. She seemed to hold his attention for a lot of the time; but whenever she turned to talk to André, Anthony immediately engaged Jessica in conversation. At one point, something Jessica said to him made him roar with laughter.

I gave up on the pompous lawyer as fast as politeness permitted and spent most of the dinner talking to – or, to be more accurate, listening to – the television journalist. By the time the cheese appeared I felt I knew all that I would ever need to know about the workings of French television, Hachette, the Agence France-Presse, l'IFOP, *sondages* in general, the Communist party in France and the frightfulness of both America and England. It was because of the English character, he said, that the English Gallup polls were always completely wrong, whereas l'IFOP was always accurate. The English, he explained to me, had not acquired their reputation for perfidy for no reason so it was quite pointless asking them a month before polling day (let alone six months before) which way they intended to cast their vote.

'It is obvious,' he said, 'that even in two weeks an Englishman's loyalties change. In any case, they always lie about these things so you can be sure that even if they know who they are going to vote for, they will tell you something quite different. They always say the opposite of what they think. That is why they have cultivated all that false politeness: it is so that you can never tell what they are thinking. I have been to dinners in England where the food was utterly disgusting and yet everyone complimented the hostess and told her how absolutely delicious it was. They are a nation of hypocrites. I mean, what on earth is the point of telling your hostess the food is delicious when it is absolutely disgusting? It is so senseless, so useless.'

As he said this, I was reminded of Edna O'Brien's *Girls in Their Married Bliss*, in which Baba, talking about Kate Brady, says, 'she was too sedate and good, you know that useless kind of goodness, asking people how they are, and how their parents are . . .' and I suddenly realized that the French and the Irish have more in common than just their hatred of the English.

By the time I started to battle my way through an impossibly cold sorbet made, as far as one could tell, of neat Pernod, I was beginning to feel somewhat discouraged and when we eventually returned to the drawing-room I felt tired and depressed. Jessica, on the other hand, looked radiant. 'I've found someone to take us to Olivier's hotel on Saturday,' she said as we drank our coffee. 'Anthony has agreed to come with us. In fact, he seemed rather enthusiastic about the idea.'

'Did you tell him what sort of a place it was?' I asked.

'Yes. He thought it was terribly funny. Better still, he's going to see what he can do to help Olivier get tapes of lectures or something to get him through his exams.'

'How wonderful,' I exclaimed. 'Olivier *will* be pleased.'

I felt Anthony Metcalfe watching us from across the room as Jessica told me all this and I found it impossible not to look in his direction. He was half listening to the pompous lawyer, nodding in agreement occasionally, but his eyes were on me. I turned back to Jessica, saying, 'I think we should go soon, don't you?'

'What's the matter?' asked Jessica.

'I'm tired,' I replied.

'You're flustered, you mean,' contradicted Jessica. 'You *are* silly.'

'Anthony whatever-his-name-is keeps staring at me,' I said. 'Exactly like he did in the bookshop on Saturday. He's staring at me again now.'

'Yes, I know he is. So what? He thinks you're very beautiful. He kept on about how beautiful you were all the way through dinner. It was frightfully boring. At least it would have been if it hadn't been about you. As it was, I told him graciously that I entirely agreed with him. I do. You *are* beautiful.' She giggled. 'I also told him

213

you were terribly clever and completely vague and
eccentric and absolutely the most wonderful person
that ever existed.'

'Oh, Jessica, you didn't!'

'Yes, I did. I told him you were frightfully shy, too.'

'Oh God, how embarrassing. I feel even worse now. I
want to go.'

'OK,' said Jessica. 'Let's go. Those two over there are
obviously leaving now, too, so we're not the first.'

As we stood thanking André, having made our farewells to the other guests, Anthony came over to us and
said, 'How are you two going to get home?'

'We're going to walk,' I replied. 'We live practically
on the doorstep.'

'I'll give you a lift,' said Anthony. 'I've got a car
outside.'

'No, it's all right,' I said, panicking irrationally. 'We
only live about five minutes' walk away at Maubert-
Mutualité. It would be pointless to drive such a short
distance; and, anyway, we like walking. I really want to
walk.'

'In that case, I will accompany you both on foot and
come back for the car,' said Anthony, firmly. 'It will do
me good to have a walk and I don't think you should be
wandering around Paris by yourselves at this time of
night.'

'That is an excellent suggestion,' interrupted André.
'I shall feel much happier if I know that someone is
seeing *mes filles* to their door.'

'How terribly kind of you,' Jessica said in her most
dulcet of tones; 'but we'd better go in your car because
otherwise we'll feel frightfully guilty about making you
walk to the rue des Carmes and back again. Anyway,
Imogen doesn't really like walking half as much as she
says she does and I don't feel like walking at all.'

Something in her tone reminded me of the occasion
when she managed to make the station-master at Little
Upton offer to take my suitcase to Upton Hall for me.
I felt suspicious suddenly, and wondered if she was

somehow responsible for manipulating Anthony into seeing us home.

As we descended the magnificent staircase, Anthony said, 'Did Jessica tell you, Imogen, that I'm going to act as chaperon to you both on Saturday when you go on your dubious expedition to a house of ill repute?'

'Yes, I did tell her,' Jessica replied on my behalf. 'She thinks I shouldn't have asked you, don't you, Imogen?'

I did not reply.

'I'm delighted that you asked me,' said Anthony. 'I think it's thoroughly disreputable of you both to want to visit such an establishment, but I shall be vastly amused to see what you make of it.'

When we reached the car, Anthony held open the door for us. As I waited for Jessica to climb in, I felt him studying me again. I tried not to look at him.

'Don't look so frightened,' he said, gently. 'I'm not going to eat you, you know,' and I looked up to see that he was smiling.

Anthony wished us good night at our door, saying, 'I'll pick you up around eight on Saturday and take you both out to dinner before we brave your friend in the underworld. We don't want to get there too early and you'll enjoy the adventure far more if you have had something to eat first.'

Once back in the safety of our flat, I asked Jessica whether she had suggested to Anthony that he drive us home after dinner.

'Of course not,' she replied, but I did not feel totally convinced by her answer.

Before going to bed I suddenly remembered Angelica. 'Did you have a chance to talk to her after dinner?' I asked Jessica.

'Yes,' Jessica replied. 'She seemed pretty pleased with life. She wants to be fearfully rich, apparently, and that awful man owns gold mines, or oil wells, or something or other. I forget what she said exactly.'

'I got stuck with him for a bit,' I said, 'and he wasn't as awful as he looked. In fact, I rather liked him. He seemed terribly kind and completely dotty about Angelica. He gave me the impression that he was playing an elaborate joke on everyone and that he was deriving an enormous amount of pleasure from the whole thing. He calls himself something most unlikely – some invented Austrian or German name like Baron von Altemberg – but he obviously doesn't expect one to believe him and I had the feeling that he might use different names in different places. He's the sort of person who could easily be a bigamist, I imagine.'

'Honestly, Imogen, what on *earth* makes you think that?' asked Jessica, laughing.

'He just is. He's my idea of what a bigamist must be like and he said something very odd about how Angelica was the wife he liked to take to Paris. The way he said it made it sound as if he had other wives.'

'Just bad English, I should think,' said Jessica. 'If he really had other wives, he'd hardly talk about it at a smart dinner party. Anyway, I gave Angelica our address. She's staying at the Crillon and she told me to telephone her tomorrow to see if we can all meet up before she goes back to Lima. I always think one should keep up with one's acquaintances. You never know when they may come in handy and we may need a friend in Peru one day, for all we know.'

'I would have thought the bigamist might be more useful than Angelica,' I said. 'He looks like the sort of person who could pull strings the world over.'

'Aren't we horrible?' giggled Jessica. 'Wouldn't our parents be shocked? And wouldn't the nuns be horrified? So would all our French friends, particularly Pierre. I don't think we should tell him about going to dinner with André, or about knowing people who stay at the Crillon. I'm not sure he'd like us any more. We might be put on the list of people they'll line up against the wall and shoot when the revolution begins.'

CHAPTER THIRTEEN

As we drove slowly past Olivier's hotel, the following Saturday, looking for somewhere to park, my courage plummeted.

'Oh, God,' said Jessica, voicing my thoughts, 'surely that can't be it?'

'Pretty frightful, I agree,' said Anthony. 'But don't lose heart. We can always leave instantly if you hate it and it may be less gloomy inside.'

The exterior of the hotel was discouraging. Its façade was decorated with cheap, turquoise ceramics reminiscent of public lavatories or down-at-heel baths, giving it a distinctly seedy air.

After ringing the doorbell, we waited some time before Olivier appeared. 'Oh, good,' he said, 'I *am* glad you've come. I'm sorry I was so long letting you in. I was trying to sort out a row. I'm afraid it may break out again. My name is Olivier, by the way,' he said, holding out his hand to Anthony. 'I hope these two warned you about this hotel.'

'They did,' replied Anthony. 'That's why I thought someone should come with them; that, and the fact that I understand you want help with the history lectures you have missed. My name is Anthony Metcalfe and I am one of the lecturers.'

'You are the one I keep hearing about. Wonderful! I didn't expect to be visited by you in person. How very kind.'

A certain amount of shouting had been going on overhead during this exchange and Anthony looked at the ceiling enquiringly as it suddenly became louder.

Olivier smiled at us apologetically. 'There is a man upstairs who claims that one of the girls is his wife and that he has been looking for her for years. She doesn't seem to know him or, if she does, she is making a good job of pretending not to recognize him. I'm not quite sure what I should do about it.'

'Leave them well alone is my advice,' said Anthony. 'You'll never find out the truth and they won't welcome interference from you, you can be certain.'

'Well, we can't stand here all night,' said Olivier. 'Do you mind coming to the kitchen? The telephone happens to be kept in there: not that anyone ever telephones, but I feel I have to be near it in case; and I have to keep making coffee and soup for the girls.'

He led us along a narrow passage which could not have been further from the dark red plush of the interior I had imagined. The entrance was bleak enough: featureless and unfurnished; but the passage, painted dark green, seemed even more unwelcoming in the bleached light shed from a bare bulb. Only in the kitchen was there any attempt at homeliness with a checked tablecloth thrown over the wooden table, some upright chairs and three dirty bowls sitting in an old, porcelain sink.

'The girls always seem to be extraordinarily hungry,' Olivier continued when we had sat down, 'and when they haven't got a client they like to sit in here and talk to me. It's quite interesting. They all have children and live in the suburbs where they are perfectly respectable in the daytime. They don't come to work until about dinnertime and they pack up and go home again at three or four in the morning. Most of them are saving up to run boarding-houses. I can't think why. They all seem to dream of living by the sea in one of those places like Dieppe. Most extraordinary.'

As he said this, there was a tremendous crash overhead, and the sound of a woman shrieking, 'You leave my sister alone or I'll call the police.'

We rushed back along the passage just in time to see a

square-shaped man in a state of disarray hurtling down the stairs two at a time. He paused at the bottom, turned and yelled up the stairs, 'And I'm not a fucking Corsican; I'm a fucking Maltese!' He then spun on his heel and shot out into the night.

'Golly,' said Jessica, but before she could say any more a furious little figure appeared at the top of the stairs shouting, 'Bloody foreigners! I don't know why you let them in, Olivier. They're always trouble. If it hadn't been for Delphine he might have killed me. She broke a chair on his head, by the way, but don't tell the manager. We're going to say it was a fat client who sat on it. *Nom de Dieu!*' she exclaimed as she suddenly caught sight of us. 'Who are those girls? We can't have any more girls here. There are too many already. Anyway, look at them. They're just children. I'm not going to compete with kids.'

'It's all right,' Olivier interrupted. 'They're nothing to do with this place. They're friends of mine from the Sorbonne who've come to visit me; and this is an English history professor they brought with them. I told them they could come.'

'I don't mind him,' the woman replied looking approvingly at Anthony, 'although I'm not keen on foreigners as a rule. But you shouldn't have kids here even if they are friends of yours. What would the manager say if he turned up? Still, since they're here they might as well stay a few minutes, I suppose; until I've had a cup of coffee, anyway. I'm dying for one. That stupid man really had me worried for a while. I thought I was really in for trouble,' she said, as we all made our way back to the kitchen.

'As it happens, I was married to him once but I certainly wasn't going to admit it to him, horrible man. Don't you tell anyone, either. What cheek! It was such a long time ago. Bloody nerve I call it, trying to make claims on me after all these years. And I'm not joking: he was a really horrible man. I've seldom met a nastier one. The funny thing is that I could have sworn he was

219

Corsican. I just hope he doesn't hang around and try to follow me. I've got another husband now and it could be very unpleasant. I can't think what my daughter would say.' She laughed. 'My daughter's thirteen,' she continued, 'and unbelievably spoilt. She asked me for a bicycle the other day. Can you believe it? Do you know how much those things cost? I don't have a bicycle, do I? But she wanted one. She seems to think money grows on trees.' She looked pensively at her feet for a moment. 'She'd be surprised if she knew where it did grow,' she suddenly added as she flung herself back in her chair, letting out a raucous laugh which echoed round the kitchen.

Olivier had barely poured out coffee for us before another figure appeared in the doorway: a large woman with a masculine face and tiny hands. 'Here's Delphine,' said the first woman. 'We pretend we're sisters whenever there's any trouble but we're not really sisters as you can see. My name is Sabine, by the way. What are your names?' We told her and she looked appalled. 'Too difficult,' she commented. 'I can't manage foreign names. We'll call you Jessie, Irma and Antoine, all right? Are you really a professor?' she asked, turning to Anthony.

'Yes,' said Anthony, 'I am.'

'Funny,' muttered Sabine. 'You don't look like one.'

'What should I look like?' enquired Anthony, looking amused.

'I don't know, really. You look too young.'

At this point Delphine decided to sit down beside me. She put her hand on my knee. 'You're pretty. Are you his friend?' she asked, looking towards Anthony.

I was not quite sure what she meant by 'friend' and I could see that Anthony was watching with interest to see how I was going to reply.

'No,' I answered, flustered, and then, 'I mean, yes. He's a sort of friend, but we hardly know each other. He's really a friend of a friend. We met him at a party last week and Jessica asked him to bring us here because we wanted to see Olivier but we were a bit nervous about coming on our own.'

'Is *she* your friend then?' asked Delphine, glaring at Jessica.

'Yes,' I replied innocently. 'Jessica's my closest and oldest friend.'

Delphine looked annoyed.

'Do you want to come and see upstairs?' she asked me.

'No, she does not,' intervened Anthony firmly.

'Delphine doesn't like men,' explained Sabine, 'but she doesn't mean any harm. It's because of what happened to her mother. Come on, Delphine; tell them what happened to your mother.'

Delphine appeared to have no inclination to tell us about anything whatever, but when Olivier decided to be provocative she could not prevent herself from rising to the bait.

'Come on, Delphine,' Olivier had jibed. 'I want to see how many people agree with me that it is not an example of the callousnes of men but rather an example of the stupidity of women.'

At this, Delphine had turned her large face like a thunder-cloud towards Olivier. There was hatred in her eyes and her tiny hands grew agitated. 'Don't you call my mother stupid!' she had shrieked at him. 'She's not stupid at all. She's a broken woman and her life was ruined by that bastard. Do you know what he did, my father?' she had demanded, turning to the rest of us. 'He asked her to marry him just so as to get her to go to bed with him. Then, when they were engaged he kept promising her a fur coat. He kept saying that when he married her he would give her a fur coat as a wedding present, but because he couldn't buy a fur coat he kept postponing the wedding. Then, when she became pregnant with me, he said, "Well, I'll have to hurry and get that fur coat for you so that we can be married before the baby is born." He told her he would go to America for six months, make a lot of money quickly, then buy the fur coat and come back and marry her. "I'll be back in

221

October," he promised her, "and you will have your fur coat and I'll marry you. I'll meet you outside the Samaritaine on the first day of October. Wait for me in front of the Samaritaine" (my mother didn't have anywhere to live because she was so poor) "and I'll find you and give you your fur coat right there. Then you can put it on and show it off to everyone going in and out. They'll all be jealous and I will be so proud of you. And then we'll go and get married straight away."

'On 1st October, my mother stood in front of the Samaritaine all day, waiting for him. In fact, she had spent most of September there just in case he came home early; but on 1st October she stood there from five in the morning right through until five the following morning. Then she wanted to go and sleep (she had some friends who sometimes let her use their room over a café) but she was afraid to leave in case his boat or train had been delayed and he turned up when she wasn't there. So she lay down in the doorway of the Samaritaine where he couldn't fail to see her, and she went to sleep until the first shoppers arrived.

'She spent the whole of the following day standing there, waiting; the whole of the following night lying in the doorway. She spent the whole of October in front of the Samaritaine. She lived on the odd bag of roasted chestnuts and she had to beg, but she did not lose heart. He had promised her he would return, you see, and there was no way he could contact her to let her know why he was delayed or when he would be arriving. As the cold weather set in she became obsessed with the dream of her fur coat and when she asked people for money she always told them that she would soon be married and wearing a fur coat, and able to pay them back. "Come back in a month or two," she would say, "and I will pay you back."

'As soon as I was born she was back there with me, standing in front of the Samaritaine, singing the occasional lullabye to me and crooning about how I would soon be wrapped up in her fur coat. She loved him, you see, so she really believed he would keep his promise.

'A year went by and her courage began to fail, but she refused to believe the obvious. She told herself that to make a fortune, even in America, must be less easy than people imagined. That it took time. That nobody became a millionaire in a few months. That it might have taken him a year to learn the language before he could really start to earn any money. That she must be patient.

'Another year went by, and another, until eventually the day dawned when she realized that he would never come back. She had stood there with me for three years. We had slept there every night.

'When she realized, she became wild with grief. "I shall never be married now," she said. "I shall never be able to give you a home. But I promise you one thing, *ma fille*: I *will* have my fur coat and when I die you shall have it."

'From that moment, she begged with a new enthusiasm, and soon she made me beg, too. I was a better beggar than she was, being a child. I stole a bit, too, though I never told her any of it was stolen. She would not have forgiven me. Every week she hid a tiny amount of money in a bag which she hung around my neck inside my clothes. "If anyone tries to get it," she would say to me, "scream for help. Scream for the police. Say the person is trying to molest you. People never want children to be molested. Nobody likes child molesters. People will rush to help. The money is safer with you than with me."

'Every year on the first day of October (her "anniversary", she called it) my mother would take the money we had saved and go to the market on the *quai* to buy a rabbit. She took it to her friends with the room above the café and the husband would kill it and skin it for her. My mother would make them a rabbit stew in thanks which we would all share. Then the husband would dry the pelt and put it in a cupboard until she wanted it again. Year after year my mother would buy another rabbit, add another pelt. From time to time we would go together to

223

visit those friends and sit sewing the pelts together. "By the time your father reappears," my mother would say to me, "I shall be wearing a fur coat and I shall be able to tell him that I didn't need his help. That I managed to earn enough money to buy myself a fur coat."

'My mother has her fur coat now,' Delphine had ended her tale. 'She is still a beggar. In the daytime, she still stands outside the Samaritaine. At night she sleeps under the pont Neuf where her place is always kept for her by her fellow *clochards*. They know she has to have a place on the north side so that she can be near the Samaritaine. Her name is Janine but she is known by the *clochards* as '*la dame aux peaux de lapin*'. People think she is just a mad, old tramp covered in a bedraggled collection of decrepit rabbit skins, but they don't realize that her heart is broken and that it took her forty years to make that coat. You will see her if you ever go past the Samaritaine. Go past any time and you will see her there.'

We all felt thoroughly depressed by this story but only Sabine had the courage to comment.

'Bloody awful, I call it,' she said. 'Bloody awful story. Always makes me want to howl. Let's go and have a drink somewhere and cheer ourselves up. Come on, Olivier. There aren't any customers except those two who are staying the night and they're quite happy. Michelle and Séverine will look after them.'

'We'll have to warn them,' said Olivier. 'Can one of you two pop up and tell them?' he asked Sabine and Delphine.

'Let's all go up,' suggested Sabine. 'Come on, you lot. Follow me. Ever been in one of these places before?' she asked, turning to me. I shook my head. 'Didn't think you had,' she sighed. 'You don't look the type. Well, you might as well see. You may never have another chance. Girls from the Sorbonne never end up in places like this.'

'I don't think it's necessary for any of us to go upstairs,' remarked Anthony, at which Jessica and I wailed simultaneously. 'Yes, it is. We want to see.'

'How disgraceful,' said Anthony, raising an eyebrow. 'In that case, I suppose I had better come with you. Then I want to talk to Olivier to see if there is anything I can do to help him with his missed courses. That was supposed to be the point of this expedition, wasn't it?'

We had barely reached the hall before the doorbell rang. 'Oh, damn,' said Olivier. 'You'll have to go back to the kitchen. I can't let people see you,' and he hurried us out of sight once more.

Jessica and I stood just inside the kitchen door desperately trying to glimpse the latest arrival but we could not see anything. A male voice asked loudly for a room for an hour and Sabine whispered to us, 'He must have someone with him. Thank God for that. I thought one of us was going to have to stay behind and look after him.'

When Olivier reappeared he said, 'I've been upstairs and warned Séverine. She says her client is asleep and was dead drunk, so she's going to come down here and hold the fort. I don't think I can let you go upstairs now because all the rooms are occupied. But there's nothing to see. It's just exactly what you would imagine: a passage with a lot of dreary little bedrooms off it. Let's go before anyone else arrives. You don't mind if we talk about my lectures over a drink somewhere, do you?' he asked Anthony.

'Not at all,' Anthony replied.

The rest of the evening passed in a whirlwind of noise and laughter. Sabine and Delphine knew the area well and dragged us from bar to bar and from café to café. The drunker they became the more they exuded hilarity and mirth. At one point they insisted on taking us into a café where there was some sort of floor show but we all made so much noise that we were soon asked to leave.

Anthony finally brought us back to earth by saying that he thought it was time he took Jessica and me home. The 'girls', by this time, had become maudlin and sentimental. They insisted on taking our address, saying they wanted to visit us and keep in touch. Delphine's large face crumpled as she said goodbye to me. 'You're too gentle,' she said. Then she turned on her heel and left without another word.

When Anthony had driven us back to the rue des Carmes he kissed Jessica on the cheek as he said good night to her. Then he turned as if to do the same to me, but paused instead and studied me for a moment.

'No,' he finally remarked. 'You're still afraid of me. The day you cease to be frightened of me, I will give you a demure kiss on the cheek. Not before.'

As an afterthought, he added, addressing us both, 'If those two "girls" turn up here – which I think unlikely, but you can never be sure – let me know immediately. You have my telephone number. Just ring me. They might prove troublesome. In any case, I'm not sure I want you corrupted by too much association with the adult world. You're a pair of scamps, but manageable scamps as yet. Now, off to bed with you both and behave yourselves until I next see you.'

A few days later, we walked past the Samaritaine and found the old woman in her rabbit skins. She was very suspicious at first when we tried to talk to her; but when she heard we knew her daughter, she became garrulous, excited. Her daughter had done very well for herself, she told us. She made men pay for love. She had got their measure. She wouldn't be fooled. She was a clever girl and, in any case, one day she would have a fur coat. 'She'll be all right,' she said. 'I used to worry about her when she was little but I don't worry about her any more. She's got a head on her shoulders. She'll be fine; and she'll have my fur coat when I die.'

It was difficult to tell whether or not she wanted sympathy or help. She looked indignant as Jessica skirted about the subject. 'My daughter looks after me very well,' she said, 'and I'm never cold. How could I be cold? I have a fur coat. Few people are as well-off as I am. Not many people have fur coats, do they? You don't have fur coats, do you? No. Well, there you are,' and she suddenly delved into a plastic bag and rummaged, her head down, for what seemed like ages. When she finally looked up, she was holding a crumpled piece of newspaper. She studied it for a moment, then tore a tiny piece off it and handed it to me. 'I tell you what would be useful,' she said. 'I wouldn't mind a sandwich. I'm getting a bit hungry but I don't like to leave my post, you know. Just in case. So if you would be kind enough to take this over to the café and ask them for a *croque-monsieur* you'd be saving me a trip. That should cover it. They know me there, in any case, but don't let them cheat you. They never give you any change unless you ask. They always try to keep it.'

While we were waiting for the *croque-monsieur* I asked Jessica what money she thought I ought to give the old lady as change. 'What do you think she imagines she gave me?' I asked. 'Ten francs? Fifty francs?'

'God knows,' replied Jessica. 'I'd give her two or three francs. She might take it badly if you gave her more.'

The old woman had a vacant expression when we reappeared with the *croque-monsieur*. 'I didn't ask for that, did I?' she demanded. Then, looking suddenly irritated, 'Is this all the change they gave you? Daylight robbery I call it.' She took a bite out of her sandwich; then, with her mouth full, shouted at us, 'Don't stand there watching me eat! I can't stand people watching me when I'm eating. Go and buy your own food. I haven't got enough to share it with you,' and she turned her back on us.

As we walked away, she was crouched behind a stall selling toys. She had her back to the stall and appeared to be looking through the windows of the Samaritaine, staring morosely at an electric iron.

It was a relief, an hour later, to be walking through the doors of the Crillon in search of Angelica.

'Antonio hasn't arrived yet,' she said when she at last appeared. 'He's been held up in some meeting but he won't be long. Look what I bought today. Isn't she heavenly?' and she held out a Yorkshire terrier puppy she had been carrying. 'And I bought a complete set of Gucci

227

luggage, and lots of clothes. Antonio told me to go shopping, so I did.'

'Won't he think you have bought rather a lot?' I enquired.

'Of course not. He doesn't mind how much I buy. You should see our house. Everything is made of marble that he had shipped from Italy; and he simply showers me with presents all the time. I wouldn't have married him if he had been mean. Mean men are the end.'

Angelica had always had a rather gravelly voice, but it seemed to have become harsher. Her slight frame had lost its childish curves and become tense and wiry, her Spanish face too thin. In a matter of months she had been transformed from an ebullient schoolgirl into a showpiece without character. It seemed odd that anyone brought up in an establishment where material things were of no significance should, in so short a time, have become grasping and acquisitive. I watched her as she ordered champagne and felt discouraged.

'I don't know anything about champagne,' she said as a bottle of vintage Dom Pérignon was placed in an ice-bucket beside us, 'but Antonio told me last night that this was OK and he knows about these things.'

Antonio arrived at this moment still, I noticed, wearing Cuban heels. He smiled at us as he crossed the room. 'Just in the nick of time, I see,' he remarked jovially as he pulled the bottle out of the bucket to examine the label. 'These glasses won't do, though.' He gave the waiter a friendly tap on the shoulder and said, 'There's been a bit of a slip-up here, I'm afraid. We want proper champagne glasses, not these things you can't get your nose into; and make it four champagne cocktails while you're at it, will you? Champagne is pretty dull stuff if it's not dolled up a bit,' he added for our benefit. His English was faultless but his accent was Spanish with an American overlay. The waiter, who was doubtless addressed in English by at least fifty per cent of the hotel's clientèle, feigned incomprehension. Antonio repeated his request in excellent French with an equally Spanish accent. The waiter asked coldly whether Antonio would like a different champagne. Antonio replied in the negative and then said, 'If you don't know how to make it just bring me some decent glasses, some brandy, some Angostura bitters, a few sugar lumps and some caster sugar. Oh, and don't forget the Maraschino cherries.'

The waiter looked sadly at the vintage Dom Pérignon before vanishing in search of the items Antonio had requested. He still looked pained as he handed me my drink. Before taking my first sip, I put my cherry in an ashtray and scraped off some of the band of sugar that had been stuck to the brim. As I did so, I caught Jessica's eye across the table. Her obvious mirth made it difficult to drink without choking. When I next dared look up, she had her head bent so that all I could see was a half-smile at the corner of her mouth.

Antonio's conversation was surprisingly interesting. He was well travelled and well read, and he knew a great deal more about Paris than either Jessica or I. Only when he touched briefly on South American politics did one sense a more sinister person beneath the urbane exterior.

When the time came for us to leave, Antonio asked if we would be kind enough to post a letter for him on the way out. 'I've got some French stamps here somewhere,' he said as he pulled out his wallet. The latter was a leather affair of impressive proportions, made like a book with numerous pages of transparent plastic folders into which were slipped the banknotes of at least eighteen countries. Opposite the banknotes of each country Antonio had put sheets of stamps from the same country. I watched, fascinated, as his plump fingers flicked rapidly through the whole of Scandinavia and the Balkans before finding the page with his French money and stamps.

'I'm so glad we're us and not anybody else,' said Jessica as we made our way home. 'After seeing Olivier's hotel I thought how grim it would be to have to earn one's living as a tart, but I think I'd hate it even more to be

Angelica. Her life seems to be just another version of the same thing only less honest. Why do so many women think men owe them a living, do you suppose?'

'Perhaps because they feel they have been ill-treated for centuries and it's their way of getting back at society: paying men back by making them pay financially,' I suggested. 'They probably feel they aren't given the same opportunities as men and that, even when they are, men are paid far more for doing the same jobs; so by making men cough up for everything they feel they are redressing the balance, perhaps. But I have to admit that I don't think I could bring myself to do it except if I had children. I think it's different when women have children because somebody has got to bring them up and I've yet to see a man give up his career to stay at home and bring up his kids.'

'That is why nannies and boarding schools were invented,' remarked Jessica. 'So that women could work, too.'

'Quite,' I replied, 'but what's the point of having children if you're going to dump them on someone else to educate? It seems wrong to have children if you're not prepared to look after them. And how many people can afford either nannies or boarding schools, anyway? I think the government should pay mothers a proper salary to bring up their children. It's a job like any other: in fact, it's a far more important job than most and it should be salaried like any other job. The children would be much better looked after and it ought noticeably to reduce the problem of unemployment both by liberating jobs taken up by working mothers and by taking hordes of others off the dole queue. Women would cease to feel inadequate because they chose to look after their own children; it would relieve husbands of a financial burden; their wives could face them on equal terms rather than as slaves and beggars; and a great deal of domestic pressure would be removed. Everyone would be happier and the whole of society would benefit.'

'It's a wonderful idea,' said Jessica, laughing, 'but can

you honestly see any government doing it? And do you really think that men want women to be on an equal footing? I bet most husbands would continue to taunt their wives for not doing a "real" job – you know, sitting at a desk reading the newspapers, or having three-course luncheons ending with port and cigars, or drinking endless cups of tea with their mates when they are supposed to be building a house. It would require a complete change of attitude from the whole of society and that won't come about until men are forced to swap rôles with women. If men were made to stay at home and bring up the children while their wives went out to work and then came home and shouted at them about their shirts not being ironed, or the dinner not being ready, things would soon change; but men aren't stupid enough to allow that to happen. They would never support a government that stood for real equality: they know full well which side their bread is buttered.'

'In that case, you have your answer. That is presumably why so many women think men should pay for everything: they feel they do all the dirty work with no help from men, and that they are being held in contempt for it to boot.'

'I'll tell you another thing,' said Jessica as we reached our front door. 'Have you noticed how many books about sex, written by men, are full of stuff about what women are supposed to like? They go on and on about "erogenous zones". Well, I can tell you that erogenous zones don't work.'

'What on earth do you mean?' I asked, astonished.

'The other night when I went to the cinema with Thibault, he kept messing about with my ears – my left ear, to be precise. Ears, you see, are supposed to be an erogenous zone. Anyway, he was sort of nibbling it and licking it and all that sort of thing thinking, I am sure, that it was exciting for me; but it wasn't at all: it was quite disgusting. I can't remember hating anything so much for ages. All I wanted to do was get my ear away from him and dry it.'

'Perhaps it's just you,' I suggested.

'Rubbish,' retorted Jessica. 'Try it some time and you'll find out. It's revolting and it's all because men have decided to tell us what we like instead of asking us. Anyway, it's the last time I go to the cinema with Thibault and that's for sure.'

CHAPTER FOURTEEN

We saw a lot of Anthony after our expedition to Montmartre. Amongst other things, we served as messengers between him and Olivier, constantly racing across Paris carrying parcels of notes and books from one to the other. André always included Anthony in his invitations, too; and, gradually, as we saw more of him, he joined our circle of friends and seemed to slip quite easily into the group who frequented the rue des Carmes. Pierre and Thibault liked him from the outset and Anthony appeared amused rather than annoyed by their incessant attacks on the English.

At the start of our second year Simon decided to pay us a visit, something he was to repeat at regular intervals during our remaining two years in Paris. It was during that original visit that Simon first encountered Anthony – not, as I would have wished, in André's flat or ours, but in faintly embarrassing circumstances in a police station in Versailles.

It was Jessica who had opined that Simon ought to see Versailles. Simon had been enthusiastic and I had acquiesced although by then I felt I knew it quite well and would have preferred to see something else.

It was a perfect late summer day and it seemed a waste to go indoors so we decided to visit the gardens first, leaving the interior of the château to the end of the afternoon. There was in the air that fleeting sensation of Indian summer when it turns to autumn and we wanted to clutch at every last moment of sunshine, aware that the good weather might vanish with the

233

morrow to disappear into the season of mists and rain.

It is a long walk to the Petit Trianon and back and we made it longer by visiting the Grand Trianon on the way. By the time we had wandered around the Hameau and made our way back to the château it was much later than we had realized and we were lucky to find ourselves there just in time to buy tickets for the last guided tour.

'Why do we have to go on a guided tour?' complained Simon. 'Why can't we just wander round on our own?'

'They don't like people doing that, for some reason,' Jessica replied.

'You have to pretend to be with a group,' I added, 'but it's quite easy to drop behind or rush ahead once the guide starts talking. We always manage to detach ourselves from the rest of them.'

'We know it so well, by now, that we could give you the tour ourselves, in any case,' said Jessica. 'Come on. They're starting.'

We kept up with our group for a while but it soon became apparent that we were as irritating to them as they were to us. Every time we said anything to each other the guide glared at us and when, at one point, Simon and I had a heated argument in Italian about whether the date on a piece of furniture could possibly be correct the whole group turned and hissed at us to be quiet.

We eventually came to a halt in a room where the guide was describing the private apartments, indicating in a vague manner that they could be reached through pressing a button on some hidden, secret door in a bookcase. This was not the only means of access, obviously, she explained to us, but it had been useful in its day for illicit meetings between lovers and their mistresses.

The private apartments were not included in the tour so our group soon moved on to the other State Apartments, leaving us to discuss the intriguing thought that we might be able to find the secret door and go exploring forbidden ground on our own.

It was Simon's idea and he organized the campaign. He posted me at one door and Jessica at the other while he climbed over a rope and headed for the bookshelves. I could see our group in the distance, several rooms away, and Jessica apparently could see no-one coming from the other direction, so we signalled to Simon that it was safe to proceed.

He was not successful. He took books out of shelves, pushed panels, felt for cracks and hinges, but no door flew open before our gaze. I was beginning to feel nervous and Jessica kept hissing at Simon to hurry up. Before long he moved away from the bookshelves and appeared to be considering the possibility of moving a picture that was hanging in the centre of one of the panels. Jessica stopped him just in time. 'Don't be ridiculous, Simon,' she exclaimed. 'The pictures are bound to be wired up to an alarm system. You'll get us into terrible trouble if you start fiddling with them.'

'Coward,' said Simon. 'How else are we ever going to find this door?'

'I think there might be a much easier way of reaching those rooms,' I interrupted. 'Do you remember that staircase that was blocked off by a rope a little further back, and that blue room that we were only allowed to peer into over a rope? Well, those must lead somewhere, mustn't they? Supposing we went back and climbed over the ropes? Ours was the last group being shown round this evening so there won't be any more people coming through.'

'Of course,' agreed Jessica. 'How silly of us not to think of it before. Let's go.'

It was not quite as easy as I had expected because there were still guards hanging around in most of the rooms. However, since they were under the impression that they had seen the last of tourists for the day, they had started thinking about going home and were either already wandering off or were huddled in groups of two and three, saying good night to each other. We carefully circumnavigated the few who were still about and when we reached the stairs it was but the work of a moment to hop over the rope and skip out of sight.

There followed a curious game of hide and seek, for these stairs did not lead immediately to rooms off the beaten track. Sometimes we found ourselves in deserted halls and chambers not normally seen by visitors, but time and again we would find ourselves back in a room we had seen earlier. Eventually, however, we ceased coming across rooms that were familiar and for thirty minutes or more we explored in peace, surprised by the minute and dreary bedrooms which, even allowing for the fact that they were for the most part unfurnished, seemed more suitable as nuns' cells than as bedchambers at the court of a glittering monarch.

'I don't think much of these rooms,' commented Simon after a while. 'If this was the way Louis XIV housed his noblemen, I'm surprised they were so keen to stay at court. No wonder he threw Fouquet in prison for "*luxe insolent et audacieux*" if this was his idea of hospitality.'

'I expect lots of them had equally poky and uncomfortable rooms in their châteaux,' remarked Jessica. 'In any case, they had to come to court otherwise they would have missed all the fun. The women in particular would have had a much less amusing time. They wouldn't have had a hope of wielding any influence if they hadn't lived at Versailles. What good would it have been to be Madame de Maintenon or Madame de Montespan if they had been stuck in some provincial castle?'

'Yes,' I agreed with Jessica. 'Madame de Maintenon couldn't possibly have met the King, let alone married him, if she hadn't been brought to court; and think of the choice of lovers everyone had, and the limitless possibilities for intrigue. Life in the country couldn't conceivably have produced such excitement. It obviously didn't matter how uncomfortably they were housed.'

'There was always a good chance they would be moved up in court circles in any case, so they had every hope of being housed more comfortably. I think it was very clever of Louis,' Jessica added.

'It might have been all right for the women,' replied Simon, 'but it can't have been such fun for the men who were all cuckolded and were constantly being poisoned by their wives. Their chances of coming out of it alive were slim and their chances of influencing anyone non-existent.'

As we talked I realized that I had gradually been losing my sense of time and direction. I looked out of the windows at a tiny courtyard that I had never seen before. 'Do either of you know where we are?' I asked the others.

'No idea,' said Simon, 'but we can always go back the way we came.'

'Don't you think we ought to go back?' Jessica asked. 'They must be just about at the end of the tour by now.'

'All right,' Simon agreed reluctantly.

We thought we knew the way back but we did not. We walked for three quarters of an hour, upstairs, downstairs, in and out of rooms which frequently looked the same. We tried to find our bearings by looking out of the windows but all the windows seemed to face inwards on to endless, small courtyards which we were never quite sure whether we had seen before or not.

As dusk turned to night outside, it became exceedingly frightening. We could barely see our way from one room to the next and Jessica suggested gloomily that we would probably remain locked in there for ever, left to starve to death and possibly only discovered as cadavers months or years from now. One thing was perfectly clear. The main entrance must by now be locked so there was no point in attempting to find our way back to the State Apartments.

Once again looking out of a window and having made our way down to the ground floor, Simon pointed out that there was an archway in the courtyard outside which might well lead to one of the larger courtyards and so out of the château. 'We're obviously not going to be able to get out through any of the conventional exits,' he said. 'The doors will all be locked at this hour, so we might as well climb out of this window and see if we can get out through that archway.'

'Even if we do, the gates to the front courtyard will be shut,' I said.

'There must be hundreds of other ways out,' replied Simon. 'There are other gates, after all. Some of them must be easy to climb and, if not, there must be endless ways out of the grounds.'

'Surely an alarm will go off if you try to force the window,' said Jessica.

'I very much doubt it,' Simon replied. 'They can't possibly have wired up every window in this place, particularly not the ones on the inside. It wouldn't be worth it for the windows overlooking internal courtyards.'

'It's our only chance, anyway,' I said, agreeing with Simon, 'and if an alarm did go off it would probably take ages for anyone to find out what had set it off or track us down. We could run away before they got here.'

The window looked easy to force but, having been shut for hundreds of years, proved impossible. In our efforts we broke a pane of glass and Jessica then suggested that it would be simpler to break more glass and climb out than to unblock the window itself.

I took my shoe to the rest of the pane and bravely started to climb out. As I did so a whistle was blown and two guards appeared from nowhere, running towards me. It later transpired that they had been on a routine last patrol when they heard the sound of broken glass falling on cobbles. They were not particularly friendly in spite of my efforts to be conciliatory and in Simon's case they were quite rough.

We were not given a chance to explain as they marched us to an office and called the police, but when the police arrived I realized that the guards had been comparatively civilized. There is something about the French police which makes it preferable not to be on the wrong side of the law.

I didn't dare say anything to the others as we were driven to the police station although I was longing to know whether they found it as embarrassing as I did to be shooting along in a police car with its siren blaring. I felt as if the whole world was staring at me even though it was dark and there were not many people about and we were going too fast for anyone to see us.

It was worse when we were marched from the car into the police station. Several interested pedestrians stopped and stared.

Once inside we soon realized we were in worse trouble than the escapade merited. We were foreigners. We none of us had identity cards and we were none of us carrying our passports. The police clearly did not believe our explanations as to how and why we had been caught in the act of breaking a window in a part of the château not open to the public, at night, after every door and gate had been locked. What were we trying to steal, they demanded? Or were we terrorists? Had we planted a bomb? The policeman in charge of questioning us became very over-excited and unpleasant at the thought of a bomb.

It looked for a time as if we would certainly be put in prison. I had produced my student's card as identification but they seemed to have little time for students and, as they pointed out, I could have stolen the card. I asked them to telephone André for confirmation as to our identity but André was out. Jessica then suggested Anthony.

They spent some time on the telephone to him and it seemed an eternity before he finally marched into the police station in Versailles. He had brought someone from the administrative side of the Sorbonne with him. He had also brought Edward Blight.

The police were surprisingly impressed. They photo-copied everybody's documents, copied out everyone's names and addresses at home and at work, took telephone numbers, filled out forms in triplicate and demanded a very large fine which Anthony paid for us.

When we were finally allowed to leave, the Blight gave us a lecture such as we had never expected to hear again once we had left school. He did not bother to introduce himself to Simon and it was apparent that even Jessica had temporarily fallen from grace. His parting words, exactly like any headmistress', were that he would have to inform Jessica's parents. He then offered to give the person from the Sorbonne a lift back to Paris and the two of them turned on their heels and left.

Anthony looked as if he was trying to be serious. 'I see you are not Imogen's twin for nothing,' he said to Simon. 'How could fate possibly have elected to throw up two of you? I'm sorry I had to ask Edward to come along,' he added, turning to Jessica. 'I know you don't like him but I thought he might prove useful in these particular circumstances. Perhaps it will have served the double purpose of finally making him think less highly of you. I must say, you two really are impossible. Next time I shall leave you to extricate yourselves.'

'It was entirely my idea,' interrupted Simon. 'I'm extremely sorry we've caused so much trouble.'

'So you should be,' said Anthony, 'although if you're anything like your sister it won't stop you doing something equally exasperating tomorrow. How long are you here for?'

'Only another two days. I could only steal a long weekend, but I'll be back.'

'You're at Cambridge, aren't you?' asked Anthony, 'Imogen told me what you were reading but I've forgotten, I'm afraid.'

'Biochemistry,' replied Simon.

'Of course,' said Anthony. 'I remember now. Do you like Cambridge?'

'Yes,' my brother replied. 'Very much.'

The two of them talked about mutual acquaintances, and about Cambridge in general, all the way back to Paris; and when Anthony dropped us in the rue des Carmes he seemed loth to leave. 'Why don't you all have dinner with me tomorrow?' he asked. 'I'll take you to a delightful family-owned and family-run restaurant I have just discovered in the place de la Bastille. If you like fish, they do wonderful fish dishes.'

Jessica and Simon both accepted with alacrity but I, to my secret regret, had to decline because I had promised to have dinner with Enrico de Mitis the following night. There were to be many repetitions of that dinner, however, because every time Simon came to Paris after that, Anthony invited us all out to dinner at some point during his stay.

Simon liked Anthony but always seemed slightly uncomfortable with him, almost as if he sensed my reactions and felt obliged to duplicate them. I still felt ill at ease with Anthony. His interest in me was tangible. I felt it as strongly as an electric current and I did not know how to deal with it. It might have been easier had I not felt a reciprocal interest.

Jessica was the only one of us who was truly untroubled by him. By the end of our second year she knew him far better than I did, having been taught by him for three terms and having spent a great deal of time with him. Just as when we were children, I admired and envied the ease with which she sailed through life.

It was around the time of Simon's first trip to Paris that Jessica's life and mine began to diverge, an occurrence caused largely by the uninvited presence of Enrico de Mitis. Very shortly after our evening at the opera I bumped into Enrico as I came out of the bibliothèque Sainte-Geneviève.

'Ah,' he said, 'I hoped I might find you here. I've just been round to your flat and Jessica said she thought this was where you'd be. Life would be simpler if you had a telephone. Can't you get one?'

'Have you ever applied for a telephone here?' I demanded. 'It takes anything up to six months to be given a line. Some people wait years. That's why there's such a demand for flats which already have phones. Anyway, we're used to not having one now.'

241

'I wanted to ask you out to lunch yesterday. I hung around the main entrance of the Sorbonne for a while but I never saw you. I couldn't wait too long because I had to attend a press conference at two thirty. What time do you usually come out?'

'It varies, but I never come out of the front anyway. I usually come out in the rue des Ecoles.'

'Well, since I didn't manage to find you yesterday, would you care to have dinner with me tonight instead?'

'I'd love to,' I replied, 'as long as you don't want to have dinner too early. I have to do some written work for tomorrow morning and I shan't feel like doing it after dinner, so I'd better get it out of the way beforehand.'

'You tell me what time suits you. Eight thirty? Nine?'

'Would nine be OK?'

'Fine. I'll be downstairs at nine.'

When I walked into our flat a few minutes later, I found Jessica in an ebullient mood.

'It's a good thing we decided not to do archaeology except as a hobby,' she said. 'I've just been to the Institut d'art to see what their courses are like and it turns out to be the most hideous building. You wouldn't believe your eyes. Horrible red brick with strange gargoyles and decorations, and it's incredibly dilapidated and dirty inside. It would have been so depressing to work in practically the only ugly building in Paris.' She grinned, then continued, 'It has several libraries, though, including one which is really wonderful. You must come and see it. They say it's better for art and architecture books than the Bibliothèque nationale. I'm obviously going to have to transfer my presence from the bibliothèque Sainte-Geneviève to the library at the Institut d'art. Will you come and keep me company?'

'Yes, of course,' I said and then, 'To change the subject completely, I'm having dinner tonight with Enrico de Mitis. I bumped into him coming out of the library. He said you had told him to look for me there.'

'Yes, I did. That's lovely. I told you he was pretty

242

interested in you. I *am* pleased. I thought he was very civilized. I hope he takes you somewhere nice. What time is he collecting you?'

'Not until nine because I absolutely must do some work first. In fact, I must start right now, otherwise I'll never finish it in time.'

'OK,' said Jessica. 'I'm going to have a bath now so I'll leave you in peace. I said I'd meet Pierre and the others in the rue Mouffetard at seven. We thought we might go to a film. They all want to see the Godard although I'd much rather go to the Truffaut, but I don't suppose my opinion will carry much weight. At any rate, we'll definitely be going to the *Rhumerie martiniquaise* around eleven because we told Thibault that we'd meet him there after the cinema. You could come too after dinner if you've finished by then.'

'I can't imagine Enrico wanting to drink a *punch au lait chaud* or any of those disgusting drinks, can you? Still, if he turns out to be frightfully boring, I might try to persuade him to go there later, but don't count on it. I don't want to be too late because I've got to get up frightfully early tomorrow.'

Enrico took me to the Closerie des Lilas for dinner. It was pleasant to be able to talk Italian for a change and we spent more time discussing Italy and our childhoods than we did talking about our present lives in Paris. We ate at a leisurely pace and, when we had finished eating, sat sipping armagnac and talking while the piano played in the background. It was not until I had finished my fourth cup of coffee that I realized how late it was. All temptation to join Jessica and the others had completely vanished. I wanted to go home and fall asleep.

When Enrico dropped me at my door, he said, 'I'm so glad I accepted that invitation of Edward's. I am delighted to have met you. I have greatly enjoyed our evening and hope that you will allow me to repeat the pleasure very soon.'

*　　*　　*

After that, Enrico was constantly to be found hanging around the rue des Carmes waiting for me to come home. At the beginning, he used to pretend that he just happened to be in the area, even though it was obvious he had no reason to be on the Left Bank.

'This is the man that Edward told us worked so incredibly hard,' remarked Jessica, recalling something the Blight had said about Enrico getting up at the crack of dawn and working until all hours. 'Really, embassies have no idea, do they? He seems to be free at six every evening. I don't call that terribly late, do you? Although I can see that by Edward's standards it must seem the middle of the night.'

At first I tried to include Enrico in our group of friends. I would invite him into our flat where Pierre and the others were usually to be found lounging around reading newspapers and arguing endlessly about the government and its latest follies. Pierre was violently anti-American and dismissive of the English as lackeys of the Americans. According to Enrico, he had a simplistic approach to foreign affairs and a childish idealism.

'Your friends,' he would say to me, 'have absolutely no understanding of the intricacies of foreign affairs. All that unrealistic purity is not going to get anyone anywhere.'

The only member of the group with whom he could be bothered to argue was Pierre's brother, Thibault, a poly-technician with an acutely analytical mind; but he made it clear that he disliked Thibault and thought him arrogant. Before long, I abandoned the attempt and accepted Enrico's invitations to go out but ceased to ask him to join our friends in the rue des Carmes.

Enrico was amusing and intelligent but his sense of humour was frequently cruel so that, although I thought him entertaining when he was demolishing political leaders or Embassy officials, I was less than happy when his wit was turned on me. He was appalled by my lack of education, thought my upbringing insane and my parents criminal for having sent me to school in England. He liked to question me endlessly on subjects about which I knew nothing. I felt hideously ignorant. I tried not to mind, but he had a knack of rubbing salt in wounds.

Because I was defenceless and at a total disadvantage, he soon took on the rôle of teacher and I of pupil; and it was then that he was at his best for he made an excellent teacher. History suddenly seemed like current affairs and economics began to have some relevance to life. Figures from the far distant past who had never seemed real, let alone interesting, were transformed by Enrico into the complex, sometimes frail, human beings they must have seemed to those who knew them intimately in their day. The newspapers began at last to make some sort of sense. As Enrico explained the reasons for each event, I began to see the globe as a chess board on which any move by a given country must produce one of the several possible responses from the other countries. For the first time in my life I was beginning to understand the world around me; and I wanted to learn more.

I was not sure how much I liked Enrico, but I was undoubtedly fascinated by him. He, on the other hand, was interested in me for other reasons. He had no particular desire to have a Trilby; he simply wanted to go to bed with me. I was frightened whenever he made a move in this direction. I had not been brought up with the idea that I would go to bed with people. The combination of Italian standards of behaviour and eight years in a convent weighed heavily against it so that the more Enrico tried to force the situation, the more I resisted the idea; and the more I resisted, the more determined he became.

We were having a drink at his flat one evening when he suddenly asked, 'Why do you go on seeing me?'

'Because you are so persistent,' I replied.

'There must be more to it than that,' he insisted.

'I enjoy your company,' I answered, 'and you have taught me so much. No-one else has ever bothered to explain anything to me and I want to understand.'

'I want to teach you other things,' he said. 'You don't know the first thing about anything. I could teach you things which are far more fun. Am I really the first person who has tried to go to bed with you? I can't understand it. It's such a waste. You've got to start some time. Why not now?'

'I don't want to. I want to wait until I'm married.'

'Don't be ridiculous! That's the stupidest thing you have said yet. What on earth makes you want to marry, anyway, when you can have all the fun without the tiresomeness? Come here,' and he pulled me towards him.

I was taken by surprise. I suddenly found myself pinned against the wall, my arms above my head, one of my wrists in each of his hands so that I was trapped, unable to move.

It was the first time I had ever been kissed. Fear battled with sensuality but fear, it transpired, was the stronger of my emotions. The moment Enrico started trying to undress me, my only desire was to escape and, before either of us knew what was happening, I had sunk my teeth as hard as I could into his shoulder.

Enrico was astonished. He let go of me very suddenly and for a moment I thought he was going to hit me. Instead, he looked briefly at his shoulder, then walked across the room and stood with his back to me. He stood staring out of the window for a few minutes then turned round and said, 'I'm sorry. I didn't realize how frightened you were. Why are you so frightened?'

'I don't know. I just am.' I replied.

He thought for a moment then said, 'All right. I'd better take you home.'

We drove back to the rue des Carmes in silence and Enrico made no attempt to kiss me when we said good night.

When I told Jessica the next morning she said, 'You

were quite right. You're not even in love with him, are you?'

'No,' I replied, 'not in the least. But I do enjoy his company.'

'How horrid,' she said, making a face. 'Really, if every man whose company one enjoys is going to leap on one, the world will soon become an absolute bear garden.'

CHAPTER FIFTEEN

Jessica reminded me of this incident as we continued to clear out the attic at Manta.

'Do you think you were always afraid of men, or did you just not like Enrico enough to try it with him?' she asked.

'A bit of both, I suppose,' I replied, 'plus all those basic fears about getting pregnant, committing a mortal sin and breaking all the rules with which we'd grown up.'

'You were already in love with Anthony, too, by then, weren't you? I expect that had a lot to do with it, don't you think?'

'Perhaps,' I replied.

We were both silent for a while until Jessica suddenly said, more as a statement than as a question, 'You really loved Anthony, didn't you?'

'Yes,' I replied with a sigh. 'I really loved him.'

'You both took long enough about it, I must say,' commented Jessica. 'If it hadn't been for that ball, I don't think either of you would ever have made a move. I wonder,' she mused, 'what would have happened if we hadn't gone to it? We could so easily not have gone back just for that.'

It is true that we would not normally have been in Paris on 14th July, but André had been so insistent.

'It's my great-niece's twenty-first birthday,' he had said. 'You will probably never have the chance to attend anything like it again. It is not often that a twenty-first birthday coincides with the *quatorze juillet* and my sister's flat, as you know, is the perfect place for it. How many people are you ever likely to meet with such a ball-room overlooking the place des Vosges? Imagine that room with the windows all open on to the balcony, in summer, overlooking the most beautiful square in the world. You will have the music and candlelight behind you as you look out at the people dancing in the streets. How can you resist anything so romantic?'

We couldn't, we replied; and so we went.

Anthony, too, was bludgeoned into it, as was Marguerite, although she required very little persuasion.

It was a perfect evening, balmy, enticing. One felt the activity brewing in the streets and currents of excitement crossing the city. As we were dressing, groups of people were already piling into restaurants; the café tables were filled to overflowing.

Most of our friends were away for the summer but the few who remained, like Olivier, were all intending to watch the fireworks later that evening. I regretted not being able to go with them but, as Jessica pointed out, we would have endless other occasions to see fireworks whereas a ball in these circumstances was unlikely to be repeated.

The evening came as a shock to us both. Our fellow guests had nothing in common with any of the people we knew in Paris. They were a different breed, out of another stable. We might never have known they existed had it not been for that ball. Until then I had assumed that the upper-class imbecile was a peculiarly English invention not to be found elsewhere. To my astonishment, I discovered, that evening, that the French can rival the English at that particular game.

The setting was unbearably beautiful: immense rooms with marble fireplaces and beams that had been painted in the seventeenth century; long windows opening on to an endless balcony overlooking the place des Vosges; a view of trees and fountains, and the sound of music. With a sudden poignancy I realized that perhaps Versailles in its heyday was not as romantic as one had always supposed, that the ruling classes might never have been those with the brains, that the aristocrats of the time might have been just as small-minded as those of today. For the first time in my life, I felt an overwhelming sympathy with the French Revolution, a solidarity with Pierre and his friends. I wandered out on to the balcony to breathe the night air and wished that on this, of all nights, I could join the population celebrating in the streets.

As I was surveying the square below me, I felt a hand on my shoulder and Anthony's voice said, 'You're not enjoying it at all, are you?'

'Not much,' I replied, 'although I love standing here and imagining what it might have been like to live in some other century. I just wish we could go and watch the fireworks, or join the dancing on the pont Neuf.'

'As soon as it is possible to leave without appearing impolite, I promise you I'll take you off; and Jessica too if she wants. Then we can go and join the rest of the world down there, if it would amuse you. The festivities will go on, all over Paris, until two or three in the morning, so don't worry. In the meantime, will you come in and dance with me?'

It was the first time I had had any physical contact with Anthony, although I had known him for the better part of eighteen months. I felt nervous and awkward, and I had the uncomfortable feeling that he must be able to feel my heart pounding. My hands felt sticky, although I felt cold.

After a time, Anthony looked down at me and whispered, 'Relax. You can't still be afraid of me after all this time. Or are you?' and his eyes held mine as if searching for an answer I might not give.

'A bit,' I answered turning my head away. 'I feel nervous with you.'

'And why is that, do you think?' he enquired. I had the distinct impression that he was laughing at me.

'I don't know.' My voice was almost inaudible and I could feel my cheeks turning scarlet. I stared at the floor pretending to study the other dancers' feet, hiding my embarrassment.

'Don't you?' asked Anthony; and then, after a long pause, 'It would be nice if you could look at me occasionally. I enjoy looking at your face, you know; and although the top of your head is a charming sight, I can't tell what is going on inside it if I can't see your face.'

I looked up, feeling foolish, and laughed.

'That's better,' said Anthony gently. 'Now look at me properly and tell me you're not afraid of me any more.' He was smiling but there was something in his expression that I had never noticed before, an anxious look, a flicker in the shadows. Seeing this, I felt less nervous suddenly.

'I don't think I am afraid of you any more, after all,' I said uncertainly.

'Good,' he replied. Then he bent down and kissed me on the cheek. After a moment he laughed. 'I've waited a hell of a long time for this,' he said. 'I doubt whether many men would have been as patient.' His arms tightened around me for an instant; then, feeling me shiver, he loosened his hold again murmuring, 'It's all right. I won't do anything you don't want me to do.'

When we finally stopped dancing, André's old lady beckoned me. She was sitting, straight-backed, by the window, on a throne-like object that André claimed had once belonged to an antipope.

'Go and talk to her,' said Anthony, 'while I see if I can find us both a drink.' He put his hand on my shoulder briefly before heading for the room where the drinks were being served.

I crossed to the window where the old lady was sitting. She stretched out her hand as I reached her side. 'Talk to me for a moment,' she said. 'Are you enjoying the dancing? You looked so young, so charming.' Still holding my hand, she looked up at me, her face suddenly anxious. 'Be careful, *chère petite mademoiselle*,' she said. 'Don't allow yourself to be hurt. It is so painful. So painful; and there is nothing one can do about it.

251

Absolutely nothing. I know,' and her gaze wandered briefly in André's direction.

'André is devoted to you,' she added after a pause, and she squeezed my hand before letting it drop. As she looked away I sensed a certain quietude disturbed.

When the first guests started to depart, Anthony came over to me saying, 'I have spoken to Jessica and she is ready to leave, if you are. I think we can go now without appearing uncivil.'

Once outside, he stopped a taxi. 'Pile in,' he said. 'I'm going to take you both to Montmartre where the evening should still be in full swing. Then we can stand beneath the Sacré-Coeur and watch the whole of Paris laid before us, and the fireworks exploding under the moonlit sky. I'm sorry that I didn't bring my car but I was right in thinking that it would be impossible to park. Shall we see if Delphine and Sabine are around? This is their night, really. They should be dancing in the streets.'

The *hôtel de passe* was closed but it did not take us long to find Olivier. We saw him marching up the hill in front of us as the taxi continued its way up to Montmartre. We stopped and asked him if he wanted to join us.

'I'd love to,' he said, 'and so would the girls. I had intended to go to the Trocadéro to watch the fireworks down there but I couldn't get away. We've been incredibly busy so we've only just closed the hotel. They went up ahead of me to the place du Tertre but it shouldn't be difficult to find them. Sabine was in a particularly boisterous mood tonight. I'm sure we'll be able to hear her a mile off.'

The square, always humming with activity, thronged with people singing and laughing and it was almost impossible to move through the crowds. There was no sign of Sabine but we found Delphine quite easily. She was sitting, looking gloomy, at a café table, clutching a *crème de menthe frappée*. She perked up at the sight of us and threw her arms around Anthony as she kissed him on both cheeks. (Anthony had given Olivier a fair

amount of help with his history and had not objected to
Delphine being present at these sessions so that he was
on very friendly terms with her by this time.) 'What a
disgusting-looking drink,' Anthony said to her. 'Where's
Sabine?'

'She's over there,' answered Delphine, pointing
across the square. 'She's having her portrait painted
by a Dutchman. He's very drunk. She'll be back in a
minute.'

I was pleased to sit down after dancing for hours.
Anthony ordered drinks for us and we sipped these as
we waited for Sabine to reappear. When she did eventually wander over, she had the Dutchman in tow and
was carrying a garish water-colour of herself. 'Lovely,
isn't it?' she asked, holding it out for us to admire. We all
nodded enthusiastically.

The Dutchman ordered us another round of drinks
and then started singing. After a while he turned to
Jessica and said, 'So, you are English?'

'Yes,' she replied.

'Then you will help me with my idioms,' he announced.
'I think they are good but I wish to perfect them. Quick as
a flash, is that right? Faster than light. To cry over spilt
milk. To sail close to the wind. To lose your skirt.'

'No,' said Jessica, 'it's "shirt" not "skirt".'

'Thank you,' said the Dutchman politely. 'I knew you
would be useful. We continue: out of the frying pan, into
the fire.'

Jessica was finding it hard not to laugh. Seeing her
grinning, the Dutchman took offence and began shouting. Sabine intervened at this point, telling him that if
he wasn't going to speak French he could leave. The
atmosphere became unpleasant suddenly. We were all,
by this time, feeling tired and faintly tipsy. Anthony
decided to take matters into his own hands. 'You're all
going to drink some coffee,' he said, 'and then we're
going for a brisk walk up the hill.'

There were people streaming in all directions and by
the time we had fought our way through the crowds and

up the steps of the Sacré-Coeur, I felt perfectly sober again. I felt Anthony's hand on my arm as we turned to look at the view.

In due course, as we headed back down the hill, we discovered that there were no taxis to be had. We walked as far as the rue de Paradis before we finally managed to persuade one to stop.

'I'm not taking all of you,' he shouted. 'I'm only allowed to take three passengers.'

We had no choice but to split up. Olivier, Delphine and Jessica climbed into the taxi and we agreed that we would look for another one and join them as soon as possible on the pont Neuf. 'There might still be something going on down there,' Olivier suggested, 'and if there isn't, we can walk from there to the rue des Carmes. Do you mind if I spend what's left of the night on your sofa? I can't be bothered to go back to my room. It's too far.'

Anthony started to tell Olivier not to let Jessica out of his sight and, should we fail to meet up with them, to make sure he saw her home safely, when the taxi-driver lost his temper. 'Eh, dis donc,' he said tersely to Anthony, 'vous avez fini de bavarder, non? Je ne vais pas rester ici toute la nuit, vous savez,' and he drove off, nearly knocking me over as he went.

We were still wandering the badly lit streets twenty minutes later when Sabine said, 'I've had enough of this. I'm exhausted and we're obviously never going to find a cab. Let's go back to the hotel.'

The Dutchman thought this an excellent idea. Anthony declined. 'No,' he said, 'I'm going to see Imogen home safely if it takes me all night.'

Sabine and the Dutchman started back up the hill again, leaving Anthony and me to continue our way southward on our own. Most of the earlier activity had, by this time, died down although there was still an occasional sound of music or laughter in the distance.

Finally Anthony said, 'I can't believe that anything is still going on around the pont Neuf at this hour. You don't really want to go there, do you? It will be morning in no time and Jessica and Olivier must have left long since. Wouldn't it be more sensible for you to sleep at my flat? We're very close to it. We could be there in three minutes.' Seeing my expression, he added, 'Don't worry. I'll sleep on the sofa. And I'll drive you back to the rue des Carmes in the morning; but, first, I want proof that you're not afraid of me any more.' He pulled me towards him and there, in a deserted street, under a half-hidden moon, he took me in his arms and kissed me.

All around us, Paris lay silent. Here and there, in the far distance, a firework exploded, a spire rose up against the sky.

Anthony was aware of the fact that for the previous eighteen months I had been relentlessly pursued by Enrico. What he did not know, though he no doubt suspected it, was that Enrico had tried so hard to persuade me to go to bed with him. The recent incident with Enrico had left me so embarrassed and insecure that I had serious misgivings about spending what was left of the night in Anthony's flat. The moment we walked through his door, I was overcome with nervousness, but I was far too shy to express my fears.

Noticing my distress, Anthony turned to me and said, 'My dear girl, I am not a monster you know. I have already said that I won't do anything you don't want me to do. I would, as it happens, like very much to go to bed with you, but I have absolutely no intention of doing anything of the sort unless you want me to, so you can put your mind at rest. I am not in the habit of violating little girls.'

I thought I detected a hint of anger in his voice, but the expression in his eyes was something other than anger.

His tone was gently mocking as he continued, 'For a long time I hoped that your friend, Enrico, might succeed in persuading you over the first hurdle, but it is painfully obvious that he has failed; and I am not intending to add myself to your list of persecutors.' He paused and then

255

added in a kinder voice, 'You're such a child. It's atrocious.' Putting his arms around me, he repeated, 'You're such a child. When are you going to grow up?'

I felt uncomfortable and unhappy and quite incapable of explaining what I felt. Flinging my arms around his neck I said, 'I'm sorry. I really am sorry. It's not you. It's me. It's not because I don't love you. I've loved you for ages; but I'm scared. I can't explain why. I don't really know why. I just am. I'm frightened.'

'That much is perfectly obvious,' said Anthony curtly. 'I'm not blind.'

I still had my arms around his neck and my face was buried against his shoulder. Neither of us said anything for a time until finally Anthony broke the silence.

'You're extraordinarily beautiful,' he remarked at last. 'I wonder if you realize how beautiful you are. If you don't want to tempt fate any further, I suggest you go and shut yourself in my bedroom before I change my mind.'

He unclasped my arms from around his neck and made no move as I walked across the room. 'Go on,' he said, as I hesitated at the door. 'It's down that passage. Second door on the left. I think we could both do with some sleep.'

He was standing motionless with his back to me as I glanced back, briefly, before shutting the door.

I woke during the early hours of the morning to find Anthony standing over me. Emerging from deep sleep, I was startled to find myself looking straight into his eyes. He had pulled back the curtains to let in the light and was bending over me, studying my face. I tried to sit up but was prevented by Anthony putting a hand on my arm and keeping it there.

'Don't move,' he whispered. 'You look so perfect lying still.'

It was misty outside, and on the horizon a cloud-embedded moon was giving way to the dawn. The corners of the room remained in the shadows but we were both bathed in a milky haze.

He continued to watch me in silence for a while. I lay in

the shadow he cast across me, a dark lagoon in a moonlit lake; and all the while his hand stroked my arm, a sculptor's palm smoothing an alabaster limb.

'One day we shall curse ourselves for the time we have wasted,' he murmured so quietly I could barely hear.

The stillness of the dawn enclosed us. The light became milkier. The shadows shifted. Anthony's eyes were like grey pools at morning when the mist has lifted and the waters are clear.

Little by little the clouds converged, the moon hid her face, reeds bowed to the wind. When, at last, he lay down beside me, I was engulfed and all time stood still.

CHAPTER SIXTEEN

Yes, I thought, remembering all this, I had indeed loved Anthony.

Night after night, as he emerged, tired, from his evening lectures, I would watch him slowly unwinding until he took me in his arms and blotted out the day. In the watches of the night, he would murmur in my ear, 'I want every corner of your mind, every corner of your heart, every corner of your soul. I want every part of you.'

Contemplating him in the early morning light, my emotions were complex and difficult to subdue. I sometimes wondered who lay beside me as I looked down on the head of this man, this child, my brother, my lover, my father, my friend. Waking, once, and catching my expression, he whispered, 'Don't. It makes me feel positively incestuous.'

I continued to see a lot of Jessica, and Pierre, and Enrico but I saw them in the daytime, reserving my evenings for Anthony who half-jokingly said, 'I can't stand the thought of you enjoying other people's company. I want to have you all to myself. I want to smother you. I want to possess you entirely.'

If Jessica felt suddenly abandoned, she certainly never showed it. 'I'm so glad about you and Anthony,' she said shortly after the night of the ball. 'It's lovely to see you so happy and with somebody who is fun. I was worried that you'd fall for Enrico eventually, and I've come to the conclusion that he's rather bad for your self-esteem. I like him, but not as much as Anthony, and I'm sure Anthony is better for you.'

In every other way, life continued as before but something fundamental had changed for me. The discovery of physical love is not, in itself, earth-shattering but the discovery of one's own sensuality cannot be reversed. Anthony, aware of this, looked at me suddenly while we were having dinner, one evening, and reached across the table to take my hand. 'Now that you have discovered what it is all about, you're not going to start sleeping with other people, are you?' he demanded.

'Certainly not,' I retorted, shocked. 'Of course not. Why on earth would I want to sleep with anybody else?'

The following evening when he collected me from the rue des Carmes, he kissed me then asked, 'Are you pleased to see me?'

'Terribly,' I replied. 'You *know* I am, don't you?'

'Yes.'

'Then why do you ask?'

'Because I want to hear you say it.'

A few months later, when he had ceased to ask such questions, I mentioned that he seemed less anxious about me than he had been at the beginning. He made no reply. 'You *are* less anxious, aren't you?' I insisted.

He smiled, looked at me and finally laughed. 'No,' he said. 'No, I'm not less anxious about you.'

Only once, in all those months, was a shadow cast for a fraction of a second. André tried to warn me; but I did not understand and, in any case, I was far too in love to listen.

'Be careful of Anthony,' André had said. 'You may think it is none of my business, but I do not want to see you hurt. Don't get involved, *ma chérie*; it's too dangerous. Don't lose your heart to him. Anthony is a dear, but he's an absolute menace. This is your old, old André speaking. Take my advice. Choose someone else.'

'Why?' I asked.

'Some things just cannot be,' he replied. 'Some things were never intended.'

'But I thought you liked Anthony,' I insisted.

'I do like Anthony. Very much. I'm extremely fond of

259

him. But I am also exceedingly fond of you.' More than this I could not wheedle out of him. 'You'd be badly hurt,' was all he would say.

I repeated these remarks to Anthony, hoping that he would put my mind at rest by dismissing them totally. Instead, he paused before answering. 'Well,' he said calmly, after a moment, 'he may be right. One thing is certainly true and that is that he is exceedingly fond of you.'

'What did he mean?' I asked.

'One of any number of things. I don't know. That I don't deserve you, I expect. That I shouldn't be seducing little girls. He doesn't realize that you are not a little girl any longer. He may suspect that we are lovers, but he is certainly not sure of it. He wouldn't have said anything if he had been sure.'

When I told Jessica she said, 'That's odd. I wonder if Anthony has lots of girlfriends we don't know about.' She gave the matter some thought for a day or two and then announced, 'I'm afraid we're going to have to do something dreadful. You're not going to like it, but we haven't any choice. Whatever André meant, it sounded like a dire warning to me and André isn't given to issuing warnings – unless, of course, there's something wrong with Anthony's family. If he can't find Anthony in one of those books of his, he might think he was unsuitable for you. Do you think it could be that?'

'No,' I replied. 'He has never shown the slightest reticence about discussing anyone's family. He would have told me immediately if that was what was worrying him. It sounded much more ominous than that.'

'In that case, we'll have to put my plan in action, I'm afraid,' sighed Jessica. 'We're going to have to spy on Anthony, day and night.'

'Jessica!' I exclaimed.

'I told you you wouldn't like it,' she interrupted, 'but you have simply got to swallow your principles. He might be a criminal or even a murderer for all you know, and you can't let rules prevent you from finding out. Rules are made for normal situations, anyway, and this situation isn't normal. It may be very abnormal for all we know. How do we know he isn't married, after all?'

'He would have told us.'

'Not if he didn't want you to know.'

'Well, somebody would have told us: André would have, surely?'

'Perhaps he doesn't know either and is simply guessing.' She paused for a second and then said, with finality, 'No. We haven't any choice. We'll simply have to follow him everywhere and see what he's up to.'

For the next few days we did just that. I felt guilty about it to begin with, but it soon became fun to skip lectures and creep along passages at the Sorbonne, hiding in doorways and flattening ourselves behind columns. Every time Anthony stopped to talk to a girl student, or walked down a corridor talking to a female lecturer, Jessica would pinch me and hiss in my ear, 'I'll keep an eye on her; you go on following Anthony.' Soon we had far too many people to follow and we had to revert to following Anthony and no-one else. At lunch one day we trailed at some distance behind him and one of the women with whom we had seen him chatting in the corridors from time to time. They ambled into a café and sat talking together. They were just visible through the windows so we stationed ourselves in a café opposite and watched them from across the street. They seemed engrossed, studying some papers which they had spread out on the table. Their heads almost touched at times and my heart sank. I hated the woman instantly. She looked conniving, I thought, and she was wearing hideous shoes. The minute they left their café, Jessica and I rushed to pay our bill and follow, but the woman disappeared into a bookshop and Anthony returned to the Sorbonne.

That night, alone with Anthony, I nearly asked him point blank. I had felt uncomfortable with him since we started this operation and I wanted to clear the air. 'Have you ever been married?' I suddenly blurted out nervously.

Anthony looked astonished. 'No, of course I haven't,' he replied. 'What on earth makes you ask?'

261

'I don't know. I just thought you might have been.'

'Did it not occur to you that I would have mentioned it if I had been?' he enquired, laughing.

'Do you have another girlfriend?'

'No. I do not. Why all these questions all of a sudden?'

'I just wondered, that's all. I thought you might have lots of other girlfriends.'

'Well, I haven't. Good God, I'd hardly have time even if I wanted to: I spend all my free time with you. When am I supposed to see these other girls?'

'You could see them in the daytime. You could have lunch with them. That sort of thing.'

Anthony looked at me very oddly for a moment. He appeared to be going to say something, then apparently changed his mind.

'I could, of course, have lunch with them. That's perfectly true,' he finally replied with a smile. 'Who are they, by the way? Have you any particular candidates?'

'No. But I don't know all your friends, do I? You must know lots of the women professors; and lots of students, if it comes to that.'

Anthony could barely contain his laughter by this time. 'Oh, I do. I do,' he said. Then, pulling me out of an armchair, he took my face in his two hands. 'Do I detect the demon jealousy suddenly blossoming in your fair bosom?' he asked. 'You've been behaving very oddly lately. What's the matter? Do you want to tell me about it?'

'Nothing's the matter. I was just curious,' I said with what I hoped was an air of gay insouciance.

'In that case,' said Anthony, 'if you're sure we've covered the subject adequately, do you mind if we go out and get some dinner? I don't know about you, but I'm quite hungry.'

As he helped me into my coat, I was still uncomfortably aware of a gleam of amusement at the back of his eyes.

*　　*　　*

A couple of days later Jessica and I were forced, in the course of our spying activities, to trail all the way out to Neuilly and back. Anthony had told me that he was going there to visit a man who was apparently going to supply him with some vital information for the book he was writing, so I warned Jessica the day before this trip was to occur.

'It's obviously the woman,' said Jessica with satisfaction. 'Well, at least we know where she lives, now, but we'll somehow have to get close enough to see which bell he pushes. That's the only way we'll ever find out her name.'

'What do we do when we have found out?' I asked feeling suddenly nervous.

'I haven't thought about that yet. We can work that one out when we know who it is.'

It is not the easiest thing to follow someone on the *métro* without being spotted. There was a nasty moment when Anthony changed trains and we nearly missed the *correspondance*. Having installed ourselves in the carriages on either side of the one Anthony had chosen, it was impossible for us to communicate with one another and not particularly easy to see Anthony. I stood as near to the communicating door and its glass window as I dared and buried my head in a copy of *Le Monde*. Jessica did the same on the other side. From time to time I saw half an eye peering round the edge of the newspaper at the far end of the neighbouring carriage but it was too far away to read any expression on her face or even to be quite certain that it was Jessica and not some complete stranger.

When Anthony descended we waited until the last possible moment before following and, when we did so, sidled out with our backs facing in his direction and our noses in our newspapers.

I let Jessica follow Anthony up the escalators, at a discreet distance, while I waited until he was out of sight before following Jessica. She was by this time near the top of the escalators; and by the time I emerged from the station she was well down the street but turned back briefly to make sure I was following. We had worked out this procedure before starting on the assumption that we would be less noticeable if we separated. Jessica took her duties seriously and had dressed the part. She was almost unrecognizable in someone else's coat, a pair of borrowed spectacles (through which she could see very little) and with her hair entirely hidden under a woollen hat which she had pulled well down over her forehead. I had relied on a pair of dark glasses, a head-scarf and a large overcoat borrowed from Pierre. I had taken the precaution of keeping my long hair out of sight inside the coat.

Every time we reached a corner, we came to a halt and peered round it cautiously to make sure Anthony had not stopped or turned round before we continued in his wake. Sometimes, looking round a corner, I could only see Jessica because Anthony had already turned down yet another street.

After proceeding in this manner for four or five minutes Jessica, standing at the next crossroad, waved her hand frantically at me, first, it seemed, urging me to catch up with her and then, as I came nearer, apparently wishing me to slow down. When I reached her she looked flushed.

'He's gone into that building over there,' she said, pointing. 'That one with the balcony on the third floor. Do you see?'

I nodded.

'As far as I could see, he just walked in without pressing any buzzer, so I don't know how we're going to find out which flat he is in. We'd better separate again. I'll go first and stay on this side, pass it, cross and creep back again keeping as close to the buildings as possible. You had better wait a minute or two and then cross immediately and keep to that side. You might want to pop into that chemist over there for a moment and then come out again just in case Anthony is looking out of a window or anything. You must give me enough time to get there first. I'll wait for you on the landing of the first floor because I don't want to hang around downstairs in case there is a *concierge* about. If we do bump into the *concierge*, incidentally, just walk past with a purposeful air. If she asks any questions, reply in English and look as if you know where you're going. I'll do the exact opposite and chat in French about the weather if I bump into her. That way she won't connect us.'

'What will you do if she asks you who you've come to see?' I enquired.

'I'll say I've simply come to deliver some papers to the *professeur*. There's bound to be a *professeur* somewhere in the building and if there isn't, she'll think there is and that she ought to know who it is. She won't ask, anyway, because she won't want to let on that she doesn't know. Right, I must be off. See you in a few minutes. If there is any problem on the first landing, I'll just keep on walking upstairs. You could take the lift to another floor and walk down to meet me. Keep out of sight if any doors open. It might be Anthony although I don't suppose he'll come out again for hours.' She wandered off with her head well down and her hands in her pockets.

By the time I reached the building my heart was pounding. What had, until then, seemed a game now seemed despicable. I could think of no excuse for such dishonourable behaviour and I was filled with dread lest I bump into Anthony.

Jessica appeared to have no such qualms. I found her on the first floor looking thoroughly pleased with life.

'This is fun,' she whispered when I appeared. 'I think I might take it up as a profession when I've finished at university.'

It was a long afternoon. Two hours seemed much like twenty. The stairwell and landings were dark and the lights worked on the *minuterie* system, automatically switching themselves off after a minute. When one pushed the button to turn them on, it made a clicking noise which, we felt convinced, was audible throughout the building. It seemed unwise to use it more than very occasionally, so we spent most of our time hovering in the semi-darkness. The lighting system and the noise of the lift did, however, warn us when anyone was coming.

Fortunately for us, not many people came and went, but when they did it was a nerve-racking experience. Uncertain what to do with ourselves and never sure that it was not Anthony, we felt simultaneously obliged to hide and to see who the person was. During the course of the afternoon we worked out an elaborate plan of action. At various intervals one or other of us crept down to the entrance and copied as many names as we could from the letter-boxes in the hall noting, at the same time, the relevant flat numbers. Once we had the full list, we stationed ourselves on different landings. Jessica remained on the first floor and I sat on the stairs between the fourth and fifth floors. As soon as the lights went on I leapt to my feet and started to walk downstairs. If we heard the lift being summoned I would run to the floor in question as quickly as possible and wait while Jessica hovered on the stairs between the first floor and the entrance, standing at a bend where she could just see who was coming out of the lift below without being easily seen herself.

We had not, however, thought what to do if more than one person threatened to cross our paths simultaneously. The lights suddenly clicked on and I heard footsteps on the landing above me. I started downstairs but whoever it was called the lift which started its slow climb with a great metallic hiccough. Jessica meantime had heard the door from the street buzz open. Looking down she watched a woman head for the lift then change her mind when she saw it was in use and start for the stairs. Jessica ran up ahead of her and bumped into me on the second floor just as the door beside us opened and Anthony emerged.

He saw us instantly but was talking to an elderly gentleman who was bidding him farewell. Ignoring us, Anthony turned to the man, shook his hand warmly and thanked him for his help. By the time he had said good-bye we were down the stairs and racing for the door into the street. We heard Anthony behind us taking the stairs two at a time and we ran.

'Quick!' whispered Jessica, grabbing my arm. 'Into the chemist before he sees us.'

The *pharmacien* looked annoyed to see me again since I had not bought anything on my earlier visit. I asked him for a toothbrush and stood with my back to the street while he pointed to a stand holding a selection of tooth-brushes. Jessica, standing beside me, thought she had better give him a more onerous task and asked him if he could find her something for a dry cough.

As he wandered off to search his shelves, Jessica glanced behind us. She turned back quickly. 'Anthony's outside,' she said with a voice of doom. 'He's watching us.'

We delayed as long as possible. Jessica rejected the first cough linctus that the *pharmacien* produced and studied the labels of several more before finally choos-ing one. I spent some time looking at toothbrushes and then took as long as possible to find the right money.

'Isn't there anything else we need?' asked Jessica desperately. 'He's still there.'

'A shower cap,' I replied.

Ten minutes later, having bought cotton wool, Kleenex, cough linctus, soap, rubber gloves, a tooth-brush, some throat lozenges, a shower cap, a comb and a bottle of nail varnish, we realized that Anthony was going to wait all day if necessary.

'What do we do now?' asked Jessica.

'We'll just have to brave it,' I replied. 'We'll have to pretend we were visiting a friend who happened, by strange coincidence, to live in that building.'

'We'd better choose the name of someone who actu-ally lives there,' said Jessica, pulling our lists out of her pocket.

We chose the name of someone on the fifth floor. 'Yvenou,' the letter-box had said, '5ème *droite*'.

'She's a girl called Isabelle,' said Jessica as we drew a deep breath and walked towards the door, 'and she's a friend of Pierre's.'

As we emerged Anthony moved to greet us. His expression was one of mingled exasperation and curiosity. Holding each of us by an arm, he marched us along the street, saying, 'Now that you have finished buying up the chemist, perhaps you would be kind enough to tell me exactly what you were up to outside Monsieur Nesteroff's flat.'

'We were on our way downstairs from seeing Isabelle,' said Jessica. 'She invited us for lunch and then we somehow just stayed and stayed. You know how it is. Then we remembered we had to rush because we had all these things to buy from the chemist and we had told Pierre he could come round to the flat at five and we were worried we wouldn't be back in time.'

'And who is Isabelle?' asked Anthony.

'She's a friend of Pierre's who lives on the fifth floor of that building,' I replied. 'Her name is Isabelle Yvenou. She's very nice.'

'What an unusual coincidence,' murmured Anthony, 'and what an unusual name.'

'I think it's Basque, or Languedocien or something like that,' said Jessica with surprising assurance. 'Isabelle comes from somewhere near the Pyrenees, doesn't she, Imogen?'

'Yes,' I replied, 'somewhere near the Spanish border, she said, as far as I can remember.'

Anthony looked at me very oddly. I did not like the glint in his eye.

'I've run out of *métro* tickets,' I announced in order to change the subject (we had, by this time, reached the *métro*).

'I have plenty,' said Anthony handing me one and then offering one to Jessica. Then, looking at Pierre's coat as if he had only just noticed it, he asked, 'That's a new coat, isn't it? It looks rather large for you.'

'It isn't mine,' I said, relieved that I could at last say

something truthful. 'I borrowed it from Pierre because I was cold.'

'What happened to your own coat?' enquired Anthony.

'I couldn't find it.'

'Odd,' said Anthony. 'I could have sworn I saw you in it standing outside the Bibliothèque nationale this morning.'

I blushed but Jessica intervened saying, 'It must have been someone else. It couldn't have been Imogen because we were both at the flat all morning. Right up until we left to come and see Isabelle, in fact.'

'I must have imagined it,' said Anthony. 'There are so many girls who look just like Imogen and that Italian raincoat of hers seems to be all the rage in this town, I've noticed. Everyone seems to be wearing it. It has become the Parisian uniform.' He looked straight at me but I could read nothing in his eyes. 'You seem to be wearing rather unusual garb, too,' he continued, addressing Jessica. 'I don't think that hat really becomes you, if you will forgive me for saying so. You never told me you were having trouble with your eyesight, either. Since when have you taken to wearing spectacles?'

'I haven't,' replied Jessica who had put the borrowed pair in her pocket before we emerged from the chemist's shop.

'Yet you were wearing specs earlier, were you not?'

'Oh, you mean *those*,' answered Jessica. 'You mean those things I had on earlier? I don't count those. They're not real ones. They have ordinary glass in them. I just wear them for fun sometimes.'

'May I have a look at them?' asked Anthony.

Jessica opened her handbag and rummaged for a while. 'How stupid of me,' she said finally, looking apologetic. 'I must have left them in the *pharmacie*.' She smiled sweetly at him. Anthony smiled back.

'Well,' said Anthony as we changed trains at the Châtelet, 'I'm going to get out at Saint-Michel because I've got to go back to the Sorbonne. What about you two?'

'We're going back to the flat,' I said.

'I won't be through until eight-thirty,' said Anthony. 'I'll come and pick you up from the rue des Carmes then if you like, Imogen. What about you, Jessica? Do you want to have dinner with us?'

'I can't,' replied Jessica. 'I'm going to the theatre with this terribly good-looking man from the Côte d'Ivoire. I can't tell you how frighteningly clever he is. I've never been anywhere with him before but I've had my eye on him for some time, and he finally talked to me yesterday. It's all very exciting. In fact, I feel quite nervous. I'll tell you both all about it tomorrow but at the moment all I want to do is rush home and make myself beautiful.'

'What about Pierre?' asked Anthony.

'Pierre?' repeated Jessica, looking blank.

'I thought you were rushing because Pierre was arriving at five.'

'He is,' said Jessica recovering her wits. 'Imogen is going to look after him, aren't you Imogen? He's only coming for an hour, in any case.'

'Do you think he has guessed?' I asked Jessica the moment we were on our own.

'I'm not sure,' said Jessica. 'He obviously thought it was rather odd and I don't think he quite believed everything, but I thought he seemed reassured by the end. He can always check up on Yvenou if he has any doubts. It's a bore that he saw you outside the Bibliothèque nationale but I think you just have to keep denying it if he brings it up again.'

Later that evening Anthony came to collect me and drove me straight from the rue des Carmes back to his flat.

'Right,' he said the minute we walked through the door, 'let's have the truth this time. What exactly are you and Jessica up to? You've been following me for well over a week, now, and I am beginning to find it tiresome.'

'We haven't been following you,' I said, remembering Jessica's advice about denying the facts.

'My dear, you are the world's worst liar so if I were you I would stick to the truth. I have been watching you and Jessica for days flitting about the passages and hiding in doorways, or installing yourselves in the cafés opposite those I happen to have chosen; or, as today, wearing one coat to follow me to the Bibliothèque nationale and another to follow me to Neuilly. I should add that I took the trouble to check up on your story and not only does Pierre seem unaware that he has a friend called Isabelle (let alone one who lives in the most expensive suburb of Paris), but there is no Madame or Mademoiselle Yvenou. Poor old docteur Yvenou is an elderly bachelor who lives on his own and who has been spending the winter with relatives in Rennes. His flat has not been occupied for some months. Yvenou is, incidentally, a Breton name. You want to be careful about that sort of thing. Odd though you may think it, Bretons, Basques and people from the Languedoc mind quite a lot about their regional identity. They do not much like being taken for someone from the opposite end of the country.' He paused for a moment.

'I'm so glad to see that you found your own coat again, by the way,' he continued. 'That one of Pierre's was far too big. I mentioned the fact to him when I reminded him that you and Jessica had been expecting him at your flat at five – an engagement he seemed to have forgotten since it was by then five-thirty and he was heading up the Boul' Mich' for a drink with a gang of his friends quite unaware that you must have been wondering what had become of him. When I told him you had rushed home specially, he looked astonished . . .'

I could no longer stand the gleam in Anthony's eyes. I hung my head and waited. Anthony also waited. After a moment, he took both my hands in his and said, 'I assume you don't want me to continue, do you? How about trying to tell me the truth instead?'

'We were following you,' I said feebly.

271

'I am aware of that. You could hardly have been more obvious. What I want to know is *why* were you following me?'

'I wanted to know who your girlfriend was,' I said in a voice that was barely audible, 'and I wanted to know if there were lots of them or just one.'

'And what did you discover?'

'Nothing precise,' I whispered, feeling absurd.

'Which would be worse: one girlfriend or lots?' Anthony enquired.

I thought about it for a moment before answering. 'One, I suppose,' I said still staring at my lap and refusing to look at Anthony.

'Why?'

'Because if there are lots they can't be as important as all that. One seems more serious somehow.'

'What makes you think that? One could be just as frivolous as many, particularly since I already have you. You could be serious and this other woman frivolous; or perhaps it might be the other way around: she might be serious and you mere frivolity on my part.' There was laughter in his voice. I continued to study my hands, saying nothing. After a time he asked, 'Who are your suspects?'

'That woman with the hideous shoes, I suppose.'

'Which woman is that?'

'The one you are always talking to; the one who sat in the café with you at lunch-time on Monday.'

Anthony laughed. 'Do you mean poor Mademoiselle Gonthier? She *would* be shocked. Such a respectable female, too. What on earth makes you suspect her?'

'You seem to see her quite a lot. You quite often have coffee with her and she often waits for you to come out of your lectures.'

'Will you look at me for a moment,' said Anthony taking my head in his hands. 'That's better,' and he smiled. 'I suggest you turn your powers of investigation in the direction of Mademoiselle Gonthier for the short time it would take to find out all about her. She is a

272

secretary and she has kindly taken on the job of typing my book. Since I do not have time to gallop back and forth to her flat between lectures, she comes to the Sorbonne to collect bits of manuscript from me. Occasionally, if it's difficult to read, or there are complicated footnotes to sort out, I discuss it with her over a coffee or a sandwich. I'd give her an occasional lunch in any case. It seems the least I can do to repay her for the trouble she takes.'

'Oh,' I muttered. I could think of nothing to say.

'Now, who are the others?'

'Students. I don't know their names. There's a fair-haired one who always wears jeans. She's about my height and she's quite pretty.'

'Monique,' said Anthony. 'Yes, she is quite pretty. She's very bright, too; but she does not, as it happens, have a particularly pleasant character. Neurotic. Extremely argumentative. *Moins douce que toi, ma folle, ma jalouse.*' He suddenly pulled me towards him and held me in his arms saying, 'My beloved, what an idiotic creature you are. What can I do to reassure you? I am bound to talk to my students occasionally and some of them happen to be girls. The world is full of women but you must have realized by now that you are the one who interests me. If there is a problem in our relationship it is that I feel unable to detach myself from you. I feel as if I'm crawling all over you. I want to smother you; I want to drown your passive power. I want to possess you entirely.'

When we finally went to bed he held me in his arms for a long time. Then, leaning on one elbow, he looked down at me and whispered,

'Yonder beyond all hopes of access
Begins your queendom; here is my frontier.
Between us howl phantoms of the long dead,
But the bridge that I cross, concealed from view
Even in sunlight, and the gorge bottomless,
Swings and echoes under my strong tread
Because I have need of you.'

'What a beautiful poem,' I murmured.

'Robert Graves,' he replied. 'He wrote two slightly different versions of it, but this is the better one, in my opinion.'

Jessica was less easily reassured than I was on the subject of Anthony's behaviour. As soon as an opportunity presented itself, she asked André whether Anthony had ever been married.

'Good heavens, no,' André had replied, apparently.

'Has he got lots of girlfriends, do you think?' she then asked him.

'Not as far as I know,' said André. 'I'd be surprised. Highly unlikely I would have thought.'

'Has he got *any* girlfriend?' Jessica demanded.

'I don't think so. Unless, perhaps, our little Imogen . . . He's been showing a great deal of interest in her of late.'

'He seemed rather surprised by my questions,' said Jessica as she recounted this to me. 'I don't know why he was so silly with you. He probably feels that he should be keeping an eye on you and that your family will hold him responsible if anything happens. He's terribly old-fashioned, in any case, so he probably thinks it would be the end of the world if you went to bed with anyone. Whatever he was fussing about, it was obviously something to do with you being seduced rather than Anthony's character which appears to be utterly stainless. I don't think we need worry about it any more.'

I did not feel it was worth pointing out to Jessica that I had already ceased to worry and that I had put the matter out of my mind some time ago.

CHAPTER SEVENTEEN

I had always known that Anthony would have to return to Cambridge eventually but I somehow imagined that I would go with him, that he would not be able to leave me. He was right, of course, to insist that I stay and sit my finals. I knew he was right, but it did not make it any easier.

'You cannot leave without your degree after all this,' Anthony said. 'It would be insane and you've been doing so well. It would be criminal of me to allow you to do anything so stupid. You'll be finished here in the summer. You've only got a few more months to go. It's only for a short time. It's not forever. I'm not going to disappear, you know. I'm not going to vanish out of your life.' Then, seeing the tears in my eyes, he added in a gentler tone, 'Please don't make it any more difficult than it already is. It isn't easy for me, either.'

The night before he left, he said. 'Try to learn to stand on your own while I'm away. You're not a child any longer, but you're not particularly grown up either. You have always relied on Jessica, and now you have me as well; but it is time you found your own feet and had a life of your own. You can't go through life with one of us holding each of your hands. You would be very strong if you would only learn to stand on your own. I want you to become strong.

'And while I'm at it,' he continued, 'let me give you another piece of advice. Don't fall back on Jessica the moment my back is turned. It would be the easiest solution from your point of view, but it would be a mistake.

Your friendship is such that it is very difficult for anyone to approach either of you individually. I'm not sure whether you are aware of the front you put up jointly, but it can be very discouraging. You make everyone else feel excluded. Only someone as thick-skinned as I am is likely to attempt it. It would benefit both of you if you could become less dependent on one another.' Seeing that I was wavering on the verge of tears again, he said, 'Don't start crying. I can't stand it. Come here.' He put his arms around me and said, 'Please, my beloved, don't cry. We have the whole night ahead of us. Let us not spoil it.'

'I'm not going to let you come to the airport with me,' Anthony had said the following morning. 'I can't bear farewells and, anyway, this is only *au revoir*.' Seeing my expression, he laughed and pulled me towards him. 'It's no use looking like that,' he said. 'I'm not going to change my mind. In a minute, you are going to walk out of here, smiling; and you are not going to look back. I'll write to you very soon, I promise.' He kissed me and then said, 'Right. Off you go. It's time for you to leave. Go on,' he insisted. 'Just walk out of that door and don't look back.'

The sky seemed to darken as I shut the door behind me.

Two months later Paris was at war. As the *Express* was to write long after the event, '*En moins d'une semaine, dans un printemps sans histoire, une tempête a fait lever sur Paris les pavés de l'émeute, les mousquetons du pouvoir, et les idées de tout le monde . . .* ' What started lightly, with a festive air, soon turned to horror; and the carnival spirit of the early days was rapidly poisoned by fear and hate.

As I looked out at the rue des Carmes, the Friday before our exams started, I felt a twinge of pain at the thought of leaving. Paris had become home and I had been very happy there until Anthony left.

It was perhaps because I had been so happy with Anthony that I had paid little attention to the storm that had been brewing since the previous November, but I do not believe that I was alone in this. It seemed that everyone was taken by surprise. We were all aware of the student unrest: one could hardly fail to be; but everyone totally underestimated it.

Every day new graffiti appeared on the walls, some hastily scrawled, some beautifully lettered in gold paint and gothic script. Our classes were constantly interrupted. Many students no longer attended their lectures but hung around the corridors all day long, agitating against the 'consumer society', against the 'mandarins', against de Gaulle – the father-figure, still there ten years after the 'coup d'Alger'. While England was carousing through the sixties, France was attempting to overthrow its gods. Both countries were in revolt but, as always, the routes they chose were very different.

As Jessica and I sat down to lunch that Friday we had no idea that within a matter of hours the volcano would have erupted and that Paris would never be quite the same again. While we dallied over our omelettes, the closing of the faculty at Nanterre could not have been further from our thoughts. Instead, we were discussing what we were going to do when our exams were over. I was bewailing the fact that before I had become involved with Anthony, I had arranged to go back to Milan to do post-graduate work and now bitterly regretted my decision. I was just asking Jessica whether she thought it was too late for me to try to go to Cambridge instead, when our doorbell rang.

We rushed downstairs and opened the door to find Pierre, Thibault, and a group of our friends all in a state of great excitement.

'Come on, you two,' Pierre ordered. 'You're not going to miss this. I told you it would happen but you would never believe me. You never listened, but now it has really happened. It has begun.'

'What has begun?' I asked, looking completely blank.

'The revolution, of course,' replied Pierre triumphantly. 'The police have moved into the Sorbonne.'

Jessica and I stared at him, unbelieving. 'They have,' he insisted. 'We couldn't get in there at all. The police are inside and they're forcing everyone out.'

It seemed inconceivable that the police could have done anything so stupid. The Sorbonne was sacrosanct. The police were not allowed inside. It was as much a sanctuary as a church or cathedral. What on earth could have made them do such a thing? They might as well have shot a child in Notre-Dame.

Françoise Giroud was later to say, 'We shall never know what would have happened if the Rector of the académie de Paris had allowed the demonstration, organized for Friday, 3rd May, in the courtyard of the Sorbonne to take place according to the normal academic tradition: that is to say, without involving the police.' True, we shall never know; but the police *were* involved and it could only mean one thing: war.

'Hurry up!' Pierre shouted. 'You've got to come. You've got to help us. We're going to fight and we need everyone's help.'

'You're not really going to fight the police, are you?' I asked, as we all ran down to the rue des Ecoles.

'Of course we are,' yelled Pierre. 'You don't think we're going to let this pass, do you? *Tu ne veux pas qu'on laisse ces cons de flics nous marcher dessus, non? Ce sont des salauds, des emmerdeurs, des fascistes, des cons! On va les écraser. Ils n'oublieront jamais; ils le regretteront, tu verras. On va les écraser!*'

I could not stop myself remembering Enrico's warnings. During the past few months his had remained the voice of Cassandra, Pierre's the voice of student optimism.

'Marchais is right about one thing,' Enrico had said. 'They are under the impression that they are helping the workers. They are trying to identify themselves with the working classes, but it cannot work. They are all middle class. They are the bourgeois children of bourgeois parents. They have nothing in common with the working classes. The best they can hope for is to force the government to build more schools and make more room in the universities; but this is already under way, albeit twenty years too late. The interesting thing will be to see whether or not they manage to get rid of de Gaulle. I'll tell you one thing, though. Whatever happens you can be absolutely certain that in twenty years' time, all these so-called revolutionaries, all your Pierres and Thibaults, will be exactly like the people they are trying to overthrow today.'

As we ran along the rue des Ecoles, I tried to piece together what information Pierre was able to give us. The students from Nanterre, thrown out when it was closed *sine die* the day before, were today roaming the quartier Latin, many of them intending to join in the meeting being held at the Sorbonne in protest against the closing of their faculty. Knowing this, some one hundred undergraduates of the far right (our old enemies) had decided to amble up the boulevard Saint-Michel in search of these 'left-wing exiles' with the aim of teasing and provoking them. Quite what had happened then was not clear but Pierre said that he had heard that someone had set fire to a desk in the courtyard of the Sorbonne, or that there had been some sort of minor fire caused, supposedly, by the extreme right, but which the 'Occident' movement was blaming on the Trotskyists. Otherwise everything had been perfectly peaceful. About four hundred students had gathered together to listen to the head of the national students union and the representatives of the various far-left groups. Nobody had the faintest idea why the police had moved in.

When we reached the Sorbonne the place was in tumult. The police were steadily pushing the students out of the courtyard and forcing them into their armoured vans. Group after group, about twenty-five at a time, were taken off to police stations. We, like everyone else present, saw friends of ours being carted off by the *gardiens de la paix*. There seemed to be no reason for it. The students were all perfectly peaceful, there was no fighting. The operation continued until about five in the evening and it was completed without one single, unpleasant incident.

A reaction was inevitable. We were shocked and angry. All around us and up the boulevard Saint-Michel the tension mounted. People started shouting *'Libérez nos camarades!'* and 'CRS, SS!' (a mistake on our part since there were no CRS present that day). The police tried to disperse us with tear-gas. They blocked off the approaches to the Sorbonne with their vehicles. It was the beginning of six hours of violence in the quartier Latin.

Signposts were uprooted and thrown around, cobblestones ripped up and hurled in all directions, windows broken, cars placed across the middle of the road and set alight. The police used tear-gas and extreme brutality. They returned paving-stones and other projectiles thrown by the students, sometimes hitting passing cars as they did so. In a totally haphazard fashion, they laid into people with truncheons and the butts of their rifles, sometimes picking on an isolated and solitary demonstrator; they charged us at regular intervals; they called up police reinforcements.

I saw things I had never seen before.

I saw Pierre, his head a mass of dark curls, his face almost entirely hidden by a large scarf he had tied over his nose and mouth, holding a dustbin lid as a shield.

I saw a student being dragged along the cobbles by his feet, one policeman pulling him, another clubbing him with the butt of his rifle. The latter looked as if he was trying to club the boy to death.

I saw Thibault covered in blood, the front of his shirt soaking in it, but I was too far away to see where he had been hurt.

I saw a girl of about sixteen being arrested for no reason.

I saw a man lying face-down in the middle of a street, lying absolutely still and straight, his arms by his sides, his fists clenched, his legs together, his feet pointed like a ballet dancer's. I could not tell if he was alive or dead. He was surrounded by rubble, his face buried.

I saw a boy being clubbed by three policemen simultaneously. One of them held his legs, another his arms, and again it seemed as if they were clubbing him to death.

I saw a young man standing motionless, facing east, a wild head of hair, a pure profile. The left side of his face was covered in blood. Blood matted his hair above his temple. Impossible to tell whether the wound was there or much higher. Blood poured down his cheek then separated into rivulets which dripped off his chin and down his jacket. His shirt was white on one side, dark red on the other. He stood quite still, his face immobile, apparently surveying the roofs in the distance. Under dark brows his eyes blazed.

Between five o'clock and eleven o'clock in the evening, five hundred and ninety-six people were questioned before being taken off to police stations. Twenty-seven of these, we heard the following day, had been put in prison. Nobody knew how many had been hurt, but it was obvious that the total was high.

From then on chaos reigned. The courts, normally closed at weekends, functioned the next day and the next. Those who appeared in court on Saturday, Cohn-Bendit among them, were released on bail. Those who appeared in court on Sunday were given prison sentences. Worse trouble broke out on Monday. Exams were cancelled and Paris witnessed rioting which made Friday's efforts pale into insignificance. It lasted twelve hours and resulted in the whole of France condemning the police.

Every day the situation became worse and the numbers involved increased. Within ten days of the first outbreak, a million people were marching through Paris and a silence fell as they entered the Latin quarter.

We saw riot after appalling riot and our world was turned upside-down overnight. Dany Cohn-Bendit became a popular hero; Jean-Louis Barrault was thrown out of the Odéon; right-wing extremists and left-wing extremists fought side by side against the CRS; the universities ceased to function; the gare du Nord closed; the petrol ran out, as did the food supplies. Violence raged. The cobbles were torn up, the trees smashed down. Soon both public and private transport ceased. One could go nowhere except on foot. The schools went on strike, the theatres shut down. One could not cash a cheque, buy a newspaper, send a letter, watch television. No rubbish was collected, no trains left Paris. Even the weather was in revolt: the middle of May was as cold as autumn.

I remember the *nuits révolutionnaires* and someone playing the piano in the main courtyard of the Sorbonne. There was a Vietcong flag flying in the *cour intérieure*, and the statues of Victor Hugo and Pasteur held red flags in their arms.

I remember Dany Cohn-Bendit looking more Irish than German with his stocky figure and bull-like head. Under that coarse red hair he had the impish expression of a clever, naughty child. His intelligent face, alert with enthusiasm, was overflowing with laughter and happiness. Most memorable of all was his wonderful smile. He was not a person one could easily forget.

I shall also remember, as long as I live, the smell of tear-gas, at once sweet and acrid, sickly and stinging.

Clearly, these events had taken everyone by surprise, above all those whose job it was to foresee such things. They regarded the small, left-wing groups in Nanterre as insignificant, easy to isolate. They were relieved that Cohn-Bendit was a foreigner: it meant that he could be expelled from France and it was convenient to blame it on a German. They thought the mass of 'reasonable' students would refuse to join in, but they were mistaken. They thought it impossible that the UNEF (the student union movement) could be resuscitated, yet it was. It seemed improbable that the teachers and professors would join the movement yet, for the most part, they did. It was impossible, at any rate, that public opinion would sympathize, yet it did.

They should never have allowed the police to move

into the Sorbonne in the first place and, having made such an error, they should have moved them out of the whole area as fast as possible. A group of university professors, including a Nobel prize-winner, wrote an open letter to the government pleading with them to remove the police from the Latin quarter, and insisting not only that the police had started the trouble but that it continued because of police provocation.

The government did not withdraw the police.

Pierre was imprisoned early in the month and Thibault followed shortly afterwards. One of my fellow philosophy students was arrested the first day and, interestingly, he was arrested before the trouble started. The others who were arrested that first day, also before the trouble started, were never anywhere near the Latin quarter. Four of them were given prison sentences.

A lot of foreigners were picked up at the beginning. Foreigners seemed suddenly suspect. Worse still, for Jessica and me, our flat was impossible to reach a great deal of the time, the place Maubert being at the centre of some of the worst rioting every time.

Enrico moved us into an Embassy flat on the Right Bank, away from the worst of the trouble; but although we were in less immediate danger, no-one could ignore what was happening.

The hospitals were inundated and the medical world up in arms. Not only were the police brutalizing people to an unspeakable degree, they were not taking them to hospital until it was far too late to treat them and, said the doctors, the police were using a new gas, something much more dangerous than tear-gas, which was causing damage to lungs and hearts. They begged the government to tell them what chemicals were being used so that they could treat the people who were brought to them. The government and the police both denied the use of any new gas.

We heard of girls being mass-raped by the police, of boys being stripped and beaten until their genitals

283

burst. Everyone was subjected to beatings and clubbings before being put in prison and then they were squashed into cages so full of injured people that there was no room for anyone to lift an arm, let alone sit down or collapse on the floor. As the lycées became involved, more and more children, under age, ran the same risks and were exposed to the same dangers. On several occasions, I saw members of the CRS caught by students and I saw the treatment meted out to them. No one could pretend that the students behaved any less brutally. I discovered a side of humanity I could not stomach and it appeared to be concentrated in the male of the species.

Anthony was frantic. So were our parents. They wanted us to come home immediately and it had become clear, by then, that we would not be sitting our finals. There were no exams for any of us that summer. Undergraduates moved effortlessly from one year to the next, passed without test. The rest of us were given our degrees regardless of whether or not we would have passed. Some were eventually offered the possibility of coming back the following term to sit the exams they could not take in the summer, but many did not avail themselves of this opportunity.

'Our degrees are going to be absolutely worthless, do you realize?' Jessica said to me despairingly. 'Do you think that it will be any better by the autumn?'

'It doesn't look as if it could possibly improve at the moment,' I replied. 'In any case Enrico seems to think that any degrees obtained this year will be worthless, regardless of whether or not we sit the exams. He says people will be bound to assume that we never took our finals and that human nature is such that they will automatically believe we would have failed if we had taken them.'

I telephoned Anthony and he said exactly what Enrico had said. 'Go and take your exams in Milan,' he said. 'You've got a place there and they have that excellent system of being able to sit the same exams at regular intervals all though the year. You'll be able to get your degree in a matter of weeks and then proceed with your post-graduate work as you planned.' I wailed that I wanted to be in Cambridge, not Milan, but Anthony dissuaded me. 'It's far too late to apply for Cambridge,' he said. 'And anyway, you wouldn't be able to re-take your exams nearly so quickly, and the course is completely different – the Latin countries are all much more similar. It would be frightfully complicated and quite unnecessary. I'll visit you in Milan, I promise. I've got to go there at some point, in any case. In fact, I think I'll come over to Paris and make sure you and Jessica get home safely.'

A few days later, Anthony put Jessica in a plane bound for London; then he drove me home to Milan. In the autumn, Jessica chose to return to the Sorbonne, but I was persuaded to stay in Italy.

Italy

Be assured, the Dragon is not dead
But once more from the pools of peace
Shall rear his fabulous green head.

The flowers of innocence shall cease
And like a harp the wind shall roar
And the clouds shake an angry fleece.

'Here, here is certitude,' you swore,
'Below this lightning-blasted tree.
Where once it struck, it strikes no more.

'Two lovers in one house agree.
The roof is tight, the walls unshaken.
As now, so must it always be.'

Such prophecies of joy awaken
The toad who dreams away the past
Under your hearth-stone, light-forsaken,

Who knows that certitude at last
Must melt away in vanity—
No gate is fast, no door is fast—

That thunder bursts from the blue sky,
That gardens of the mind fall waste,
That fountains of the heart run dry.

                              Robert Graves

CHAPTER EIGHTEEN

Manta was a haven of peace after Paris. I arrived home exhausted, confused, and more than a little ashamed of myself for having run away from what was, I suspected, an important social upheaval: one in which I believed in theory in spite of the fact that I could neither condone nor stomach the violence. I had, by that time, spent so much time arguing with friends about whether or not the end ever justifies the means, whether violence is ever the solution, whether one was ever going to be able to change anything anyway, that I no longer knew what I really thought.

I decided to try out my ideas on my family but my parents were of no help. My father thought that all extremists, right or left, should be shot. 'If either you or Simon ever became fascist, or Communist, I would never let you set foot in this house again,' he said. My mother put on a distracted air and sighed, 'It's utterly abominable what human beings are capable of doing to one another. You would have thought that we might have progressed a bit by now: but no, we still go on fighting, as if that ever solved anything. I don't want to hear any more about it, *cara*. The whole thing is *odioso*. I find it totally depressing,' and she returned to her piano to play Rachmaninov as if to wash away unpleasant thoughts and empty her mind of all but music.

When Simon returned from Cambridge, I asked him what he thought. His attitude, predictably, was much the same as mine: troubled, muddled, guilt-ridden, cowardly; but he used as his excuse the fact that, not having

291

lived in Paris and not really understanding what it was all about, he was not in any position to judge.

Only my grandmother was prepared to discuss the matter with me. 'There are,' she said, 'two diametrically opposed ways of dealing with life: either you join in, or you withdraw from the fray. Once you have made up your mind which route you wish to take, the rest falls into place. If you withdraw, you have opted for a purely personal peace – or, if not peace, at least a certain calm you don't want disturbed. In that case, there is no point whatever in looking too closely at humanity: it merely upsets you and achieves nothing. You are better occupied concentrating on Man's achievements: music, art, literature, all the things which have risen above degradation and horror. With effort, you may be able to add to that achievement in which case your life will not have been wasted.

'If, on the other hand, you decide to join in, then you must work out how best to be useful. There are limitless ways of improving the lot of others and few of them involve violence. Obviously, doctors, teachers, scientists, social workers and so forth are all in a position to improve the human lot but these are not the only ways. Journalism can be as useful as it can be trivial, writers can draw attention to injustice, political agitators can change the mood of a society for good as well as for bad. Financial aid can achieve a great deal, though this is the easy way out for people like me who can afford to write cheques. Still, the fact that it costs the donor little in no way reduces its usefulness from the recipient's point of view.

'Since you appear to have developed a social conscience (and I am glad that you have) you must simply make sure that you use your education and your time to good purpose. It is so easy to be corrupted by trivia, to be seduced by rubbish. Don't fall into the trap of wanting to be like everyone else or, worse, competing with everyone else; ignore all that rubbish about knowing the "right" people and living in the "right" place: it's all nonsense and an unfailing sign of small-mindedness and lack of intelligence. Don't take your standards from everyone else: your standards should be far higher. To put it in its simplest terms, don't join the cocktail-party circuit, don't earn your living writing gossip columns or women's pages, don't imagine there is anything special about yourself because you are on christian-name terms with a few famous people, and avoid the media at all costs, television people in particular: their values are truly deplorable.

'But I know that you know all this.' She patted my hand. 'What you don't, perhaps, realize – and it is equally important – is that guilt is a thoroughly debilitating emotion. Don't cripple yourself with guilt. It was luck, and only luck, that you were born into a family living in comfortable circumstances, but the fact that you did nothing to earn it does not mean that it is your fault. You didn't ask to be born well-off any more than anyone asks to be born poor. There is no point in behaving as though you thought you had personally trodden on the faces of the poor. Do you think you could have been more use to society if, instead of being who you are, you were starving, penniless, uneducated, persecuted? Instead of feeling pointlessly guilty, go and do something of value with your life and thank your lucky stars that fate allowed you such an easy passage.'

Her gaze, as it always did sooner or later, shifted back to the lake. She appeared to be scanning the far shore, but I knew from the expression in her eyes that she was somewhere much further away.

'I can't think why I am rambling on like this,' she sighed after a moment. 'I'm hardly in a position to give anyone advice. I must be the least active member of the human race. I gave up long ago and I shouldn't really be here at all: but I do at least know that what money I have is not mine, that I did nothing to earn it, that it belongs to anybody who needs it. I don't know that I've been much use on this earth, but I suppose I have helped a few people financially if nothing else.' She paused for a moment and then added, 'Although I dare say they would have found someone else to help them if I hadn't been around.'

'Think what would have become of us,' I exclaimed. 'What would Simon and I have done without you? What would Mummy have done? You know we couldn't have managed without you. Don't you feel you have been useful as far as we're concerned? Doesn't that matter?'

Dragging herself back from the lake, she smiled at me. 'You have been my greatest pleasure,' she said. 'You are my only interest in life: you children and your mother.' She took my hand and squeezed it affectionately. 'Now, I think you should go and find Simon and have that game of tennis before the light begins to fade; and I shall go for a stroll. The tennis racquets have been moved, by the way. You'll find them in the chest outside the music-room.'

Twenty minutes later, as Simon and I walked towards the tennis court, we saw her down by the summer-house standing with her back to us, staring out across the water.

I had never, until then, looked at Simon objectively on a purely aesthetic level, but while we were playing tennis I for the first time noticed his striking beauty. He possessed extraordinary purity of line and expression. His tall, slim form moved about the court with the grace of a cat and his face, under his fair hair, was intelligent, sensitive and slightly drawn as he concentrated on the ball.

I suddenly remembered what a shock I had had, in our early teens, when his voice began to break and the beginnings of a beard first became visible. I had always thought until then that he would have made a beautiful girl and I hated the sudden leap into male adolescence.

Another thing I noticed, which had always been true, was that he really wanted to win. He shared with me an overwhelming determination never to do a thing badly but his panther-like movements gave away a stronger desire than this. Whereas I, having no sense of competition and only a sense of perfection, never wanted anybody to lose, Simon still wanted (although in a more civilized manner than as a child) to beat the living daylights out of me. Where, I wondered, had the rest of his frustration with the world been hidden? Into what had his fury against my father been converted? There was no sign in this tall young man of the rivalry and uncontrollable temper demonstrated by the child.

I wondered whether, during all those years at school and university, I had changed as much as Simon appeared to have done. He was the person most likely to have noticed and I determined to ask him at the first opportunity.

'You haven't changed,' he said to me later that evening, 'except for your political opinions. You really didn't have any before. Neither of us did. Have I changed, do you think?'

'Yes,' I replied. 'You seem gentler and more considerate. You used to be such a bully, and so noisy and rough. I was afraid of you quite a lot of the time.'

'Were you? Why?'

'You know I was and you know why.'

'Yes, I suppose so, but I prefer to forget. You were so terribly easy to bully,' he said apologetically.

'You had an awful temper, too. Just like Daddy. Ghastly. You don't seem the least bad-tempered any more. I can't tell you what a relief it is.'

'Do you realize that we've been separated for most of the last eleven years? That's more than half our lives to date.'

'Yes, but it hasn't made any difference except that you seem more like me now. I half expected public school to turn you into an English country gent. You know, all hunting and shooting and reactionary ideas. I'm glad you've taken up baggy corduroys, though. They suit you.'

'Not all the English are the way you see them,' said Simon. 'They're not all narrow-minded and reactionary. There are lots of interesting people at Cambridge who are not the least like that. Why don't you come and visit me there? You'd like it.'

'Yes,' I said, thinking immediately of Anthony, 'I'm sure I'd love it and it looks as if I'll have to come and visit you since you seem determined to spend years there. I want to see Anthony, in any case.'

I did not need to tell him that and he did not need to answer. We both understood perfectly well. One might have expected to become estranged after spending so much of our lives apart, but this was not the case with us. If anything, the genetic link seemed stronger now that the childhood threats had been removed and whereas, when Simon first moved from childhood to adolescence, I felt him to be less my twin by reason of his sudden masculinity, he by this time seemed to me to be simply my male counterpart and barely distinguishable from myself. Now that his childhood anger appeared to have been spent or, if not, buried very deep, our characters were almost identical. We were both shy, secretive and self-controlled and neither the difference in our sexes nor his blond beauty could hide the fact that our features were the same.

'Why have you decided to go back to Cambridge?' I asked.

'It seems the obvious place for my particular postgraduate research but, in any case, I like Cambridge. I like England. It was only school that I hated.'

Although I missed both Jessica and Anthony, the summer was easy because I had Simon. In a curious way, his presence replaced them both. The relationship between twins is an entity which can manage without others and between twins of opposite sexes this becomes doubly powerful. You have your mirror-image, your love of yourself and your dislike of yourself, your total knowledge of the other person because they are you. You are protected, flirted with, shown off to others, teased, confided in and sometimes bullied; but it all takes place on neutral territory. You are with yourself. It is a no-danger zone.

Once term began and Simon was back at Cambridge, all

my old aches reappeared. I longed for Anthony. I needed Jessica. Their letters seemed my only hold on life. Worse, my course did not start until November so I had time on my hands and nothing to distract me. I wandered the streets of Milan re-inspecting childhood haunts, visiting museums, drifting in and out of churches.

Then the winter set in and the fog descended.

Would things have turned out any differently if I had not stayed in Milan, I wondered, as Jessica and I continued to clear out the attic at Manta? Probably not, I decided. If I had returned to Paris, Jessica would still, presumably, have met Dermot; and Anthony . . . Well, that was another story.

'You never liked Dermot, did you?' asked Jessica. 'Not even in the beginning.'

'No. I couldn't stand him,' I replied, 'but then I wasn't predisposed to like him. The whole thing was such a shock. I was devastated. It seemed inconceivable that anything so important should have happened to you without my sensing it coming, without my feeling *anything*.'

'Well,' retorted Jessica, 'if you didn't feel anything, you should have known that it wasn't important.'

'It seemed important at the time,' I remarked, 'and given the number of years it took out of your life, it jolly well was important. How could I possibly not have thought it important?'

It had seemed more than just important at the time. I had just sat down to breakfast, I remembered, when I noticed the letter lying beside my plate. It had an English postmark and the flamboyant handwriting was as familiar to me as my parents' faces across the table. I helped myself to some coffee before opening it, savouring the moment, and I do not believe I even wondered why Jessica was in England when she should have been in Paris.

'Do have something to eat, Imogen,' said my mother as she said every morning. 'You can't just drink coffee. It's very unhealthy.'

My father peered irritably over the top of his copy of *The Times*. 'Really, this paper is *not* what it used to be,' he muttered. 'I think I shall have to give it up.'

As I turned over Jessica's letter to open it, my attention was caught by the name and address on the back of the envelope: *Mrs Dermot O'Flaherty*, it said, *The Grange, Chillingford, Cambridgeshire*. I looked at it, stunned, for several seconds before tearing it open. Who was Dermot O'Flaherty? What was Jessica doing in Cambridgeshire? What on earth had happened? But though I asked myself these questions, I knew in my heart of hearts, from that first horrible instant, that Jessica must have married.

Darling Imogen,

I was married yesterday in a horrid registry office. Dermot is Irish as you might guess from the name. He's an oceanographer who was working at the CNRS most of the time we were in Paris. Anthony knew him before that in Cambridge apparently, but he didn't realize Dermot was in Paris until he came over for a few days last month and bumped into him at la Coupole. He introduced me to him because I was wailing about the fact that I was missing you and everybody, and that all our friends had left, and I had nobody to talk to any more.

Anyway, Dermot is colourful and boisterous and very clever. He's also quite, quite mad. He spends a lot of time in plastic bubbles at the bottom of the sea, and I'm told he's pretty good on underwater archaeology so he knows Leroi-Gourhan and all those people.

Last week he suddenly announced that he was returning to Cambridge, so I had to come too or I would never have seen him again.

It's all been a bit of a rush and my parents weren't too pleased, but they came to the wedding anyway. As soon as we've organized ourselves a bit, you must come and stay. I've learnt to make *lasagne verde* and since it's about the only thing I know how to cook, we're going to have to eat an awful lot of it. I've also taken to painting my toenails green which makes them look more interesting.

Cambridge is terrible. Full of people who are too, too academic for words. Goodness, they are boring. You must come and see.

How is Milan? Are you learning anything? Since we always spent our entire time at Manta, I can't remember much about it except that hideous cathedral and the fact that Santa Maria delle Grazie is always shut. You really should *do* something about it. I bet they don't really have the 'Last Supper' at all and they are only pretending.

Tell your grandmother I want her to come and see us here. I know she'll say she doesn't travel any more, but she's jolly well got to, tell her. Give my love to your parents. Simon and Anthony are both about, fortunately, so I expect that between us we can drown out the dreary dons' wives.

I miss you dreadfully. Do come and see us soon.

Love,
Jessica

I put the letter down and looked out of the window. It was the end of February and the Milan sky was the colour of slate. The fog, waist-high, was drifting slightly so that the pedestrians looked ghostly and legless. Out in the suburbs I could see a cloud of pink and yellow smoke belching from the factory chimneys to form an acrid layer in the fog. The world was of that suicidal darkness that only northern Italy can produce, and an iron hand was clutching at my heart.

'You had better hurry, *cara*.' My mother's voice brought me back to my surroundings. 'You are going to be late for your classes.'

'I can't think why you want to spend the best years of your youth mouldering amongst academics,' my father grumbled. 'University is a complete waste of time. Most professors are solid ivory from the neck up.'

'I don't know how you can criticize,' I replied. 'You had already been to two other universities before you went up to Oxford.'

'It is precisely for that reason that I am perfectly placed to know that they are all a complete waste of time,' my father said.

'Do leave the poor girl alone,' my mother interrupted. 'She's late as it is.'

I fetched my coat, put Jessica's letter in my pocket, kissed my parents goodbye and descended the marble staircase. As I crossed the courtyard, the *portinaio* eyed me balefully from behind a grilled window. He buzzed the door open without saying a word. It clanged shut behind me as I wandered out into the fog.

I felt not the slightest inclination to attend my lectures. Instead, I ambled aimlessly across tram-lines, through the park, past the castle and eventually into a drab café where workmen were standing at the bar drinking *espresso* and *grappa*. I sat down, ordered a coffee, and re-read Jessica's letter.

I felt betrayed and jealous and colossally hurt. I could not believe that Jessica could have fallen in love and not even have mentioned it to me. How could she have married someone without warning me first? I felt cheated, and forgotten, and rejected. Jessica had suddenly excluded me from her life. She had left me behind, grown up, gone off without me. She had chucked me aside like an old toy wantonly abandoned. She had transferred her affections to someone else, not temporarily, but for life. I had lost her completely without prelude or farewell. Who was this man who had removed her from me? What had made her do it? What was so special about him? Why hadn't she told me?

The more I thought about it, the angrier I became; and because my sense of loss was all-embracing my anger included everyone. I was angry with my parents for having made me come back to Milan; I was angry with Anthony for having helped persuade me; I was angry with myself for having listened; I was angry with Jessica for having forgotten me the moment my back was turned. Most of all I was angry with this Irishman who had muscled in on our friendship and I was furious with Anthony for having introduced them to each other.

By the end of the day, for lack of anyone else on whom to vent my feelings, I turned in my anguish on Anthony. After dinner, as my mother played Scriabin, I sat down and wrote him an infantile letter. 'I hope,' I ended it, 'that you have at least produced someone who will make Jessica happy, otherwise I shall never forgive you.' It was as pointless an outburst as the wailing of a child under shell-fire, but it made me feel better briefly. Exhausted by all the emotion, I took myself off to bed.

Anthony wrote back:

My dear Imogen,
That was a very childish tantrum and quite unnecessary. Why should you cease to be friends with Jessica just because she is married? And what right have you to stop her being happy with anyone else? You surely didn't expect her never to marry, did you? And were you thinking of eschewing marriage yourself simply because you are friends with Jessica? I seem to remember that she was unswervingly generous when we became lovers. What kind of love do you feel for her that you cannot return her generosity? It is not a limited commodity, you know: it does not have to be removed from one person in order to be given to another. If this is not so, how can you claim to love me since you also claim to love Jessica? Love is not exclusive, it is infinite, otherwise it can hardly claim to be love; and jealousy is a most unattractive emotion which becomes you ill.
As for Dermot, who can say whether he is what Jessica needs? He appears to be what she wants at this moment and he has a great many qualities, not

301

least bags of brains. You could easily have fallen for him yourself. He has loads of Irish charm and Wildean good looks. Most women seem to find him attractive. He's very good company, although on the noisy side, and he is an excellent raconteur. I have to admit that I find him tiresome when he is in his cups – and he does have a tendency to drink too much. What else can I tell you about him? He is a curiously emotional man and he likes to be the centre of attention. I should think he'd be absolute hell to live with, but I am sure Jessica can cope. She's by far the stronger of the two.

Now, I shall be in Milan in three weeks' time and hope to see you. As you heard from Jessica, I was in Paris briefly last month and I must say it is not the same without you. In fact, it seemed quite ordinary. I can't think why I miss you – you've done nothing but disrupt my life – but I do miss you all the same.

Unsatisfied with Anthony's description, I wrote to my brother to ask what he thought of Dermot. Simon's reply added little except that Dermot was obsessively interested in world affairs.

He went to Vietnam last year. He says he wanted to see for himself, but it is obvious that he would go anywhere where there is a war. He likes the excitement and drama. He had a bad time there traipsing about with some journalist and pretending to take photographs for an English paper. They were caught in a patch of fighting when a bomb was dropped. They weren't close enough to be badly hurt but it gave him a hell of a fright. He claims to have been thrown through the air by the force of the explosion and to have ended up concussed and with a broken arm. It certainly hasn't done him any good: it has left him jumpy, explosive and wildly anti-American.

There is something of the animal about him:

powerful, interested in women, a born seducer. I don't know how one would sum him up – brilliant, drunken, shell-shocked, sexual: no doubt, all very exciting from Jessica's point of view.

I had to be content with this until I saw Anthony and could ask him more.

Anthony's visit to Milan was brief and during the few days he was there I only managed to be alone with him once. On that occasion, he had taken my face in both his hands and studied me for a while before kissing me.

'Have you got over Jessica's marriage?' he asked.

'Of course,' I replied, not quite truthfully.

'Have you?' he repeated. The intensity with which he studied my face frightened me but when I looked away, he pulled me to him roughly. 'Look at me,' he said. 'I want to know the truth.'

'Well, more or less,' I whispered, shaken.

'Sometimes,' he said, 'I feel like crushing your head between my hands and emptying it of everything. I'd like to crack·it open and spread the contents on a table and find out exactly what it is you feel for Jessica.'

To my surprise, Anthony and my father took to one another instantly. I had thought they seemed slightly wary of one another when Anthony had driven me back from Paris, but this wariness had vanished by the time they met again. When, in the course of conversation, Anthony explained that he had finally embarked on his history of the Waldensian movement but that he never had time to get on with it, my father immediately invited him to stay with us in the summer so that he could write his book 'in peace and comparative comfort'.

'If you want to escape us all,' said my father, 'you can always install yourself in this flat since we spend the whole summer on Lake Maggiore; although I have to warn you that Milan is a nightmare in August – hellishly hot and humid and everything tight shut. Still, it's there if you want it, and otherwise come to Manta where at least you'll be decently fed and there is more than enough room for everyone to keep out of everyone else's hair.'

I was overjoyed when Anthony accepted.

CHAPTER NINETEEN

Some time in March Simon wrote to say that he had decided to stay in Cambridge for Easter and around the same time I received a letter from Jessica inviting me to stay with her. It would be difficult to say whether my curiosity to meet Dermot or my desire to be near Anthony was the stronger of my motives in accepting.

I had not set foot in England for nearly four years and I felt unexpectedly emotional as I boarded the train for Cambridge. The chaos at Liverpool Street, the fact that everything was running late as usual, the stale smell and shabbiness of the English trains, the damp fields under grey skies, all brought memories flooding back.

I saw Jessica the moment I stepped down from the train. Beside her stood a large man with a wild head of dark hair. He must, I assumed, be Dermot. He made no move as Jessica ran to greet me, no move to help her when she picked up my case. He stood staring at us as we walked towards him and when Jessica introduced me to him, he said, 'So you're the beautiful Imogen,' and kissed me on the mouth before I had time to turn my head away.

He grinned as I instinctively took a step backward; and when I tried to take my case from Jessica, he stopped me saying, 'Let Jessica carry it. She's far stronger than you; stronger than any of us.' It did not occur to him, apparently, to offer to carry it himself.

'There is a reception committee waiting for you at home,' said Jessica as we bowled along in the car. 'We left Simon and Anthony making tea and crumpets. I hope they haven't burnt them all.'

The front door opened as we drove up to the house and Simon emerged, immediately followed by Anthony. 'We've made you proper English tea,' said Simon as he embraced me. 'Crumpets, watercress sandwiches, the whole works.'

The kitchen was large, warm, and pretty in a comfortably farmhouse fashion. 'It's friendly, isn't it?' said Jessica as I followed her in. 'It's the only really friendly room in the house so we live in it all the time.'

Dermot pulled out a chair for me and stood behind me while I sat down. 'You must be tired and hungry,' he remarked, putting a hand on each of my shoulders and squeezing them hard.

'We've got all sorts of plans for you,' Jessica told me as I drank my tea. 'You're going to be so busy that you'll be exhausted by the time you go home. You're going to have to learn to punt, by the way; but before we tell you all the things we're going to do with you, I want to hear about Milan. Is the university at all like the Sorbonne? And are the students really in revolt in the way they were in Paris?'

'It's not at all like the Sorbonne,' I replied. 'For a start, it is physically much more beautiful. The university building used to be a hospital in the fifteenth century, the Antico Ospedale Maggiore. I can't think why we never took you to see it when you were staying with us: very remiss of us. It is one of the most exquisite examples of fifteenth-century architecture in Milan; damson-coloured, with cloisters and tiled roofs, and a double row of arches under the vaulted ceilings. It is vast and airy, with a huge lawn in the main courtyard, and clumps of trees in the corners. You can see other courtyards beyond: another and then another, all with wonderful windows and columns and staircases. It is unbelievably lovely and remains, in spite of the recent upheavals, totally redolent of peace and learning. The riots don't have the same murderous feeling as the Paris riots. They certainly haven't impinged on the university's atmosphere of ancient tranquillity.'

306

'Why have you changed from philosophy to modern history?' asked Jessica.

'I just suddenly felt I had had enough of philosophy, and I was always torn between the two. Daddy made one of his classic comments. "It's the first sensible decision you have made of late," he said, "although you'd learn far more by travelling." Considering that he had made such a song and dance about wanting me to leave Paris and then joined Mummy and Granny in persuading me to stay, I felt quite peeved; but when I pointed this out to him he turned the tables on me and attacked me, saying that I should be learning another language. "The fact that you are unable to speak German is really an astonishing lack in your education," he said. "I can't think what we're going to do about it." It's lucky I don't take his remarks too seriously any more. He was really terrible pleased I'd taken up history. He told Granny he couldn't be more delighted.'

While I was talking, Dermot never took his eyes off me. He leant forward, his eyes on mine, as if hanging, breathless, on my every word. It was disconcerting. Under the great mass of his hair, two lambent eyes held mine. Like two dark suns they burned, liquid and beguiling. The charm of the man was too powerful to be anything but repellent. Anthony watched, snake-like, from the far side of the table.

After tea, while I was unpacking, I could hear Dermot downstairs bellowing songs and roaring with laughter. As I was brushing my hair, Simon knocked on my door and came in saying, 'You've been quite long enough. Come and join us before Dermot becomes any noisier. He has been drinking all day and he'll soon start shouting about politics if you don't come and distract him.'

'What do you really think of him?' I asked.

'Unpredictable,' replied Simon. 'He's quite fun some of the time. In fact, he can be very pleasant when he feels inclined. But you want to keep him off politics. He's convinced he is the only person who knows anything about what is going on in the world, and he becomes accusing and angry whatever you say to him. It's absolutely impossible to have a rational discussion with him. He takes it all personally; and he doesn't understand the first thing about politics which makes it worse. For an intelligent man, he says some of the stupidest things. It's like trying to have an argument with an uninformed, spoilt, hysterical child. He genuinely believes that all governments are out to crush the poor, the Jews, the immigrants; that all police forces practise torture on a daily basis; that everyone in prison is a saint; and that those of us who don't throw rotten tomatoes at the Prime Minister are all shits and persecutors. You know the sort of thing – if you happen to have a friend who is Arab, you're anti-semitic, or if you go to Spain or Portugal on holiday you condone political torture. It's frightful. And he yells and screams if you disagree. He can be unbelievably rude to people. He drinks too much, which doesn't help. He can become extremely aggressive.'

'You don't like him, in other words.'

'To be perfectly honest, I think he's poisonous.'

'How does Anthony get on with him?'

'Oh, Anthony doesn't pay any attention to his outbursts. I think he quite likes Dermot and just thinks he's childish. He admires Dermot's flair in his own field. He is supposed to be quite brilliant at what he does and Anthony likes people who are good at what they do. We'd better go downstairs soon, incidentally, or they'll wonder what has become of us.'

'Do you still like Anthony?' I asked as we headed for the stairs.

'Yes. Very much,' replied Simon.

It was obvious from the sound of voices that everyone was still in the kitchen. As we walked in, Dermot leapt to his feet, took me by the arm and said, 'Come and have a drink.' His face was flushed and his hair dishevelled but he otherwise appeared perfectly sober. 'We were talking about the King's College Christmas carol service,' he

308

said. 'I was suggesting to Jessica that she should take you along to King's at some point to hear the choir since I gather you're interested in music, and somehow we managed to be sidetracked by Anthony into discussing the Christmas carol service. Anthony is still in a rage about the man they chose as the cross-bearer.'

'They chose him,' Jessica interrupted, 'because he goes to chapel every Sunday. It seems a reasonable enough choice to me but Anthony disapproved because he had pimples.'

'He was a horrible-looking youth,' commented Anthony.

'What's that got to do with it?' I enquired.

'They never used to choose them just because they attended chapel regularly,' said Anthony, grinning. 'It's outrageous. They used to be chosen solely for their good looks.'

We all laughed and Dermot shouted, 'That's the spirit. That's what I like to hear. Keep it aesthetically pleasing and to hell with the pimply churchgoers. It's all a load of drivel anyway.' He clambered on to a chair and started to sing the *Credo* loudly in Latin.

'Do stop it,' begged Jessica. 'You've got the wrong church, anyway. They wouldn't sing the *Credo* in King's chapel.'

Dermot promptly abandoned the *Credo* and began singing *Jerusalem*.

'Oh, come on, Dermot,' pleaded Jessica. 'We all know you've got a good voice. Do sit down and be quiet. You've no idea how noisy you are,' but Dermot was determined to sing it to the end.

When he finally sat down, he turned to me and said, 'I have a very powerful voice. I'll sing you some of my Irish songs after dinner. There are some very pretty ones about Irish eyes and that kind of thing. There are some splendidly bawdy ones, too. You have Irish colouring, do you know that? Your face is Italian but your colouring is Irish. I've always thought it a heartbreaking combination, dark hair and blue eyes. I shall enjoy singing to

309

you,' and he leaned so close to me that I could smell the whisky on his breath.

I looked across at Jessica who was preparing dinner for us. She was standing with her back to us, stirring something, but she turned briefly and smiled at me.

During dinner, Dermot regaled us with funny stories. He was an excellent mimic. As we were eating our pudding, he told an exceedingly funny story against himself, and I began to see what it was that had appealed to Jessica.

Shortly after midnight, Simon rose to his feet saying, 'I think it's time Anthony and I left. Do you mind giving me a lift, Anthony? Imogen, you and Jessica are meeting me at ten tomorrow morning. I'm going to take you both round my college and then show you some of the sights. Keep your fingers crossed that it doesn't rain.'

As Simon was kissing me good-night, Dermot suddenly said, 'I don't believe you two are twins, I've never heard of twins looking so different.'

'You can't have looked at them properly, in that case,' said Anthony. 'They have very strong similarities once you overcome the difference in colouring. Anyway, we'd better be going. Come on, Simon. I'll give you a ring tomorrow, Imogen. Perhaps you'd like to have dinner if Jessica has nothing special planned for you. I'll call you in the morning, anyway,' and he bent and kissed me on the cheek.

Dermot disappeared upstairs the moment Simon and Anthony had left. I helped Jessica clear up and then sat and talked to her for a few minutes before going to bed. 'I'm so pleased you are here,' she said, giving me the smile I remembered from school, the smile she gave when she thought one might be cross with her. 'I've got so much to tell you. In fact, I hope you don't mind but I told Simon and Anthony that the day after tomorrow I want to have you all to myself for a day. Dermot is going to be in London and I want to get away from Cambridge. Anthony has said he'll lend us his car. I've learnt to drive, did I tell you? I'm not fantastically good at it but I'm a lot better than Mummy or Grandpa so you shouldn't be too frightened.'

'Where will we go?'

'I don't know yet. Somewhere beautiful where no-one will bother us. We can think of somewhere tomorrow. By the way, Mummy wants to see you, so she's coming here on Friday.'

'How lovely,' I said.

'I thought you'd be pleased,' Jessica smiled.

As we were starting up the stairs towards bed, Jessica suddenly stopped. 'Damn,' she muttered, 'I've forgotten to put out the rubbish and they come to collect it in the morning at some unearthly hour. Don't pay any attention, incidentally, if you hear noises like a medieval joust going on outside at the crack of dawn. Just turn over and go back to sleep. It'll only be the dustmen. They make the most amazing racket, for some reason. I think they must hate the idea that anyone else might still be asleep. Anyway, I'd better go down again and take out the bins. Sleep well. I'll wake you if you haven't surfaced by nine.'

I was opening the door of my bedroom when Dermot, in pyjamas, emerged from the door on the other side of the landing.

'Off to bed, are you?' he enquired. 'Anything you need? You've got water and a glass and all that sort of thing, have you? Let's just make sure,' and he pushed past me into the bedroom. 'Yes, that looks OK,' he said, squashing me against the door as he turned to leave. 'Sorry,' he laughed putting a wandering hand on my backside. 'Right. Well, sleep well.' He grinned and walked out.

At breakfast the following morning Dermot seemed morose. He gave us a lift into Cambridge with considerable ill grace and I was relieved when he dropped us outside Trinity.

We spent a pleasant day and by the time Simon left me with Anthony (with whom I had arranged to have dinner) we had caught up on most of our news.

'I understand that Jessica is planning to take you off

311

somewhere tomorrow,' said Simon as he was leaving, 'so I'll see you on Wednesday. With luck I may have a bicycle for you by then so, if it's a nice day, we could all go out into the country and have a picnic.'

'A *picnic*?' I teased. 'A real, English picnic? Shame on you, Simon. What would Mummy say if she discovered you had been converted?' We both laughed, then with one voice chanted, 'One inevitably ends up eating ghastly buns in a thistle patch.'

'What on earth are you two going on about?' enquired Anthony.

'Mummy brought us up to despise the English habit of going on picnics,' I explained. 'She thinks picnics are one of the worst aspects of English life – along with shooting, being unromantic and the fact that they like swimming in cold water.'

'Where is Jessica taking you tomorrow, in my car?' asked Anthony as soon as Simon had left.

'I've no idea,' I replied. 'She didn't seem to have the faintest idea herself. She just said. "Somewhere beautiful where no-one will bother us".'

'Clever of her,' remarked Anthony, adding, 'Your mother certainly couldn't accuse *her* of being unromantic: or was that criticism reserved solely for the English male?' Before I could answer, he murmured to himself in pensive tone, 'I wonder whether Dermot has the faintest idea what he is up against.'

'What do you mean?' I asked.

'Nothing,' he replied and then, abruptly changing the subject, 'Where do you want to have dinner? I thought I might drive you to London for the evening. Would you like that? Cambridge is somewhat stifling, I find, and the choice of restaurants is limited.'

'Yes, that would be lovely.'

'Well, we'd better be on our way in that case. Come on.'

On the way up to London, Anthony suddenly pulled into a lay-by. 'I want to kiss you before we drive any further,' he said. Then, having done so, 'Right. We can proceed now. I've been wanting to kiss you ever since you arrived. As I've said before, you are a thoroughly disruptive element in my life. I can't think why I ever became embroiled with you.'

'Well, what do you think of Dermot?' Anthony asked me over dinner.

'He's exactly as you described him,' I replied. 'You were certainly right about him wanting to be the centre of attention. I find it difficult to believe that he is such a success with women as you make out, though. He is certainly not my idea of the born seducer. Do you know, last night he barged into my bedroom for no reason, squashed me against the door quite unnecessarily, and grabbed the opportunity to feel my backside: is that his idea of seduction?'

'That was inevitable,' said Anthony. 'He seemed to be having a pretty good try at attracting your attention in the kitchen, yesterday afternoon, as far as I could see. He thinks of himself as a ladies' man. My guess is that he won't like it if you don't fall for his charm. He claims that all women fall for him.'

'What on earth does Jessica think?'

'Oh, I wouldn't worry about Jessica. She's quite able to take care of herself.'

'Do you think she's happy?'

'You're the one who should be able to answer that. If you don't know, how can I possibly tell? Perhaps you'll have a chance to ask her tomorrow.'

'You sound cross.'

'Well, I'm not cross. Only faintly irritated.'

'Why are you irritated?'

'Because I seem unable to shake Jessica out of you. She is ever-present wherever you are, either in person or in essence. Wherever I take you, the ghost of Jessica is with us. You may think me selfish, but I want you entirely to myself. I think I am going to put you on to severe rationing, starting now. For the rest of this evening we

313

are not going to mention Jessica again, all right?'

'Fine,' I said.

On the return journey to Cambridge, Anthony said, 'They're not really expecting you back tonight, are they?'

'Yes,' I replied. 'At least, I assume so.'

'Did they give you a key?'

'Yes.'

'Then they're not going to worry if you are very late – or, to be more accurate, very early. You're going to spend the night with me. I'll take you back in the early morning, before they're up, if you feel it is impolite not to be there at breakfast.'

Anthony rented a small house in Cambridge which he shared with another don. The latter, conveniently, had chosen to go away for Easter.

Once inside, Anthony seemed to relax for the first time since I had arrived in England. 'At last,' he said, taking me in his arms. 'It seems an eternity since I said goodbye to you in Paris; and Milan, though pleasant, was nothing if not frustrating.' He smiled at me. 'You're even more beautiful than you were, if that is possible. You're too thin, though. Haven't you been eating? One expects people to put on weight in Italy, not the contrary. Why have you become so skinny?'

'I don't know. I think I lost weight during last May and I've gone on losing ever since; I felt sick, or frightened, or both, the whole time. I still have nightmares about it. I find it difficult to look at anyone now without imagining them clubbing people, or beating them to a pulp, or raping girls who should be at school instead of playing at being volunteer nurses. And it wasn't just the police, although they started the whole thing. It was the students too, our friends, boys we knew, people we liked and admired. Of course, they didn't rape and do some of the things the CRS did but I swear to God they were nearly as bad. I saw Pierre and Thibault once when they caught one of the CRS. I don't even feel able to tell you

314

about it. I can't bear to remember it. I can't bear it.' The nightmare had started to return and I began to cry.

Anthony held me tight, stroking my head. 'Talk about it,' he said. 'It's better to talk about it than to bury it. What do you remember most other than the fact that you were afraid?'

'I remember the smell of tear-gas, and I remember the CRS and the other police forces: great walls of terrifying creatures in helmets charging at us with rifles and shields; and I remember the way they beat everyone up as if they were trying to smash them to a pulp, kicking them and dragging them along the cobbles and clubbing them, and clubbing them, and clubbing them as though they would never stop. They wore enormous goggles as well as their helmets – I suppose they were gas-masks of some sort – at any rate it made them look like aliens with their helmets and shields and all their equipment: straps across their breasts, buckled belts, revolvers on one hip, tear-gas on the other, and these huge rifles – at least I suppose they were rifles: nasty looking things with huge spikes on the end. I never felt we stood a chance against them.'

'What else do you remember?' Anthony asked.

'The contrast between the feeling of war and the feeling of being at a party. It was weird – a sort of street festival gone wrong. After we occupied the Sorbonne, it was unreal inside, with someone playing the piano in the *cour d'honneur* and concerts going on in some of the *salles*. There always seemed to be jazz playing in the courtyards, and the amphitheatres were full, day and night, with interminable discussions going on in them all the time – about how we were going to change the world and that sort of thing. Lots of the people there had nothing whatever to do with the university. Some of them had never set foot inside the Sorbonne before. One group threatened to sell the Puvis de Chavannes frescoes in the Grand Amphi' at one point but, fortunately, they didn't know how to peel them off the walls.

'Then there was Cohn-Bendit, too. He has a really

315

open enthusiastic face and the most enchanting smile. He crashed into me once, by accident, when he was charging at someone, head-down, like a bull. When he got me by mistake, instead of the person he had meant to flatten, he looked up and smiled his astonishing smile; then he apologized and lifted me to safety behind a barricade. His face was alight with laughter and happiness, and it was such an intelligent face. When I find the rest unbearable to remember, I force myself to think about the nice things like Dany's face and the *nuits révolutionnaires*. I suppose it's wrong of me but it seems the only way to obliterate the horror.'

I had stopped crying but Anthony continued to hold me tightly and stroke my head. 'You are so waif-like sometimes,' he said. 'It makes me feel I'm simply sheltering an orphan from the storm.'

CHAPTER TWENTY

It was five in the morning by the time Anthony drove me back to Chillingford.

'I'll bring the car back around nine so that you and Jessica can set off early if you want to,' he said as I climbed out. He waited while I opened the front door, then drove off.

As I tiptoed across the front hall towards the stairs, the sitting-room door was flung open and there, standing against the light, was Dermot. He looked dishevelled and he was plainly drunk. He hesitated for a second, then wove his way towards me with a menacing smile.

'Where have you been all night, my lovely?' he asked.

I did not answer. As I started towards the stairs, he lurched in my direction and grabbed my arm. 'Not so fast. You haven't answered my question.'

'I went to London,' I replied.

'Pussycat, pussycat, where have you been? I've been to London to visit the queen. Pussycat, pussycat, what did you there? But I can guess. And now you're here. Shall I frighten a little mouse under the stair? Shall I?'

I tried to free my arm but he tightened his grip until I winced. 'Please let me go,' I said as calmly as I could. 'You are hurting me.'

'You'll have to give me a kiss if you want me to let you go,' he said. 'Come on, my lovely. Just one little kiss.'

I tried to push him away but he was too heavy for me. His eyes were huge. They glistened in the half-light. Triumphant? Entreating? I could not decide.

His weight suddenly shifted as he lunged to kiss me,

317

his eyes blurring as he did so. As I stepped backwards he lost his balance and crashed to the floor, pulling me with him. I felt him grab my ankle as I scrambled to my feet but I kicked my foot free and rushed for the stairs.

'Damn you!' he yelled. 'Damn and blast your innocent eyes!'

As I reached the top, Jessica came out of her bedroom saying, 'What on earth is going on?' At that moment I could have killed Dermot for putting me in a situation where I had to lie to her.

'I bumped into Dermot by mistake. I'm terribly sorry. It was so dark down there and I didn't see him in time. I tripped on the carpet and knocked him over. It was stupid of me. I'm dreadfully sorry.'

'Poor you,' said Jessica. 'It's all my fault. We had a silly row last night while you were out and it put him in a rage, so he started drinking and wouldn't come to bed. Don't worry. It doesn't last. He'll be fine when he's had some sleep.'

'I'm going to sleep for a few hours myself, if that's OK,' I said. 'Anthony said he'd bring the car back around nine in case we wanted to set off early.'

'Fine. Dermot has to leave for London at nine thirty so I'll get him to bed and wake you both at eight.'

As I was shutting my bedroom door, I heard Jessica laughing. 'Oh, Dermot, you do look funny,' she giggled. 'You are a fool. I wish you could see how silly you look.' I could hear Dermot growling in the background but this did not, apparently, upset Jessica. She was still trying to stifle her giggles as she helped him upstairs. 'Don't be absurd,' I heard her saying just outside my door. 'It's too late. You must have some sleep or you will never make it to London. You should have come to bed at the right time instead of going off in a huff.'

The door across the landing closed and silence descended.

Jessica woke me with breakfast on a tray. She sat on my bed and talked to me while I drank my coffee.

'Anthony should be here with the car soon and then we can go,' she said. 'I hope you're not utterly exhausted. I want you to be at your best.'

'Where are we going?' I asked.

'That's a surprise,' she replied, 'but I've put all sorts of delicious things into a hamper in case we get lost. I'm not very good at map-reading and I have to concentrate on driving so I never seem to have time to read the signposts. I'm counting on you to do all that which is why I want you to be feeling wonderful. Anyway, I've prepared for the worst. We have masses of smoked salmon and champagne, and that sort of thing, in case we end up in the middle of nowhere, or stranded in some horrid place with nothing but cafés and Wimpy bars.'

I assumed, because the house was unusually quiet, that Dermot must already have left for London; but when I wandered downstairs, I discovered him sitting in the kitchen reading the morning papers. He appeared to be in a cheerful mood and it was difficult to believe that a few hours earlier he had been blind drunk. If he remembered anything about it, he acted as if nothing had happened. As I walked in, he greeted me with a sunny smile and said, 'Hello, young lady. I hope you slept well. Do you want any of these papers? You can have them all in a moment, in any case, as I shall have to be off shortly. There's some coffee over there, on the Aga, if you want it.'

'I've already had some, thank you,' I replied. 'Jessica was kind enough to bring me some in bed.'

'Fine. Well, you've chosen a good day for your expedition by the looks of it. They say it's going to be fine and reasonably warm all day. Not your idea of warm, of course, but warm for the time of year in this country.'

I heard a car pulling up outside as he said this and a moment later the doorbell rang. 'That must be Anthony,' I said.

Jessica shouted from the top of the stairs, 'Can one of you answer that, please? I'll be down in a second.'

Dermot opened the door and seemed delighted to see

Anthony. 'Hello, dear boy,' he said in mock-pompous tones. 'You've arrived at the right moment. Perfect timing. I'm about to leave for London so I'll give you a lift back into town on the way. I must say, it's extremely civil of you to lend the girls your car. What were you going to do? Get the bus back to Cambridge?'

'Either that, or ask Jessica to run me back on her way,' replied Anthony.

'Well, come with me. Best to leave women to their own devices I always feel.'

Jessica appeared at this moment, looking particularly pretty under a large hat. She had another hat in her hand and a basket on her arm. She threw the second hat at me and said, 'That's for you. One shouldn't visit beautiful places unless one is wearing a hat. Imogen and I are leaving now,' she announced to the two men. 'Thank you so much for the car, Anthony. You're a true friend. Come on, Imogen, we're in a hurry. Bye you two,' she shouted at Dermot and Anthony as we scrambled into the car, but before they had answered we were on our way.

'Why are we in a hurry?' I enquired as we bowled along.

'We're not really,' replied Jessica with satisfaction. 'We were only in a hurry to be on our own. Now that we are alone, we can do exactly as we please. I'm taking you to Ely, by the way. I want you to see it rising out of the fens.'

'Have you been there before?' I asked.

'No. That's why I wanted to go there with you. I want to see it with you, not with anybody else. The fens are full of magic and ghosts, you can be sure, so you are utterly suited to them. You have that Will-o'-the-wisp aspect which comes from having spent so much time on Italian lakes in the mist. At least, I assume that's what caused it; that, and your grandmother. You should feel quite at home in the fens; and together we shall find the Isle of Ely. I imagine it to be exactly like all those places in Trollope, full of canons in flat, broad-brimmed hats wandering around the cathedral close; and the

320

cathedral will be perfect – a happy, self-confident cathedral that has never had to prove itself because it has always been secure and much loved.' She paused for a second and smiled to herself. 'If it isn't like that, I shall take you away immediately.'

It was not a long drive from Cambridge to Ely, but Jessica managed to make it last hours by embarking on endless detours to investigate side roads which she thought looked enticing, or farmhouses seen from a distance which she thought looked pretty and deserving of closer inspection. After a while she said, 'I brought some breakfast with us – coffee and croissants – in case you didn't enjoy being forced to wake up and eat when you'd only just gone to bed. If you don't feel like a second breakfast, you'll have to pretend it's elevenses, because I want to stop and sit in that field.'

We lay in the grass in silence for a time. The sun was surprisingly warm and there was no sound except for the chirping of birds. It reminded me of my early childhood at Manta when I used to lie in the long grass beyond the orchard, staring up at the sky, knowing that I was hidden by the height of the grass around me. It gave me a sense of great freedom and I would rejoice at the knowledge that no-one could see me as I watched the white wisps of cloud scudding across the sky.

The same feeling of freedom and exaltation returned to me in that Cambridgeshire field and I was certain that Jessica, lying beside me, had come here for precisely the same reason. She wanted to breathe. She was in full flight from captivity.

Suddenly, she broke the silence. 'I'm pregnant,' she said. 'Isn't it lovely?'

'Yes,' I replied. 'I guessed you were and it is lovely.'

'You're going to be its godmother. You realize that, don't you?'

'Of course. And I shall take it very seriously. Is Dermot pleased?'

'I haven't told him yet. I couldn't tell him before I told you, could I?'

'Who is going to be godfather?' I asked.

'Simon, of course. But I suppose I'll let Dermot choose someone too.'

'What does it feel like?'

'It feels self-contained and peaceful. The outside world suddenly becomes redundant.'

'Are you happy? I mean, happy about everything, not just this?'

'Yes, I think so. Except, as I say, the outside world becomes redundant. I don't really need other people. Except you, of course, but you are part of the inside world.' She smiled, then reached for one of the hats and put it over my face. 'Come on,' she said, 'you've had quite long enough looking at the sky. We're supposed to be going to Ely, or had you forgotten?'

Ely was precisely as Jessica had painted it from imagination. We saw the cathedral from a distance, rising up out of the fens, like some fairy-tale city coming out of the mist.

'Goodness, how eerie and wonderful,' whispered Jessica. 'It makes one think of King John, for some reason, and marauding Vikings; and Will-o'-the-wisps, of course.'

Ely itself was not eerie; rather, it was tranquil with the peace of another century and the solid, God-fearing respectability of *Barchester Towers*. The cathedral was magnificent, yet quite devoid of the overbearing grandness of the majority of European cathedrals. It seemed the ideal place for family worship, warm and welcoming. For once, Jessica's use of the word 'friendly' seemed apt; and the cathedral close was, as she had expected, pure Trollope. Rubicund clerics pottered in and out; and canons in broad-brimmed, flat, circular hats sauntered across the grass with tomes in ancient bindings clutched under their arms.

'I see, now, why Grandpa was always so keen on Trollope,' remarked Jessica. 'This must be the most reassuring place left on earth. The last relic of less troubled times. If we ever live together again, I'd like it

322

to be here. Perhaps when we're old ladies, cantankerous and long-since widowed, we'll end up here.'

'I thought we were going to push each other in wheelchairs along the promenade des Anglais and ride motorbikes to Monte Carlo to gamble away our fortunes,' I teased.

'Yes, we are going to do that,' replied Jessica seriously, 'but we'll do that in winter when it's too cold here and then we'll come here in summer when the tourist hordes move into the south of France and it all becomes too crowded.'

We wandered about Ely until three in the afternoon, at which point Jessica said, 'Let's drive out in to the fens and find somewhere perfect for a late lunch.'

Half an hour later she stopped the car and we carried the picnic basket and rugs down a track to a clearing well hidden from roads and human habitation.

'Do you think your mother would change her views about picnics if she were lying here on the grass drinking champagne with us in the afternoon sun?' asked Jessica.

'No,' I replied. 'She would say, "Smoked salmon and champagne are always delicious, darlings, but don't you think we'd be more comfortable lying in a hammock at Manta?" She hates lying in fields. It makes her feel under constant threat. She imagines that irate farmers and herds of bulls are about to burst upon her at any instant. She wouldn't appreciate the scenery that much, either. She doesn't like the English countryside. She hasn't spent enough time here. English views only grow on one with time; one doesn't fall in love with the Englishness of it all at first sight. At least, I didn't; and nor did you if I remember correctly. You were always going on and on about how you missed Maryland and Virginia and the Potomac and all that stuff; and I used to feel unbearably homesick looking out at those beautiful school grounds. They didn't seem the least bit beautiful to me in the beginning. The sight of those lawns and cedars used to fill me with gloom and despondency and

I simply longed for the poplars and willows of my Lombardy plains.'

'Imogen, what are we going to do about you and Anthony?' asked Jessica, suddenly serious. 'It's hopeless for both of you living in different countries. I can see you wilting for lack of him. Can't you find an excuse to come and live here?'

'Not really. Not until I've finished at Milan University, anyway. And even then, what could I do here?'

'Is it true that your parents have invited him to Italy for the summer?'

'Yes. I thought it was my father's idea but, according to Mummy, Simon had already suggested it to Daddy.'

'That was kind of him. I think he's as worried about you both as I am. He likes Anthony a lot, so I imagine he approves of your choice. He says your father likes Anthony, too.'

'Yes, he does. It's only Mummy who doesn't.'

'Doesn't she? Why?'

'I don't know. I don't know what she really thinks. She is very guarded about him.'

'And what about your grandmother?'

'She hasn't met him, but she knows about it, of course. She took one look at me when I came home from Paris and said, "Darling child, I can see you're in love." There didn't seem to be much point in denying it and I wouldn't have fooled her in any case.'

'It will be interesting to see what she makes of him. I shall feel so envious thinking of you all at Manta. Goodness, I wish I could be there too.'

On the way back to Cambridge, Jessica told me her plans for her baby. 'If it's a boy, it's going to be called Sholto and if it's a girl she'll be Sophie. I'm going to wrap it in swaddling clothes so that I don't have to worry about whether I've bought all the right bits and pieces. Don't you think that's a good idea?'

CHAPTER TWENTY-ONE

'Oh, God, something awful must have happened,' said Jessica as we turned into the short drive at Chillingford Grange.

Standing in front of the door were the remains of Dermot's car. We rushed into the house and found Anthony and Simon waiting for us. Before we could say anything, Anthony said, 'It's all right. It's not as bad as it looks. Dermot has a broken leg, a bump on the head and a few cuts, but he's not seriously damaged.' Seeing Jessica's ashen face, Anthony put his arms around her and she burst into tears. It was only then that I noticed that he had a huge bruise on one side of his face and a cut over his eyebrow.

'What happened?' I asked.

'When we left you this morning, or rather when you left us,' replied Anthony with a sardonic smile, 'Dermot kindly gave me a lift back to Cambridge. We had barely set off before he apparently thought he saw a lorry coming at him full speed on the wrong side of the road. He must have been very tired because there wasn't a thing to be seen. At any rate, he thought he had no choice but to drive off the road which he proceeded to do. He went into a field and hit a tree but by that time the car was going quite slowly, fortunately, so it suffered rather more than we did.'

I could see from the expression in Anthony's eyes that he was not telling the whole story. He made it perfectly clear that I shouldn't ask any more questions. Simon, too, cast me a glance indicating that we could talk about the whole thing some other time.

'Why is the car in front of the house and not in a field or a garage?' asked Jessica, who had by this time sat down but appeared to be in a state of shock. I thought it interesting that she had not enquired as to Dermot's whereabouts.

'A startled farmer who was trying to plough, or spray or something of the sort when we charged into his field very kindly allowed me to use his telephone and then, when Dermot had been taken to hospital, dragged the car out with his tractor and brought it back here.'

'Dermot's in hospital?' Jessica leaped to her feet looking frantic. 'What are we doing here? We must go to the hospital. Come on.'

'I think you could do with a drink first. You look as if you need a stiff brandy,' said Simon. 'I promise you, Dermot is quite all right. We've both seen him. He was in high spirits when we left but I should think he'll be sleeping by now. He must have had a fright as well as a hefty bump on the head and he claims not to have been to bed last night, so if I were you I'd let him sleep.'

Nothing, however, would dissuade Jessica from leaving immediately, so we all piled into Anthony's car ('I'll drive, if you don't mind, Jessica,' said Anthony. 'No reflection on your driving but I feel safer driving myself after this morning'), and set off for the hospital.

Dermot was lying in bed looking exceedingly pleased with himself, his right leg in plaster strung up to some contraption, and a large bandage tied at an angle around his head. 'Well, you've taken your time to come and see me,' he bellowed at me. 'While you two were playing truant, I was nearly killed.'

'Oh, Dermot,' said Jessica, putting her arms round him. 'Don't make me feel any worse than I do. I'm terribly sorry.'

'I hope you brought me something to drink,' continued Dermot. 'It's all very well being surrounded by pretty nurses, but they've trussed me up like a chicken and they won't give me a drink. I could do with a large Scotch or two.'

'If you hadn't drunk so much, it wouldn't have happened,' Jessica replied. 'Anyway, you know you're not allowed to drink in hospitals.'

'I think we should leave these two on their own for a bit,' Anthony suggested. 'I'll take Simon and Imogen off for an hour and then come and collect you and drive you home,' he said to Jessica.

Once we were outside again, Simon said, 'Do you mind if I leave you two and go back to my college? I'm supposed to be having dinner with the man who is lending Imogen a bicycle. He'll wonder what on earth has become of me. I'm already late. I'll ring tomorrow.'

'Are you all right?' I asked Anthony as soon as we were on our own. 'It looks as if you had quite a bad bump, too.'

'I'm perfectly OK except for a headache,' said Anthony. 'Let's go and have a drink. How was your expedition?'

'Lovely. We went to Ely. It's extraordinarily otherworldly. Have you ever been there?'

'Frequently. It's restful to the spirit, isn't it? What did you think of the cathedral?'

'I loved it. It wasn't awesome in the way cathedrals usually are. Just very beautiful.'

We went to Anthony's house for a drink but instead of drinking lay in each other's arms for an hour. 'I missed you atrociously today,' murmured Anthony. 'It is bad enough being separated from you when you are in Italy; but to be separated from you when you are on the doorstep is intolerable. I felt quite cross with Jessica for having so selfishly removed you. I wouldn't care to be in her shoes tonight, though; Dermot has made up his mind to blame the whole thing on her for some reason.'

'What actually happened?'

'He must have been exceedingly drunk. The odd thing is that it didn't show at all until he started imagining herds of cattle round every bend. He really will succeed in killing himself if he keeps this up much longer. I tried to persuade him to let me drive and he flew off the handle. Then he yelled, braked violently, cursed a few times and drove off the road. It was only because I grabbed the wheel and pulled it hard in my direction that we weren't both killed. I trust it was a salutary lesson for him, but my guess is that he will choose to forget all about it.' He pulled me towards him and held me in silence for a while.

'Shouldn't we be going to collect Jessica?' I asked eventually.

'Yes, we should, I'm afraid. Do you think she would mind if I stayed the night in Chillingford? I don't think it would be fair to take you away and leave her on her own tonight, do you?'

'No; but I'm sure she wouldn't mind you staying. I'll ask her if you like.'

'No, I'll ask her myself, thank you. I don't need a go-between, my dear. Come on, we'd better be on our way.'

Dermot was asleep when we returned to the hospital, and Jessica was sitting beside his bed in tears. 'I told Dermot I was pregnant,' she said, 'and he was furious.'

'I wouldn't pay too much attention,' said Anthony gently. 'He's had a considerable shock and it was perhaps not the best time to tell him. I'm sure he's delighted really. You've had quite a shock, too. Would you like me to take you home, or would you rather we took you out to dinner somewhere and cheered you up?'

'I'd like to go out somewhere, just the three of us. That would be lovely.'

During dinner, Jessica regained her spirits. 'It's just like being back in Paris,' she said. 'I wish we could all be back in Paris again.'

At one point she asked Anthony the question I had half wanted to ask all evening. 'Why was Simon there when we came home?' she demanded. 'And where is he now?'

'He's having dinner with someone from his college in order to wheedle a bicycle out of him for Imogen,' Anthony replied. 'As for why he was there, I had arranged to have lunch with him so when I turned up and told him what had happened, he offered to go out to the house during the afternoon while I went back to the hospital. We were both worried that you might come back and see the state of the car and imagine we were dead.'

Jessica foresaw Anthony's question. As we waited for the bill, she put on her pleading look. 'You couldn't be mean enough to leave us on our own tonight,' she said. 'I want you to be in the house and Imogen needs you. I wouldn't suggest it if Dermot were there because he can be funny about things like that, but it's so lovely to be all together again that I don't want it to end.'

The house seemed extraordinarily silent with Dermot absent. Jessica looked weary and very pale. 'Do you mind if I go straight to bed?' she asked. 'I don't feel terribly well, suddenly. I don't think the baby liked that wine.' She kissed us both goodnight and started slowly up the stairs.

It was clear, the following morning, that Jessica was not well. Although she tried to make light of it, she was obviously in pain and Dermot's return did nothing to help. The fact that his leg was in plaster made him feel deserving of attention and, like a child with an Elastoplast, he wanted to show it off every minute of the day.

He had us both running in circles from the moment he arrived home, and the fact that Jessica was not at her strongest exasperated him. I kept begging her to go to bed but each time Dermot exploded, 'Why should she go to bed? There's nothing the matter with her. If she hadn't been so careless as to become pregnant, she wouldn't be feeling tired and most women make less fuss about it. Good God, the world is full of pregnant women working the fields and planting rice and what not and they're perfectly all right. What is all this nonsense? I'm the one who is unable to move. Blasted nuisance. Can't even work.'

I tried to fetch and carry in her stead, but Dermot was having none of it. It was Jessica he had elected to have as

329

handmaiden and he wished to be waited on by her, not by me.

'If you were doing it to please me, it would be different,' he growled at me once. 'But you're doing it to please her, aren't you? And I think you and I already have a little score to settle, do we not? Maybe we should deal with that matter first.' He grabbed my arm and tried to pull me towards him.

'Oh, for God's sake, leave me alone,' I snapped at him.

'Still very high and mighty, madam, aren't we?' he sneered. 'Then Jessica had better drive me into Cambridge. I've got to teach.'

'Dermot, for heaven's sake, she can't drive today. She should be in bed. Anyway, you no longer have a car. Can't you cancel it, or get people to come here, or something? She had a frightful shock yesterday and shocks are bad for pregnancies.'

'Who asked her to get pregnant? I don't want any bawling babies around this place. She made her bed; let her lie in it.'

I heard a sob, looked round and discovered that Jessica had been standing in the doorway, listening. She turned and fled.

'Jessica!' roared Dermot. 'Ring the garage, get hold of a car – rent one, borrow one, I don't mind – and take me to Cambridge. I have students attempting to learn something, people needing me, and all you two can do is snivel!'

I organized a taxi for Dermot, watched with relief as he departed and then tucked Jessica up in bed. She looked at me with huge eyes and I could barely stand the pain in them.

'I'm losing it,' she whispered. 'I'm losing the baby. I know I am.'

The end of my stay in Cambridge was overshadowed by Jessica's miscarriage. Her mother arrived the moment she heard and instantly built a wall of protection between her daughter and Dermot. He subsided beneath her cool charm, knowing his weapons were not adequate against hers. I knew Jessica would be all right as long as her mother was there.

As I left, Dermot was holding Jessica in his arms and telling her he loved her.

Manta

CHAPTER TWENTY-TWO

'Goodness, this is exhausting,' said Jessica, sitting down on the cushions again. 'I'm going to need a drink soon. This is obviously going to take us all day.'

'The trouble, I think,' said I, picking up the threads of our earlier conversation as I chucked a couple of hats and a bundle of letters at her, 'is that we were brought up to admire brains and talent rather than character. We always loved people who were good at what they did. We *only* loved people who were good at what they did. Dermot, after all, was exceedingly good at what he did. Even I would admit that he was interesting when he talked about his own subject. He was amusing when he wanted to be; and he was good-looking. All that was wrong with him was that he was unspeakably selfish and he drank too much; but one could say that about a lot of men.'

'You wouldn't put Anthony in that category, though, would you?' asked Jessica.

'No, I don't think so. He certainly didn't drink too much but I'm not sure about the selfishness. I didn't know him long enough to find out. To this day I don't really understand it. I really thought he loved me. I honestly and truly believed he loved me as much as I loved him.'

'He did,' sighed Jessica. 'He loved you. There's no doubt about that.'

'Then how do you explain what happened?' I asked. 'I simply don't understand it.'

'I don't either,' said Jessica. 'I never did. I don't think it was as important to him as it was to you. I don't think these things are important to men. I don't understand it at all. They quite casually, and for no apparent reason, wantonly destroy what matters most to them. And then they wonder what has happened. They don't even know why they did it half the time – just for a change, or for fun, or not even for fun. Most of the time they don't think it was worth it afterwards. It all seems to be quite meaningless to them. It is difficult, sometimes, to credit them with any intelligence at all. But I think it was more complicated in Anthony's case. In fact, it obviously was more complicated. He must have tried to explain, didn't he? You must have felt something was different about him that summer. Didn't anything warn you?'

I tried to remember. There had been signs I had missed, there were moments when I felt uneasy, but I did not remember having felt any great sense of foreboding. Had Anthony seemed in any way different when he arrived? I did not think so. I described what I remembered of it to Jessica to see whether she would have been quicker at picking up the clues.

It had been hot for a month before the holidays started, but that day we knew we were in for a storm. The sultry weather of the day before had turned oppressive and the sky was dark. As I helped my mother close the shutters of the apartment, the clouds were amassing and the air was still. Milan lay torpid as I looked out of the window and the city was bathed in a yellow-grey hue.

'You'd better start ahead with the luggage,' my mother said to my father. 'I'll take Imogen to the airport in the Renault and come on from there.'

'You'll never make it to Manta before the weather breaks,' my father said. 'Are you sure you wouldn't like me to collect Simon and Anthony?'

'No,' my mother replied firmly. 'I always like seeing the brats reunite.'

By the time Simon and Anthony had arrived at Linate, the first flash of lightning had shot across the sky.

Seconds later, there was a huge crash overhead and we had only just managed to pile the luggage in the car when the rain began. All the way to Manta the storm continued, the rain hurled down, Vulcan raged about the skies. As we reached the lake, the noise subsided but the downpour continued as heavily as ever. We could just make out the Borromeo Islands as we drove towards Manta, but many of the things I wanted to point out to Anthony were obscured by the rain.

I remember my grandmother waiting in the doorway, hiding her curiosity behind a gracious air; and my father, looking vaguer than usual, embracing me warmly as if he had not seen me for months.

'You must all be exhausted,' he had said to us collectively, 'so I don't think we'll change for dinner tonight. We can return to civilized habits tomorrow,' and Anthony had cast me an amused glance which seemed to say, 'My God, in this heat?'

My grandmother had placed Anthony next to her at dinner. Her obvious contentment at having all her family about her cast a warm glow over the evening and I watched her with interest as she surveyed us all in stately fashion. I wanted to know what she thought of Anthony. She looked interested in what he was saying, and mildly amused quite a lot of the time. She knew a surprising amount about the Waldensians, it transpired, and discussed the subject with him at some length.

'Your general was not a Waldensian, of course,' she said. 'He simply went to live among them and took up their cause. But you know that, I am sure.' Then, after a pause, she added, 'A very courageous people of high moral character. I have friends in the high valleys if it would be of any help to you. Like all persecuted people they have tended to keep themselves to themselves and a great deal of their history has been passed on from father to son without written record. They could tell you some remarkable tales. It might help fill in the gaps in your story.'

My grandmother retired to bed shortly after dinner, saying, 'Well, my darlings, it's lovely to have you all home again. Clémence has left more coffee in the kitchen should you want it and you know where the drinks are. Forgive me for abandoning you but I like to read for a while before I go to sleep. I'll see you all at breakfast.'

I followed her upstairs, shutting the door of the drawing-room on the others as I went. 'Is it all right if I come and talk to you for a bit?' I asked her as we reached the first landing.

'*Certo, cara mia,*' she replied, smiling. 'I rather thought you might want to,' and she took my hand and patted it.

I sat on the end of her bed while she brushed her hair. 'Do you like Anthony?' I asked.

She left her dressing-table and came to sit beside me. 'He is charming,' she said, 'and very good-looking. It's not surprising you have lost your heart to him. I would have done the same.'

'I feel as if I can't live without him,' I said.

'*Lo so, cara mia, lo so, l'ho capito.* I know, my darling, I know, I can see,' and she smiled at me, then looked down and appeared to study her hands for a moment. Her posture, always so upright, seemed slightly bowed as she returned to her looking-glass.

That was the beginning of our Italian summer. It was more like a honeymoon than the end of an affair. All along the lake shore the gardens were in bloom. There were other houses like ours, with stone steps winding down to the water, and camellias and tiger lilies to be glimpsed behind walls. There was the constant lapping of water in the background and we ate watermelon and peaches, with the juice running down our fingers. I remember swimming in the Ticino and nearly being swept away by the current, and the dragonflies flitting here and there in the sun.

There was that expedition to Isola Bella. Anthony had

not been overly impressed by the *palazzo*. Simon came back to look for us at one point and was embarrassed to walk in on us kissing in a corner.

'Did Imogen tell you that Napoleon and Joséphine slept in that bed in 1797?' Simon asked as if to lighten the atmosphere.

'The number of beds those two slept in would fill a continent,' remarked Anthony. 'It looks extraordinarily uncomfortable to me. I must admit that I prefer the gardens to the *palazzo*. I don't think the combination of highly ornate and Empire furniture is an unqualified success. Neither of them is my favourite style at the best of times. Shall we go downstairs and see the famous *grotte*?'

Once down in the so-called caves, Anthony gasped in horror. 'Good God,' he exclaimed, 'how could anyone have built anything so devastatingly ugly? What on earth have they used on the walls?'

'They're made of lava and marble and something I don't know the name of in English – *tufo* – it's some sort of stone,' I replied. 'I think it's the lava which makes it so particularly unpleasant. I knew you'd hate these rooms. I've always detested them. What you might like to see are the unicorn tapestries: not as perfect as the ones in the musée Cluny, but lovely all the same. The unicorn was the Borromeo symbol, incidentally.' I was about to head upstairs again when Anthony held me back, pausing to look at a figure of a sleeping divinity.

'It reminds me of you,' he said and then whispered, 'Do you think we could disappear somewhere together this afternoon?'

He repeated this request during lunch. We were sitting with Simon outside a restaurant in Stresa and Simon had turned away from us briefly in order to say something to the waiter. Anthony put a hand on my arm and said, very quietly, 'I want to spend this afternoon alone with you.' He had removed his hand before Simon turned back towards us.

During lunch, Anthony's little finger occasionally stroked the back of my hand under the table.

If it had not been for Simon accompanying us everywhere and tactfully disappearing whenever he thought we wanted to be alone, Anthony and I might not have had much time on our own that summer. As it was, Anthony worked a good deal of the time and then Simon and I would go sailing together, or play tennis, or swim. I wanted to thank him for making it easier for me and Anthony, for acting as cover and chaperon, but whenever I attempted to say something he brushed it aside as if he did not wish to discuss the matter. It was the first time I had ever felt that I did not know exactly what he was thinking and I found the experience distressing.

As the summer progressed, Simon seemed to become more and more remote. It was as if, in the process of growing up, we had each had to amputate a limb. When I mentioned this to Anthony, he looked thoughtful but said nothing; but my grandmother, never slow to pick up her grandchildren's moods, was patently worried by the situation. I overheard her, one evening, saying to Anthony, 'I have contacted my friends in Piemonte and they would be delighted to give you any help they can if you feel like visiting them. I think it would be good for Imogen and Simon if you went away for a few days. I am sure you are aware that twins have a more complicated relationship than other siblings. They need time together. Time on their own.'

I was unable to see Anthony's expression because he and my grandmother were walking away from me towards the tennis court, but whatever he replied seemed to reassure her for she nodded her head in agreement before they disappeared from sight down an alley of cypress trees.

The evening before Anthony left for Piemonte, as we walked along the lake shore at dusk, he put his arm around my shoulders and drew me towards him.

340

'I want you to know,' he said, 'that whatever happens I love you very much. But you mustn't try to turn it into a conventional set-up. You mustn't run your life to suit me. We are not a couple in the classic sense. You must be free to live your life and love other people. You mustn't become so attached to me that you can't love anyone else.'

'But I don't want to love anyone else,' I replied.

'You will, though, and you must. I am not suited to conventional arrangements. I'm not the marrying kind and I don't want to live with you permanently. You must realize that. It doesn't mean that I don't love you, but we live in different countries and our day-to-day lives are very different. You still have a lot to discover about yourself and about life. You are very young and you must be free to explore. I have done my exploring and I am very set in my ways. I've been a bachelor too long to change; and although your attachment to me touches and pleases me, to be honest it also worries me. You want more from me than I can offer. I don't want to be pinned down. I don't want to feel responsible for you. I want us to go on loving each other without being tied down by it. When we are not together, we must be able to live our lives as we wish, without the fetters that bind most couples. We should be able to love one another without restrictions and rules.'

'But we lived together in Paris, to all intents and purposes, and it didn't create any problems, did it? You seemed incredibly happy to me. I don't believe you found it restrictive. You certainly didn't give that impression.'

'No, I didn't find it restrictive and, yes, I was extremely happy. Happier, probably, than I have ever been. But we both knew it was only for a limited time. That always gives an added poignancy to any situation. We were living for the moment. And there was the added fact that I was bowled over by your physical beauty. I still am. You are astonishingly beautiful. And then, like all men, I suffer from the desire to seduce. I like conquest. But I suddenly realized at Easter, when

341

you were in Cambridge, just how selfish I had been to try to keep you for myself when I had no intention of living with you permanently. You wouldn't be happy living with me in Cambridge, in any case. It was very different in Paris because you had your own life already established. Your days were taken up with your own pursuits, you had friends of your own and, as I say, we both knew it was temporary. You are not suited to living in England. You know it isn't where you want to live. You would simply fall back on your relationship with Jessica; and I would find myself living in a threesome again – or worse, a foursome, with Dermot hanging around too. You must see that it couldn't work.'

Desperation had overtaken me as Anthony was saying this but I tried to keep the anguish out of my voice as I asked, 'What are you trying to say? That it's all over?'

'On the contrary. That is precisely what I do not want. I was trying to explain it to you so that you would not misinterpret it. I want us to continue just as before, I want us to continue to be lovers, I want to be able to go to bed with you whenever we meet, but I don't want to feel guilty about you. I don't want you to think of it as anything other than it is, wonderful, happy, exciting, but not something leading to marriage and not something which excludes you from other relationships.'

'You mean that you want to be free to have other relationships. Is that what you mean?'

'Well, I must be free, too. After all, we are unlikely to see each other that often and nobody normal can live in total celibacy for the major part of every year. What I'm trying to say is that the other relationships would not in any way impinge on ours. They would be entirely different and they shouldn't affect us.'

'But you can't do that if you really love someone. You don't want to go to bed with other people. You can only go to bed with lots of people if you don't love any of them. I can't think of anything more horrid. I don't want to go to bed with more than one person. It would mean we'd stop loving each other, anyway.'

'On the contrary, it would mean that we would love each other more than ever. That's what love is. It has to be freely given, without conditions and restrictions. Look at Sartre and Simone de Beauvoir. Two highly intelligent people who love each other totally and have understood what love means.'

'I doubt whether Simone de Beauvoir is happy, however much she may try to impose reason on her emotions. I bet she's only doing it to please Sartre.'

'Rubbish. It's the ideal relationship.'

I was upset and frightened by this inexplicable change in Anthony. 'I don't understand how, only a matter of months ago, you told me you couldn't live without me and now you are saying you don't want to live with me and you want us both to have other relationships,' I protested.

'One says things in moments of passion which are perhaps a slight exaggeration,' Anthony replied with a self-deprecating smile. 'I suppose one might term it "poetic licence". As you know, I tend to get carried away when I'm in bed with you. You can't blame me for that. If you weren't such a pusillanimous little horror, we'd be in bed in some hotel at this moment instead of standing here talking while the night descends.'

'I can't go off to an hotel with you around here. You must realize I can't. For a start, everyone in the family would wonder where we were and we'd have to lie to them and, secondly, everyone knows me. It would get back immediately. We'd never be able to get away with it.'

'As I say, you're a pusillanimous little horror, but since you won't risk it I think we might as well join your family and have a drink. It's suddenly becoming rather chilly, don't you think?'

When I had first introduced Jessica to my family, Simon had been jealous of my friendship with her and I had therefore assumed that his odd behaviour of late was caused by a similar jealousy of my relationship with

Anthony; but Anthony's absence did not make Simon any happier. Something was troubling him and, whatever it was, it was serious. He remained distant and unapproachable, and unusually silent. When I felt his eyes on me, one evening, I looked at him across the dinner-table. For a couple of seconds we stared into each other's eyes, mine full of query, his full of sadness; then he turned away as if he had given up trying to explain. For days afterwards, I was haunted by his expression. He seemed to be pleading with me and I felt I was failing him by not understanding. It was like some ghastly repetition of Jessica's desertion. How could I not have felt when she fell in love? What had happened to all our telepathy? And now Simon, too. I had never had to ask him anything about himself. I knew him. All his secretiveness, used to keep the rest of the world at bay, did not exclude me. Yet suddenly, when he was patently suffering, he had cut off the blood supply. I could not bear it so I turned to my grandmother for help.

'Let me talk to Simon,' she said.

I never found out what happened then. She made sure that they were well out of sight and earshot. But I do remember their return to the house. She was exceedingly angry and Simon was in tears.

When Anthony returned from Torre Pellice things continued as before, happily as far as I was concerned, although Simon kept very much to himself. Then came the day Anthony and he returned to Cambridge.

I had a dentist's appointment in Milan that day, so I said goodbye to them both before they went to the station. It was just a routine check and I never had anything wrong, but sometimes there were queues, people sitting around in the waiting-room for hours. As it happened, I was in and out in ten minutes so I decided to go to the station and wave them off.

The whole thing was a nightmare. That awful station of Mussolini's – all that marble, and carved birds with talons, and pretty good imitation German-grand-civic-architecture stuff. And the crowds. I'd never seen so many people and I hate crowds. I had to fight my way up the marble staircase, and then try to find out what platform they were on. The announcements sounded unreal. The trains seemed to be going everywhere and I kept being hit on the ankles by luggage trolleys. Why couldn't people look where they were going, I wondered? And then I saw them. Further down the platform, behind a huge mountain of suitcases: a thing like a small train, piled high with luggage. There they were, in the corner. They'd thought they were hidden, of course, behind all the luggage. And, then, they weren't expecting me to turn up. They thought they were quite alone. I couldn't think why I hadn't thought of it before. It was so obvious. It just hadn't crossed my mind. There they were, two slim shapes, two perfect forms; and Anthony's head was as fair as Simon's. Staggeringly beautiful, really. Much better than Anthony and I could ever have looked. Talk about transfixed ... and then their heads separated. They still had their arms around each other but they had stopped kissing. Their eyes never left each other. I could see Simon from where I stood, and the expression on his face tore at my gut. I didn't realize until then that men could *love* each other. Oh, God ... I couldn't bear it ... and then Simon saw me.

He moved so fast that I thought he must catch me. I did not wait to see whether Anthony had realized. I just ran. I remember knocking a woman's handbag to the ground, I remember a man shouting at me, I remember hitting my knee really hard against a trolley, I remember tripping and nearly falling the whole way down the escalator, I remember nearly being run over by a taxi.

I ran and ran but I had no idea where I was running. It was the first time I had been hit by a blast of cold air from the real world and I had no idea how to deal with the pain. I wanted to hide from everyone. I felt ashamed and humiliated; I felt ignorant and betrayed. How *could* they? Anthony and my own brother. First Jessica and now both of them. My God, what was happening to me?

I wanted to howl and scream and tear the claws out of

my heart, but I did not want anyone to see. I was determined not to let anyone see. I knew that, somehow, I must hang on to myself until I was alone; and I wanted to be alone more than anything in the world.

I fought back my tears until I thought I was going to suffocate. Some line I had read years before kept reverberating around my head. *Squalet et ipse dies*, it went, *squalet et ipse dies.*

I ran across a street and somebody honked on their car horn. Surprised by the noise, I shot in front of a tram, hardly aware that I was within inches of being hit. On the opposite pavement, I saw a sea of strange faces staring at me. I wished they would go away. There seemed to be people everywhere. Suddenly, Sartre's line came back to me: *L'enfer, c'est les autres.* I pushed my way through the shoppers wondering why everyone moved so slowly. Why can't they hurry up, I wondered in desperation? Why can't they leave me alone? I mustn't cry. I must not cry. *Squalet et ipse dies.* What was it? Where had I read it? I must concentrate. I must be able to remember who had said it. I must be able to remember what it was.

I had reached the canal when at last it came back to me. It was Adam when he first woke outside Paradise:

> Daylight grew squalid: underneath his feet
> He saw a narrower earth; above his head
> Hung a remoter heaven, with moaning stars

That was it, of course. How could I have forgotten? 'Daylight grew squalid.' I must be alone, I thought. There must be somewhere in this world where I can be alone.

After a time, I could run no further. I stopped in a doorway and stared across the street without seeing. I had a photographic image in my head which I could not obliterate. It was of two fair heads locked in a kiss, the lines of their necks like the lines of a statue, their two slim shapes almost one. Suddenly, I could bear it no longer. I hid my face in my hands and wept. Tears

346

poured between my fingers and I was racked by sobs. I cried and cried until I felt as if I was going to sick up my heart all over the street. I wanted to tear out my insides and demolish the pain. I could not believe that anything could hurt so much. I turned my back on the world, leant my head against a door and howled.

After some time, I felt a hand on my shoulder and turned round, tears streaming down my face. An old woman with a basket on her arm was looking at me anxiously. 'Is it someone in your family?' she asked and looked towards the other side of the street. Following her gaze, I noticed for the first time that the entrance of the house opposite was draped in black. A huge, black curtain covered the double door into the courtyard and great bunches of black taffeta were looped over the top of the door and hung in long trails down either side until they touched the ground. In the middle of all this black a hideous wreath had been nailed. Apparently someone had died within.

I could not bear to think about it, even now. The awful state I was in when Anthony finally found me. I was standing on the little bridge with the mermaids, my favourite place, below the castle, looking at the ducks on the rather dirty water. I was not thinking of anything very much by then. I felt numb.

'I knew I would find you here, eventually,' Anthony's voice said from immediately behind me and before I could move he had grabbed me by the shoulders in a grip which hurt. 'No, you're not going to run away,' he said. 'I want to talk to you.'

'Leave me alone,' I sobbed as he made me turn to face him. 'Just leave me alone. Please let me go. Oh, God, please, I beg you, let me go.'

'No, I'm not going to let you go,' said Anthony. 'But since I think we are beginning to cause a certain amount of interest, I suggest we go for a little walk while you calm down.' He took me by the arm and, gripping it so hard that I thought it would snap, marched me across

347

the moat, into the castle and through to the courtyard of the Ducal Court. There, in those magnificent surroundings, we found ourselves entirely alone.

'You are going to listen to me, whether you like it or not,' he said. 'You've got to understand. I want you to understand. Are your parents expecting you back at Manta tonight?'

I nodded.

'Well, you're going to ring them and tell them that you have decided to stay in the flat overnight, that you'll be back tomorrow. We need time to talk and I'm not going to do it out here. I'm going to take you home.'

I became hysterical. 'I'm not going anywhere with you,' I sobbed. 'I don't want to go home. I don't want to see you ever again. I don't want to see anyone. Why can't you leave me alone? I want to be alone.'

Anthony became quite angry in the end. I remember him taking me by the shoulders and shaking me, and suddenly the life went out of me: all emotion seemed to drain away, leaving me listless and blank.

As we walked slowly back to the Via Alberto da Giussano, Anthony continued to hold my arm in a tight grip, but I was beyond struggling by then. I suddenly realized that he must have missed his train and then I wondered where Simon was.

'Where's Simon?' I asked.

'At the flat. He went to wait for you there in case you went home.'

I stopped dead. 'I'm not going home, then. I don't want to see him,' and I started to cry again.

'I'll telephone him and ask him to go to an hotel,' said Anthony. 'You can't wander the streets for ever. You'll have to go home some time; and Simon can go somewhere else.'

We stopped in a café while Anthony rang Simon. I could not have cared less whether I lived or died.

I did not understand anything Anthony said to me. It seemed like hour after hour of meaningless words – 'a completely different kind of love . . . nothing to do with us . . . the need to dominate . . . the need to humiliate . . . blind urges' – endless phrases which conveyed nothing but disaster. The only facts that I took in clearly were that Anthony and Simon had been lovers since Easter and that they were intending to live together in Cambridge.

When Anthony finally carried me to bed, I viewed all three of us with such revulsion that I almost wanted to be humiliated further. I think I hoped that I would die in the attempt; or that, while making love to me, Anthony would plunge a knife through my heart.

When I woke, in the morning, Anthony was gone.

Paris

Why have such scores of lovely, gifted girls
   Married impossible men?
Simple self-sacrifice may be ruled out,
   And missionary endeavour, nine times out of ten.

Repeat 'impossible men': not merely rustic,
   Foul-tempered or depraved
(Dramatic foils chosen to show the world
   How well women behave, and always have behaved).

Impossible men: idle, illiterate,
   Self-pitying, dirty, sly,
For whose appearance even in City parks
   Excuses must be made to casual passers-by.

Has God's supply of tolerable husbands
   Fallen, in fact, so low?
Or do I always over-value woman
   At the expense of man?
              Do I?
                  It might be so.

Robert Graves

CHAPTER TWENTY-THREE

It was the only time I ever saw my grandmother cry: and that was worse than all the rest. '*Sei soltanto una ragazza, una ragazzina,*' she whispered. '*Non è giusto! Non è giusto!*' She rocked me in her arms, hour after hour, as the tears poured down her sad, old cheeks.

In the end, she let me go. 'It won't help,' she said. 'It's a sickness of the soul: but your parents seem to think it would be good for you to get away. Call me, my darling, and let me know how you get on,' and she held me to her and stroked my head.

To this day, I am not sure why I did it. Paris seemed the only place to go, and I wanted to get away from them all. Perhaps Enrico's incessant telephone calls had made a dent in me somewhere. Perhaps the endless flow of letters from him during the past year had touched me after all. I remembered one of them in particular: he said he preferred telephoning to writing but that, in writing,

at least I don't run the risk of hearing your voice which can sound so glacial (yes, it can also sound very tender, it sounds tender when you talk to me in a whisper and I see your beautiful eyes becoming as gentle as your mouth and it's as if you emerged, for an instant, from your solitude, from your fear, to give me that minimum of tenderness without which every woman is lost). When you emerge from that terrible indifference, that anaesthesia of the soul, you suddenly become as adorable as a tiny leaf or a

355

shell; I see all your fragility, I see you as obscured by an eclipse – and then I want to take you in these tired hands of mine and carry you, I don't say to paradise, but at least a little way into the light (I, so dark!). How I wish I could hold you tightly to me. How I wish I could stretch my fingers across this monstrous distance (not only of kilometres!) and gently caress your lips, and feel your eyes on me, and watch them as one watches a horizon at daybreak, and see your expression change from fear to tenderness and gently melt into a kiss.

On some other occasion he had written, '*il faut avoir le pessimisme de l'intelligence et l'optimisme de la volonté.*' Why had he written it in French? It was not a quote, as far as I knew. And Pierre, I remembered, was forever saying to me, '*il est fou amoureux de toi.*'

Did I simply want someone to love me, or was it a straightforward flight from the wastelands? Perhaps I wanted to make Anthony jealous. Perhaps I simply wanted to hurt myself. Whatever the reasons, I married Enrico; but I told him, first, all that had happened.

I should have known better. Enrico was Italian. I must have known my countrymen well enough to know that. But in those days I was honest and it seemed out of the question to embark on a marriage not telling the truth.

That first night was awful. I thought Enrico would kill me. He thumped my head against the pillow again and again. '*Sei mia, sei mia!*' he said through clenched teeth. '*Soltanto mia!*' he shouted, 'Why him? Why not me?' He shook me and shook me but there were tears in his eyes.

All the same, he had married me. He did not have to marry me. I told him everything beforehand and he married me just the same. I thought, during our honeymoon, that he had learned to accept it. It was the past, after all. It was dead and gone.

My grandmother wrote the moment I left, before she heard that I had married.

Dearest Child,

This is Sunday – a lovely, fine day with practically no wind. I hope it is the same for you in Paris but I have misgivings about those gales in France that we have been reading about in the papers. I hope the wind will have blown itself out without crossing your path.

The scenes when I saw you off at the station are something I would rather not remember. I still have a dazed feeling about the number and type of the passengers on your train. They seemed to fill every corridor and carriage so that it was impossible to get near anyone responsible and my plans to have a word with one and another, and slip them some money here and there, faded into impossibility.

I hated to leave you, standing tall and charming among a rabble like a *Club Méditerranée* gone mad, but I felt I could do nothing for you and was only in the way.

I do wonder how you are managing. I hope you will tell me and not try to spare my feelings. I am recovering today but yesterday I just felt stunned.

Try and get a little rest here and there in Paris. Manta is very dull without you. Come home as soon as you feel you can bear it.

She did not need to say anything when she heard my news. She understood it all. 'I am here if you need me,' she said on the telephone.

Two weeks after our honeymoon came another bolt from the blue. It was a Saturday afternoon and Enrico suddenly said to me, 'I shall be out to dinner tonight. Don't wait up for me. I may be very late.'

'Is it an Embassy dinner?' I enquired, surprised.

'Yes, in a sense,' he replied. 'The girl who is going to replace me as Press Attaché has just arrived from Rome and I'm taking her out to dinner to explain the set-up to her. As you know, we're having a bit of trouble

357

with the French at the moment because of this ludicrous Petrocchi affair and it is going to require careful handling. She's obviously very bright but she doesn't have the contacts yet and she needs briefing. I shall have to spend a bit of time with her for the first couple of weeks – introduce her to the right people and all that sort of thing. I must say, I'm relieved they're moving me. I much prefer economics to all this rubbish.'

That evening, just after Enrico had left, the telephone rang. It was André. '*Ma petite, comment vas-tu?* How was your honeymoon? Not so much as a card from you! I want to hear all about it. And how does it feel to be married? You haven't made a sign of life for over a month. I feel positively deprived. When are you going to come and see me? Would you and Enrico care to join me for luncheon tomorrow?'

'I'd love to,' I replied, 'but I don't know what Enrico's plans are. He's out this evening so may I ring you back in the morning?'

'Of course. But not before ten if you don't mind. I like to be terribly lazy on Sundays. I haven't made any plans for the afternoon but I thought we could all go out, if it's a reasonable day. I have rather a yearning to go and admire the *Ecuries* in Chantilly. I have a feeling they're *haunted*, my dear, by the Prince de Condé. For all his conviction that he was going to return as a horse, I don't believe he's a horse at all. I think he's there in person. I find it very encouraging. I have reached the age where I want to feel that I shall be able to return to my favourite places as a ghost. Will you come with me? It never does any harm to see something beautiful and I feel like a little outing.'

'I'd love to,' I replied. 'I haven't been to Chantilly for ages. But, as I said, I'll have to check with Enrico. I'll let you know in the morning.'

'*D'accord, ma chérie. Je t'embrasse très fort. A demain, alors.*'

After this conversation, I spent an uneventful evening listening to music. I tried not to think about Anthony and

Simon but my thoughts kept wandering back to them. What, I wondered, were they doing at this moment? Had they heard that I had married? What made men love one another to the extent that they had to go to bed with each other? Had Anthony ever really loved me? If he had, what had made him change? Was it somehow more exciting physically with another man? For all Anthony's explanations, I had seen Simon's face ... That never-erased, photographic image of the two blond heads floated before my eyes and I could see the look they exchanged. I clutched myself, silently, as if to hold the hurt inside; but the pain did not diminish. I rocked in my armchair, trying to listen to Boïeldieu until, at last, I could bear it no longer. I bent my head to my knees and wept. When my tears subsided, I felt worn out and old.

Before I finally took myself off to bed, I looked out at the Sacré-Coeur standing white against the skyline.

At one in the morning I woke with a start. I had not closed the shutters and it was a very bright night. There was a full moon and the light was streaming on to the bed. Enrico had not yet returned and I felt uneasy. Still, I thought, he had said he might be very late. I turned over and fell asleep again.

I woke again at four o'clock. A lorry was unloading further down the street, and still there was no sign of Enrico.

He finally rolled in at five in the morning.

'Where on earth have you been?' I asked. 'I've been terribly worried. I thought you must have had an accident. Are you all right?'

'Yes, fine,' he replied as he started to undress.

'What happened?'

'Nothing,' he said.

'Something must have happened,' I insisted. 'It's five in the morning. What have you been doing?'

'I've been in bed with the new Press Attaché.'

It is extraordinary how slowly the human brain absorbs new information when that information does not conform to anything in its past experience or conditioning. It behaves like a computer that has been asked a question not contained in its program. I have known the case of a man, brought up in Europe, who was unexpectedly caught in a third-world revolution and was, to his astonishment, arrested as he walked into his own house one morning. In spite of the fact that his landlord had been executed, that the place was swarming with the revolutionary army brandishing machine-guns, and that he was accused of being a CIA agent because he possessed an American Express card, when they carted him off for interrogation and thence to prison, the only thing that troubled his mind was the fact that he had a lunch date that day and that he was unable to telephone the person with whom he was supposed to be lunching to tell them he could not make it. It was, as he put it, so inconvenient. It was some time before he began to understand what was really happening.

I found, that Sunday morning, that it was equally difficult to take in what Enrico had just said to me. I had not yet come to terms with the fact that Anthony and my brother were lovers and I was in no state to cope with another betrayal. My brain simply refused to understand what had just been said.

'Do you mean you've been making love with her?' I asked.

'Yes.'

'My God, I don't believe it,' I exclaimed. 'Why?'

'Because I wanted to. I don't know why you should be so surprised. You know what life is about. You weren't a virgin when I married you, after all.'

'But we've only been married a month,' I protested feebly.

'What's that got to do with anything?'

'Well, I don't know, really. It's just not what I'd imagined. I thought marriage was a commitment. I don't know. I suppose it seems terribly soon after getting married. It's only two weeks since our honeymoon.'

'You mean I should have waited another month? What

difference would that have made? This has got nothing to do with marriage, in any case. It's just fun. It doesn't *mean* anything.'

'If it doesn't mean anything, why do it? I can't believe it. What was the point of getting married?'

'I told you, this has nothing to do with marriage.'

'But I thought you said you loved me. Don't you love me?'

'For Christ's sake, what has this got to do with love? You're not expecting me to be faithful, are you? You can't be that naïve? It's not as if I'd married a virgin. And don't tell me you're not still in love with that queer. God, he must be laughing! An innocent little beauty, never touched by anyone and looking like a cross between the Madonna and Sophia Loren, and she falls straight into his bed – and he doesn't even like women! It's repulsive! He should have been on his knees grovelling to you, begging you, not the other way round. He isn't fit to wipe your shoes and you let him walk all over you. He's a typical Englishman: a pervert from a degenerate race. And you and Jessica are equally degenerate: ruined by your frightful upbringing, your ludicrous families and that insane school. Look at Jessica! What does she do with all her precious upbringing? Runs off with an Irish drunk who is old enough to be her father. And you, you go to bed with the first pervert you meet! You turned me down, remember? You put on a wonderful show of hysteria at the mere idea of bed; but it didn't prove a problem when a queen offered his services. How *could* you? How could you fall in love with a homosexual? How could you have gone to bed with him? Did you pretend to be afraid of him, too? Did you bite him and scream? Come on, I want to know. I wonder whether you realize that I collected you out of the gutter. You were sullied; you were rubbish. You had ruined yourself. Nobody would have wanted you. And you have the gall to make a fuss about an insignificant, totally trivial incident! I am *not* going to discuss it any more. I'm tired and I want to get some sleep.'

'Is she pretty?' I asked.

361

'Yes, she is quite. But I mean it; I'm not going to talk about it any more. It's none of your business and I'm not going to have you interfering in my private life. Now, I *must* get some sleep.'

He turned over and fell, instantly, into a deep slumber. I, on the other hand, knew that further sleep was out of the question. I decided to make myself some coffee. Once made, I took it into the drawing-room where I sat for hours in a state of shock.

At about eleven, I heard Enrico bellowing from the bedroom, '*Caffè! Voglio un caffè!*' This was another of the surprises that marriage had held in store for me. Every morning, without fail, Enrico shouted for coffee. He never said 'please', or 'thank you'; he simply roared, 'Coffee! I want coffee!' Had he been English I might well have said something but I knew full well that it was normal behaviour for the great majority of the Latin world. It went with the virginity cult: slaves and virgins, virgin slaves. I was Italian enough not to be able to reject it entirely and at that point I still wanted to be the perfect wife. My ancient fear of men was reawakened, too, and I was nervous of his bad moods, afraid to argue. It nevertheless irked me and in order to obey, docilely, I had to keep telling myself that having survived eight years in a convent I must surely be able to bow to a man's intolerable rudeness.

On this particular Sunday morning, I was in no state to argue about anything. As I handed Enrico his coffee, I remembered André's telephone call.

'André rang last night,' I said.

'What did he want?' asked Enrico.

'He was inviting us to lunch today. He thought we might like to go to Chantilly afterwards, if we had nothing better to do. I said I'd have to ask you but I did promise I would ring him after ten and it's eleven now so I think I'd better let him know.'

'That's fine. You go. It's a good idea.'

'Don't you want to come?'

'I can't.'

'Why not?'

'Because I've got Paola coming here.'

'Who's Paola?'

'The girl I had dinner with last night. The new Press Attaché. You'd better go to Chantilly. I don't want you rushing home in the middle of the afternoon. Ring me before you come back to be on the safe side. I don't suppose you want to bump into her, do you?'

'Are you going to go to bed with her again?'

'That's the general idea, yes.'

'Do you mean you arranged this last night?'

'Yes.'

'What was I supposed to do?'

'I was going to suggest that you went out for the afternoon. Fortunately, you've already organized yourself to do so and guess who with? *Another* queer! They don't grow thick on the ground here, the way they do in England, but one could count on you to find one here, too. Do you find him irresistibly fascinating? I've been meaning to ask you for some time.'

'Enrico, don't be ridiculous! André is a family friend. You know he is. And, anyway, he's about a hundred years old.'

'I haven't noticed that age matters much. Look at Jessica. And your family seems to have a *penchant* for homosexuals – breeds them, in fact.'

I burst into tears and fled back to the kitchen.

After a while, Enrico appeared and came and put his arms around me. 'Do stop crying,' he said. 'You shouldn't take it all so seriously. You're the only person I love. You must know that.'

'Then why do you want to go to bed with this horrible girl?'

'She isn't horrible. She's very nice. She's intelligent, attractive and has a good sense of humour – something you seem to be losing, incidentally. You'd like her.'

'I bet you'd lose your sense of humour if I did the same thing to you. What would you feel like if I hadn't come

363

home until five in the morning and I then told you I'd been in bed with somebody else? What would you say?'

'I wouldn't say anything. I'd kill you.'

'Well, there you are. How do you justify that?'

'It's different. You're a woman.'

'What difference does that make?'

'It's well known that women take these things more seriously. If you were unfaithful, it would mean something to you. You'd get involved with the person emotionally. One would never be able to have children if one had an unfaithful wife, either, because one would never be certain the children were not someone else's – that weighs very heavily in the male subconscious, don't forget. It is in every way a much more serious business when a woman is unfaithful. All men are unfaithful but it doesn't mean anything. It's just fun. It's a game. It's the excitement of the chase, the fun of flirtation, the desire to impress and the thrill of conquest; but it isn't love. It has nothing to do with love.'

'Why should it be any different for women? That's absurd. Women want fun and excitement too. They always have done. If that weren't the case Shakespeare would never have written that speech of Emilia's. I can't imagine how you can say it's different just because I'm a woman. It's terribly unfair.'

'Well, just remember what happened to Emilia. Killed by her husband and quite right too. She probably had slept with the Moor. If you ever look at another man, you'll end up dead, too. *L'ho già detto. Sei soltanto mia.* Now go and ring André.'

'I don't want to go out any more. I don't feel at all like seeing anyone today. Can't you cancel the Press Attaché?'

'No, I can't. I want to see her. If you loved me, as you pretend, you'd want me to be happy and I shall not be happy if you try to make me faithful. In any case, I'd only deceive you and invent lies, but I'd still be unfaithful.'

'Why do you have to do it here? Why can't you go somewhere else?'

'Because Paola is staying with friends while she looks for somewhere to live, so we would have to go to an hotel. I took her to one last night and I don't want to have to do the same today. In any case, I want to see whether you really love me. You let that pervert go to bed with you after you knew he had slept with your brother. What you could do for him, you can do for me. You would have gone on sleeping with him after that if he had asked you to go to bed with him again, wouldn't you?'

'No, I don't think so.'

'Yes, you would. You're not being honest with yourself or with me. If he had wanted you, you would have continued to go to bed with him. So let's see what you're prepared to do for me. Go and ring André.'

Coming so soon after discovering that Anthony and Simon were lovers, I was not at my most resilient. If I felt destroyed by Anthony – desolate and humiliated – I simply felt numb about Enrico. My capacity to suffer anguish seemed entirely used up; I had sweated out my misery, I had bled myself dry. I needed time to absorb this new shock and react. There seemed no reason not to ring André, not to do as I was told; no reason why Enrico should be faithful or why he should not chuck me out of my own flat. It all seemed perfectly reasonable. I had been stunned into a state of paralysis.

When I telephoned André to accept his invitation on my own, but not on Enrico's, behalf, I found myself obliged to invent some story to explain Enrico's absence. Brought up never to lie even in dire circumstances, it was an uncomfortable experience. It was the first of an endless stream of lies that I was to pour out over the years in order to cover up for Enrico but I would have been astonished, at the time, had anyone told me that I would soon be lying on his behalf to his parents, to my own parents, and even, in due course, to our own children.

365

Washington

Quand je parle d'amour mon amour vous irrite
Si j'écris qu'il fait beau vous me criez qu'il pleut
Vous dites que mes prés ont trop de marguerites
Trop d'étoiles ma nuit trop de bleu mon ciel bleu

Comme le carabin scrute le coeur qu'il ouvre
Vous cherchez dans mes mots la paille de l'émoi
N'ai-je pas tout perdu le Pont-Neuf et le Louvre
Et ce n'est pas assez pour vous venger de moi . . .

Louis Aragon

CHAPTER TWENTY-FOUR

The next ten years were a walk along a tightrope. I managed to hang on to some semblance of myself as long as we continued to live in Europe, largely because I could run back to Manta and visit my grandmother whenever my marriage seemed intolerable.

Once Enrico was posted to Washington, my last links with the past were severed; and we had barely arrived there before my grandmother died. She had said to me before I left, 'I shall not see you again, my darling. I have packed my bags and I'm ready to go.' She was not ill. There was nothing whatever the matter with her. She simply did not wish to live.

Washington (or, at any rate, Georgetown) had a certain charm but I would have enjoyed it more if I had been happier. I could probably have ignored Enrico's incessant infidelities had he been better humoured when he chose to be around; but the fact that every woman we knew was a putative mistress seemed to underline his contempt for everything concerning me. My family, my education, my 'Englishness', my friends were all the subject of constant attacks. Even my love of music was interpreted as idiotic romanticism. Everything I thought was dismissed out of hand. Like many another woman who has lost her self-esteem, I gave myself up entirely to the bearing of children. I had three in swift succession; and I loved them the more because I could not love their father.

From time to time an old acquaintance would appear. Dermot came over regularly but never brought Jessica.

Angelica came once, still on the arm of Antonio, but told me in private that she was about to leave him. 'He has three other wives, I've discovered,' she said. 'Anyway, I've found a much better arrangement. I've met this politician with an *hôtel particulier* in the rue de l'Ancienne-Comédie and I'm going to live with him, but I've also got a lover who is terribly useful: he's the manager of the Ritz and he lets me take all my friends to lunch there for nothing, and he also lets me do all my long-distance telephoning free.'

To my delight, one evening, I bumped into Pierre at a cocktail party. The room was very crowded and I had not noticed him when we arrived. Suddenly, there he was, the same old Pierre, and he nearly reduced me to tears by saying, '*Salut, camarade.*' With that once-familiar, wonderful, long-forgotten greeting, I was carted straight back to Paris and May '68.

'What are you doing here?' I asked him when I had embraced him.

'I'm working for the AFP. They've sent me here to cover the State Department. As long as I don't disgrace myself, I should be here for a couple of years.'

'When did you arrive?' I asked.

'Last week,' replied Pierre. 'Thibault's here, too. He's at the Embassy. He's longing to see you, so don't be surprised if you suddenly get bombarded with invitations to the French Embassy. He's become frightfully arrogant, you'll find. I don't know what it is about embassies: they have the most awful effect on people, and I'm not sure that the ones with brains aren't worse than the ones with no brains. I suppose it's difficult not to think you're clever when you're surrounded by dolts. Thibault seems to have seduced the Americans as well as impressing the Ambassador. He's surrounded by admiring television journalists and Pulitzer prize-winning art critics from the *Washington Post*, and that sort of thing. Anyway, you'll see for yourself. Now, what about you? I hear that Enrico is doing pretty well, too. I've heard a few other things as well. Is he here?'

'Yes,' I said, pointing across the room. 'He's over there, talking to that woman in blue.'

Pierre looked at me rather oddly, I thought. 'How about lunch tomorrow?'

'That would be lovely,' I said.

The following day, at lunch, Pierre asked, 'Did you tell Enrico you were having lunch with me?'

'No.'

'Why not?'

'Cowardice. He doesn't much like me having lunch with people.'

'What on earth do you mean?'

'He doesn't like me to see anyone on my own: specially men, of course; but he doesn't really like me to see anyone. He'd like me to stay shut up in the house all day.'

'I knew he was possessive about you, but that's insane. Why don't you simply tell him to get lost?'

'I hate rows.'

'Some rows cannot be avoided, or should not be avoided. My God, you're both behaving like a couple of Calabrian peasants! After all, you're not impeding his freedom, from what I hear.' He must have noticed my expression for, relenting, he leaned across the table and said, 'Ecoute, ma vieille, you don't have to talk about it if you don't want to. It's none of my business, anyway; but you don't have to pretend with me, either, if you want to talk. After all, I do know you better than most of your Washington acquaintances do; and as for Enrico, everyone knows about him. It's public knowledge. Washington is such a gossipy place and Enrico has never made much attempt at being discreet, from what I'm told.'

'I don't know if I can talk about it,' I replied. 'I've never tried to talk to anyone about Enrico – except, in letters, to Jessica sometimes.'

'What does she think about it?'

'She fluctuates, as I do, between thinking I should leave him and thinking that I have no choice but to stay.

373

Enrico and I have had three children, you see, since I last saw you and he's mad about them even if he's never prepared to do anything for them. I don't quite see that I can take them away from him. It wouldn't be fair on him. It wouldn't be fair on them either, if it comes to that. In any case, he wouldn't let me. I think he'd kill me rather than allow me to leave. Quite apart from the fact that he imagines he loves me, there is the question of loss of face. Enrico couldn't cope with the loss of face.

'I have occasionally suggested a trial separation,' I continued, 'but he won't even discuss it. He breaks down completely at the mere idea, saying he couldn't live without me, that all these girls mean nothing, that they are none of them fit to wipe my boots, that he couldn't chase anyone or be interested in anything if I weren't there to come back to; that I'm his base, his foundation; that I'm the only person he loves; that without me he'd be nothing. He says it again and again, and he really means it. He thinks he loves me, you see. It's pretty ironic, as it happens, because it's exactly what happened to my grandmother. Here I am, condemned to re-live my grandmother's life, married to a man who constantly swears eternal love but can never be bothered to come home.'

'What's his mother like?'

'Why?'

'I'll tell you in a minute. Tell me what she's like.'

'A born organizer, with more energy in her little finger than the combined forces of fifteen armies. She's ambitious: for Enrico in particular. She's very hard-working, with a hectic temperament. She's manipulative, overbearing, noisy, highly intelligent, highly educated, highly political and entirely used to getting her own way. She's extremely proud of Enrico (he's by far and away her favourite child) and pretty possessive about him. She has always been fine to me, though.'

'Too intelligent, by the sounds of it, not to want you on her side. It's just what I thought. Mother-fixated. You

374

are a replacement for his mother. In a sense, he's right about the others not meaning anything. As long as he goes to bed with every girl he meets, you're in no danger whatever. He may seem totally adolescent but it is certainly not a threat to you. Does he ever see any of them more than two or three times?'

'No.'

'Does he always tell you about them?'

'Yes; and he makes a point of leaving photographs of them all over the house, and letters lying about, and so on.'

'It's obviously all done for your benefit. He may secretly long for you to break a few plates over his head. Does his mother shout at him?'

'Yes, she shrieks at everyone.'

'He probably expects you to do the same, in that case.'

'It's not in my character to shout at people.'

'Pity. It would do him good. However, as I said, I don't think you have anything to worry about. If he suddenly grew up and started having a serious affair, something which lasted a bit, then you might have trouble; but he won't. He needs you.'

'I wish he would. I'd give anything for him to go off with someone else permanently. It's the only way I can think of that I shall ever escape from this trap.'

'He won't, though. I'm prepared to bet you anything you like that he won't. People don't leave their mothers, not people like Enrico; and they don't expect their mothers to abandon them, either, so beware.'

When I next spoke to Jessica on the telephone (something I did when I was feeling particularly fed up), I mentioned my lunch with Pierre and repeated some of his remarks to her.

'He's quite right,' she said. 'Women are caught in a trap because what they want men cannot give. Men always make of their wives a mother-figure, whereas women want their husbands to be lovers, not sons. Men don't want women around all the time and they don't

375

want the same woman all the time, either. The only women they tolerate on a permanent basis are mothers, or mother-figures. Mothers, of course, are there to be reviled, abused, misused, adoring. Sons can behave as badly as they please and know their mothers will still love them just the same. Mothers do all the dirty work, so they are useful; and it doesn't matter how much they complain, you know they will never leave. It's a wonderful invention, a mother; and it's a very secure relationship for the son because a mother never abandons her son.' She paused for a second.

'In a way,' she continued, 'the rest is probably just showing off to Mummy. It sounds as if Enrico is trying to prove something to you although I suppose he may be trying to prove something to himself as well.'

'Or showing off to the other boys,' I interrupted.

'Yes, I expect there's an element of that, too,' said Jessica. 'There is also, I suspect, a very primitive man-the-hunter aspect. They obviously adore the chase: seduction, conquest and all that stuff; and they seem to need a limitless supply of new flesh. I've never made up my mind whether variety is the essence of the pleasure for men, or whether it is simply a competition against other men, notching up the hits and trying to beat everyone else's score. I have a feeling it is a competition because it is so hideously like shooting. You can never kill enough of them. It doesn't matter if there are hundreds, or thousands, dead. Anything that moves you want to kill and however many you may have shot, you'll go on looking for one more that moves. But don't forget that at the end of the day, men always want to go home to crumpets and tea. I think that's all they're made of: the desire to kill and the desire to be cossetted.'

I did not feel particularly cheered by Jessica's discourse. 'Why do we fall for it?' I demanded. 'After all, I can't imagine many women want to be a mother-figure.'

'We haven't any choice,' replied Jessica. 'It is simply nature. Either we allow ourselves to be killed or we accept the unappealing rôle of mother. Anthony killed

376

you, if you like; Enrico has turned you into his mother. And because we *are* mothers and we *do* love our children, our husbands expect us to be like that with them too. It is one of the endless misunderstandings between men and women. They want a mother, we want a lover. We want someone to carry us off on a white charger. They simply want to lay their heads on our laps. It's hopeless.'

'And yet,' I said, 'some women genuinely don't seem to mind their husband's or lover's infidelities.'

'I've never really believed that, not if the woman is in love with the man. I've looked at a good many cases over the years and those women always fall into one of two types: either they want an excuse to sleep around themselves, or they are materially grasping and feel it is worth the price because they have acquired what they wanted (a title, a fortune, a secure job, a house, a step up some ladder either socially or in terms of career – all that sort of thing). There is always a quid pro quo.'

'So you don't think allowing the other person freedom is a proof of love?' I asked.

'No, I don't. That's all rubbish. It never works. It's just destructive. Anyway, I've had an idea,' said Jessica, characteristically changing the subject. 'You know we're moving back to Paris?'

'No, I didn't know,' I replied.

'Well, we are,' said Jessica. 'Next month. Dermot is going back to the CNRS permanently. Anyway, we've decided to rent a house in the Lot for a month in the summer because of everything being shut in Paris in August, and I've asked Dermot to persuade Enrico to bring you all over. It's huge, the house we have in mind. There'd be masses of room for all of us.'

'In that case, I'd better get off the phone. Enrico certainly won't consider such extravagance if I run up any more bills.'

'Don't say anything to him. Leave it to Dermot,' were Jessica's last words before I put down the telephone.

*   *   *

377

Three months later, to my immense joy, we were all reunited under one roof in the Lot. It was the only time, during all the years I was married to Enrico, that Jessica and I managed to meet. We were simply never in the same country. As a result, we had both really looked forward to that summer.

It was an awful holiday and it was not helped by the presence of Dermot's mother. Mrs O'Flaherty was a self-pitying woman whose only reason for living was her son. Dermot was not particularly pleasant to her but this seemed to suit her. It gave her an excuse for playing the rôle of perpetual martyr. One might have thought from her attitude that it was she who was responsible for all the shopping and cooking and bathing of children. She gave one the impression that she was permanently over-worked; and, like her son, she drank. Unlike Dermot, however, she never did it when there was anyone about. Whenever any of us offered her a drink she would sigh and put on her martyr's expression.

'No, thank you, my dear,' she would say, heaving another great sigh. 'I'd absolutely love one, but I really *haven't* got time. You have one. Just put your feet up and take it easy. I'd join you willingly if I could, but I simply *must* get on.'

Why, one wondered? With what? And yet, by six in the evening she was pickled. Then came the rows with Dermot. He would behave intolerably and she would become long-suffering and make fatuously stupid remarks in a voice that was slurred. They were both exasperating and they made each other worse. The height of the drama was reached one night, after dinner, when Dermot's mother insisted on making the coffee. Jessica and I never let her anywhere near the kitchen if we could help it because it always ended in disaster, but on this occasion she made such a song and dance about it that we gave in to her. She had, since the beginning of the holiday, steadfastly refused to learn how to work the *espresso* pot, but she was convinced she understood it better than any of us. I knew she would manage to make it explode one day and she chose that night to succeed. The noise was impressive and we all rushed out to the kitchen in a state of panic. All over the kitchen there were jagged pieces of metal sticking out of the ceiling and walls, and there was coffee everywhere. It seemed unbelievable that such a small amount of liquid and grounds could have covered so large an area. Dermot's mother was slumped over the kitchen table and for a moment I thought she was dead (I had visions of her pierced to death by a piece of flying metal). She was not dead, however. She had simply passed out.

Enrico and Dermot left Jessica and me to clear up the mess and returned to the drawing-room without offering to help. Neither of them ever set foot in the kitchen except to come and shout at us when they wanted something but on that particular evening the shambles was such that we were not in the mood to have Dermot come in, ranting and raging, because he could not find any ice. He tore into Jessica, blaming her for his mother's behaviour, for the fact that she drank, for the fact that the coffee pot did not work and for the fact that the children had woken up as a result of the noise. I had never heard anyone being so rude to another human being in my life. It left me shaking.

Jessica looked furious but she did not say a word in reply. She waited, white-faced, until Dermot was out of the room and then she exploded.

'What a complete, fucking jerk that man is!' she said turning her back on me and thumping her head against the wall. I had never heard her use bad language before and when she turned back to face me I could see she was trying not to cry. It was not the first time we had had one of these scenes: they were regular occurrences.

'Why do you put up with it?' I asked. 'Why on earth don't you defend yourself?'

'Because I can't stand rows and because it doesn't make any difference. He doesn't pay any attention and he doesn't behave any less contemptibly. It upsets the children, in any case. I used to react in the beginning, but I soon realized that it was a waste of time; and it was extremely frightening for the children. I'm damned if I'm going to allow my children to grow up amid raging arguments. One might as well condemn them to grow up on a battlefield. God knows, Dermot makes enough noise for twenty. He can sound like an army all on his own. If I, too, were to draw my sword, life would become intolerable. Anyway, I can't be bothered any more. I'm too tired and I hate rows. I feel such contempt for him for being unable to control himself, and for being so unfair, and for never thinking about the children. I am not prepared to descend to his level.'

'The problem with that approach is that you and your children are condemned to living in terror. You are all permanently on tenterhooks waiting for the next outburst. You're frightened of him, aren't you? And so are the children. That isn't a very healthy way to live. And don't tell me that Dermot isn't perfectly well aware of it. He plays on your fear and your desire to protect the children. Like all selfish people when they find the way to get what they want, he's not going to give up. Why should he abandon this infallible system for making everyone jump to attention? He wants the whole world to dance attendance on him. Worse, he wants everyone to admire him to the point of infatuation. There was always a Mrs O'Flaherty, mother, ready to flatten herself at his slightest whim; and now he has a second Mrs O'Flaherty, wife, ready to do the same. Don't let him get away with it.'

'Come on, Imogen, you do exactly the same. Enrico is vile to you and you never say a word.'

'But Enrico can argue for hours, and he's so disagreeable about it. It simply isn't worth it.'

'Well, there you are.'

'Yes, but it's different because Enrico isn't as explosive as Dermot is. He has a much more calculated way of destroying one. He still manages to make me feel like the lowest of prostitutes and the most deformed of perverts simply because I fell in love with Anthony. He actually says things like, "All women are prostitutes. The only ones who are honest are the ones who demand money ... You were rubbish when I married you. I rescued you from the sewers. Nobody would have touched you. You should be grateful that I saved you from your own squalor." It's not exactly encouraging but it doesn't seem worth having yet another argument about it, particularly not with Enrico. He never changes his mind about anything and he can argue for ever even with no one arguing back. I've known him keep it up for an hour or more when I haven't said a word from start to finish. He is like an actor practising his part. He says all my lines for me so that he can get on with his next line. It doesn't matter whether or not it is what I would really have said as long as it keeps the argument going.'

'God, how boring.'

'It's not just boring, it's exhausting. He goes on, and on, and on. I wish somebody would invent a pill to make him shut up. And I really don't need to be told daily, almost hourly, that I'm degenerate (his favourite word), and a tart, and a pervert. I know all that now. I don't need to be reminded of it all the time. There's nothing I can do about it anyway. I can't change the fact that years ago I fell in love with Anthony. I can't make it never have happened, however much I might like to, so there's no point in going on about it all the time.'

'Imogen!' Jessica exclaimed, looking appalled. 'You are talking as if you really believed you were at fault for having loved Anthony, as if you genuinely think you were immoral and perverted.'

'Well, I probably was, but it's such a long time ago that I can't understand why I can't be forgiven. Why does Enrico still hate me so much for having loved Anthony? Actually, I think he minds more about the fact that I went to bed with him than that I loved him; but, anyway, why does he still mind about it? I haven't done anything awful since; and I told him about it before he married me. Why did he marry me if he can't live with the fact that I wasn't a virgin? Why do Latins mind so much about virginity? It's so depressing. I don't think I knew what it was to feel seriously depressed until I married.'

'You should leave him. He's destroying you. He has actually managed to convince you that you are all the things he says you are. Can't you see that it is he who is at fault? You are *not* degenerate (what a ridiculous word), and you are certainly not, and never have been, a tart. My God, most of our generation have gone to bed with countless hordes, and have lied and cheated, and have gone in for two-timing people and one-night stands, and started going to bed with people at sixteen or even younger – and love never entered into it anywhere. *That* is squalid, *that* is being degenerate (if you have to use that word), that is prostituting oneself. And what have you done? You fell in love with someone at eighteen, waited until you were nearly twenty to go to bed with him, suffered the misfortune of losing him, married and have been a faithful wife ever since. Faithful, I may say, to an incredibly unfaithful husband. In all your life you have only slept with two men and you have never been unfaithful to Enrico in spite of the fact that he has never been anything but unfaithful to you, and callously public about it at that. *He* is the one of easy virtue, not you. You are the least promiscuous, the least decadent person I know. You and I would be considered puritanical freaks by most people these days.'

'How could I have been so stupid as to have believed Anthony? How could I not have noticed what was happening to Simon? I must be half-witted. I ruined everything, really, didn't I? No wonder Enrico despises me.'

'Don't be ridiculous, Imogen. Why do you let Enrico pull you down? You are obsessively honest and loyal, and you are highly intelligent, yet you allow him to convince you of the opposite. You don't even realize how lovely you are to look at. To hell with what Enrico says (and, actually, he never stops telling other people how wonderful and beautiful you are: it's only to you that he pretends the opposite). Can't you see that you are

382

beautiful? Don't you know that you're just as clever as Enrico and far more fun than he will ever be? Far from despising you, he admires you; and to admire you seems to him belittling. Only by making you despise yourself and by removing the last vestiges of your self-confidence will he ever feel freed from his own inadequacies. He can't stop criticizing you because he hates himself for loving you and so he demolishes you daily.'

'I don't think he means to,' I interrupted.

'Yes, he does,' retorted Jessica. 'I've watched him doing it. Like one of Cromwell's men knocking the heads off gargoyles and defacing statues, he has decided to destroy you. He hacks away at you by the hour like some barbaric warrior who daily has to sharpen his sword on the carved face of a madonna. Don't let him do it, Imogen. I beg you to stop him or one day the madonna will no longer have a face.'

I was on the verge of tears by the time Jessica had finished. 'Oh God, Jessica,' I whispered. 'I don't know how to stop him. I'm trapped and I feel as if I'm drowning. I knew I was trapped the moment we were married. I don't believe I'll ever escape. I don't believe I'll ever be allowed to be me again. I can't breathe. There isn't a moment of the day or night when I don't feel I'm suffocating, and I have all the rest of my life to live. How am I going to survive this for another thirty or forty years? How are you going to survive life with Dermot for another thirty or forty years, if it comes to that?'

'I don't know. I suppose that when the children are older we shall be able to work and then it may be easier. It would help if we could ever escape the chores and get out of the house occasionally.'

'You say that, but that isn't the real problem. Do you remember when I had that job at the American Film Institute? Well, it was an absolute disaster on the domestic front.'

'I remember you saying that, yes.'

'Of course, life was more bearable and a hell of a lot more interesting while I was at work, and God knows it's less tiring to go to an office than to bring up small children; but it was eight times worse when I came home in the evenings.'

'Why?' asked Jessica.

'Because Enrico was so awful about it. He simply could not stand me working. He never wanted me to work: he didn't want me to have money of my own, he didn't want me to meet other people, he didn't want me to set foot outside the house. He became unbelievably jealous and suspicious. He was absolutely unspeakable. I can't tell you how awful he was. Life simply wasn't worth living so in the end I had to give up the job.'

'What I find exasperating about both Enrico and Dermot,' remarked Jessica, 'is that they behave as if they believed we did absolutely nothing from dawn until dusk, as if they thought we simply frittered away our days with our feet in the air, lazing about doing nothing.'

'I'm sure they do think that. It is what they honestly believe.'

'Yet they wouldn't be seen dead doing any of the things we have to do. They simply would not do it for a moment. One morning of our lives would finish them.'

'They want the boring things done, though,' I said. 'They're the first to complain if some button is missing, or the house is a mess, or they can't find a clean shirt.'

'They are just the same at work, too,' added Jessica. 'Their secretaries do everything for them. Have you ever noticed how men expect their secretaries to organize things that are nothing to do with their work? They don't think twice about using office time and staff to organize their personal affairs. It apparently doesn't occur to them that there is anything dishonest about using their own and other people's salaried working hours on purely personal business, and the more important and successful a man is the more he does it; or do you think it is the other way round? Is it that the more a man uses the women around him – wives, secretaries, personal assistants, mistresses – the more successful he is?'

384

'His argument would be that it gives him time for the important things,' I said.

'The trouble with women,' said Jessica, 'is that they never have time for the important things because all the unimportant things, which would kill any normal man, are dumped on them.'

'I know,' I agreed, 'and we are never supposed to be tired or fed up, either, because we haven't ever done anything. Only men have the right to be bad-tempered and exhausted.'

'Yes, I know,' sighed Jessica. 'I find it utterly exasperating. We had a perfect example of it about six months ago when Dermot suddenly decided he needed a holiday. There was no question of my needing a holiday, naturally, and when I said I would quite like a break too, Dermot said that it was out of the question – too expensive. This, I might add, was the fourth holiday he had taken without me. In fact, this is the first holiday I've had for three years and you don't need me to point out that it isn't really a holiday either for you or for me since we still have to do all the shopping, cooking, washing-up, bed-making, bathing children, changing babies and all the usual routine.

'Anyway, Dermot's attitude is that I don't qualify for a holiday since I don't go to an office or a classroom, or whatever. While he was away, that week, Barnaby and Elizabeth both developed violent gastro-enteritis – and you know what that's like with very small children: terrifying. They had such high temperatures that they nearly went into convulsions and I had to do all those drastic things like plunging them into tepid baths and turning the fan on them while they lay on wet towels. I had visions of them dying. They couldn't even take boiled water without being sick and they were becoming totally dehydrated as the week wore to its close. I sat up all night, every night, with a basin in each hand, alternately mopping up sick and diarrhoea; and, in between, endlessly remaking cots with clean sheets. It was simply ghastly. The doctor told me afterwards that they should

385

both have been in hospital, but he didn't bother to tell me that at the time.

'The whole thing was a nightmare and by the time Dermot came back from his week's holiday, looking brown and rested, we were all shattered. Dermot chose this moment to invite ten people to dinner. He kept saying, "You don't have to do anything terribly elaborate, you know. I can't think why you're making such a fuss about it," but you know what it's like: shopping with three children is impossible, and it takes hours. Cooking anything half-way decent whilst giving babies bottles and baths and making up feeds and changing nappies is equally impossible. Dinner happens at the wrong time of day for mothers: it happens at the worst possible moment of the twenty-four hours, and by the time Dermot came home I was weaving on my feet.

'He didn't come home until about five minutes before the guests arrived, in any case. He never does when we are having people to dinner because he wants to avoid any possibility of being asked to lay the table, or move a chair, or anything exhausting of that sort. Elizabeth had just had another explosion and was in such a mess that I'd had to give her a second bath, so I was only just putting her into her cot at that point. I hadn't laid the table, or put the vegetables on, or anything, when people started arriving.

'When Dermot came into the kitchen to fetch ice for their drinks, I said to him, "I'm not nearly ready. I haven't even had time to lay the table yet," and he replied, "So I see," and returned to the drawing-room without suggesting that he might help. When, from time to time, I looked briefly into the drawing-room to see if everybody was all right, Dermot, sitting happily, drink in hand, would shout, "I assume dinner is going to be ready soon, is it? We're all starving."

'In spite of everything, I managed to produce a reasonable dinner and there was a total shambles to clear up when they finally departed. The first person didn't leave until one thirty in the morning so you can imagine what I was feeling like by then. When the last person had gone, Dermot glanced at all the dirty coffee cups and ashtrays in the drawing-room, followed me through to the dining-room which looked as if a bomb had hit it, and then on into the kitchen which looked even worse. There, he leant against the fridge for a moment and watched me starting to clear up the mess. "Well," he said after a second, "I'm absolutely exhausted. I'm going to bed." That, after a holiday! That is the sort of thing which enrages me. The complete selfishness of men, their total lack of consideration. Do you know, I spent two hours clearing up, and the few remaining hours of the night were disturbed three times by the children waking and needing to be changed? Dermot didn't move a muscle each time I clambered out of bed and in the morning he had the gall to say to me, "That was what I call a really good evening. I think everyone enjoyed themselves." '

'I want to kill men when they behave like that,' I said. 'I really *hate* them sometimes. Do you know what Enrico once did? He invited eight people to dinner, not one of whom I had ever met, and he kept telling me how important they all were for his work. They were all from the State Department or other embassies. Anyway, I had the same frightful business of shopping and cooking with a newborn baby and a toddler; trying to do things between feeds and all that stuff. You won't believe this, but I promise you it's true. As the first guest rang the doorbell, Enrico suddenly said, "I can't stand any of them. They bore me stiff. None of them understands the first thing about anything. I'm damned if I'm going to put up with a whole evening of them. I can't think why we ever invited them. I'm going somewhere else. Tell them I've been called back to the Embassy," and he skipped out through the drawing-room into the garden and down into the alley like a flash, leaving me to deal with them all on my own.

'It was one of the most embarrassing evenings I have ever experienced. I made pathetic excuses about something urgent having come up and Enrico being suddenly called back to the Embassy, but since every single one of them would have heard if anything dramatic had happened anywhere, they must have all known it wasn't true.'

'I don't believe it,' exclaimed Jessica.

'I promise you, it's true,' I said, 'and as for holidays, Enrico hardly ever takes me on holiday. He always takes a girlfriend instead and then comes back and leaves photographs of her lying around the house for weeks afterwards. But to be perfectly honest, our holidays together have always been so unhappy that I prefer to stay at home while he goes off with someone else. It's such a relief to be on my own that it's the best holiday I could have. I've secretly wished for years that he would just go and never come back. If it weren't for the children, I'd have left myself years ago.'

'I wonder if it really is the best solution from the children's point of view. We've all had it drummed into us that it is better for children if couples stay together but I am beginning to wonder whether that is correct. It's obviously the best thing if the parents are fond of each other, but when they are miserably unhappy and do nothing but fight I don't believe it can be better for the children than if their parents split up and were happy.'

Farewell to Marriage

... j'ai entendu ta voix heureuse
ta voix déchirée et fragile
enfantine et désolée
venant de loin et qui m'appelait
et j'ai mis ma main sur mon coeur
où remuaient
ensanglantés
les sept éclats de glace de ton rire étoilé

Jacques Prévert

CHAPTER TWENTY-FIVE

It was during that holiday that I finally realized that I must somehow leave Enrico.

'You still took ages to do it,' remarked Jessica when I said this to her in the attic at Manta.

'I know,' I said. 'It was only when I discovered what it felt like to be happy that I realized how pointless and stupid it was to go on being unhappy. Sébastien not only pushed me, from the moment he met me, into leaving Enrico, but – more important – he gave me back my taste for living. If it hadn't been for him (or, to be accurate, if it hadn't been for our bet) I don't think I would have ever made a move. For some reason, I had resigned myself to the idea that life was over and that nothing would ever be fun again. I wonder why. Something to do with our Catholic upbringing, do you think? Marriage being for life, this world being nothing but a vale of tears, the more you suffer the holier you are, punishment for having fornicated in your youth? I expect all that had something to do with it; but I think it was also something to do with Granny's incessant warnings about men and the fact that, in my experience, she was proved right. I suppose I thought that we would have been miserable whoever we had married since all men were equally unbearable: hideously selfish, violent, bad-tempered, unkind, unfaithful and thoroughly unpleasant. I worked on the assumption that all women were doomed to this misery and that any other man would make me equally unhappy. I remember making a list of all the couples I knew and thinking that there wasn't one of those women with whom I'd care to swap places. It wasn't just Enrico who was foul, I realized. After all, both your father and mine had, and still have, appalling tempers; Anthony was a liar and a cheat; my own brother was prepared to betray me; Dermot was as ghastly to you as Enrico was to me; Antonio turned out to be a bigamist (as I had always suspected – do you remember how you used to tease me?); and Thibault was unbelievably unpleasant to his poor wife in Washington – patronising, intellectually arrogant and nearly as unfaithful as Enrico.

'Then we made that bet and miraculously, out of the blue, along came Sébastien. As it turned out, he proved to be just as awful as all the others, but I don't hold it against him because he gave me the impetus to leave Enrico – and, anyway, it was fun while it lasted. What about you?' I asked. 'Can you remember at exactly what point you decided to leave Dermot? When did you first *know* that it couldn't go on forever?'

'I'm not sure,' replied Jessica. 'The same time we decided to take lovers, I suppose. After that bet. It wasn't in our natures to cheat on our husbands, was it? I mean, from the moment we took lovers it really meant it was all over. Although I don't think I worked it out consciously until much later. After Gilles walked out of my life, perhaps. It was rather odd the way he just disappeared one day. After all, we had been lovers for two years by then and he still seemed just as obsessed with me as he was at the beginning. It wasn't as if it was the first time he went off to the Ardennes, either. He was forever going off there. Whenever the mushroom season hit us, off he would go to the Ardennes for weeks on end. Only that time he never came back. When he had been gone long enough for me to start worrying, I made a few enquiries and discovered that he had sold his flat before leaving. He simply vanished without trace. I suppose I should have guessed from the last batch of poems he sent me, but I had had so many poems from him by then that I had ceased to look for special messages in them.'

'What did the last ones say?'

'I'll show you. I saw them here, somewhere, earlier this afternoon. I think they are in that pile over there. Wait a second. Yes, here they are. Read them.'

She handed me four sheets of paper, held together with a safety-pin, on each of which was a short poem, written in a large, firm scrawl. I read them in the order in which they had been sent:

> 1) Entre ma joie et la vôtre
> il y a le nerf de la guerre.
>
> Chez nous
> la monnaie courante est l'éther.
>
> 2) Piquées aux chardons
> vos mains
> peu à peu de l'ombre victorienne
> se dégagent
> pour monter vers la lumière.
>
> 3) Souffrir
> quand on prend son luth
> ça va.
>
> 4) Ce soir
> vous êtes seule au milieu des chiens.
> Quel dogue
> en même temps que le morceau
> emportera le secret?

'Yes,' I said, 'I think you might have guessed that something was wrong. It sounds as if he knew you'd fallen in love with Mircea.'

'I suppose he must have done. At any rate, I never heard from him again although I did hear from someone else, years later, that they had seen him in

Strasbourg and that he was just the same. It was bound to end some time, but it was an odd way of doing it.'

'You didn't sound particularly devastated at the time, remembering your letters,' I remarked.

'No, I wasn't. I think I knew that I had exhausted that relationship; but it was a shock, all the same. He was very odd,' she mused, and then laughed. 'I wish you could have seen him, always wandering about in a dark blue overcoat that had once been smart but had lost all its buttons; and he always had this curious little basket on his arm. It was full of tiny phials of different coloured poisons. He used them for analysing mushrooms. For some reason he had to drop minute amounts of different poisons on them with a dropper. I never understood why. Then he would study the results against a colour chart. I'm sure he would have ended up using his little bottles of poison on me if he hadn't chosen to vanish instead.' She paused for a moment, looking thoughtful. 'In any case, I was on the verge of falling in love with Mircea at that point.'

'And yet you married the Blight.'

'Not immediately,' objected Jessica.

'No, not immediately, but still . . . What on earth made you do it?'

'I don't know, really. I hadn't even got my divorce from Dermot before he had that accident and even though I couldn't stand living with him, I was quite fond of him in a way. At any rate, I wouldn't have wished that on him. And then Mircea didn't look as if he was likely to leave Amélie for years (hilarious, when you think of it: I did actually believe he'd leave her eventually); and I began to worry about the children not having a man around, and their financial security with Dermot dead, and all that sort of thing. I suppose I was in a state of shock – the news about Dermot came just after that awful man tried to leap on me at the Berendon Club, and I was thoroughly thrown and upset about everything – and there was dear old, boring Edward, still as keen as ever, nothing if not faithful: it

seemed the only thing to do at the time. He seemed positively reassuring and then, you know, I still believed in
marriage.'

'I was appalled at the time, when I heard,' I said. 'I
didn't understand at all. Of course, we were neither of
us to know that poor old Edward would die instantly
from all the excitement.'

I remembered Jessica's letter at the time. She told
me, virtually in one sentence, that Dermot had gone
down in one of his plastic bubbles, somewhere off
Mexico, when he was blind drunk and had, as far as
anyone could tell, decided to climb out of it for some
reason. At any rate, he had died and his remains had
been found more or less intact (which everyone said
was extraordinary, given the shark population in the
area).

Then Jessica had had some sort of upset with Mircea
and had married the Blight on the rebound, if one could
call it that. Poor Edward was so excited that he had a
heart attack on his wedding night. Jessica had sounded
quite resigned, if somewhat surprised, in her letter.

When I finally started divorce proceedings against
Enrico and he shortly afterwards committed suicide,
she wrote saying, 'It's odd, isn't it? Men don't seem to
have much of a hold on life and yet we were brought up
to believe they were so strong.'

My father also wrote to me, I remembered. He could
sound surprisingly callous at times. 'What in God's
name is going on?' he enquired in his letter. 'Have you
and Jessica taken to bumping off husbands as a way of
life?'

I was upset by my father's letter, at the time. He had
no idea how difficult the whole thing had been. Apart
from everything else, I had felt terribly sorry for
Enrico. It had been painful and violent because he still
believed he loved me.

I remembered his reaction when he finally understood that I was going to divorce him whatever he said
or did. I remembered watching him from an upstairs

window as he left for work the following morning. He walked through our garden in the sunlight, past banks of azaleas, and I could hear the sounds of Washington, smell the smells, see the maple and the ginkgo tree, a child's tricycle, the terrace with its deck-chairs, the Virginia creeper. I watched him open the gate at the end of the garden, then stop and look back; but he did not look up, he did not see me. He simply stared at the house for a few seconds, then turned and left. Seen from behind, he looked lonely and sad. He walked away down the lane as if he knew he had already lost it all, as if he were saying goodbye to me, goodbye to our life, goodbye to the children, goodbye to our house, goodbye to the rare moments of happiness that he could never admit were happy, that we always managed to spoil: a forlorn and tragic figure.

Then, two days later, I was telephoned by the police. They had found him dead in an underground car-park miles away. It was obviously not just a gesture gone wrong: he had taken an overdose, *and* slit his wrists, *and* left the car engine running just for good measure. The Ambassador insisted on coming to see me. He kept apologizing, as if he thought it was his fault.

I would have given a lot to have Jessica around at that moment, but it was a long time since we had last seen each other and she was embroiled in her own problems, three thousand miles away. I did not know of course that she had remarried or that the Blight had died. It all happened so quickly. The last letter I had had from her was all about Mircea and it sounded as if they would sort something out in the end. She had had to explain to me who Mircea was because, although I remembered the story, I had never known his name.

It dated back to our time at the Sorbonne. Olivier had been hopelessly in love with a girl whom he had every intention of marrying but, instead of marrying him, she had married a Rumanian in order to help the latter acquire French nationality. (I remembered quite clearly how depressed Olivier had become.) It had been obvious from the start that the Rumanian had every intention of treating it as a serious marriage, but Olivier had continued to hope that Mircea would eventually disappear. According to Jessica, Olivier (who had never married) was still in love with Amélie and it was through Olivier that she had met Amélie's husband.

Mircea and Jessica fell in love and it was an affair which went on for years. Olivier was delighted because he thought that at long last Mircea might leave Amélie and he could have his heart's desire; but Mircea appeared to feel he had a moral obligation to remain with his wife. He was a Catholic, and believed absolutely in his marriage bond; but stronger even than this was the feeling that he owed her a debt of permanent gratitude for what she had done for him. Jessica said, in her letter, that though he talked a great deal about the Rumanian sense of honour, she was always left with the impression that eventually she and Mircea would leave their respective spouses and be free to live with each other. Mircea, she said, was waiting for Amélie to make the first move, knowing that sooner or later she would run off with Olivier; and Olivier certainly believed Amélie would leave Mircea.

I had telephoned Jessica after receiving one of her letters on the subject, because I sensed her despondency beginning to overwhelm her. She sounded unhappy, but resigned, on the other end of the line.

'It doesn't matter,' she had said. 'It's a lifetime thing. I can wait twenty, thirty, forty years. It really doesn't matter. It's just the waste of time which is so sad. It seems such a terribly sad waste of time.'

I suppose she imagined when Dermot died that Mircea would finally leave Amélie and marry her. When he showed no signs of doing anything of the sort she turned in her despair to Edward.

Once Edward Blight had had his heart attack, Jessica returned to having an affair with Mircea exactly as if nothing had intervened.

('Would you have gone on having an affair with Mircea if Edward hadn't died?' I asked her in the attic.

'No, I don't think so. I would have thought it unfair on Edward,' she replied.)

At the time of Enrico's suicide, however, I was unaware of all this. I guessed, of course, that she was in a state of shock because she sounded quite unlike herself when she rang me to tell me of Dermot's demise. Even before that, I knew she was shaken by her incident in London, at the Berendon Club. The fact that she managed to be funny about it did not, I knew, mean that it had not frightened and upset her.

During our sorting operation in the attic I looked particularly for that letter and eventually found it.

Darling Imogen,

Mummy's in hospital having an operation on her hip. I've just been over to visit her and she sends you her love. She says she agrees with everything you say about Washington. All women find it boring, sooner or later, she says, and it has been responsible for more divorces than you would believe. She says you'll miss some things when you return to Europe, though: things like playing tennis all the time, and Georgetown in the autumn. That's what you'll miss the most, she thinks, because the North American fall is as powerful as English gardens, or Canadian lakes, or those village squares in the *midi* with the plane trees, the café tables and the old men playing *boules* in the shade. God, I wish I could visit you. Still, it's no use feeling miserable, is it? I'll tell you a funny story instead.

It happened when I went to see Mummy in hospital last week. She's in this frightfully expensive place in Hampstead, miles from anywhere one could possibly want to go; and the visiting hours are such that you haven't time to go into the centre

400

of London, or see an exhibition, or anything between visits.

The third day I was there, it poured with rain – it simply came down in torrents all day – and I had to do something to fill in the time between visits. I had walked all round Hampstead and the Heath on the previous two days, so I didn't want to do that again, especially in the sopping wet. I hate Hampstead, anyway; I've always found North London terribly depressing. So I tried to think of a way of keeping dry and passing the time until the ferocious matron at the hospital would let me see Mummy again. I thought about going to a hairdresser, but you know how I loathe them and how they always want to chop off all one's hair and make one practically bald, so that didn't seem very tempting; but it gave me the idea of something to do with making oneself look beautiful. I finally had what I thought was a brilliant idea – something I've never done in my life – and that was to have a 'facial'. I have always thought it sounded wonderful, and at least I would be dry and warm instead of out in the rain.

I went to a telephone box, looked up beauty salons in the yellow pages and the only one I had ever heard of that was within striking distance was a hairdresser-cum-beauty-salon in the Berendon Club – you know, that place where all Daddy's smart friends used to play squash and where we once had lunch with him before we went back to school. I telephoned them and the woman said, 'We can't give you a facial today, I'm afraid. The girl who does them is away because she's sick.'

I explained my problem and the limited time before I had to be back at the hospital, and she said, 'I suppose you don't want to have your legs waxed? We could manage that if you want. Yvonne normally does that, too, but Monsieur

Pierre is helping us out while she's away.'

It reminded me of how I used to worry as a child that I was turning into a man. Do you remember? It seemed quite a funny idea, so I said 'yes'.

'Monsieur Pierre is very nice,' she added. 'He runs the gym for us and his children always come here to have their hair cut.'

It struck me as slightly odd that a gym teacher would want to do people's legs, but then people do the strangest things and I've never understood why men want to do women's hair, or why anybody wants to be a dentist, or any of those things.

Anyway, when I arrived I was greeted by a very friendly woman who kept repeating the same story about Yvonne being sick and Monsieur Pierre helping out. 'Ever so nice, he is, dear. We've known him for years and his boys always come to us to have their hair cut. Such a thoughtful man. You'll like Monsieur Pierre. If you'll follow me, dear, it's along here.'

I followed her along a corridor, up some stairs, along another corridor and finally into a small room miles from everywhere. 'Here you are, dear,' the woman said. 'Monsieur Pierre won't be long,' and she disappeared.

I sat on a bed-like affair and was looking at the bowls and cooking equipment (which looked jolly primitive to me) when an ape-like figure leapt into the room.

' 'Allo, 'allo, 'allo!' he hailed me. 'And how are we today? I'm Monsieur Pierre. Come to 'ave your legs done, 'ave you? Well, that's nice. Won't take a jiffy and your husband won't recognize you afterwards. Got a husband, have you? Thought so. I can always tell. He'll be pleased and no mistake. Smooth as a baby's bottom your legs will be. Just you wait and see. 'Ere!' he suddenly exclaimed, producing a flask from his hip-pocket. 'Want a sip?'

'No, thank you,' I replied, politely, having no idea what he was offering me.

'It's whisky,' he said. 'Have some. It'll do you good.' (This was at about three o'clock in the afternoon.)

'It's very kind of you,' I replied, 'but I won't, thank you.'

'Come on, dearie. It'll warm you up after all that rain. You want to relax and enjoy yourself,' he insisted.

'No, thank you,' I said again, putting on my disapproving voice. 'I'm not in the habit of drinking at three in the afternoon.'

'Dear me, you *are* a tease, aren't you? Very tense, too. Never mind, you'll soon feel better. Well, I'll have some if you don't mind. Sure you won't join me? No? All right,' and he took a quick slug from his flask, smacking his lips when he'd finished. 'Right,' he continued, 'I'd better start warming that wax. You get those stockings off and hop back up there,' he said, waving at the bed. 'Don't be shy, there's a good girl. I'm a father with kids, you know, and we're only dealing with your legs. It's not as if I were asking you to strip to the buff, is it?' He laughed uproariously at this last remark.

While I was peeling off my tights and clambering back on to the bed-like affair, the gymmaster was cavorting about in front of a Bunsen burner, throwing lumps of wax into a saucepan and, all the while, sipping at his flask with loud, slurping noises.

'Right, dearie,' he finally said. 'That should be about ready, now. Sure you don't want some Scotch first? Loosens you up and makes you relax, you know. No?' (Had I had the faintest idea what was coming, I would have accepted with alacrity.) 'Here we go then,' he shouted gaily, brandishing the saucepan in his left hand. Then, he started slapping boiling wax on to my right leg. It hurt exceedingly.

'Ouch!' I yelped.

'Not too bad when you get used to it,' he remarked, amiably. 'It'll all be worth it in the end, you'll see.'

'I think you're burning my leg,' I said.

'Have to leave it on for a while, dearie, otherwise it won't work,' he replied cheerfully. 'Let's do the other one while that's cooking, shall we?' he asked and proceeded to hurl a saucepanful of boiling wax over the front of my left leg.

Never having been through this operation before, it was difficult for me to know whether or not this process was abnormally painful. I had the vague idea that someone had told me that it hurt, but at the same time I felt sure they would have mentioned the fact that it was absolute agony. Would so many women be prepared to go through this, not just once but on a regular basis, I asked myself? We all know women will put up with the most astonishing things, but I had serious doubts about it all the same. It wasn't as if one were going to come out with a baby at the end of it, or anything. And our mothers were neither of them the type to go in for torture, yet they were forever rushing off to have their legs waxed. It seemed out of character. They liked to be pampered. I couldn't imagine either of them going in for this.

The gym-master was reheating his bowl of wax when he suddenly turned round and said, 'I say, dearie, you don't look as if you're enjoying yourself. You want to let your hair down. How about a massage? A massage would do you the world of good. Soon make you relax, a massage would.'

'No, thank you,' I replied, aghast at the thought.

'Ever tried a massage?' he enquired.

'No,' I said firmly, 'and I do not wish to try

404

today, thank you. Quite apart from everything else, I'm in a hurry. I've got to be back at the hospital within three-quarters of an hour.'

'That's what it is, is it?' enquired the gym-master, solicitously. 'Friend sick, is he? Or your Dad or something? No wonder you're tense. You'll feel much better when you've had your massage. Let's get those things off,' and he leaped on me and started trying to pull all my clothes off.

'Stop it!' I cried, pushing him away. As I leapt off the bed, he started taking his own clothes off, still waving the whisky flask around. I fled from the room, bare-footed and half-undressed, with wax all down the front of my legs, and flew along passages and downstairs to the hairdresser's salon. There, I burst in on the unsuspecting group of women sitting placidly under hairdryers.

'You have a maniac up there!' I stormed at the woman in charge. 'What on earth do you mean by allowing him to work here?' I was extremely annoyed and not a little shaken. The woman looked appalled when I told her what had happened. 'What's more,' I shouted, 'not only is he a sexual maniac, a raving lunatic and an alcoholic, he's a sadist as well, an incompetent sadist. Look at my legs! I should think he has given me third-degree burns.'

All the women were crowding round by this point and one of them helped me to peel off the wax, exposing raw, red burns the entire length of my shins. The manageress was utterly apologetic, but irritated me by saying, 'We won't charge you anything.'

'I should think not!' I retorted. 'You'll be lucky if I don't sue you and I'm going to report it to the police immediately.'

'Let me go and talk to him first,' the manageress said. 'Who ever would 'ave thought it? We've done his children's hair for years. Such nice kids, too.

405

You stay here. I'll fetch your clothes for you.'

When she returned, clutching my shoes, tights and coat, she looked worried. 'He's gone,' she said. 'He must have jumped out of the window. There's no other way out. I'll have to call the police.'

The police turned up almost instantly in the form of PC Higgins, quite an amiable fellow who took reams of notes. At the end of it all, he warned me that if I wanted to press charges (and he wanted me to press charges for assault) I would have to return from Paris, in due course, at my own expense as far as I could make out; and that I would be treated very unpleasantly in court. He said they would try to make out that I had some-how provoked the whole thing and that I had delib-erately set about trying to seduce the horrible little man. I said I wasn't at all enthusiastic about having to buy a return ticket from Paris in order to be insulted and humiliated, and that I would like to think the matter over for twenty-four hours before deciding whether or not to press charges.

I then, very belatedly, tottered feebly over to the hospital feeling thoroughly upset and barely able to hobble because my legs were so sore. I showed my shins to a nurse who promptly took me into the Outpatients' Department where they anointed and bandaged the burns which they said were quite serious.

At the end of all this, I staggered up to the wards to visit Mummy and, partly to explain why I was late and partly because I was so shaken by the whole event, I told her in great detail exactly what had happened. I think I was hoping for some sympathy but Mummy put on her pained expres-sion and said in a tired voice, 'Really, darling, I do *wish* you would go to Lizzie Arden,' so that was that.

I was lucky, as it turned out, because I didn't

have to do anything about the gym-master. The police caught him in Leighton Buzzard the following day and he'd committed two rapes in the interval so there were plenty of other charges against him.

I must dash. I've got to collect the children from school in a minute. I miss you.

All my love,
Jessica

Once I had re-read it, I handed it to Jessica. 'Read this,' I said. 'I don't know how you managed it but you remained funny throughout. I always admired you for that. I was quite incapable of hanging on to my sense of humour. I became revoltingly self-pitying and boring.'

'Did you?' asked Jessica. 'I don't remember you ever being boring.'

CHAPTER TWENTY-SIX

'As a matter of fact,' said Jessica suddenly, 'I think you did rather lose your sense of humour in Washington. I'd forgotten, until I re-read this, how gloomy you became. Read it,' and she handed me an old letter of mine.

Darling Jessica,

I am sitting under a horse chestnut tree in the gardens of Dumbarton Oaks. My immediate surroundings look so English that I can hardly believe I am in America.

I come here to rest my spirit whenever I find Washington too much to bear. The lawns and cedars remind me of school; the rose-garden and ponds of your parents' garden; and the statues and fountains, and the way everything slopes downhill, remind me of Manta. There are potting sheds and a kitchen-garden with lots of herbs. It brings back memories of many a summer day when we picked ripe currants, tomatoes, raspberries and all manner of delicious things together: very nostalgic.

Washington is a most peculiar place and not at all the way you remember it. It is very provincial and the Europeans are appallingly gossipy and tiresome: everybody showing off to everyone else about the important people they know and no-one having anything to do with the Americans outside work. The French, as you can imagine, make incessant, cutting remarks about how the Americans don't know how to dress, or what to drink, or how to cut meat (I even heard a child the other day saying '*Ils ne savent pas couper*'); and everyone ridicules their political ignorance. Dermot would have a field day. In fact, they are rather sweet – at least the Americans I've met are – much less pompous than everyone else here and with a child-like innocence which makes them rather endearing as long as one keeps off politics.

I am fascinated by their lawn-mower-garage culture. There is an entire breed of American men whom I have nicknamed 'the garage men'. They seem to spend the whole of every Saturday mowing their little patches of lawn in front of, and behind, their houses: up and down, up and down, like a *New Yorker* cartoon, and the rest of their free time is spent in dreary little sheds or garages at the back of their 'yards' (as they insist on calling their back gardens. Actually, 'garden' is perhaps too grand a word for what is, in fact, simply a small patch of grass or pebbles).

Next door to us, in Georgetown, there lives an American with an Irish name and a hatchet-faced wife. He is retired, but he sets his alarm at six every morning (I can hear it from our bedroom) in order to dress, breakfast and install himself in his garage at the end of the garden before his wife rises. He stays in his garage all day, except for one morning every fortnight when he takes the car to some supermarket to stock up on beer and tins of this and that to bring back to his garage as supplies for the next two weeks. There is no room for his car in there so it remains parked in the back alley, winter and summer.

He has invited me in a couple of times to show me his domain: a worktop on which he rests his feet while he smokes his pipe (he is not allowed to smoke in the house); a supply of booze, beer mainly;

shelves and shelves of tinned ham, beans, peas, etc.; a refrigerator; a transistor, and then lots of tools with which he fiddles all day long. He sings loudly, out of tune, when he isn't smoking his pipe and his friends from the other garages in the alley pop in and out all day long and stay for a chat and an iced beer. When he is feeling particularly adventurous, he sets forth (all of ten or twenty yards) to visit one of his friends in their garage for a change of scene.

When the sun sets and all is dark, one can still hear him humming and pottering about in there and, if I look across from our terrace at nightfall, I can see the feeble glimmer of a torch moving slowly about his lair. He packs up at about nine, climbs the steps up to his veranda and vanishes inside to be greeted by his wife, a bowl of soup, and bed. This routine is only broken once a fortnight, as I described, when he takes the car to the super-market to replenish his supplies.

His wife never appears, never sees anyone, never goes out and only figures as a raucous voice in the background.

Our neighbour on the other side does exactly the same, except that he neither hums nor ever receives visits. Up and down the alleys, hundreds of little men are similarly passing their lives away amid the sound of hammering, the blaring of transistors and the smell of tobacco and beer. They seem quite content as far as one can tell. I wonder whether it is better to be contented in a garage than to be bored in embassies.

I often wonder how your mother stood the diplomatic life. She always seemed so serene. How did she do it? I cannot tell you how dull the embassies are. Their dinners and cocktail parties are a nightmare and the people are frightful beyond belief. The worst shock was the discovery that so many countries are represented by complete cretins:

mean, snobbish, stupid ambassadors; small-minded consuls who have never bothered to go further afield than New York and Washington because they made up their minds before they arrived that America had nothing to offer; cultural attachés whose jobs seem to consist solely of supervising exams in the International School and who have never heard of Twyla Tharp or Alvin Ailey, who have never seen Baryshnikov dance, who have never visited the Space Museum or even the Hirshhorn. We dined with one cultural attaché, a few nights ago, who has been here for two and a half years yet has never been to any concert, opera or ballet at the Kennedy Center and had never been further south than Richmond or further west than the suburbs of Washington. He seemed to think that politics were an excuse for having neither the time nor the curiosity for anything else and yet he was extraordinarily arrogant and clearly despised anyone who did not spend their days running like a hare from one government official to another.

I have to say in Enrico's favour that he is the only one who doesn't take himself seriously and who isn't bowled over with self-importance at the knowledge that he spends a fair amount of time with Kissinger and the like. Having said that, he is working fiendishly hard and is permanently exhausted and bad-tempered.

I don't know how long I'm going to be able to stand it: night after night dressing to the teeth in order to go and make trivial conversation with people about whom I couldn't care less; or cooking endless dinners for people I don't like and never wish to meet again. Why am I doing it? Why are all the wives doing it? Why isn't there one woman brave enough to say, 'Sorry, I'm not going to any reception tonight. I don't care whether Rocky is the guest of honour, and I've already met Kissinger quite often

411

enough. I want to stay here and read my book.' Or, 'You can invite as many people from the State Department as you like but you'll have to organize the dinner because Baryshnikov is dancing at the Kennedy Center and I cannot bear to miss him.'

We only do it because it is expected of us. No-one in their right mind wants to shake hands with a row of stuffed shirts, or listen to dull people making dull conversation, just so as to say they have met a list of important people. The trouble is that I am too cowardly to refuse. I am afraid of Enrico's bad humour. I can't face the scenes, the shouting, the threats and accusations, the sulking, the revenge and all the rest. Presumably at least fifty per cent of the wives here are doing the same thing for the same reasons. It's quite absurd.

'I've just re-read *A Room of One's Own* and I had forgotten how much to the point it was. V.W. put in words a question I have often asked myself (particularly whenever I have seen a Bergman film), to wit: 'Why are women, judging from this catalogue, so much more interesting to men than men are to women?'

Do we in fact understand anything about each other? Do women understand anything about men? Do men understand anything about us? Do either of us want to understand the other, and is it possible? Why do we try to live together? Is there any common factor which obliges us to try? Yes, sex, I suppose. But does sex not simply underline the differences, the complete hopelessness of attempting to meet or merge? Do you remember Abelard? 'Never yet hath he possessed her wholly. Never yet have twain been one.'

I feel lost and empty. Not lonely, but forlorn. Is it any better for you?

I miss you.

Love,
Imogen

412

The letter that was attached to this was much shorter and quite different in tone.

Darling Imogen,

I always miss you most on the *quatorze juillet*. Do you remember how we celebrated that year, with Anthony? All that dancing in the place des Vosges, and the fireworks and that ridiculous trip to Montmartre. It makes me want to cry, I feel so nostalgic. Anyway, guess who I saw yesterday? Dear old André Brillac d'Hocquincourt. My *dear*, you wouldn't believe how he's aged: he seemed antique when we were at the Sorbonne but now he looks positively translucent, like porcelain. He was *beautifully* dressed and as witty as ever, and so kind. He seemed terribly lonely. He took me from one *chocolatier* to another all afternoon assuming, I suppose, that I was still a little girl; and we ended up having tea in the bois de Boulogne, by which time I was feeling thoroughly sick. He has kept in touch with Anthony and Simon, apparently, and of course he still sees your parents to whom he is as devoted as ever. He had just come back from staying with them so he gave me all their news. It doesn't sound as if they've changed much.

He still splatters the conversation with 'My cousin, the Countess of What-Not' and gives you the full pedigree of everyone he mentions, but he did tell me one thing which would interest you. Apparently he and Marguerite were married once, centuries ago. It was a complete disaster, as you can imagine. It only lasted a few weeks. It explains a lot about Marguerite, though. No wonder she was worried about you and Anthony.

Anyway, I've promised to keep in touch and he sends you masses of kisses and *hommages* and all that sort of thing.

He'd love to see you again. So would I.

Love as always,
Jessica

I remembered how homesick I had felt when I received that letter and how I tried to telephone her but was told she was out. I had rung my parents instead and they had been pleased to hear from me.

'I've had a letter from Jessica,' I said to my father, 'and she says that André's been staying at Manta. Was it exhausting?'

'No,' my father had replied. 'As a matter of fact, he was less irksome than he sometimes is. Less talk about princesses. He sewed all morning and he slept most afternoons.'

'*Sewed* all morning?' I asked incredulously.

'Yes,' my father replied. 'He kept sewing revolting little pieces of fur onto other revolting little pieces of fur. He was endlessly occupied taking up, and taking in, and letting down a collection of dreadful, moth-eaten objects saying that the fashion had changed and that lapels were half a centimetre narrower this year and that he was saving a lot of money by not going to his tailor. It kept him very busy. Then, as I say, he slept a lot in the afternoons, so it was really much easier than his previous visits.

'I'm terribly fond of him in any case,' said my father. 'I find him rather heartbreaking. He is such a lonely man – a loneliness entirely created by himself but none the less sad for that. All those legal battles over inheritance . . . the French are so litigious . . . I think we must be the only friends he had before the war with whom he hasn't fallen out. He has fought with everyone . . .

'He was having trouble with his circulation,' added my father as an afterthought. 'He kept getting pins and needles in his feet. It was rather like having a horse about the place. Wherever one went, one heard the distant stamping of feet. Anyway, darling, I must go. Are all of you all right? Children OK?'

'Yes, fine, thank you.'

'Excellent. Glad to hear it. Give them all my love. I've sent you something quite interesting to read. You should

get it in a day or two. Let me know what you think of it,'
and he hung up before I had time to say goodbye.

'Do you still feel nostalgic on the 14th July?' I asked
Jessica.

'No,' she said, 'Why should I?'

'You did,' I replied. 'You said so in this letter. Read it.'

Jessica glanced at it and then said, 'Yes, but that was
when you were living the other side of the world. That
was different. I thought I'd never see you again.'

CHAPTER TWENTY-SEVEN

'When we decided to take lovers, did you find it difficult to be unfaithful to Enrico?' Jessica asked me after a moment's silence.

'Yes, unbelievably. Quite apart from feeling hideously guilty, I wasn't very self-confident. I wasn't at all sure that anyone would be interested. I was so worried about making a fool of myself that I decided I'd better practise flirting on someone not too dangerous before I made any serious move. And that's exactly what I did. Do you remember that letter you found this afternoon, about the 'garage men'? I told you about our neighbour with the hatchet-faced wife, the one who hummed and messed about in his garage all day. Well, he used to invite me into his garage sometimes; usually because he wanted to give me something for the children. He was perfectly sweet. Anyway, I practised on him. I flirted like mad (I felt pretty safe because I knew he wouldn't do anything about it). He didn't know what had hit him, poor man. You can't imagine how embarrassed he was. I feel dreadfully guilty in retrospect, but I think he was quite pleased, in a way, too. I don't think garage men have much experience of that sort of thing. It doesn't really go with their life-style.'

'Honestly, Imogen!'

'Well, I had to practise on someone and I like to think it made his life more exciting for a few days.'

'Did the hatchet-faced wife know?'

'Of course not. I doubt whether she knew that such an activity existed, judging by her face the only time I saw her.'

416

'Did you find it useful, this practice run? Did you start flirting with Sébastien the minute you met him?'

'No, I didn't need to. I saw him, he saw me, and that was it.'

'It sounded a lot of fun, your affair with Sébastien.'

'It *was* a lot of fun. I can't tell you how much I enjoyed it. In a perverse sort of way, I think it was all the more exciting because it was so dangerous. I mean, imagine what would have happened if Enrico had found out. And it's almost impossible to keep anything secret in Washington. You can't sneeze without everyone knowing it. It was my first and only experience of utter deviousness: I spent most of my time plotting and scheming and making secret telephone calls. It would have worn me to shreds if I'd had to keep it up much longer.'

'Did you mind splitting up with him?' Jessica asked.

'Not really. I knew it had to be done. It would have been suicide otherwise. It was such a shock to discover that he was an exact repetition of Enrico – just as jealous, just as possessive, just as obsessive, just as determined to keep women in their place, just as unfaithful. I panicked the moment I realized. I saw that trap about to snap shut on me again and I fled. I was so aware of my narrow escape that I was far more relieved than sad; but once Enrico was dead I would have lost interest in any case. I completely lost interest in men after that.'

'Have you thought much about Sébastien since?'

'Not really. Hardly ever, in fact. But you have to remember that I only chose him for his looks. I told you that at the time. I took, if you like, the masculine approach. If women took that approach all the time, we'd be just as unfaithful and callous as men.'

Thinking about it for the first time for years, I realized that my only regret was that Sébastien and I had not managed to end on the same, light-hearted note that had carried us along until then. That last week, with the autumn smells about us and the leaves turning red, things had suddenly turned very sour.

*   *   *

Autumn, in most countries, brings with it a feeling of approaching death. It is the saddest time of year in Europe; but this is not the case in North America. The North American fall is beautiful beyond all reason and carries with it a sense of great optimism.

I was in love with Georgetown in the fall and Sébastien seemed to share my enthusiasm. As we drove through the streets in his open car, the breeze ruffled his hair and his eyes were alight. All the excitement and joy that I felt were summed up by one, small gesture of his. We had stopped at a red light and he put his hands above his head, high in the air, and clapped them with delight. Like a small boy excited at being let out of school, he clapped his hands in the air and laughed. His three years were up, he was being given the job he had always wanted, and he was thrilled at the thought of being transferred to Rome.

It was an unpleasant surprise when, later that week, I discovered that all the time we had been having an affair he had been having an equally passionate affair with one of the secretaries at *Le Monde*. If he was to be believed, he did not even like her very much. 'I like power,' he had said to me. 'I like the power of girls wanting to sleep with me.'

I, by that time, had finally decided I must divorce; and Sébastien, aware of this, wanted me to join him in Rome as soon as I was free. We had talked for months about living together – in fact, Sébastien wanted us to marry – but it was only during that last week that he mentioned that he would prefer me not to work. '*Vous avez l'air d'une petite fille criminelle avec ces nattes,*' he whispered to me as I registered this latest piece of information.

All the danger signals were there. Instead of thinking, as I frequently did, how pleasant it was of him to continue to address me as '*vous*', I suddenly remembered how angry he had been when he had found me flicking through a copy of *Vogue*. He had thrown it away in disgust and accused me of reading trash when I should

418

be reading about world affairs. Did I want, I asked myself, to live with a man who insisted on leaping up at five every morning in order to listen to every available version of the news, installing numerous wirelesses and television sets around himself so that he could simultaneously listen to, and watch, all the different channels? I had had more than my fair dose of half-hourly news bulletins from Enrico, and I was inclined to feel I deserved a break. There was the endless analysis to put up with as well (interesting much of the time, but perhaps not interesting enough to merit a lifetime of cohabitation). The warning bells rang just in time as I realized I had been within inches of repeating my marriage.

Sébastien did not take it well. We had a horrible lunch in a restaurant which we had frequented when we were happy. I tried to explain to him that I wanted to be free, that I could not go through a divorce just to repeat the same thing. He stormed out of the restaurant halfway through our main course, leaving me to pay the bill and heave a sigh of relief.

The only things I missed about him, and that was only for a time, were the notes he used to leave in my coat pocket when we attended the same gatherings but were unable to talk to each other for more than a minute. They were not love letters: that would have been too risky. They were simply signs of life, odd little messages, such as 'On annonce pour le week-end l'arrivée à Washington d'une cohorte de Danois, d'un régiment de Hollandais et de 15,000 Italiens disant tous la même chose et tous vêtus du même costume blanc,' or 'the spider, the fly and the web: il faudrait, pour écrire la fable, distribuer les rôles une fois pour toutes. En tout cas, l'image de la toile d'araignée vous va très bien. Vous êtes la Parque fileuse.'

Left penniless, with three children to bring up, I had little time to think about Sébastien, in any case. My thoughts were taken up with the necessity of finding a job. I answered an advertisement for someone to teach French and Italian to senior employees in a large, multi-national corporation based in New York. Until then, I had had little to do with the business world and had never experienced life in a corporation, so I was somewhat surprised by my interview.

The building was impressive and the office into which I was ushered was large. Behind a huge desk sat a man whose suit appeared to have been ironed on to him. He looked exactly like the dummies for men's clothes that one sees in the windows of large department stores. His tie was enormous and very ugly. He rose to his feet as I came in and leant across his desk as he greeted me. When he sat down again, he bent one arm and draped his tie over it. Throughout the interview, the arm remained bent, the tie hanging in space.

He could not have been more affable although I could not see the point of the interview. He was not in a position to test either my French or my Italian and he seemed unworried about the fact that I had never taught anyone anything. His only preoccupation was whether I would settle happily in New York, after Washington, and whether my children were going to cause problems. He asked me very few questions and seemed more interested in whether or not I could add up than whether I could speak languages. Most of our forty minutes together were taken up by his elaborate explanations about how the corporation worked, who answered to whom, and what the monthly profits were in each division.

He ended our conversation by telling me that he seldom went out to lunch. As he said this, still with his tie draped over his left arm, he pulled open the bottom right-hand drawer of his desk with his free hand and asked me to admire the contents. It was full of tins of what appeared to be cocktail sausages. He told me they were called 'weanies' and that he kept them to hand in case he felt hungry. 'The clock is always ticking,' he said, tapping his watch to make the point. 'People spend too much time over lunch.' Then he told me the job was mine.

Once I started the job, I discovered that they were all built on the same model. I gave private lessons to individuals, mainly from the sales side of the company. Some of them had mastered the rudiments of the language they were learning, some were clearly never going to be able to construct the simplest sentence. All of them were hoping to be sent to Europe for the corporation.

I tried, in conversation classes, to find subjects that interested them, but we always fell back on two subjects about which I knew nothing: money and baseball. Their main preoccupation in life appeared to be budgets and it seemed that they had barely finished one set of budgets before they had to launch forth on revised budgets, then budget 'up-dates', then budget reviews. Budgets seemed to take up the major part of the year but if, for any reason, there was an unexpected break in the pattern, they employed their time, profitably, drawing up five-year plans.

Not having anyone to talk to about this curious way of life and the men who went in for it, I decided that Jessica might be amused to hear about it.

Dear Jessica,
Since I started this job, I have discovered a new breed of man. It is the corporation man. They are quite unlike anyone you have ever met. They like to pretend that they are all one, big, happy family, but they spend their lives stabbing each other in the back. They are not particularly educated men – they know a lot more about baseball than they do about anything else – but they all make a point of learning company politics. Internal politics rule their lives and an awful lot of them don't seem to have any job but that. They don't seem to do anything but manoeuvre themselves around the corporation, up if possible, sideways if the worst comes to the worst. A great deal of jockeying for position carries on and there is an incomprehensible structure which, at first, seems a perfectly

421

straightforward distinction between 'divisional responsibilities' and 'corporate responsibilities' but, when you look at it closely, is confused by something known as a 'dotted-line relationship'. Dotted-line relationships are utterly baffling.

The corporation man is easily recognizable physically. They wear the strangest suits and they have huge ties which they drape over one arm when they sit down.

I have nicknamed these droll characters 'the Cardboard Men' and I have studied them in great detail. If you were to dissect them, I am sure that you would discover that instead of a heart they have a cash-register, that nickels and dimes course through their veins, that their heartbeat is the steady thump-thump-thump of coins dropping into the till.

Cardboard Men do not like creative talent and, oddly enough, they have never heard of the god they worship. There was a wonderful *New Yorker* cartoon, recently, which I pinned to the wall of my office because I thought it was so apt. It was a picture of a businessman at his desk, late at night, poring over figures in the light cast from an anglepoise lamp and mopping the sweat from his brow with a towel. Behind him, in the shadows, stood a ghostly figure grinning maliciously and bending towards the man who was looking round enquiringly. The caption was, 'Good evening, sir, I'm Mammon.' One of the Cardboard Men (one of the more educated ones) spotted this on my wall, peered at it and then said, 'I don't understand the joke. Who is Mammon?'

Somebody sent me a witty poster the other day which was entitled 'Five Stages of a Project'. These were (1) Wild enthusiasm, (2) Disillusionment, (3) Search for the guilty, (4) Punish the innocent, and (5) Reward the uninvolved.

There you have corporate life in a nutshell, and

now you know all you will ever need to know about it.

Love,
Imogen

Jessica, meantime, had also embarked upon earning her living. As a result of her contacts at the CNRS, she was offered the job of translating and interpreting from English into French for the oceanography department. When a group of their scientists were sent to Berkeley for six months, she was offered the chance to go with them to help with the language difficulties. Thinking that it would be fun for her children to have a spell in the sun and that their English might improve as a result, she accepted. She was unaware, when she agreed, that my company had given me the chance to move back to England as a trainee in their advertising department in London.

Jessica left Paris the day after I left New York. We seemed doomed to miss each other, condemned to living on opposite sides of the Atlantic; but I knew that it could not go on forever, that sooner or later we were bound to meet again.

Manta

Non pianger più . . .

Vieni; usciamo. Il giardino abbandonato
serba ancóra per noi qualche sentiero.
Ti dirò come sia dolce il mistero
che vela certe cose del passato.

Ancóra qualche rosa è ne' rosai,
ancóra qualche timida erba odora.
Ne l'abbandono il caro luogo ancóra
sorriderà, se tu sorriderai.

Ti dirò come sia dolce il sorriso
di certe cose che l'oblìo afflisse.
Che proveresti tu se ti fiorisse
la terra sotto i piedi, all'improvviso?

Sogna, sogna, mia cara anima! Tutto,
tutto sarà come al tempo lontano.
Io metterò ne la tua pura mano
tutto il mio cuore. Nulla è ancor distrutto.

Gabriele d'Annunzio

CHAPTER TWENTY-EIGHT

I was not quite sure how it would happen, or when. So much time had gone by that I imagined a certain amount of preparation on each side and something resembling a stage set for the encounter - among the potted palms at the Ritz - or a lunch somewhere neutral.

Inevitably, it happened unexpectedly. The telephone rang one morning, early, and Jessica's voice said, 'It's me. Have I woken you? Can I come and see you?'

I thought she was in California. 'Where are you?' I asked.

'At Liverpool Street,' she replied. 'I've just missed my train.'

'What train? What are you doing at Liverpool Street? What are you doing in England?'

'We've finished our stint at Berkeley,' she replied. 'I've come back via London because the CNRS want me to persuade Dermot's old college to part with some of his papers. They don't seem at all willing, but I've said I'll try. I'll have to take a later train. It doesn't matter. I've sent the children to my parents for a week. It's ages since they were last at Upton and they want to show off their American English. This station hasn't improved, has it? And it's jolly cold here. Can I come and see you?'

'Of course.'

'You won't run away?'

'I won't run away.'

Twenty minutes later, I opened the front door and Jessica was standing there, looking tired.

'What an amazing nightie!' was all she said, with an amused expression on her face.

'Isn't it *hideous*? Enrico's mother gave it to me when we were first married. She thought it would make me look sexier, I suppose. I like wearing it. It reminds me of what I've escaped.'

'It's so utterly dreadful that it's almost beautiful in a weird sort of way. I approve. You haven't changed. Now, can I kiss you?'

'*May* I, not *can* I.'

'You haven't changed. *May* I?' and she took my head in her two hands for a moment which seemed almost eternal. Then her lips fluttered gently against mine like a butterfly landing briefly on a petal to dance in the sun and fly away again.

As soon as Jessica had achieved her mission in Cambridge, she rushed straight back to Paris to find Mircea. Had it not been for my parents deciding to sell my grandmother's house, we might not have seen each other again for months, but Jessica's reaction to the news was the same as mine.

'They *can't* sell Manta!' she wailed down the telephone. 'You *mustn't* let them do it, Imogen. You can't let them do it.'

'I've tried to make them change their minds, but it's hopeless. They say they can't afford to keep it up and that none of us uses it any more. It's true, you have to admit. In the last ten years, I've only been to Manta three times: twice for Christmas and once when Granny died. Simon and Anthony have always refused to go back there. Mummy thinks it makes them feel guilt-ridden. Clémence is on her last legs: she can't possibly run the place any longer; and Mummy says it's so redolent of Granny that it makes her miserable because she misses her so much. I can't bear the thought of them selling it, but I can't see what alternative they have.'

'Well, we'd better go over there immediately,' said

Jessica. 'We *must* go and say goodbye to the place;' and so we went.

It is doubtless a mistake to re-visit anywhere that holds so many memories, but we both felt a need to clutch at the deserted remains of our childhood before they were finally gone forever.

'In any case,' said Jessica, 'didn't Kierkegaard say that only robbers and gypsies refuse to go back to a place they have once been?'

My parents wanted to come with us but they accepted the fact that we wanted to go alone. We wished to make our farewells in private, with neither parents nor children as witnesses.

It was an odd experience seeing the place again in such different circumstances. With my grandmother's death, ten years earlier, the house and grounds had also died. We had, however, fooled ourselves into believing that as long as we could still go there and see the place physically, we could somehow recapture her presence and re-live our lives. In a sense it was proof that our childhood selves had truly existed and that the things we remembered had been real, not a dream. It all seemed so long ago that we sometimes felt we must have imagined it. That night, however, we recaptured it all.

On the terrace at Manta, we caught up with each other at last. I sat watching Jessica, her face mobile in the twilight, as she talked about her father, her lovers, her unhappiness with Dermot and her despair over Mircea. As I studied her face in the shadows, her hair falling down around her shoulders, I reflected on how much I admired women, how much I liked them.

Three years earlier, Jessica had said to me, 'It doesn't matter. It's a lifetime thing. I can wait twenty, thirty, forty years. It really doesn't matter. It's just the waste of time which is sad. It seems such a terribly sad waste of time.'

That night, at Manta, she said she had finally understood and given up. 'I've seen Mircea with Amélie and I think they're perfectly happy together. I think he's very comfortable with her. He has no intention of leaving her. In fact, I don't think he ever had the slightest intention of leaving her, or the slightest desire to do so. All that rubbish about his Rumanian honour and not being able to leave her because she helped him acquire French nationality! I think he's been perfectly happy with her all along. I don't know why he had to pretend. Why couldn't he just tell me?'

Jessica's lovely, fragile features were beginning to blur in the dusk. Night comes very suddenly in Italy. It does not creep up on you gently, the way it does in England. There is an immensely reposeful period when one can sit and watch the evening rise; then, suddenly, with no warning, the night comes tumbling from the sky.

For a few seconds, just before this velvet darkness enveloped us, I could see Jessica's head and neck outlined against the distant lake. Behind her and beyond the terrace, the gardens ran down to the water's edge. The summer-house was still standing, but some of its glass panes were cracked and the wood was rotting. The gardens were desolate and overrun with brambles. The terrace needed sweeping and someone had broken one of the many stone urns along the balustrade. The whole place felt abandoned and forlorn and I suddenly understood, too late, my grandmother's melancholy moods. In the distance I could see a little fishing boat far out on the lake.

The twilight had made us nostalgic but once the darkness descended our mood changed.

'At least we've had interesting lives,' remarked Jessica, her habitual optimism returning. 'And we've lived intensely. Imagine how boring it would have been to have lived all our lives in one country, with one person, never having been wildly happy or wildly miserable, like all those frightful people in the *seizième* who spend their entire lives having to know the right people and passing on each other's tedious gossip. Imagine *having* to know the right people. Worse still, imagine never having known the wrong ones. No

432

wonder they're so boring. *Think* how lucky we are.'

She came and sat beside me on the low stone wall that separated the terrace from the garden. Suddenly, she leant her head on my shoulder and cried. She cried for a long time, then clutched my hand, sniffed and muttered, 'Oh God, I haven't even got a hankie.'

'I've got a rather bedraggled Kleenex you can have,' I said, offering her the item in question.

'Honestly!' exclaimed Jessica. 'What on earth was the point of being brought up always to have a clean hankie if this pathetic piece of Kleenex is the best we can produce between us? I never seem to have a clean hankie when I need one, do you?' She giggled.

'No,' I replied, 'but then I haven't cried since Enrico died. I seem to have become frozen inside.'

'You never wrote about what happened to you after he died. Do you realize how silent you have become since? All your letters said nothing. I mean, you said lots about your job and that sort of thing, but you didn't really *say* anything. Your letters gave away nothing. That period before I came to London and saw you again was the only time in my life when I felt I might have lost you . . .'

'There wasn't anything to say. Nothing happened, I didn't feel anything about anything. It has all been one long struggle to earn enough to support the children, and to try to make them happy. I've been fighting to survive, that's all.'

'I know,' said Jessica, 'but you still didn't say anything about it. You didn't tell me anything about *you* or about your life inside. For instance, now that you're living in England, do you see Simon at all?'

'I've seen him a few times, but it's difficult.'

'And Anthony?'

'Yes. I saw him, too, a couple of times when I first arrived in London but I haven't seen him since because it's impossible. I didn't write to you about it because I couldn't bear to think about it, but Anthony turned up on my doorstep the first week I was in England. He tried to

433

make out that it was all a mistake, that he was still in love with me, that he wanted us to get together again. He actually asked me to marry him, if you can believe it. He pretends he has never been happy with Simon and that Simon is incredibly promiscuous. I told him I really didn't want to hear about it, that I actually found it all quite upsetting, and he tried to bully me. He tried to bully me into going to bed with him. It was awful. All I could think of was that sonnet of Shakespeare's:

Why didst thou promise such a beauteous day,
And make me travel forth without my cloak,
To let base clouds o'ertake me in my way, etc.

Then he tried to bribe me into marrying him. He took me to see some frightful house done from top to bottom in original William Morris wallpapers. One of the pre-Raphaelites had lived there and it was under some sort of preservation order so that whoever bought it would not be allowed to touch the décor. Anyway, Anthony said he'd buy it for us if I agreed to marry him. I can't think why he thought I'd like it. I loathe William Morris . . . and I was bloody insulted that he thought he could buy me. I wish I'd never seen him again. It was better left alone.'

'That's why you were silent,' said Jessica. 'I knew something must have happened.' Then, after a pause, she looked at me and asked, 'Would you mind if we walked down to the walled garden, the place where all the herbs grew? I want to see it again.'

We wandered down the stone steps and along paths that had not been mown for years. At last we found ourselves in the walled garden, the place that had once been the glory of Manta. The herbs had run riot, but they were still there. We fought our way through shrubs that came up to our hips until we came to what had once been a lawn. The grass had been entirely smothered by heather.

We came to a halt and surveyed the scene. The air was warm and the night sky bright. The smell of herbs was

434

overpowering as we sat down on the heather and looked up at the stars.

'How stupid we have been,' remarked Jessica quietly. 'How *could* we have wasted so much precious time?'

She took me in her arms and the whole world changed. There were no beards, no sweat, no prickly stubble on chin or lip; no powerful hold, no weight to crush us. We were both light and slight and silken. Touching each other we seemed to be touching ourselves. Her caresses were my caresses, her soft, smooth skin my own. Impossible to tell where one person ended and the other began. It was my own light body pressed against me, my own long hair falling like a curtain on our embrace. We both smelt of heather, and rosemary, and thyme. The years rolled back and all pain vanished. Nothing else mattered. I felt as one does if one stands on the highest ridge of the Atlas looking down at the land below, the whole world spread at one's feet; looking down, as God must do, and knowing one has no further to climb. There was nowhere further to go. The struggle had ended.

I smiled up at Jessica as she bent her head to kiss me, and I suddenly realized that all those years I had simply been waiting for her face to come between mine and the stars.

Epilogue

The time will come
When, with elation,
you will greet yourself arriving
at your own door, in your own mirror,
and each will smile at the other's welcome,

and say, sit here. Eat.
You will love again the stranger who was your self.
Give wine. Give bread. Give back your heart
to itself, to the stranger who has loved you

all your life, whom you ignored
for another, who knows you by heart.
Take down the love letters from the bookshelf,

the photographs, the desperate notes,
peel your own image from the mirror.
Sit. Feast on your life.

                    Derek Walcott

EPILOGUE

'I've brought you a drink,' said Jessica, suddenly reappearing in the attic carrying a tray and glasses. 'The children are all home, now, and I've told them we'll be down in a minute. They're watching some awful thing on television so they're perfectly happy for the moment.'

As she said this, there was a shout from below. I went to the top of the attic stairs and looked down. Two of Jessica's children were standing there, and behind them one of mine stood laughing.

'Imogen,' Elizabeth called up to me, 'what have you done to the chocolate cake?'

'I haven't done anything to it.'

'How did you make it?'

'The usual way – chocolate and butter and flour and that sort of thing,' I replied.

'It tastes *extraordinary*. Come and try,' said Elizabeth.

'I'll bring you a piece,' said Barnaby, always polite.

They all trooped up into the attic and gave Jessica and me a piece each. Jessica took one small mouthful and nearly choked. 'It's disgusting,' she exclaimed. 'It tastes of nothing but bicarbonate of soda. Why has it got bicarbonate of soda in it?'

'Because I couldn't find any baking powder,' I answered. 'I thought we were taught at school that they were the same thing.'

'Well they are not,' said Jessica. 'This is the proof. Try a bit and you'll see.'

I did and it was uneatable. 'Honestly, Imogen, you are hopeless,' said Jessica laughing.

441

'Do you think it's poisonous?' asked Barnaby. 'We tried some on the budgie and he's developed hiccoughs. He can't stop hiccoughing.'

The three children started to laugh and Luciana added, helpfully, 'Perhaps he'll die, like the Pope.'

'Try giving him some water,' I suggested.

'Or a fright,' added Jessica. 'We'll be down in a minute. Go and see what you can do until we get there.'

The three children clattered downstairs again, giggling, and Jessica turned to me still laughing. 'Why did anyone give us a budgie, anyway?' she demanded. 'I can't stand budgies. Let's give it away. Incidentally,' she said, 'do you realize that it is exactly five years today since we moved into Manta? I thought we might take the children to Stresa for dinner, to celebrate.'

'Good idea,' I said. 'Shall we invite my parents, too, or do you think it's too late?'

'Well, it wouldn't take them long to get here if they haven't planned anything else for this evening. They can always stay the night if they don't want to drive back to Milan afterwards. I think it's the least we can do, considering how sweet they were about letting us buy Manta when they knew it would take us the rest of our lives to pay off the full amount.'

'They were wonderful about it, weren't they? But they were so pleased to find a way to keep it in the family, and still be able to come here when they wanted; and I think it suits them better to have us paying them monthly instalments than to have a huge lump sum which would all be taken in tax. My father always says that he likes to feel that if he blows all his money on a horse and has nothing to leave us, at least we'll have a respectable roof over our heads.'

'He's been unbelievably good about the whole thing. Do you think he was very shocked about us?'

'Not in the least. He told me that he thought both he and I were "indigestible" and that only you would be barmy enough to want to live with me, or strong enough to survive it.'

442

'What about your mother? Was she upset?'

'Difficult to say with Mummy. I think she had such a shock over Simon that nothing could throw her again to that extent. She was brought up by Granny, too, don't forget, so she genuinely believes men and women are unsuited to living together. I have a feeling she is slightly envious. It is the only time I have ever known her show any curiosity about anything she would consider personal, or not her business. She hates prying. But she asked me a lot of questions at the beginning.'

'What sort of questions?'

'Questions about our relationship. She wanted to know how close it was to childhood love, whether it was emotional or intellectual; and she wanted to know how important sexual contact was to us.'

'What did you answer?'

'I answered that it was extremely close to childhood love but that because we were no longer children, our feelings had had an additional layer added to them – i.e. sex. I said that every adult needed to express themselves physically but that that didn't mean that sex was the reason for the relationship, or the basis of the relationship. I tried to explain to her that it was to do with *friendship*, being with somebody you had always known, somebody like your own family with whom you didn't have to pretend anything or explain anything and whom you loved whatever they did or didn't do: somebody who was part of you.'

'And did you say it was emotional or intellectual?'

'I said it was both. I said it was extremely emotional but that all our interests were the same, basically (which doesn't mean to say that I'm not more interested in music than you are, or that you are not more interested in archaeology than I am – but we are interested in each other's interests), and that we found each other's company amusing and stimulating. I tried to make her understand the vast relief of an equal relationship where we share everything right down to the chores; where we both see what has to be done and do it, where we don't have to clear up after each other, where all the boring things like shopping and peeling vegetables are made less boring because we do them together and keep each other entertained. I told her that we laughed a lot and that I thought that was perhaps the real secret of our relationship.'

'Did she comment at all?'

'Yes. She said she thought it must be very agreeable and easy to live with a woman but she still wondered whether women living without men could eliminate all those age-old problems of domination, possessiveness, jealousy, and so forth.'

'Well, she's right, or course: those problems are part of human nature. We'd be jealous if one of us went off with someone else. I used to be jealous of Anthony.'

'Well, you certainly didn't show it.'

'It was easy to hide because I liked him; easier than it was for you, at any rate, since you so obviously loathed Dermot.'

The telephone rang at this moment and the children shouted from downstairs for one of us to come.

'I'll go,' said Jessica. 'Can you just find out what's in that last box while I'm downstairs?'

While Jessica was answering the telephone, I wrenched open the lid of the last box. It contained mainly photographs, including one of Dermot on the back of which someone had written a quote from Edmund Burke: 'It is a general popular error to imagine the loudest complainers for the public to be the most anxious for its welfare.' I did not recognize the handwriting.

When Jessica returned I said, 'I'm bored with this. We've been at it all day. That box has practically nothing but photographs in it, anyway, and it can jolly well wait until tomorrow.'

'OK,' she said. 'That was your mother, by the way. I asked her if they'd like to have dinner with us and she seemed delighted. They'll drive straight to the restaurant to save time, and then come here afterwards for the night. All right?'

444

'Fine,' I said. 'Incidentally, are you ever going to take off that ridiculous dress?'

Jessica laughed. 'Yes,' she said, 'I'll take it off just as soon as you take off that hat.' She crossed the attic and stood in front of me with her back towards me. 'You'll have to undo all these silly little hooks, though. No wonder they needed maids to dress them if this is the sort of thing they wore.'

She suddenly turned to face me 'Everything has been such fun since we've been together again,' she said, putting her arms around me. 'I'm so glad you came back in the end even though you always tried to live as far away as possible just to be difficult. It was so boring without you. Why on earth did you leave me in the first place?'

'I didn't leave you. You left me.'

'No, I didn't. You went off to Milan. It was perfectly beastly of you. Anyway, I'm glad we're together again. It was horrid without you.'

24.95